praise for Sister of My Heart

"Divakaruni's talent and originality lie in her ability to discern [the] basic emotional motifs beneath the flashy 'exotica' of Indian, and American, lifestyles. She finds the real points of departure between the two cultures and, in putting her finger exactly there, activates the universal."
—*LA Weekly*

"An extraordinary tale. . . . A serious tragedy in which the protagonists' requisite fatal flaw lies in thinking that one can know what is in another's heart."
—*San Jose Mercury News*

"Beguiling and cleverly plotted."
—*Los Angeles Times Book Review*

"[A] magical mix of art and feminism."
—*Houston Chronicle*

"Divakaruni's gift asserts itself in her moving portraits of Gouri, Nalini, and Pishi, the three acrimonious women—sharp-tongued one minute, compassionate the next—who bring the girls up."
—*The New Yorker*

"Wonderfully unpredictable. . . . One of the book's many pleasures is anticipating where the two women will end up."
—*Milwaukee Journal Sentinel*

"Hard to put down."
—*Detroit Free Press*

"A wonderfully satisfying novel, full of surprises and emotional truths."
—*Hartford Courant*

"What an irresistibly absorbing immersion in the pleasure and anguish of growing up passionate in a world of duty, where each comfort is hedged with a constraint and love unsettles every plan. *Sister of My Heart* may be alive with exotic detail but its emotions are very recognizable."
  —Rosellen Brown, author of *Before and After* and *Tender Mercies*

"Chitra Banerjee Divakaruni's account of family life in Bengal is warm and richly detailed. Hers is one of the most strikingly lyrical voices writing about the lives of Indian women today."
  —Amitav Ghosh, author of *In an Antique Land*
  and *The Calcutta Chromosome*

"Shimmers with radiant energy. . . . Unfolds with hypnotic rhythm. A book sparkling with invention, a complex tapestry of worlds ancient and new."
  —*Toronto Star*

"Thoroughly engages the reader. A unique and instructive mix of unflinching social criticism and old-fashioned romance."
  —*National Post* (Toronto)

"An absorbing tale, underlined by Indian myth and fable. . . . A lush display of the Indian romantic imagination, in which the twin narratives encompass both fantasy and fatalism."
  —*Toronto Globe and Mail*

"Strikes a delicate balance between realism and fantasy. . . . A touching celebration of enduring love between two women."
  —*Sunday Times* (London)

CHITRA BANERJEE DIVAKARUNI
Sister of My Heart

Chitra Banerjee Divakaruni is the bestselling author of the novels *The Mistress of Spices* and *The Vine of Desire*; the story collections *Arranged Marriage*, which received several awards, including the American Book Award, and *The Unknown Errors of Our Lives*; and four collections of prize-winning poetry. Her work has appeared in *The New Yorker, The Atlantic Monthly, Ms., The Best American Short Stories 1999*, and other publications. Born in India, she lives in the San Francisco area. The dedicated Web site for the author is www.chitradivakaruni.com.

ALSO BY CHITRA BANERJEE DIVAKARUNI

Black Candle

Arranged Marriage

Leaving Yuba City

The Mistress of Spices

The Unknown Errors of Our Lives

The Vine of Desire

Sister of

My Heart

Sister of My Heart

CHITRA BANERJEE DIVAKARUNI

ANCHOR BOOKS A Division of Random House, Inc., New York

First Anchor Books Edition, January 2000
Copyright © 1999 by Chitra Banerjee Divakaruni

All rights reserved under International and Pan-American Copyright Conventions. Published in the United States by Anchor Books, a division of Random House, Inc., New York, and simultaneously in Canada by Random House of Canada Limited, Toronto. Originally published in hardcover in the United States by Doubleday in 1999.

Anchor Books and colophon are registered trademarks of Random House, Inc.

All of the characters in this book are fictitious, and any resemblance to actual persons, living or dead, is purely coincidental.

The Library of Congress has cataloged the Doubleday edition as follows:

Divakaruni, Chitra Banerjee, 1956–
Sister of my heart / Chitra Banerjee Divakaruni. — 1st ed.
p. cm.
I. Title.
PS3554.I86S57   1999
813'.54—dc21   98-30254
CIP

Anchor ISBN: 0-385-48951-X

Book design by Leah S. Carlson-Stanisic

Author photograph © R. J. Muna

www.anchorbooks.com

Printed in the United States of America
20 19 18 17 16

For those who told me stories
and those to whom
I tell them now:
my grandfather, Nibaran Chandra Ghosh
my mother, Tatini Banerjee,
and
my three men, Murthy, Anand, and Abhay

My deepest thanks to:
My agent Sandra Dijkstra for her continuing belief and support
My editors Martha Levin, Peternelle van Arsdale, and Marianne
Velmans for guiding me through the labyrinth
Deepika Petraglia Bahri, Amitav Ghosh, Martin Nouvelle,
and Susanne Pari for their vision
The California Arts Council for financial support
Foothill College for the gift of time
My family, especially my mother and mother-in-law, Tatini Banerjee
and Sita Divakaruni, for encouragement and blessings
My three men, Murthy, Anand, and Abhay, for all the microwave
dinners they ate uncomplainingly
and
Baba Muktananda and Gurumayi Chidvilasananda
for opening my heart

It is only the story . . . that saves our progeny from blundering like blind beggars into the spikes of the cactus fence.

—CHINUA ACHEBE

Anthills of the Savannah

— BOOK ONE —

The Princess
in the Palace of Snakes

ONE

Sudha

THEY SAY in the old tales that the first night after a child is born, the Bidhata Purush comes down to earth himself to decide what its fortune is to be. That is why they bathe babies in sandalwood water and wrap them in soft red malmal, color of luck. That is why they leave sweetmeats by the cradle. Silver-leafed sandesh, dark pantuas floating in golden syrup, jilipis orange as the heart of a fire, glazed with honey-sugar. If the child is especially lucky, in the morning it will all be gone.

"That's because the servants sneak in during the night and eat them," says Anju, giving her head an impatient shake as Abha Pishi oils her hair. This is how she is, my cousin, always scoffing, refusing to believe. But she knows, as I do, that no servant in all of Calcutta would dare eat sweets meant for a god.

The old tales say this also: In the wake of the Bidhata Purush come the demons, for that is the world's nature, good and evil mingled. That is why they leave an oil lamp burning. That is why they place the sacred tulsi leaf under the baby's pillow for protection. In richer households, like the one my mother grew up in, she has told us, they hire a brahmin to sit in the corridor and recite auspicious prayers all night.

"What nonsense," Anju says. "There are no demons."

I am not so sure. Perhaps they do not have the huge teeth, the curved blood-dripping claws and bulging red eyes of our *Children's Ramayan Picture Book*, but I have a feeling they exist.

Haven't I sensed their breath, like slime-black fingers brushing my spine? Later, when we are alone, I will tell Anju this.

But in front of others I am always loyal to her. So I say, bravely, "That's right. Those are just old stories."

It is early evening on our terrace, its bricks overgrown with moss. A time when the sun hangs low on the horizon, half hidden by the pipal trees which line our compound walls all the way down the long driveway to the bolted wrought-iron gates. Our great-grandfather had them planted one hundred years ago to keep the women of his house safe from the gaze of strangers. Abha Pishi, one of our three mothers, has told us this.

Yes, we have three mothers—perhaps to make up for the fact that we have no fathers.

There's Pishi, our widow aunt who threw herself heart-first into her younger brother's household when she lost her husband at the age of eighteen. Dressed in austere white, her graying hair cut close to her scalp in the orthodox style so that the bristly ends tickle my palms when I run my hands over them, she's the one who makes sure we are suitably dressed for school in the one-inch-below-the-knee uniforms the nuns insist on. She finds for us, miraculously, stray pens and inkpots and missing pages of homework. She makes us our favorite dishes: luchis rolled out and fried a puffy golden-brown, potato and cauliflower curry cooked without chilies, thick sweet payesh made from the milk of Budhi-cow, whose owner brings her to our house each morning to be milked under Pishi's stern, miss-nothing stare. On holidays she plaits jasmine into our hair. But most of all Pishi is our fount of information, the one who tells us the stories our mothers will not, the secret, delicious, forbidden tales of our past.

There's Anju's mother, whom I call Gouri Ma, her fine cheekbones and regal forehead hinting at generations of breeding, for she comes from a family as old and respected as that of the Chatterjees, which she married into. Her face is not beautiful in the traditional sense—even I, young as I am, know this. Lines of hardship are etched around her mouth and on her forehead, for she was the one who shouldered the burden of keeping the family safe on that thunderclap day eight years ago when she received news of our fathers' deaths. But her eyes, dark and endless-deep—they make me think of Kalodighi, the enormous lake behind the country mansion our family used to own before Anju and I were born. When Gouri Ma smiles at me with her eyes, I stand up straighter. I want to be noble and brave, just like her.

Lastly (I use this word with some guilt), there's my own mother, Nalini. Her skin is still golden, for though she's a widow my mother is careful to apply turmeric paste to her face each day. Her perfect-shaped lips glisten red from paan, which she loves to chew—mostly for the color it leaves on her mouth, I think. She laughs often, my mother, especially when her friends come for tea and talk. It is a glittery, tinkling sound, like jeweled ankle bells, people say, though I myself feel it is more like a thin glass struck with a spoon. Her cheek feels as soft as the lotus flower she's named after on those rare occasions when she presses her face to mine. But more often when she looks at me a frown ridges her forehead between eyebrows beautiful as wings. Is it from worry or displeasure? I can never tell. Then she remembers that frowns cause age lines and smoothes it away with a finger.

Now Pishi stops oiling Anju's hair to give us a wicked smile. Her voice grows low and shivery, the way it does when she's telling ghost stories. "They're listening, you know. The demons. And they don't like little eight-year-old girls talking like this. Just wait till tonight . . ."

Because I am scared I interrupt her with the first thought that comes into my head. "Pishi Ma, tell no, did the sweets disappear for us?"

Sorrow moves like smoke-shadow over Pishi's face. I can see that she would like to make up another of those outrageous tales that we so love her to tell, full of magic glimmer and hoping. But finally she says, her voice flat, "No, Sudha. You weren't so lucky."

I know this already. Anju and I have heard the whispers. Still, I must ask one more time.

"Did you see *anything* that night?" I ask. Because she was the one who stayed with us the night of our birth while our mothers lay in bed, still in shock from the terrible telegram which had sent them both into early labor that morning. Our mothers, lying in beds they would never again share with their husbands. My mother weeping, her beautiful hair tangling about her swollen face, punching at a pillow until it burst, spilling cotton stuffing white as grief. Gouri Ma, still and silent, staring up into a darkness which pressed upon her like the responsibilities she knew no one else in the family could take on.

To push them from my mind I ask urgently, "Did you at least hear something?"

Pishi shakes her head in regret. "Maybe the Bidhata Purush doesn't come for girl-babies." In her kindness she leaves the rest unspoken, but I've heard the whispers often enough to complete it in my head. *For girl-babies who are so much bad luck that they cause their fathers to die even before they are born.*

Anju scowls, and I know that as always she can see into my thoughts with the X-ray vision of her fiercely loving eyes. "Maybe there's no Bidhata Purush either," she states and yanks her hair from Pishi's hands though it is only half-braided. She ignores Pishi's scolding shouts and stalks to her room, where she will slam the door.

But I sit very still while Pishi's fingers rub the hibiscus oil into my scalp, while she combs away knots with the long, soothing rhythm I have known since the beginning of memory. The sun is a deep, sad red, and I can smell, faint on the evening air, wood smoke. The pavement dwellers are lighting their cooking fires. I've seen them many times when Singhji, our chauffeur, drives us to school: the mother in a worn green sari bent over a spice-grinding stone, the daughter watching the baby, keeping him from falling into the gutter. The father is never there. Maybe he is running up a platform in Howrah station in his red turban, his shoulders knotted from carrying years of trunks and bedding rolls, crying out, "Coolie chahiye, want a coolie, memsaab?" Or maybe, like my father, he too is dead.

Whenever I thought this my eyes would sting with sympathy, and if by chance Ramur Ma, the vinegary old servant woman who chaperones us everywhere, was not in the car, I'd beg Singhji to stop so I could hand the girl a sweet out of my lunch box. And he always did.

Among all our servants—but no, I do not really think of him as a servant—I like Singhji the best. Perhaps it is because I can trust him not to give me away to the mothers the way Ramur Ma does. Perhaps it is because he is a man of silences, speaking only when necessary—a quality I appreciate in a house filled with female gossip. Or perhaps it is the veil of mystery which hangs over him.

When Anju and I were about five years old, Singhji appeared at our gate one morning—like a godsend, Pishi says—looking for a driver's job. Our old chauffeur had recently retired, and the mothers needed a new one badly but could not afford it. Since the death of the fathers, money had been short. In his broken Bengali, Singhji told Gouri Ma he'd work for whatever she could give him. The mothers were a little suspicious, but they guessed that he was so willing because of his unfortunate looks. It is true that his face is horrifying at first glance—I am embarrassed to remember that as a little girl I had screamed and run away when I saw him. He must have been caught in a terrible fire years ago, for the skin of the entire upper half of his face—all the way up to his turban—is the naked, puckered pink of an old burn. The fire had also scorched away his eyebrows and pulled his eyelids into a slant, giving him a strangely oriental expression at odds with the thick black mustache and beard that covers the rest of his face.

"He's lucky we hired him at all," Mother's fond of saying. "Most people wouldn't have because that burned forehead is a sure sign of lifelong misfortune. Besides, he's so ugly."

I do not agree. Sometimes when he does not know that I am

watching him, I have caught a remembering look, at once faraway and intent, in Singhji's eyes—the kind of look an exiled king might have as he thinks about the land he left behind. At those times his face is not ugly at all, but more like a mountain peak that has withstood a great ice storm. And somehow I feel we are the lucky ones because he chose to come to us.

Once I heard the servants gossiping about how Singhji had been a farmer somewhere in Punjab until the death of his family from a cholera epidemic made him take to the road. It made me so sad that although Mother had strictly instructed me never to talk about personal matters with any of the servants, I ran out to the car and told him how sorry I was about his loss. He nodded silently. No other response came from the burned wall of his face. But a few days later he told me that he used to have a child.

Though Singhji offered no details about this child, I immediately imagined that it had been a little girl my age. I could not stop thinking of her. How did she look? Did she like the same foods we did? What kinds of toys had Singhji bought for her from the village bazaar? For weeks I would wake up crying in the middle of the night because I had dreamed of a girl thrashing about on a mat, delirious with pain. In the dream she had my face.

"Really, Sudha!" Anju would tell me, in concern and exasperation—I often slept in her room and thus the job of comforting me fell to her—"How come you always get so worked up about imaginary things?"

That is what she would be saying if she were with me right now. For it seems to me I am receding, away from Pishi's capable hands, away from the solidity of the sun-warmed bricks under my legs, that I am falling into the first night of my existence, where Anju and I lie together in a makeshift cradle in a household not ready for us, sucking on sugared nipples someone has put in our mouths to keep us quiet. Anjali and Basudha, although in all the turmoil around us no one has thought to name us yet. Anjali, which means offering, for a good woman is to offer up her life for others. And Basudha, so that I will be as patient as the earth goddess I am named after. Below us, Pishi is a dark, stretched-out shape on the floor, fallen into exhausted sleep, the dried salt of tears crusting her cheeks.

The Bidhata Purush is tall and has a long, spun-silk beard like the astrologer my mother visits each month to find out what the planets have in store for her. He is dressed in a robe made of the finest white cotton, his fingers drip light, and his feet do not touch the ground as he glides toward us. When he bends over our cradle, his face is so blinding-bright I cannot tell his expression. With the first finger of his right hand he marks our foreheads. It is a tingly feeling, as when Pishi rubs tiger-balm on our temples. I think I know what he writes for Anju. *You will be brave and clever, you will fight injustice, you will not give in. You will marry a fine man and travel the world and have many sons. You will be happy.*

It is more difficult to imagine what he writes for me. Perhaps he writes *beauty,* for though I myself do not think so, people say I am beautiful—even more than my mother was in the first years of her marriage. Perhaps he writes *goodness,* for though I am not as obedient as my mother would like, I try hard to be good. There is a third word he writes, the harsh angles of which sting like fire, making me wail, making Pishi sit up, rubbing her eyes. But the Bidhata Purush is gone already, and all she sees is a swirl—cloud or sifted dust—outside the window, a fading glimmer, like fireflies.

Years later I will wonder, that final word he wrote, was it *sorrow?*

TWO

Anju

SOME DAYS in my life I hate everyone.

I hate Aunt Nalini for constantly telling Sudha and me about how good girls should behave, which is exactly the opposite of whatever we're doing at the moment. I hate the endless stories she insists on repeating about her childhood. I know those stories aren't true—no one could possibly be so virtuous, especially not *her*. Worst of all is when she makes up little rhymes with morals tagged onto them. *Good daughters are bright lamps, lighting their mothers' name; wicked daughters are firebrands, scorching the family's fame.*

I hate her friends, all those waistless women with their hair pulled back in greasy buns who gather every afternoon in our drawing room to drink liters and liters of tea and eat too many sweets and show off their jewelry and knit sweaters with complicated ugly designs. And gossip, which is what they've really come to do.

I hate Pishi when she puts on her patient smile and sits in the back of the hall on feast days, not participating, because widows mustn't. And if I tell her that's rubbish, why, just look at Aunt N or even my mother, she only pats me on the cheek and says, That's sweet of you, dear Anju, but you're too young to understand these things.

Once in a while I hate even Mother because she believes so much in me. It's like a rock in the center of my chest, her certainty that I'm special. That I'll make something beautiful and brilliant out of my life and be a fitting daughter of the illustrious Chatterjees.

Most of all—when I allow myself to think of him—I hate my father. I hate the fact that he could go off so casually in search of adventure, without a single thought for what would happen to the rest of us. I blame him for the tired circles under Mother's eyes, the taunts of the children at school because I don't have a father. None of it would have happened if he hadn't been so careless and got himself killed.

But never Sudha. I could never hate Sudha. Because she is my other half. The sister of my heart.

I can tell Sudha everything I feel and not have to explain any of it. She'll look at me with those big unblinking eyes and smile a tiny smile, and I'll know she understands me perfectly.

Like no one else in the entire world does. Like no one else in the entire world will.

Early in my life I realized something. People were jealous of Sudha and me.

At first I thought it was because our family's so old and respected. But it couldn't be that, because everyone knows that we've fallen on hard times, and the bookstore that Mother runs is the only source of income we have left. Aunt N is always lamenting in her melodramatic fashion that she's sitting on poverty's doorstep, and it's a good thing that her dear parents are departed, this way they're spared from seeing their daughter's sufferings. It couldn't be our possessions—Sudha and I don't have many. There just isn't the money for that, in spite of the long hours Mother puts in at the store and her determination to get us whatever a daughter of the Chatterjees must have. (That's something else I don't understand. My mother's the most intelligent person I know, and the most efficient. Still, the store never seems to make a profit, and each week she has to go over our household expenses in her careful, frowning way, trying to cut costs.)

But finally I've figured it out. What people hate is how happy Sudha and I are when we're together. How we don't need anyone else.

It's been this way ever since we were born. Even before I could walk, Pishi has told me, I'd crawl down the maze of corridors looking for Sudha, both of us shrieking with baby laughter when I finally found her. We'd amuse ourselves for hours at a time, playing with each other's toes and fingers and hair, and when Aunt N came to take Sudha away we'd throw such tantrums that she retreated, complaining bitterly to Pishi that she didn't know why she'd gone through all the trouble of labor and birthing, because it was as if she didn't have a daughter at all.

All through childhood we bathed together and ate together, often from the same plate, feeding each other our favorite items: the crunchy brown triangles of parothas, fried eggplant, spongy-sweet rasogollah balls. Our favorite game was acting out the fairy tales Pishi told us, where Sudha was always the princess and I the prince who rescued her. At night we lay in twin beds in my room, though officially Sudha had a room of her own next to her mother's, a dark ugly mausoleum filled with old oil paintings and heavy mahogany furniture. We whispered and giggled until Pishi came and threatened us with separation. And when we had nightmares, instead of going to our mothers for comfort, we squeezed into one bed and held each other.

As we grew older, the nuns who ran our convent school were concerned at our closeness. It wasn't normal, they said. It would stunt our development. They put us in different classes, but all it did was make me sulk. And it made Sudha cry. At recess I'd rush to meet her in the playground, feeling as though the morning had been a pillow held down over my face. When I saw her swollen eyes, rage burned my skin as if it had been rubbed with chili powder, and I'd want to kill someone. That's when we started planning our escapes. At first we complained of stomachaches or headaches so we could stay home. When that didn't work with Pishi, we sneaked out of the school compound at noon, along with the girls who went home for lunch, and spent the afternoon somewhere, anywhere, just so we could be together. We ate peanuts by the lake, walked through the animal market admiring the baby chickens, or rode the tram to the end of the line and back again just in time to meet Singhji at the school gate with our most guileless smiles.

Somehow we'd believed we could get away with it. But of course our teachers complained, and the mothers called us into the study, that dank room filled with dog-eared ledgers and the smell of mildew, where we were summoned only when we were in real trouble. Aunt N insisted we should be given a good spanking, and even Mother, who's usually so reasonable—her face was white with anger. But when I explained everything, a strange, sad look came into her eyes. And although she told us that our teachers were right, and our education was too important to ruin in this way, the sternness left her voice, and she put out a hand to touch my shoulder.

Later I overheard her telling Pishi that she worried about us. Loving someone so deeply was dangerous. It made you too vulnerable. And Pishi sighed and said, "Yes, we both know that, don't we?"

The following morning Mother didn't go to the bookstore—something which hardly ever happened. Instead, she took us to school and, having waved good-bye to us, went into the principal's office. She never discussed with us what she said in there. But from the next week we were put back in the same class.

All of this didn't make us popular at school, or later, when news traveled—as news always does in Calcutta—with our neighbors. "Oh those Chatterjee girls," people said, "forever acting like they're too good for our daughters. And Anju's mother, what was she thinking, indulging them this way? Nalini was right, a good beating would have taught them to behave. To obey rules. You simply wait and see, their troubles are just starting. Everyone knows what happens to girls with that sort of high-nose attitude."

They didn't understand that Sudha and I never felt we were better than other people. It was just that we found everything we needed in each other. As Pishi says, Why go to the lake to fetch water when you have a well in your own house already?

One time a neighbor lady said to me, "You'd better not waste all your time with that Sudha. You should be making friends with girls from other important families, especially those who have eligible older brothers with whom your mother could fix up a match for you." Then she'd added, in a low, confidential voice, "Why do you want to be around a girl who's so much prettier than you, anyway? Don't you know that when you're together people notice your bony legs and teeth braces more than they would have otherwise?"

I was so angry I couldn't stop myself from telling her it was none of her business. Besides, I didn't care if a bunch of silly people who didn't have anything better to do compared our looks. I already knew Sudha was more beautiful. Did that mean I should love her less?

"So virtuous, aren't you, Miss High and Mighty," the neighbor woman said. "Watch out! The jealousy's going to hit you bad one of these days." She huffed away and I knew exactly what she'd go around telling everyone: what a junglee that Chatterjee girl has become, baap re, but what else can you expect when there's no man in the house.

But yesterday was the worst of all.

Yesterday Sarita Aunty, one of Aunt N's fat teatime friends who prides herself on her frankness, saw us entering the house hand in hand. Right away her eyebrows scrunched up in a horrendous frown. "Goodness," she said, "don't you girls ever do anything without each other? I swear, you're like those twins, what do they call them, born stuck together."

I was about to say, So what if we are? But Sudha, who's the

polite one, gave my hand a warning squeeze. Then she surprised me by saying, "Didn't you know, Aunty? We *are* twins."

Sarita Aunty's nostrils quivered like an overwrought buffalo's. "Ei, girl, don't back-answer me," she said. "You think I don't know what's what? You're not even first cousins, let alone sisters. Your father was just some kind of distant relation of Anju's father's, nothing like a real brother."

Odd, isn't it, how some people take pleasure in hurting others.

I tried to say something scathing to shut her up, but I couldn't speak. If Mother had been there, she would have come to my rescue with one of her cool, calm sayings. *Who are we to judge relationships, Sarita? Are we not all related in God's eye?* But she was at the bookstore, and the words *You're not even first cousins, let alone sisters* pounded inside my head like hammers gone berserk.

Aunt N looked as if someone had made her bite into a lemon. She's always going on and on about how much better things were in her father's house—servants and children knowing their place, even the cows producing, obediently, more milk than any of the neighboring cattle—until you would have thought she wished she wasn't related to us at all. But she doesn't like anyone else reminding her of her tenuous connection to the Chatterjees.

Sarita Aunty went on triumphantly, "The two of you weren't even born at the same time, or under the same star either. Am I right, Nalini Di?"

For a moment Aunt N acted as if she didn't hear the question. But then she couldn't resist the opportunity to be melodramatic. She gave a martyr's sigh and said, "You're quite right, because although Anju was born right at noon, Sudha"—here she looked accusingly at my cousin—"didn't come until midnight. What a labor I had with her! The pain was like a thousand jabbing knives! I screamed and screamed, and I was losing blood also. The midwife, a youngish woman, not experienced like the ones at my mother's confinements, was so frightened she said maybe they should send for the English doctor, although everyone knew he always cut open the mothers' stomachs and quite a few of them died of the fever afterward."

We'd heard all this a hundred times. But Sudha looked up wide-eyed and said, as though it were a whole new story, "But he didn't have to do that to you, did he?"

"No . . ."

"That's because Anju saved you, isn't it?"

Aunt N glared at her daughter. She didn't like being interrupted in the middle of an exciting story, particularly when she was the suffering heroine.

"Actually I think it was the lucky childbirth amulet I'd had the forethought to buy the month before from a traveling roja—"

"Tell what happened next," Sudha interrupted, surprising me again. Usually she's so quiet around her mother. "Tell about Gouri Ma."

Aunt N clicked her tongue in annoyance and made like she'd stop. But after a moment she continued, because at her heart she loves a good story as much as we do.

"When your Gouri Aunty heard what was going on, she climbed out of bed. The midwife kept telling her she mustn't, because she'd lost a lot of blood too, but she paid her no attention. Somehow she walked all the way across the hall with Anju in her arms and put her face-down on my stomach. Anju lay there for a moment, draped over my huge belly—I was very big, even though it was only the end of the eighth month. I tell you"—here Aunt N gave another dramatic sigh—"I simply never recovered my figure afterward. Anyway, I guess Anju didn't like being there, because all at once she gave a loud cry, and right then I felt a contraction so strong it was like my backbone was snapping in two. Next thing I knew, the midwife was handing Sudha to me, saying It's another girl."

"That's why Anju's my twin, don't you see?" Sudha said, and it seemed to me that she was talking to her mother as well as to Sarita Aunty. "Because she called me out into the world." And she put her arm around my neck, my usually quiet cousin, and smiled a brilliant smile that left the two women wordless.

I couldn't have done it better myself.

There are other reasons why I can never hate Sudha. Once I made a list of them.

Because she's the most beautiful person I know, just like the princesses in the fairy tales Pishi tells us, with her skin that's the warm brown of almond milk, her hair soft like monsoon clouds all the way down her back, and her eyes that are the softest of all.

Because she can put her hand on my arm when I'm ready to kick the world for its stupidity, and it's like a drink of clean cold water on a hot day.

Because she believes in magic, demons and gods and falling stars to wish on, the way I never could.

Because she's the best storyteller, better even than Pishi. She can take the old tales and make them new by putting us in them. Us, Anju and Sudha, right in there among the demon queens and fairy princes and talking beasts.

Because I called her into the world and, therefore, must do all I can to make sure she is happy.

THREE

Sudha

ANJU GROWS UPSET whenever I ask Pishi about the day our fathers died. Why can't you forget it? she says. Why can't you just let it go? If you always look backward, you'll never get anywhere in life. Besides, what's there to know about two men who didn't have the sense to stay home where they'd have been safe, instead of going gallivanting in search of some stupid adventure?

There is truth in what she says, I admit it. And for once the mothers are on her side. My mother thinks it's bad luck to talk of that day. Gouri Ma says it is better for us to focus our thoughts on more positive things. And Pishi, our enthusiastic informant in matters of the past, will give us only a few reluctant details before she changes the subject.

I trust Pishi. I know she must have a reason for her silence. And yet I am strangely pulled to that day twelve years ago, day of my father's end, day of my beginning, when perhaps our spirits crossed in mid-air, his rising to heaven, mine descending to earth. Recently the pull has grown more urgent, for any day now we will shed our child-selves, Anju and I, and become women. And how can we take on that new history if we know nothing of what came before?

For my mother's sake too, I want to know what happened that day—and what led to it. Perhaps it will help me understand why her heart is so bile-bitter, why she has only words of complaint and chastisement for me. Perhaps it will help me grow more daughterly toward her.

So on Sunday morning when Anju is busy with a new American novel she has borrowed from the bookstore, I go looking for Pishi. I find her on the terrace setting out trayfuls of salted mangoes for drying. Pishi is an excellent pickle maker and knows it. Ever since she returned to her father's house, she has told us proudly, the Chatterjees have never had to soil their lips with store-bought achar. In three days' time, when the mango slices are crisped thin by the sun, she will mix in spiced mustard oil and chili powder and seal them in squat jars for us to enjoy through the year. Meanwhile she must stay up here to guard them from the black-faced monkeys which appear magically—for monkeys are not common here in the heart of Calcutta—every pickling season. Anju thinks they must escape from the Alipur Zoo, but Ramdin-mudi, who owns the corner grocery, insists they are descendents of the god Hanuman, whose image, with its great coiled tail, hangs in his store above the tins of atta and oil.

Pishi looks unhappy. There's going to be a big kirtan in the neighborhood temple this afternoon, singers and dholak players who have come all the way from Nabadwip, and all the women she knows are going. Kirtans are one of the few pleasures Pishi considers suitable for widows and thus allows herself. But drying mangoes is an important job, not something she can trust to a maidservant, for everyone knows that if the slices are touched by a woman who hasn't bathed, or has lain with a man that day, or is menstruating, they will turn furry with fungus.

I'll be happy to watch the mangoes for her, I say. I'll be very clean and careful and turn them over at the right time so both sides get equal sun. If she will tell me a special story, one I've been wanting to hear all my life.

Pishi knows at once which story it is that I desire. Her face grows dark and pinched with disapproval. Is it apprehension I see in her eyes? She orders me to go downstairs. But there's a faint note of unsureness in her voice, which gives me the courage to resist.

"Why won't you tell me?" I cry. "I have a right to hear about my father. Haven't you always told us that we'll never really know who we are if we don't learn about our past?"

Pishi stares past me at the blank sky. Finally she says, "At the heart of the story you want to know, a secret lies buried. I am the only person left alive who knows it, though sometimes I think your aunt Gouri might have her suspicions. But she's an intelligent woman—she knows that there are times when one should search for answers and times when one should let matters be.

"I've always believed in the importance of telling you girls about your past—you know that. But this secret is so terrible that I've been reluctant to burden you with it. I'm afraid it will take away your childhood and destroy the love that you hold dearest. I'm afraid it will make you hate me."

"Pishi Ma," I cry, my voice breaking with excitement, "you *must* tell me. I need to know. And nothing could ever make me hate you."

"I hope that's true," says Pishi, "because you and Anju are the daughters I was not lucky enough to give birth to. Through you the Bidhata Purush has allowed me to experience the blessing of mother love, and for that I always thank him. But it's not myself I worry about, it's you. And your relationship with—"

Here Pishi breaks off, and in the silence that wells up around us I notice how her voice has changed, grown dark and deep-grained as it never was before. And in dizzy fear I know this is a dangerous story, one that can burn me in its sudden blaze.

"Are you sure you really want to know this secret?"

Pishi watches me. I know that if I betray the tiniest fear she will stop, the sun will cease its white-hot circling around me, and I will have my old, safe life back again.

I hold my body tense against the temptation. "I am sure," I say.

"Very well," says Pishi, and her breath is ragged and resigned.

"Come, sit close to me, and I'll tell you. It is your right after all, this story about your father. And your mother, yes, for it is her story too. And if your love survives this telling, then you'll know it's true, and that nothing can break it, ever."

That is how I finally learn about my father's life, and his death.

"Your father came to this house in the hot month of Sraban," says Pishi, "in a parched year when the crops were beginning to fail and there were more beggars than usual in front of our gate. Even Bijoy, Anju's father, had worry etched deep and black under his eyes because in those days much of our money came from our ancestral paddy fields. His anxiety hurt me, for more than anything in my life I wanted him to be happy, my younger brother who had taken me into his home when mine shattered and had never for a moment let me feel that I was a burden.

"With him your father brought a locked blue trunk, a long, thin music case stitched in red silk, a newlywed wife, and rain. For the very night he came, the sky filled with fat-bellied clouds the color of steel, and a cool wind began to blow, smelling of faraway wet earth and champak flowers—a smell that even now, remembering, makes my old-widow blood beat faster. And the monsoons began. Lying in bed we could hear the jhup-jhup of the raindrops on the roof, the coconut trees rustling their pleasure. The rain lasted all month, just heavy enough, with sunshine in between to keep us from getting tired. By the end of it our garden was filled with more flowers than I recall ever seeing, bel and jui and the white king-flower, gandharaj, that makes you drunk with its sweet smell, and the crops were saved.

"Perhaps that is why Bijoy took your father so fully into his heart, because he believed he was good luck. But I think he would have even otherwise. For your father was a man of great charm, and part of his charm lay in his recklessness, his belief that every day was a new one untouched by yesterday's deeds, and that he could get away with anything for the price of a smile.

"All this Bijoy loved because it was so completely different from the way he was, always proper, always responsible. The way he, as the only son of the Chatterjees, had been trained to be. But some of his seriousness fell away from him when he was with your father, and he laughed more boyishly, more openheartedly, than in years. For this, I too loved your father.

"Your father told us his name was Gopal, and that he was the only son of our youngest uncle. All we knew of this uncle was that he had taken his share of the family inheritance and left home a long time ago, after a fierce quarrel with our grandfather. Now Gopal told us that his father had settled in the city of Khulna, across the border, where he had thrived as a merchant until the partition. But in the riots that followed he had lost everything—the business, the house, his savings—and, brokenhearted, died soon after. His last words to Gopal had been to go back to his ancestral home and tell his people his story.

"We welcomed our lost cousin into the family with joy, honored that he had chosen to come to us. He was so handsome and fair-skinned, so obviously well born, and laughed so merrily when describing the trials of his travels to Calcutta. He would burst into song for the least reason. And he played the flute—for that was what had been in the red silken case—as sweetly as his namesake Gopal, the god Krishna, must have done when he charmed the milkmaids of Brindaban into leaving home and husband to follow him.

"There was much that he didn't tell us about himself and about your mother. Some of it I would learn from words Nalini let fall carelessly from time to time, and some I would learn when you were born, by piecing together her delirious words as she tossed about in her bed of fever and grief and childbirth pain. That he'd met his new bride as she washed clothes by the river at one of the villages where his boat had stopped. That he promised her riches and honor, marriage into one of the oldest Calcutta families, promised her eternal love in a voice so sweet she thought it surely would pull down the stars from the sky. It made her forget years' worth of cautions impressed on her by mothers and aunts, the old women of the village. At dawn she slipped away from her parents' home. She let your father take her hand and pull her onto the rickety boat filled with men like himself who hoped to make their fortune in the big city.

I want to interrupt Pishi. Surely she is wrong. How can this runaway adventuress be my mother, who is built of sighs and complaints, who guards every propriety as though it is a fragile crystal heirloom she has been personally entrusted with? My mother, who has implied often enough that the laxities of our household would never have been tolerated in her father's perfectly run one—how could she have been washing clothes like a common village girl? And yet, as the scene shapes itself inside my eyelids, I know it is true.

In the scene, my mother is slim and scared. The hot stares of the men on the boat make her blush and draw the edge of her sari over her face. She wonders in fear as she breathes in their unwashed odors if she has made a horrible mistake, if distaste for the unending drudgery of her chores—scouring pots that blackened her nails and broke them, lighting coal fires that turned her eyes a stinging red, plastering cow dung on the walls of the hut that leaked every monsoon—has led her to ruin. She wipes at her tears silently as night falls and the sky fills with strange stars, and when my father tries to kiss her, discreetly, behind a bale of hay, she pushes him from her with sudden energy.

Fortunately, my father is not without honor. When after changing many boats and trains they finally reach Calcutta, he takes her to the Kali temple. There a priest mumbles a few mantras and impatiently gestures at them to exchange garlands. Then he tucks into his waistband the coins my father gave him and turns to the next couple, for Kalighat is popular with lovers who have eloped. And thus my parents are married.

It is not what my mother dreamed of all those years as she

swept the mud floor of her home with a coconut-leaf jhata and ground red pepper paste for curries and wiped the snot noses of her younger brothers and sisters. Where is her red Benarasi, glittering with zari thread? Where is her wedding jewelry, the gold bangles with the alligator-head design, the thick seven-strand chain that when unwound will reach from her head to her feet? Where are the hooped earrings so large they knock against her cheeks when she turns her head, the tiny diamond that sets off her perfect nose? (For my mother is pretty, she knows this, pretty enough to deserve a better life.) Where are all her childhood friends, fellow-sharers in fantasy, to look on enviously and whisper behind their hands as the conch shell sounds its auspicious notes? Still, she allows herself a tiny smile as her husband rubs vermillion into the parting of her hair, the good luck sindur that proclaims to the world that she is a married woman, with a new life ahead of her.

That new life must have seemed good to my mother as they approached the white mansion that shone in the late afternoon sun, its brick neatly painted, its marble polished, its wrought-iron gates topped regally with prancing lions. The driver honked impressively—for although they'd hired a wheeled cart to carry their baggage most of the way, when they were close to the house, her husband had hailed a taxi. It wouldn't do to ride up to his cousin's house as though they were penniless, he said. Indeed, if he hadn't been set upon by robbers early in his trip, he would have hired a taxi all the way.

Did my mother believe the story about the robbers? She had no option. To doubt him would have meant doubting herself, allowing that insidious voice to start up again inside the spaces of her skull, *you shouldn't have, you shouldn't have.* So she chose not to hear the stridency in my father's voice as he told the gatekeeper to announce his arrival to barababu, the master of the house. *Yes, I'm his cousin brother, that's right, from Khulna, what's the matter, something wrong with your ears?* And when the barababu did appear, looking a trifle puzzled, she tried not to see the strained lines at the corners of her husband's mouth as he smiled, and how he held himself, too careful of the creases of his dhoti, as though he had something to prove. It pained her that she could see all this about her husband already, and she no more than a day-old bride. Somehow it made the pain worse to see that the barababu, a true gentleman—you could tell it by the way he never raised his voice, never had to, in his life—believed every word her husband was saying. So she was glad when the widow, the barababu's sister, took her by the hand and said, Come along, my dear, you must be so tired after the long journey, not to mention terrified, having those robbers attack you like that. (For that was what Gopal had said, to explain his bride's bare arms, her unjeweled neck and ears. And my mother, lowering her startled eyes quickly, guiltily, had realized that it was not the ceremonial knotting of garments that binds a wife to a husband but the chain of collusion.) Fortunately, the widow did not notice my mother's blush of shame. What is the world coming to these days, she continued. It is kaliyug for sure. Come, let the men catch up on their man-talk. I'll get you a glass of sweet michri water and show you the room where you are to sleep.

"Oh, she was beautiful, your mother," says Pishi. "Maybe the most beautiful woman I'd seen, though recently it seems to me that you've surpassed her. Even on that day, with the dust of Calcutta lying like a veil over her face, and wilted like a lotus flower plucked and left too long in the sun, she could turn a man's head. Yet how docile she seemed as she followed me, docile and a little stunned. How full of young wonder when I showed her to her room and explained how the switch to the ceiling fan worked, and the flush toilet. But that was to change soon."

I imagine the years passing my mother by as she sits on the high four-poster bed, staring out through the window grills at the passing vendors calling their wares outside her room. But it is not really her room, just as the peacock-silk bedspread is not hers, nor the saris she wears, or the jewelry. She cannot even claim the food she eats as rightfully hers, earned by her own husband. She is here on charity, a poor cousin by marriage, and even though the barababu and his wife are truly kind and welcoming, even though the widow-lady, his sister, takes her everywhere she goes—the market, the temple, the *jatra* performances of tales from the *Mahabharat*—the truth of her situation gnaws at her endlessly. She feels cheated, and as each year rolls like karma's iron wheel toward its end, the lines of discontent take over her face like spiderwebs do an abandoned house. She begins to nag at her husband more and more. *Are you ever going to make any money, when are we going to move into our own home, where are all your fine promises now, hai Mother Kali, this is my punishment for following this man, for smearing black on my ancestors' faces.*

"Your father was a dear man," says Pishi, "but not lucky in matters of money. It was as though the Bidhata Purush, having given him good looks and charm enough for two, felt he had received his due. Oh, he had great ideas, Gopal, but they were like unbaked clay pots. You went to fetch water, lowered them into the lake, and all you were left with was mud on your hands. That's how it was with the handmade perfume factory he proposed, the radical newspaper he wanted to run. He would go to Bijoy for the capital, promising big things. *This time it'll work, I know it, Biju Da, I'll return you double money within two months.* Bijoy was always happy to help. He was a generous man, my brother. Too generous sometimes, we told him, your Gouri Ma and I, but he wouldn't listen. He just said, 'What's the good of money, Didi, if I can't use it to make my own brother'—that's how he thought of your father—'happy. By God's grace, don't we have enough?'

" 'Not really,' Gouri would say. 'Have you seen the accounts this month?' Even in those days she was the clear-eyed one, fooled by little. She would point out how the bookstore was running at a loss, and how Harihar the nayeb hadn't sent the full revenues from the village, claiming that the paddy prices had fallen again. 'You've got to go and check on him,' she said. 'He's stealing from us with both hands.'

"But Bijoy would just smile his gentle smile and say, 'Gouri, where's your trust? Hari Kaku has been with our family for thirty years. He used to carry me around on his shoulders when I visited the village as a little boy. He would never do a thing like that.'

" 'If he's so honest,' Gouri would say, her face reddening, for she hated that anyone should take advantage of her husband's generous heart, 'he shouldn't mind you asking a question or two, checking his facts and figures with other people.'

"Bijoy would shake his head. 'I can't go snooping around for the sake of a few rupees, Gouri,' he'd say. 'It would be an insult to Hari Kaku. We Chatterjees have never done things like that.' His voice would still be soft, but firm also, and final, so that your mother knew there was nothing to be gained by arguing. In any case, she believed that a woman's first duty was to support her husband.

"She was the perfect wife, your aunt Gouri, and her perfection was beautiful because it sprang from a source of goodness deep in her heart. I admired her greatly for it, and envied her a little too. But later I would wish it had not been that way. If she had fought with Bijoy, if she had wept and sulked and threatened and charmed, like ordinary women do with the men they love, perhaps he would still be alive.

"Deep within himself Bijoy must have known Gouri was right, that the fortunes of the Chatterjee family were like a moon spinning toward eclipse. I think that is why he agreed with your father about the ruby cave.

"But first came the pregnancies.

"We were all pleased when Gouri and Nalini became pregnant within weeks of each other, but Bijoy was overjoyed. He had been wishing for a child ever since he was married, seven years ago, and he took the double pregnancy as a miracle of sorts, further proof of the good luck Gopal brought to the house. He showered the two women with gifts—of equal value, that's the kind of man he was—and made sure the baidya came each month to check on their progress. Special food was prepared for them, whatever their hearts desired. When your mother, who had not been doing too well, took a fancy for mangoes in the winter, Bijoy sent all the way to Hogg's market, where the sahebs shopped, to get a dozen of them at an exorbitant price. He wanted her to be happy."

But my mother was not happy, and she no longer attempted, as she had done early in her marriage, to hide it. Nor did she care that an unhappy mother is said to pass on her sorrow to the baby in her womb. For with the onset of her pregnancy, a strange desperation had come over her. As her waist thickened and her feet grew swollen, as her only treasure, her beauty, disappeared within the bloated sack she saw her body turning into, she felt that her one chance at life was over. Things would only get worse now. She was doomed to grow old and die in the borrowed room she had lived in for the last three years. And thus her tirades grew worse. *Are you a man or a ground-crawling insect?* she would shout at my father. *How long are you going to beg your daily food from your cousin-brother, just because he is kind? Running after no-good schemes like a dog chasing his shadow. Why can't you get a job in an office like all the other men? Chee chee, don't you see how even the servants look at us, with no respect in their eyes, how they whisper about us in the kitchens?* And finally, *If the baby knew what kind of father he had, he too would be ashamed. He would rather die than be born to you.*

For a while my father would have tried to ignore her. She didn't really mean it. Everyone knew how pregnant women were. Water spouted from their eyes for no reason, and flame from their tongues. He would sit on the terrace after dinner and play on his flute while Bijoy listened, and the darkness would be cool against his skin, cool and calm and deep, the water of a black lake that extended out forever, and the high notes of the flute would be perfect ripples on its satin surface.

But the part about the baby—ah, that stung, as though someone had wound him around and around in poisonous bichuti vines. So that one morning he left, very early, before even the servants were awake, and was gone for three days. And just when a frantic Bijoy was about to inform the inspector saheb at the police station that his brother was missing, he returned. With the ruby.

"The sun was setting when he flung open the gate and hurried up the gravel driveway," says Pishi, "and its last rays caught his disheveled hair in a brown halo. A two-day stubble covered his face, and his clothes—the same he had worn when he left the house—were crumpled and muddy. But his eyes—they glittered in his face with such intensity—like he was a prophet, or maybe a madman. He was laughing as he shouted for us all to come and see what he had with him."

Rolled across his palm the ruby must have sparkled like fire and ice together, like a teardrop wept by Jatayu, the mythical dragon-bird. It was so large that all who saw it drew in their breath in sharp amazement, and even my mother was silent while he told the household about the cave.

"He'd met a man, said Gopal, though he would not tell us where or how or his name either, a man who knew of a cave deep in the jungles of Sundarban where a million rubies such as these grew from the walls. His great-grandfather had been told of the cave by a sannyasi he'd met while on pilgrimage. He had found the place and chiseled three stones from it, and on his return had them polished by the finest jewelers in Calcutta. Yes, this stone that we were passing around in amazed silence was one of them.

" 'Why three?' Gouri asked, frowning.

" 'That was all that was allowed by the demons who guarded the cave, the sannyasi had warned,' Gopal replied, and by his laugh you could tell he did not believe in such warnings. He went on to tell us that over the years the ruby-finder's family had come upon one misfortune after another until they'd had to sell the other two rubies—but this one, the loveliest of them all, they'd held on to. Now, though, they faced disaster unless they sold this last one too—or unless the great-grandson could find the cave again.

" 'And can he?' Bijoy asked eagerly, as though he really believed this story, which sounded to me as if it had been lifted from a book of old tales.

" 'He thinks he can,' said Gopal. 'His great-grandfather left directions, but he warned the family that the caves were cursed and the guardians easily angered. They were not to undertake such a journey unless the family were in the direst straits. But now they are, and the great-grandson is prepared to take the risk. What he needs, though, is a partner, a man of honor and adventure, a man who can raise the money needed for the expedition.'

" 'How much?' asked Bijoy.

"I was surprised that he would even consider such a crazy scheme, and looking at Gouri, I saw that she was too. There was something else in her eyes which I'd rarely seen—fear. She crossed her hands over her belly—she was in her eighth month—and pressed her lips together to keep in all the things I knew she wanted to say.

" 'A hundred thousand rupees,' said Gopal, his voice like a child's who has run all the way home.

" 'A hundred thousand?' Gouri burst out incredulously.

" 'Yes, I know it's a lot,' Gopal said. 'It's because he'll have to pay the bearers extra to go into that forest—they believe it's haunted. He's willing to leave the ruby with us for surety—we can have it evaluated by any jeweler we choose. He says it's worth more than what we loan him. On his return he'll pay us back double the money.

" 'I told him I thought I could raise the money—but only if he let me come with him. If he let me get my own rubies. Then he wouldn't owe me anything.

" 'We bickered back and forth, and finally we agreed that I'd go with him. I'd let myself be blindfolded the last part of the journey, and I'd bring back only one ruby. Even then, brother, a ruby like this one—can you imagine how much that would be worth? Enough for me to repay you—not that I ever could, in my heart—for all these years you've been taking care of me. Enough for Nalini and me to start a new life in our own home. Brother, please say you'll loan me the money.'

" 'And Bijoy, my gentle, conscientious brother, who had never traveled more than a hundred miles outside of Calcutta, who had never expressed any desire of doing so, said, 'I will if I can come with you. If I can bring back a ruby too.'

"Oh, chaos broke loose then, myself and Gouri crying, *Are you mad? It's some kind of a trick, can't you see? And even if it weren't, it sounds terribly dangerous.* And *Where will you get money like that, anyway,* and *How can either of you think of leaving at this time, there's no more than a month left for the babies to come.* Only later did I realize that Nalini hadn't said a word.

" 'Please, Didi, Gouri, calm yourselves,' Bijoy had said, and when I heard his voice I knew his mind was made up. Gouri must have heard it too, for she left the room then, weeping, though she'd never been one for tears, and took to her bed and did not come down for the night meal. But Nalini's eyes shone as they hadn't in a long while, and she ate well, and while she ate she asked many questions.

"News of all this spread like flames in wind—with servants, it's never any other way. In the telling the ruby grew to be big as a pigeon egg, the cave became a treasure house of the jinns, and the stranger was a magician, a jadukar who'd mesmerized the two brothers, surely, for although Gopal Babu had always been crazy, Bijoy Babu had too much sense to believe such things. And yet, and yet—the eyes of the tellers would take on a faraway look at this point—what if there *were* such a cave, what if the brothers *did* bring back those rubies—and anyone could see that they wished they were going too."

I think I understand how my father felt, and my uncle. And

even my mother with her sudden-sparkling eyes (though always it is her I know the least, less even than the two men whom I have never seen). For each of them, in a different way, it was a last opportunity.

The cave of rubies would allow my father to redeem himself with his wife and his brother—yes, he too thought of Bijoy this way, he was surprised to discover, and not merely as the rich cousin to whom he was beholden. Ah, when did this change, which he had never intended, occur? When had he begun to love them both, to want them to look on him with admiring eyes?

For my uncle, the only son of the Chatterjees, trapped since birth in the cage of propriety, it was the one chance at a life of adventure. At a life which had seemed to him until now as remote and impossible, as holy—yes, that was the word—as that of fairy tale princes on a magic quest. How could he let it pass? His hand was steady as he signed the papers pawning the family lands— even their country mansion—to raise the needed money. When Gouri Ma protested, reminding him that the house had been owned by the Chatterjees for more generations than anyone re- membered, he held her hands tightly and assured her he would get it back before the year was out. The hunger in his eyes stopped her from saying anything more. She knew what he was thinking ahead to: The way he would sit, years from now, in the purple Calcutta twilight, speaking of it all to his sons—and their sons as well. The look of wonder on the young faces, adoration such as he had never hoped for.

And my mother? Perhaps she longed for my father to succeed in *something*, so that she could see him once more as she had done, briefly, on that first evening by the glittering river. Perhaps a part of her longed to love him—for surely all women long to love their husbands—even while another part condemned him as unworthy of her love. Perhaps she wanted the father of her un- born son to be a hero. Perhaps this victory—so long awaited— over the fate which had doomed them to dependence would make it finally right, that decision she made early one morning, stealing from bed, leaving the shelter of her parents' home for the sky that yawed and pitched above a creaking riverboat.

But maybe I am wrong. Perhaps she was thinking only of the rubies. Strings of rubies at her neck and ears, bangles studded with them, rubies encircling her slender ankles like the fire's laughter, causing all the neighbor women to murmur their envy as she walked by.

"They left a week later," says Pishi, "dressed in the clothing of adventure: khaki pants, thick leather boots like neither had ever worn in his life, round safari hats which Gopal must have seen in a movie. They took a taxi to Howrah station, not the house car, for their mysterious partner insisted that no one must see him. There must be no breath of gossip, it was a matter of his honor. He told them that his own family did not know anything about Gopal and Bijoy either.

"After the train journey they were to take the boat along the river and then into the swamps. Next they would hike into the heart of the jungle. The partner had arranged everything, proper equipment, tents, adibasi coolies to cook and carry for them. Beyond that they did not know, except that they were sure to be back in two weeks, long before the babies came. The ruby, which was indeed genuine, they left safely locked in the bank vault.

"For weeks we waited, fretting for news. Then one morning the telegram arrived. It informed us that the Sundarban police had found two bodies and the charred remains of a launch in the swamp. No, only two bodies, said the police when we telephoned them, though of course there might have been others, the crocodiles may have got to them first. They were a small police force out there in the backwaters, after all, with a large area to cover. No, it wasn't a robbery, one of the men still had his gold watch and cuff links. In the other's pockets were two plastic-wrapped moneybags. Possibly Bijoy had given his to Gopal for safekeeping—it was the kind of thing he liked to do. The bags held a few rupees and some papers with our address on them. That's how the police were able to track us down.

"For weeks I would wake in the middle of the night, my chest aching with a sorrow so deep it was physical—as though someone had been pounding on my heart with a grain-crushing pestle. But even in my grief I realized that my loss was small compared to that of the two wives. Ah, I couldn't bear to look at their faces as they took off their jewelry and put on widow's white and wiped the marriage sindur from their foreheads as I had once done. Especially your Gouri Ma. I'd known her since she came to this house as a bride of seventeen. I'd held her and comforted her in the first homesick days when she wept for her parents, just as she would hold and comfort me a few years later after my husband's death. I couldn't stop thinking of the morning of the ill-fated journey when she had asked Bijoy, one more time, not to go. And then, when he said he must, she had said, 'What if you don't come back?' He had laughed and touched her cheek and said, 'Don't be silly. I'll be back before you even expect me.' But Gouri had not smiled. She'd said, 'But what if you don't?' And Bijoy, suddenly serious, had said, 'Then I expect you to bring up my child as befits a descendent of the Chatterjees. Will you promise me that?' And Gouri had looked at him with a sadness in her eyes, as though she knew already what was to come, and said, 'I promise.'

"She never forgot those words. In the days after the funeral, she wouldn't allow herself to break down as your mother did. When I tried to get her to weep, to let the sorrow out of her heart, she said, 'I don't have the luxury. I made a promise and I must use all my energies to keep it.' That's when she started going to the bookstore every day—the pawned lands were forfeit already—and when people, even her own relatives, said that it was a scandal, no Chatterjee wife had ever done such a thing, she looked at them with a hard face and told them she would do whatever was necessary to ensure her daughter's future."

We sit together, silent, pondering the mystery of the deaths, feeling once more their far, tragic reach into our lives. Finally,

Pishi pushes herself to her feet with a sigh. The kirtan will start soon, and she must go. The past is the past, and regrets, as the priest at the temple said in his katha last week, imply a lack of piety, a resistance to God's will.

"Wait," I shout as she reaches the edge of the stairs. "You didn't tell me the secret."

"It was there in the story," says Pishi. "One of them. If you didn't hear it, maybe it's for the best." And she starts down the staircase with slow, unsteady steps, leaning painfully on the banister because lately her arthritis has been bothering her. But for once I do not care for her pain.

"It's not fair," I shout. "You tricked me." Anger turns inside me like a broken spear tip. Ah, how helpless we children are, how dependent on the whims of adults. I'm shaken by the injustice of this, my life. And so I fling at my aunt the most hurtful words I can think of. "You broke your promise! I hate you. I'll never trust you again."

The footsteps pause.

"Very well, my poor Sudha," Pishi says from the bend of the stairs, "so eager to lose your brief innocence, I'll tell you what you want. Not because of your childish threats but because I am bound by the promise I made." And sitting there in the gloom, her face turned away from me, her voice echoing eerily up the stairwell, she speaks the rest of the tale.

"It was the night before Bijoy and Gopal were to leave for the ruby cave. I was checking the house doors to make sure they were locked when I saw the light in Bijoy's office room. I went to see why, and there he was, holding a letter. When he noticed me, he started putting it away, then sighed and handed it to me. It was from a man I didn't know, a certain Narayan Bose. From his letterhead I could tell he was a lawyer. The postmark was from Khulna in Bangladesh.

"Khulna, remember, was the city our uncle, Gopal's father, had gone to after that enormous fight with our grandfather.

Gopal had grown up there—he often spoke with longing about his father's beautiful home, seized by the rioters along with the rest of his property during the partition riots.

" 'I'd written to Narayan Bose to see if we could buy back my uncle's house in Khulna,' said Bijoy, and as he spoke I noticed how stricken his face looked. 'I thought it would make Gopal happy.'

"Narayan Bose had written back that it was not possible to buy the house in question. The daughter of the original owner—and here he gave our uncle's name—was currently living there with her husband and children. She had inherited the property ten years ago when her father died, as there had been no male heirs."

"What do you mean, no male heirs?" I break in from the top of the stairs. "What about my father—"

"No male heirs," says Pishi, staring woodenly at the wall. "And the daughter, the only child, had no wish to sell the house. It was probably a good thing, Narayan Bose wrote. The house had been broken into during the riots and parts of it set on fire. There were many other homes, far superior, that Bijoy could purchase for the same price.

" 'So he isn't related to us at all,' I said to my brother. My voice shook with rage, and my hands also, as I remembered how I had trusted Gopal—but perhaps even that name was a lie, made up for the benefit of his gullible 'cousins.' But it wasn't just rage I felt. It was pain too. I'd loved your father, the way he would come and ask me for a cup of tea, *Didi, you make the best cha I've ever tasted,* the way he'd stop at the Paush fair to buy for me the syrupy nolen gur I particularly liked. I had loved—but what was the use of thinking of it, when it was all a lie.

" 'The cheater, the fake,' I cried. 'He should be whipped out of the house tomorrow, first thing. I'll tell the gatekeeper myself. No. We should turn him over to the police. He deserves to rot in jail.'

"I would have said more, but the look on Bijoy's face made me stop. I hadn't known a man's face could show such heartbreak. And I realized that however much I'd loved your father, Bijoy had loved him far more.

"We stood there, silently, for a long time. When the clock struck midnight we jumped, as though we were the guilty ones.

" 'What are you going to do?' I asked, and Bijoy pressed his fingers to his temples and said, 'I don't know, I don't know, I can't think.'

" 'You mustn't go with him tomorrow,' I said. 'He can't be trusted.'

"But Bijoy fisted his hands and said, 'I've got to find the ruby cave—for myself more than anyone else.' And then he said, 'Maybe I'll talk to him when we're alone on the river.'

" 'You mustn't do that,' I said. 'He might get desperate and do something, who knows what. And you don't even know how to swim.' But even as I said it I felt I was being melodramatic.

"Bijoy must have thought the same, for he shook his head with a half-smile. 'Oh, Didi!' he said. 'This isn't the movies! What are you thinking? That Gopal will push me overboard and watch me drown?'

"He was right. Gopal might be a liar, a fortune hunter, but he was no murderer. Besides, Bijoy was the head of the family. I had to believe that he would know how to handle this situation.

"We did not speak of the matter again.

"Bijoy did pranam to me before he left, touching my feet for blessing, and asked me to keep a lamp lit in front of the gods in the puja room. I held him as I whispered prayers into his hair, and for a moment a forgotten memory surfaced, from where I don't know: how, before I left for my husband's house, I would rock Bijoy in my arms—he was just a few years old then—his little body slumping into sleep, the smell of his hair like melted sugar.

"I kept that lamp lit every day, I prayed each morning and

night to Ganesh, remover of obstacles, and Kali, protectress against evil. But I couldn't stop the arrival of that death-bearing telegram."

How much time passes before I realize that Pishi is gone and I am alone on the terrace? Vaguely I remember her coming back up the stairs when the story had ended, with tears in her eyes. Her trying to comfort me, and me holding my body hard and stiff against her, shoving her from me.

Now you see why I didn't want to tell you, Sudha.

Go away, go, leave me alone.

For how long did I cry, and when did the tears get used up? Now laughter is spilling out of me in great, bitter gusts, because the past is not reliable and solid, the roots of a huge banyan, as Pishi has always led me to believe. The past is a Ferris wheel like the ones at the Maidan fair. A giant Ferris wheel, spun faster and faster by my father until it careens out of control. Until it is wrenched from earth, flung into the emptiness of the hot yellow sky.

My father, the handsome rascal, the masquerader with the dangerous, diamond laugh, blown in on a bad-luck wind. Who took the lives of this household into his hands and with his thoughtless wanting broke them like rotted drywood.

And my mother, who—it comes to me now—is my other secret.

My beautiful mother with that haughty look always on her face. My mother hinting through a toss of her head, an angling of her elegant neck, how much better things had been in her parents' household. My mother, who was really the daughter of peasants, washing soiled clothes by a muddy river, who thought to erase her ancestry with a clever tongue.

The shame of their lies floods my head with thick crimson. Shame and more shame because others had watched them masquerade, first with suspicion and then with knowledge. Pishi, and surely if Pishi, Gouri Ma too. Watching them and me, knowing us for who we were long before I did.

There's a stabbing in my belly, again, again, so that I must double over with the pain. A cramp wrenches my whole body. Perhaps one can really die of shame, as the old tales say?

Then I feel the hot trickle between my thighs, and know. Will the blood be the same color as the rubies my parents longed for, and with that longing brought catastrophe to the Chatterjee family?

Ah, my sweet Anju with a world of love in your eyes, what would you say if you knew?

The thought is a wave I could drown in. I hold my breath against it as I walk to the darkening mango strips. The sun has slid down until it is impaled on the thorny fronds of the coconut trees. It is long past the time when I should have turned the mangoes over, as I promised Pishi. I bend to them and begin my task even as blood soaks my underwear, even as I know what the result of my action will be. But I don't care. I *want* my touch to rot it all, to turn everything in this faithless world black with fungus.

I try to focus on the salt-coarsened strips in front of me, but one final thought breaks over me, takes my breath. It makes me rock myself back and forth, with pain or fear, I don't know which. And the thought shapes itself into a wail that spirals tornado-like through the old mansion of the Chatterjees, shaking every stone: I, Sudha, am nothing to Anju. Not twin, not sister, not cousin. Not anyone except the daughter of the man who with his foolish dreams led her father to his death.

When I come back to myself—is it an age later?—the terrace darkening like dying coals around me, Anju's voice calling me impatiently downstairs, mock-scolding, and my own voice answering her, joking back, I know this: Something has changed between us, some innocence faded like earliest light. The air we breathe now smells of salt and seaweed, as when, the fishermen on the Ganga say, an ocean storm is about to rise.

Anju

TODAY'S A SPECIAL day, our thirteenth birthday. When Sudha and I come home from school, Mother gives us each a slim packet of rupee notes and the permission to buy whatever we want with them. The top of my head goes all tingly with excitement because we've never been given any money before.

Aunt N frowns. "I don't think you should put cash into children's hands like that, Didi," she says. "Who knows what they'll be up to."

"You forget, Nalini," my mother replies, smiling. "They're no longer children, they're women now. It's time we started trusting them."

Aunt mutters something darkly about what happens when a mother lets her daughters dance on her head.

I wish Mother would say something sharp and stinging back to her, but she only smiles again.

"Don't worry so much," she says. "They're good girls. They know what they're allowed to do."

"I hope you're right," says Aunt N, but from the look in her eyes as she fixes them on me, I can tell she has no hope at all.

Sudha and I are just finishing up our homework when Ramur Ma comes by to say Mother wants me in her bedroom, alone. No, she doesn't know why.

I'm so pleased I run all the way up the stairs. Mother's usually so busy managing the household and the bookstore that I hardly ever get her to myself. I love those rare times when I get to sit next to her in the big double-armchair in her room while she asks me what I learned at school. She's not so stern at those moments, nor so worried, and when she cups my face in her hands and tells me how proud she is of my achievements, I feel my whole body softening with happiness, all the rebelliousness melting out of it. Maybe today she'll take that ancient leather photo album from her almirah again and point out my various ancestors to me. I really couldn't care less about all those faded faces with their pince-nezs, their silver-tipped walking sticks, and their crimped dhotis. But I'll pretend a fervent interest just so I can lean against her arm and breathe in the sandalwood scent that rises from her skin like the smell of goodness.

When I get to her room, Mother asks me to close my eyes. Then she puts into my hands something at once hard and velvety. It's an old jewelry box, and opening it I gasp at the pair of bird-shaped earrings inside, sparkling against blue silk. They're beautiful—even I can see that. Usually I'm not the least bit interested in jewelry. I'd rather have a good book, as I've told all my relatives, not that they listen. But these earrings—I fall in love as soon as I see them. They're made of filigreed gold as delicate as a web, and studded with tiny diamonds. Even before Mother says anything, I know they're meant to be part of my trousseau—as they'd been hers. From now on, she adds, each birthday she's going to present me with a piece to match—bracelet, ring, ornamental comb—just as her mother had done.

"They look very nice on you, dear," she says when I try them on. "But I'll have to put them back in the vault for now. You're too young to wear them."

"Wait, first I have to show them to Sudha," I say. "You know how much she likes jewelry. I bet she'll want to try them on too." I can already see the pleasure on her face as she runs her fingers over the gold curve of a bird's neck. She'll adjust each earring in her ear with a frown of concentration. And then she'll give a small, satisfied smile, because the earrings will make her look even lovelier.

I need to see that smile. Because something's wrong with Sudha lately. She'll hardly talk to me, and she's been avoiding the mothers as well—especially Pishi, who I always thought was her favorite. What's more puzzling is that Pishi hasn't questioned or scolded her for her sullenness, as she usually would have. She's only watched Sudha with an expression I can't figure out and given me extra chores, almost as though she wanted to keep me away from her.

Whenever Sudha thinks she's alone, she gazes into the distance with her great dark eyes, and sadness seeps over her face like a stain. I must've asked her a hundred times, Sudha, What is it, what's wrong? But all she'll say is Nothing. Then she'll make an excuse and go to her room, and if I follow her she'll say she has a headache and wants to lie down.

I want my Sudha back. I want her to swing her head so the diamonds flash in the sun, to say, You've got to let me wear these the first day of Durga Puja. I want her to cajole me into trying on whatever her mother's given her—a pair of chappals, a sari—polishing the buckles, adjusting the anchal over my shoulder, buttoning me up and laughing when I complain that the blouse doesn't fit me right. It's our special birthday ritual, all the way back to when I'd take her my dolls who could open and shut their eyes and she'd tie back my hair with her satin ribbons, or take a shiny bindi from the box where she kept her few ornaments and stick it carefully in the center of my forehead.

It never bothered us that I got a lot more gifts than Sudha, or that hers were a lot less expensive. We thought of them as joint property and never hesitated to rummage through each other's almirahs for whatever we wanted. The mothers didn't seem to mind either, though once in a while Aunt N would grumble when she found a mud stain or a tear on one of Sudha's frocks that I'd worn, because I never could learn to be as careful as my cousin.

But today when I'm about to rush to Sudha's room, my mother says, "Anju, maybe you shouldn't."

"Shouldn't what?" I say in surprise.

"Show her your earrings."

"Why not?"

"Maybe they'll make her unhappy."

"Why?" I demand. "Why should they make her unhappy?" I can feel the anger beginning to flare like a fire spark inside my skull even before Mother says another word.

I've never seen Mother look embarrassed before. "Because her mother doesn't have such costly things to give her," she finally says. "And it's going to get worse from now on, as you grow older and I start putting together your dowry jewelry. I love Sudha, and I'll try to buy her something each year, but I just don't have the money to get her this kind of gift." She looks down at her hands, and I wonder if she's thinking how she'd always insisted to me that people mattered far more than possessions, or how she'd always said that there was no difference between Sudha and me as far as she was concerned.

Watching my mother, I see something else that I've been too busy or too thoughtless to notice. Or maybe it's just that she's always been good at hiding what she doesn't want us to see. Her face is pale, and her skin, usually a warm brown, looks mottled, like a frostbitten flower. I remember how she'd stayed up very late all of last week because there had been a crisis at work. What it was I didn't know; she liked to keep these matters to herself. Looking at her tired face, I feel ashamed of all the times when I'd wondered why she couldn't do better with the business. I want to hold her and tell her it's okay, neither Sudha nor I want expensive things, she doesn't have to drive herself so hard. Times have changed. A dowry isn't going to be as necessary for us. After all, we're both going to college. And as soon as I'm a little older, I'll start helping her in the store.

But Mother's next words change all my sympathy to fury.

"At some point," she says, "Sudha's bound to start comparing herself with you and feeling some envy."

"How can you say that?" I say fiercely. "You know Sudha's not like that. She doesn't have a jealous breath in her—"

"And it'll make Aunt Nalini more discontented—"

"Aunt Nalini's always discontented about something or other. Anyway, I'm not going to show these to her. Only to Sudha." And before my mother can say anything else, I hurry out.

I find Sudha up on the terrace, which surprises me. Aunt N doesn't like her to be up here in the daytime because she says all that sun will make her dark, and Sudha's usually so obedient. And ever since the time she ruined all those mangoes, she's tended to avoid the terrace. She won't even come up here with me in the evening, after Ramur Ma washes down the bricks, and the cool breeze brings up the smell of jasmine. I miss that. It used to be our private time, when we could talk without fear of eavesdroppers.

Sudha's leaning against the balustrade, staring out at nothing, dejection clear in every curve of her slumped body. When I call her name she jumps, and when I show her the earrings she gives a wan smile and says they're nice.

"Don't you want to try them on? Don't you even want to hold them in your hand?"

She shakes her head, a gesture that tries to be nonchalant but ends up only being sad.

"What else did you get for your birthday?" I ask, but inside I'm wondering if Aunt N's said something to upset her. Aunt has a tamarind-and-chile tongue and isn't shy about using it on my cousin.

Sudha tells me that Aunt N gave her a bedspread with an

elaborate design traced on it, and a boxful of silk embroidery thread with which to fill it in.

"Don't tell me—it's to be part of your trousseau, just like these are part of mine, right?"

Usually when I say things like this, Sudha rolls her eyes and bursts into conspiratorial giggles. But today she merely looks at me. Then she says, "Anju, don't compare us all the time. We're not the same."

Her voice is so emotionless it sends a shiver through me. "Why d'you say that?" I ask. "What's wrong? No, don't say *nothing*."

Sudha's silent for such a long time that I begin to wonder if Mother's right. Maybe things, *objects*, have indeed come between us.

"Sudha," I say, grasping her hand. "Look, will you do something for me? Take these, okay?" I put the earrings in her palm and close it up. "I want to give them to you for our birthday." I'm not sure what I'll tell Mother, how angry she'll be. I'll worry about that later. Right now I have to take care of Sudha. Because her eyes look as if she's drowning, as if in a minute she'll be deep underwater, beyond my reach.

I think Sudha's going to throw her arms around me, like she always does when I give her a gift, but she says, in a cold, newly adult voice, "I don't want your gifts. Or your pity. My mother and I might not have a lot, but at least we have self-respect."

I gasp. The words are like a slap so hard that for a minute it stuns the flesh. There's a coppery taste in my mouth and my palms are clammy with a sick rage that makes me want to hurt—really hurt—my cousin. I hear myself spit out, "If you're so full of self-respect, how come for the last thirteen years you and your mother have been eating our rice and taking up room in our house? If you're so full of self-respect, why don't you go tell your mother to find a home of your own?"

From the sudden pained flush on Sudha's face, I know my taunt has hit home.

And then I'm sobbing, detesting myself. Ever since I've been old enough to understand such things, I've known how ashamed Sudha's been of the way Aunt N goes around acting proprietory about everything in this house when we all know she has no right to any of it. It's the one topic we've always been careful to avoid.

I grope for her hands, crying.

"Sudha, I didn't mean it, I swear I didn't. This is your house as much as mine, you know that. Sudha, I'm sorry, I said it only because I was so angry, only because I love you."

I think she'll pull away, or fling the earrings over the ledge onto the busy street below, to be crushed under a lorry or snatched away by street children. That's what I would have done. But Sudha only says, in a cool, thinking kind of voice that amazes me even through my tears, "Anju, why do you love me?"

"What kind of a question is that?"

"Tell me, Anju."

"I love you because you're my sister, you know that."

Sudha turns the earrings over and over in her hand. I can tell she isn't even seeing them. "Suppose I wasn't who you thought I was, suppose—" She bites her lip. Then she asks unsteadily, "Would you still love me?"

I start getting angry again, this time because I'm scared. There's a certain note in her voice—as if she knows something I don't. "That's a stupid thing to suppose," I say.

"Please," Sudha says. Her eyes have gone slate-black, and I can see she really needs me to give her an answer.

I try to think of a Sudha who's different, a stranger Sudha perhaps who'd come into my life by chance and would pass out of it the same way. I try to judge whether I'd be able to love such a person. But my entire being is so tied to my cousin's, I can't even imagine it.

"Anju—" Sudha's tone trembles on the edge of anguish. What terrible thing could have happened to shake her belief in our relationship like this? The fear's like a big boulder inside my chest now, leaving no room for breath, and though I'm usually determined to pursue a question to its bitter end, this once I prefer not to know.

But I do know what she needs to hear.

"I'd love you," I say, "no matter who you were. I'd love you because you love me. I'd love you because no one else knows us as we know each other."

"Would you really?" asks Sudha, her voice loosening with relief.

"I would," I say. There's a strange prickling—like a premonition?—along my backbone as I speak. Even to my own ears my voice sounds green and raw, too young to shore up the promise it's making.

What nonsense! I'm getting as superstitious as Sudha.

I take a deep breath. "Because no matter what, I'm still the person who called you out into the world," I say firmly.

Sudha leans her head on my shoulder and releases a sigh so deep I know it carries the full weight of her heart. "You are, Anju," she says. She starts to say something else, then changes her mind and kisses my cheek instead. Her fingers brush my palm like the tip of a bird wing as she puts the earrings back in my hand. "You keep these for me. I'll ask you for them whenever I want to wear them."

And I know she will.

Walking down the stairs hand in hand, we discuss what to do with the money we've been given. It isn't a lot, but it's the first time we've had money that doesn't have to be accounted for. It makes us feel rich and reckless.

"I'll buy clothes with mine," says Sudha dreamily. "Salwaar kameezes soft as a baby's skin, colored like dawn. Saris made of the finest translucent silk, the kind that can be pulled through a ring. Scarves shimmering like a peacock's throat. I'll buy satins and stitch them into puff-sleeved sari-blouses with tiny mirrors embroidered in, and white lace nighties light as gossamer for summer nights, all of it as different as possible from the drab, decorous dresses we're forced to wear—"

I'm taken aback by the longing in her voice. Sudha's always seemed so calm and accepting—I had no idea she hated our clothes—which are admittedly unexciting—so much. What other surprises might my cousin have in store for me?

"You'd never even be allowed to try on such things," I say sadly. "You know how strict the mothers are about what a daughter of the Chatterjees should look like when she goes out in public."

Sudha smiles. "I don't care. I'll wear them in my own room. I'll wear them for you. But what'll you buy?"

"Books! I'll send away for books that are hard to find in this country. Books by writers the nuns mention disapprovingly. Kate Chopin. Sylvia Plath. Books where women do all kinds of crazy, brave, marvelous things. I want the latest novels, to give me a taste of London and New York and Amsterdam. I want books that'll spirit me into the cafés and nightclubs of Paris, the plantations of Louisiana, the rain forests of the Amazon, and the Australian outback. All the places"—here my voice grows a little bitter—"I'll never get to visit, because the mothers won't let me."

Sudha gives me a quick hug. "Oh, Anju, I'm sure you'll see many of them! Maybe after marriage—"

"Sure! I'll probably end up married to some stodgy old fellow who'll never want to step out of Calcutta, someone whose idea of a good time would be to lie on a divan, chewing paan and listening to filmi songs. Someone who'll—"

"Now who's getting all worked up about imaginary things?" says Sudha, laughing. "Don't worry, I'll make a wish for you, that you'll travel all the way across the world. But oh, I'll miss you so much when you go."

"I don't believe in wishes," I say grumpily. But inwardly I hope my cousin is right.

We spend the rest of the afternoon in Sudha's room, examining her birthday bedspread. It's an ambitious design that'll take even someone as diligent as my cousin a good many months to embroider. There's a large sunflower in the center, and a border of dancing peacocks intertwined with a saying in an old-fashioned script that takes us a while to decipher. Then we both burst out laughing, because the letters read *Pati Param Guru, the husband is the supreme lord.*

"Where on earth did Aunt N dig that up from?" I say, grimacing.

"Maybe she special-ordered it," Sudha says, wiping her eyes.

"She must have said to the bedspread maker, I want something that will teach my wild and wicked daughter the proper womanly virtues," I add, "and the bedspread maker must have said, Madam, by the time she's finished embroidering the hundredth Param Guru, I gurarantee you she'll be the perfect wife."

We laugh again, our voices high and shaky, the way you laugh when you've been too close to the edge. We decide that if Sudha puts extra-long tails on the peacocks, it'll cover up the writing and no one will know the difference. We seal our conspiracy with a kiss.

But that night, lying in a tangle of damp bedsheets in the hot dark, my heart still aches like someone ripped it in two and then stitched the torn edges roughly together with one of those thick needles the streetside muchis use to repair our sandals. I can't stop wondering why Sudha had made that strange comment about not being who I thought she was. What could have possibly happened to shake her belief in herself? In us? And why, for the first time in our lives, had she chosen to keep something so important from me?

FIVE

Sudha

THE NEW MOVIE had taken Calcutta by storm. Everywhere there were billboards, larger and brighter than life, depicting the hero and heroine. She in her exquisite gold-worked dancing skirt and dupatta, the innocent virgin in the midst of a corrupt court. Or weeping in the clutches of the evil nabab as her prince rushes on horseback to her rescue. At school the girls couldn't stop whispering about how romantic it was, the lovers singing of eternal passion as they sail on a moonlit river. And then, just as they are to marry, his stern patrician father denouncing her because she is only a dancing girl. Her lovely eyes filling with tears as she decides to leave rather than ruin her beloved's good name. Every paan shop in the city played the songs, "Chalo dildaar chalo, Come with me, heart of my heart, to the other side of the moon." And "Saari raat chalte chalte, Traveling all night, miraculously, I have found you." Every young woman's heart beat faster as she listened, humming the words under her breath. Every young man's heart must have beat faster too. But of that I was not sure. Thanks to the vigilance of the mothers, Anju and I did not know any young men.

We moved in a world of women, my cousin and I, at home and outside. It was a world of filtered, submarine light, languid movements, eyes looking out from behind a frieze. Small muted sounds: the tinkling of bangles, female laughter. In our house the few menservants did not come up beyond the ground floor. And

Singhji—although his deformity seemed to place him in a separate, androgynous zone—never entered the house at all.

At our all-girls convent school, no men were allowed past the darwan who guarded the gate, zealously twirling his metal-tipped lathi, making even the fathers wait on the street. At the few social occasions we attended, weddings or pujas, we sat among our women relatives, webbed around with gossip and song and old tales. Perhaps because we had no fathers, that other world—sweat and sunlight, male cologne, a man's voice raised in a command to a passing servant—seemed distant and full of mystery, like the dim roar of an ocean seen through a telescope.

Our existence was restrictive, yes. But I found it curiously comforting too.

I knew most sixteen-year-old girls in Calcutta didn't live like we did. I saw them on our way to school, pushing onto crowded buses, bargaining loudly with the roadside vegetable sellers as they shopped for their mothers, unabashedly fingering the lau and karala, pinching the sheem beans to check for freshness. Groups of teenagers gay as butterflies summoned the Qwality man and bought orange ices, giggling and wiping at their bright mouths when they were done. Women, young and old, hailed taxis and climbed in, on their way to New Market or Dalhausie; some maneuvered their scooters to work through streets packed with buses and pedestrians and stray cows, honking authoritatively. And once in a while in the dim alleyways where the flower sellers had their shops, I saw a girl holding hands with a young man, lowering her shy eyes as he pinned a garland to her hair.

And their clothes. Salwaar kameezes shot through with metallic thread, gauzy dupattas allowed to slide artfully off shoulders. The westernized ones in jeans, or narrow-cut skirts that showed off their rounded hips, their slender ankles. Their saris, when they did wear them, were in the latest filmi designs and not the traditional bordered handlooms the mothers bought for us. Their summer blouses, generously sleeveless and cut low in the back, drew whistles from the streetside Romeos who leaned endlessly against the corner buildings, and made me blush.

How bold and fascinating these women were. How uncaring of that fragile glass flower, reputation, that lay at the heart of Anju's life and mine. They were all that we, as daughters of the Chatterjees, yearned for and knew we could not be. Had our fathers been alive, the mothers might have been more lenient with us. But Gouri Ma's promise to her dead husband seemed to have frozen our entire household, like the magic spell which, in Pishi's stories, shrouded palaces in timeless sleep.

I accepted this, but Anju never stopped fighting. "Why must Ramur Ma go with us every time we leave the house, even to get books from the neighborhood library?" she'd ask. "Why can't we go to Sushmita's birthday party when all the other girls in class are going, instead of sending a gift with Singhji? No wonder everyone thinks we're stuck up." And "I'm tired of these old-women saris you make us wear. You'd think we were living in the Dark Ages instead of in the eighties. I bet there isn't another girl my age in all of Calcutta—except poor Sudha, of course—who's forced to dress like this. Why can't I wear pants, or a maxi, or at least some kurtas once in a while?"

"*Why, why, why,*" my mother would say. "Uff, my head hurts with all your questions. Why can't you be quiet and let your elders, who know more of the world than you, make the important decisions?"

"We'd know as much about the world as you," Anju would retort, "if you didn't keep us penned in at home all the time like—like prize cows."

"Did you hear that, Didi?" Mother would cry, turning to Gouri Ma. Loud with outrage, her voice made my ears hurt and my stomach muscles clench up. "Did you hear how your daughter talked back to me? Never in all my years did I hear a child in my parents' home speak so rudely. Are you going to let her get away with this kind of behavior? No wonder my Sudha's getting so stubborn nowadays. I can see where she's learning it."

Then everyone would be talking at once, Anju shouting, "Leave Sudha out of it, she never said a word, you're always criticizing her for no reason." And my mother: "See, Didi? See what I mean." And Pishi, placating: "Don't mind what the girl says, Nalini, you know how she is, born under the sign of the bull, never thinking what to speak and what not to speak before the words tumble from her mouth." Until finally Gouri Ma would look up from the accounts book, which she brought home each evening, worry smudged like lampblack into the creases of her face.

"Please, quiet everyone. Quiet!"

And in the reluctant silence that followed she'd tell Anju, "The last promise I made to your father was that if anything happened to him I'd bring you up the way he wanted. The way a daughter of the Chatterjee family should be. You know that."

Those words would have been enough to silence me. And her voice, somber and a little removed—the kind of voice I imagined the queens of Pishi's tales to have.

Anju didn't give up, though. "What's more important, a living daughter's happiness, or a promise you made to a dead man, who's dead because he abandoned us to run after some stupid scheme?"

"Don't talk about your father like that," Pishi cried sharply. "You ungrateful, disrespectful child."

"Or is it because I'm a daughter that my happiness doesn't matter?" Anju's breath came in gasps, and her voice wobbled as it always did just before she cried, "I bet if I were a boy you wouldn't be saying no to me all the time like this."

"Hai bhagaban!" my mother said, turning her appealing eyes toward heaven. "Now she demands to be treated like a son."

"I *am* thinking of your happiness, keeping doors open to houses you might want to enter someday," Gouri Ma said. "But I don't expect you to see that yet." It seemed there was a wistfulness, subtle as the echoing end of a raga, in her usually practical voice. But perhaps I was only being fanciful, for the next moment she sent us off to our rooms to do our homework.

She convinced me. But she never convinced my headstrong Anju, who kicked at the marble banister carved with lions all the way up the stairs.

And so this morning Anju whispers, as we stand in the senior girls assembly line at school, "Let's cut class in the afternoon and go see the new movie, okay?"

"Are you crazy?" I say. Shock makes me forget to whisper, and Sister Baptista, the assembly monitor, turns toward me, her steel-rimmed glasses glittery with disapproval.

"Don't be such a coward," Anju says without moving her lips—a feat which never fails to impress me—while she offers Sister an angel-innocent smile. "We've run off before, remember?"

"And got caught, which you've conveniently forgotten. Don't you remember how upset Gouri Ma was?" I whisper as softly as I can, but a wave of sibilant sound seems to ripple from my lips and Sister gives me a frightful frown.

"We were a lot younger then," Anju says, "and we didn't know how not to get caught." She ignores the last part of my sentence.

"But we promised Gouri Ma—" I start to say. Her face rises in my mind, austere as a Bodhisattva statue I had once seen at the Calcutta museum. She had looked at me and Anju with such reproach—or is it the future I am envisioning? Since that terrible afternoon when I had learned that mothers could lie and fathers deceive, time coils in upon itself at moments, confusing me.

"I should've known better than to ask you, little Miss Holiness," snaps Anju. "All you ever want is to get into Mother's good books. You're probably just waiting to get home so you can tell her my plan. Well, I don't care! I'm going to go whether you come or not."

Somehow I cannot be upset with Anju when she is in a temper like this, for I can see that behind the anger, her eyes are bright with tears she will not let fall. Dear Anju, for whom love means that we must want the same thing, always. That we must be the same. She has not yet learned that ultimately each person— even Anjali and Basudha—is distinct, separate. That ultimately we are each alone.

The thought catches me by surprise. When had I realized this? Was it on that afternoon of secrets, that afternoon of new blood and old tears? Was it on the day of the diamond earrings when I asked Anju why she loved me, and she gave me her answer, sweeter than a sudden spring in the desert of my heart? When had I made the decision not to burden her with the terrible knowledge that ate at me like a canker bug? When had I promised myself that I would spend the rest of my life making up to her for the way in which my father had deceived hers? The way he had tempted him to his death?

Ah, how much older than Anju my promise makes me feel.

"Sudha," Anju hisses, and I turn to her to say—what? What words can I speak with my throat, which has turned blue as Lord Shiva's from the poison I've swallowed so that Anju might continue to laugh and love and quarrel and make up? So that she might take for granted the surety of our intimacy the way I no longer can?

But I am saved by Sister Baptista, who announces in her sternest tones to the entire room that Basudha Chatterjee is to move to the troublemaker's row in the front of the room, this instant, for talking in assembly.

As I walk forward, feeling the prick of a hundred eyes on my face, the smirks that say, Ah, finally one of the Chatterjee girls gets what she deserves, I hear Anju say, very softly, "If you were my true, true sister, you'd come with me."

On the streets it is so hot that the melted pitch sticks to our chappals. The cold-drink vendors with their carts filled with bright orange Fantas and pale yellow Juslas, the slabs of ice sweating under jute sacking, have gone home, having sold out of everything. But the cool darkness of the cinema is a magic country, no less wonderful than the images glimmering bright as jewels on the screen. Air-conditioned breezes wash over us like a blessing, and the slow whoosh of the ceiling fans is as comforting as a whispered lullaby.

Not that I can even imagine sleep.

I've been to the cinema a few times before—to educational English films with Gouri Ma and, with my mother, to the sentimental Bengali movies that always make her cry. But I've never felt this excitement, this tingling that starts in my toes and fingertips and rises hotly up my body to my throat, my cheeks. To my lips, until they feel swollen and pleasantly sore, as though they've been kissed (but here I have to rely on imagination) by a man's rough mouth.

Part of the reason is our new clothes. Anju stopped in the bazaar next to the cinema and bought us each one of the forbidden kurta outfits. "We can't go to see the movie in our school uniforms," she'd said, quick-thinking as ever. "Everyone would know we'd cut class. They'd be sure to stare, and then someone might recognize us."

"Where did you get the money?" I asked, watching the wad of notes that had appeared, miraculously, in her hand.

"It's my birthday money," she said, laughing. "This year I didn't buy books with it. I had a feeling I'd need it for something else."

And so in the damp, dimly lit jenana bathroom we changed into the bright kurtas that lay light as wings on our skin. I looked down at my legs in tight-fitting churidar pants, and marveled at their shapeliness. I couldn't take my eyes from my breasts, how they rose and fell under the thin fabric colored like pomegranate flowers. How rapidly the pulse in the hollow of my throat beat above the oval neckline of the kurta.

"Final touch," said Anju as she took from her schoolbag a black eye pencil and—yes, a lipstick. *From where?* But I didn't ask. I was learning that my cousin had her secrets too.

We darkened each other's eyes with inexpert fingers and outlined each other's mouths with the lipstick, which was a rich maroon quite unsuitable for young girls. But we were reckless by now, giggling as we loosened our braided hair to fall in waves around our flushed faces. When we turned to the mirror to admire ourselves, I was shocked at how grown-up we looked, as though we had crossed over a threshold into the house of adulthood. As though there would be no turning back.

"Oh, Sudha," Anju breathed. "You look stunning. People will be looking at you instead of watching the actresses on the screen."

"Don't be silly," I replied, giving her a little push. But I was pleased. We stuffed our uniforms into our schoolbags and went to get our tickets.

We are lucky: We have good seats, with an unobstructed view of the screen, and though the theater is crowded, there's an empty seat next to mine where I thankfully drop my schoolbag. I had been nervous about who I would have to sit next to. Whenever we went to the movies with the mothers, they sat on the outer edges, buffers between us and the world. For a heartbeat, I miss their protective presence.

But the hall is so fascinating with its high ceilings and cornices embossed with plaster flowers, the rich red velvet of its stage curtain, its aisles that give off a sweetish smell like the zarda that women chew after meals. And the people. Even after the start of the film, which is marvelously romantic and sad, just as I had imagined, I can't stop watching them. The light from the screen casts an unearthly glow on their rapt faces, wiping away lines, lifting away years. As they smile, or touch a handkerchief to their eyes, they appear strangely, heart-catchingly innocent. And yet so mysterious. Even Anju, in the seat next to mine, emotions flitting like moonlit clouds over her face, seems like someone I do not know at all.

Then a male voice says, "Excuse me, is someone sitting here?"

Just my luck! The last thing I want is a strange man sitting next to me, ruining my pleasure in the movie by whistling or making crude kissing sounds during the romantic scenes. I'd heard schoolmates complaining of such things. Maybe I can tell him that a friend is sitting here, that she's just stepped out for a moment?

But when I look at him, I know I need not worry.

"How could you know, Madam Experience? How many men have you talked to in your lifetime?" Anju would say later. "As it happens, he got us into an awful lot of trouble."

Sometimes you just know, I would tell her. And the trouble we got into was not his fault.

In the pearl-blue light of the theater, the man's—but he was not much more than a boy himself—eyes glimmer, dark and bright in turns. His smile is at once open and apologetic. His hair tumbles over his forehead. Charmingly, I think.

"Awfully sorry to disturb you, but I think this is my seat." He holds out his ticket toward me, pointing to the number. The cleft in his chin can break a girl's heart.

I lift my schoolbag from the chair. To keep myself from smiling I stare sternly, fixedly at the screen, where the hero has just boarded a night train. In a moment he will see the sleeping heroine and fall in love, unequivocally, irreversibly, in the way of true passion, world without end.

But I can't stop myself from looking, just once, out of the corner of my eye.

He's intelligent, I can tell that just by how he holds himself, his body relaxed yet alert. Probably a college student, from St. Xavier's maybe. Or Presidency. Open at the throat, his white shirt is very clean and smells of mint. And when, heart pounding, I raise my eyes a little higher, his lips are smiling. At me.

How long do we look at each other in that movie hall that is neither in the world nor out of it? How long do we remain suspended in that timeless opal light that gives us strange permission? I don't know. I must have glanced at the screen from time to time, though I'd long since lost track of the story. (The heroine is weeping as she reads a letter. Then she's dancing—is it at her beloved's wedding party? She throws down a glass to shatter on the ground and keeps dancing, her feet smearing with blood, but the pain is less than that which tears her heart. And then it's the end of the movie, with her in his arms—but how did *that* come about?) It seems to me as though I haven't looked away from his eyes at all, that I cannot, even when the houselights come on, and people push each other along the aisles in their hurry to catch the buses before they get too crowded.

Lying in bed that night I would marvel at the chance that made Anju choose this very day to persuade me to go to the cinema, that arranged this young man's seat next to mine in a hall that held so many hundreds. But even then I had known it was no chance but the inexorable force of destiny, hushed and enormous as the wheeling of the planets, which brought us together. And as our glances met, like that of the prince and the princess in the story of the palace of snakes, the final word the Bidhata Purush had written for me blazed on my forehead. But this we had no eyes to see.

They say in the old tales that when a man and woman exchange looks the way we did, their spirits mingle. Their gaze is a rope of gold binding each to the other. Even if they never meet again, they carry a little of the other with them always. They can never forget, and they can never be wholly happy again.

That is why in families that kept the ancient traditions, girls were not allowed to meet men until the moment of auspicious seeing, shubho drishti, when the bride and groom gave themselves to each other with their eyes. It wasn't, as Anju said, to keep the woman ignorant and under control. The elders in their wisdom had done it to prevent heartbreak.

"Sudha." Anju shakes my arm urgently. "Sudha, what's wrong with you? Let's go!"

I try to focus on her words, but her voice comes from someplace far away. I start to say something reassuring to her, but instead I find myself smiling at my—yes, foolishly, possessively, I think of him as such—my young man.

"Come on," says Anju, and now I see that her face is tight with worry. How ironic that she, the valiant one who had initiated this adventure, should be afraid just when my own timidity has disappeared. "Let's go, we still have to change into our uniforms. If we don't hurry we'll never get back to the school gates before Singhji arrives."

"Okay," I say. But all of them—Singhji, the nuns at school, even the mothers with their inevitable anger—belong to another universe, one that has nothing to do with me.

The young man speaks thoughtfully, musingly. "Sudha," he says, and in his mouth my name takes on a sweetness, an elegance I have never thought it could possess.

Anju draws herself up. "Please move out of the way so that we can get past," she says in her best grown-up voice.

"Yes, of course," he says, courteous without being apologetic. As Anju pushes past him he says, "Sudha, I'm Ashok, Ashok Ghosh. What's your full name?"

Ghosh. The word tolls inside my head like a warning bell. I can hear my mother saying, in her most disapproving patrician tones, *What? A lower-caste man?* I squeeze shut my eyes, willing her voice to fade.

"Sudha, stop, don't say anything," Anju cries, abandoning sophistication. "We don't know who this man is, what he might do, whom he might tell." She claps her hand over my mouth, but I move it aside. *Ashok. The one who banishes sorrow.* I know he'll never use the knowledge of my name against me.

"I'm Basudha Chatterjee," I say, and I smile my most enchanting smile for him.

Anju's trying to pull me toward the door. The hall is almost empty and her voice echoes as she says, "Come on, Sudha. God, am I sorry I suggested coming to the cinema."

"It's okay, Anju, don't worry," I say. A great tenderness fills me. Because she is my sister. Because she wants to protect me from harm. Because she is the one who brought Ashok and me together.

"Don't *worry*!" Anju's voice is brittle with desperation. "Don't worry, she says. How can I not, when you stand here like your head is filled with cow dung instead of brains? Someone's sure to see you talking to a strange man, and then what'll we do?" She yanks hard at me.

"Wait." Ashok extends an arm as though he would stop me. I wonder how his touch would feel, his fingertips electric, but warm also, like summer rain. But he hasn't forgotten the proprieties completely. At the last moment he fists his hand and jams it into his pocket. "Don't go so soon. Can I buy you a soft drink? Can we talk? Even a few minutes—"

"No," says Anju angrily. "Is your head filled with cow dung too? Didn't you hear me say we'd get into terrible trouble at home if anyone saw us here with you? Please, just go away."

"At least let me call you a taxi—"

"We're going to take the bus," Anju says as she pushes me to the door of the jenana bathroom. I look over her shoulder at Ashok's fallen face. I wish I could tell him not to worry—we will surely meet again. But there's just enough time, before Anju slams the bathroom door, to say, "We live in Baliganj."

"How can you be so stupid?" Anju bursts out even before the

echo of the door fades. "You're acting just like one of those silly lovesick girls in the movie. The first stranger you meet, just because he happens to sit next to you—"

"Not just happens, Anju. Nothing just *happens*. I know—"

But before I can say more, the door to one of the ladies' stalls swings open.

"Girls," says a familiar voice. "Girls, is it you? I thought I recognized your voices, but then I thought, no, not possible. *What* are you doing here? You should be in school, isn't it so? And what's this I hear? A man? Sitting next to you?" The large, billowy form of Sarita Aunty emerges from the stall. She shakes out her sari pleats and stares at us, goggle-eyed. "*What* are you wearing? And look at that *stuff* on your lips! Like women of the street. Goodness, I'd better take you home right away. Oh, just wait till your mothers hear of this!"

And, enormously elated, Sarita Aunty grips our arms and holds on, as though she is afraid we might dissolve magically into the ammonia air of the bathroom and deprive her of the season's best gossip story. Her steely fingers dig into our flesh all the way home.

SIX

Anju

WE'VE BEEN sent to our separate rooms in disgrace, to wait until the mothers have decided on a fitting punishment. I lie on my bed staring at the ceiling. The watermarks left there by years of seeping rain usually distract me, they're in so many fantastic shapes—forests and fortresses and the winged beasts which peopled the fairy tales Sudha and I used to act out. It was on this bed, too, that we lay together and dreamed of our futures. I would have a brilliant career in college. It would enable me to visit all the countries I wanted. And Sudha would have a magnificent marriage and wear silk saris every day if she wished. Her children would be beautiful as moonbeams. But today I can't think of anything except how much trouble I've landed us in.

It seems like an awfully long time before Ramur Ma comes to summon me to the office room. All my bravado is gone by now. But at least I'm glad I didn't give in to tears. Otherwise she'd have seen the traces, and the gossip would have traveled through the servant mahals of the old Calcutta houses faster than diarrhea germs in the height of summer: *Wonder what terrible thing the Chatterjee girls have done this time to make Anju Didi break down like that.*

I stand outside the office room, gathering the courage to knock. Then I hear Sudha's soft step behind me. Her hand clasps mine, clammy but firm, telling me we're in this together. Our footsteps ring on the cold mosaic floor as we walk in. Shadows dip and swerve against the bookshelves like frightened bats, and the portrait of our great-grandfather, painted in the gloomy oils popular in his day, glowers down at us.

Beneath the portrait the mothers sit so still on the old velvet sofa, they could have been painted too. Pishi stares into the dim air beyond our shoulders, her mouth a thin, pained line. She hates scenes as much as Aunt N loves them. Aunt has worked herself up already. I can feel self-righteousness rising from her pores like sulfur gas, ready to explode. And my mother—her eyes are in shadow, I can't read her mouth. But when I see her silhouette, the head bent as if it's too heavy for her neck to hold up, I wish with a pang that I'd listened to Sudha.

"Here they are," says Aunt N. "Look at them sauntering in, hand in hand, the shameless hussies. Do they care that all of Calcutta is talking about their escapade? Of course not. Do they care that they've smeared blackest kali on our faces? Of course not. Do they care that in this one afternoon they've undone everything we've been trying to build up for years. All those hours and hours of hard work you put in at the store, Gouri Di"—here I feel a tremor go through Sudha's hand, but Aunt, unaware or uncaring, continues—"and all my scraping and bowing to women from the important families of the city? Of course not. Do they care—"

For heaven's sake, I want to say. We just went to the cinema. You're making it sound like we went and got pregnant.

But the least I owe my cousin now is not to make matters worse.

Then Pishi speaks, surprising me because usually she's a silent watcher at Aunt's scold-sessions. "They behaved badly, I agree," she says. "But must you be so hard on them, Nalini? Look at their faces, I can tell they're sorry about—"

"With all due respect, Didi"—Aunt's voice is chill and black, like the inside of a coal cellar—"you've done enough harm already, filling their heads with old romantic stories. Please don't interfere in this business between mother and daughter."

How well Aunt knew each of our weaknesses. How ruthlessly she went for them. My childless Pishi's eyes glint with pain like broken glass before she lowers them. But Sudha suddenly looks up at Aunt, her body hard and dangerous like an arrow. She doesn't flinch when Aunt lunges forward to grip her by the elbows and shake her, shouting, "Haven't I told you over and over that men can't be trusted? And still you do this! Tell me, who is he? Who's the man you went to the cinema with? How did you meet him? Tell me right now. Don't think being silent is going to save you. And you'd better not make up one of those lying tales you're so fond of."

Aunt shakes Sudha so hard that her head snaps back, and my mother cries angrily, "Nalini! Stop that! Anju has already said they only sat next to him by chance." But there's no stopping Aunt.

"Ogo," she cries, raising her eyes heavenward to address my dead uncle, "where have you gone, leaving me to bring up this wicked girl all by myself? If only you could have been alive to see my suffering and shame today, if only you—"

"He would have been alive," Sudha says. She speaks slowly, each word falling from her as distinct as chiseled stone. "If you hadn't pushed him to desperation with your constant nagging."

The room is still with the absolute silence of shock, even my aunt left openmouthed in mid-sentence. But what astonishes us isn't so much Sudha's boldness. It's the absolute authority with which she speaks.

As though she really knew.

I'm not quite sure what happens next. One moment Aunt Nalini's crying, "See, my own birth-daughter, how she's turned against me. When everything I do is only for her happiness." The sorrow in her voice is raw and rough-grained, and it hits me that for once she really believes what she says.

But when Sudha speaks it's like she hasn't even heard her mother.

"As for lying tales, haven't you told your share of them?" She says this with such contempt that I'm chilled. What could she possibly mean?

From somewhere Pishi's hand covers Sudha's mouth. "Hush, girl, hush." And then my mother, her voice uneven as if she's climbed a long hill, holds up her arms, saying, "Enough, we're all overwrought, let's end this before we say things we'll regret for the rest of our lives. Sudha and Anju, since you seem incapable of being trusted, no more pocket money for you until you start college. Give the clothes you bought to Ramur Ma—she'll dispose of them. I will let the nuns know that from now you are to be kept in your classrooms each day through recess."

The punishment's fair enough, I have to admit. Already my mother's calm sternness has shamed me more than a thousand yellings. Silently I follow Sudha to the door, thankful the evening's over.

Then Aunt N says, "Wait! Is that all you're going to say to them?"

"I think it's sufficient," Mother says. Her cheeks are a hectic red—I can't tell if it's from anger or distress—and she's breathing hard.

"Then I've got something to add," says Aunt. "Your Anju is a bad influence on my daughter. All the ideas she gets from those English novels you allow her to read, she passes on to Sudha. Sudha would never have dared an escapade like today's on her own. I can't interfere in how you deal with Anju—she's your daughter, after all, and her situation is very different from Sudha's. She's the only heir of the Chatterjees, while Sudha's just the poor cousin come from nowhere—oh yes, don't think I don't know what people say behind my back. Anju's position will shut a lot of gossiping mouths. But my poor Sudha—what does she have? Only her mother to watch out for the reputation she's determined to ruin. That's why I've decided that she's not to leave the house, not even for school, unless Ramur Ma accompanies her."

Oh, the insult of it! As though Sudha were twelve years old!

But what Aunt says next makes me feel as though someone's dropped me into a cold, dark well.

"I've also decided on an early marriage for her. As soon as she's finished at the convent, I'll start looking for a suitable boy."

"But she wouldn't even be eighteen," says Mother from somewhere above me, her voice echoing with shock. "That's much too young—"

"If she's old enough to fool around with men in movie houses," Aunt says, "she's old enough to care for her husband's family."

It's hard to speak from under layers and layers of freezing water, but finally I manage. "What about college? Isn't Sudha going to go to college?"

"What good is *that* going to do?" says Aunt. "It'll just put more wayward ideas into her head. Instead I'll have a lady teacher come to the house to give her cooking lessons. I'm only letting her finish school out of respect to your mother, who's put so much of her money into it." She inclines her head at my mother as though she's doing her a favor.

The water smells dark and musty. It presses down until my chest is about to burst open. "How can you do this?" I shout, only it comes out as a damp whisper. "How can you ruin Sudha's future—"

"That's enough, Anju!" warns my mother—but it's the pity in her eyes that frightens me into silence. "We'll discuss it later, when our heads are working more clearly. Sudha and Anju—to your rooms. Now! Ramur Ma, go with them."

We climb the desolate staircase, emptied of words. My heart feels like all the light has leaked away from it. Sudha's eyes are wide and feverish. A small, new muscle jumps in her jaw.

Oh, why had I been so impetuous? Why hadn't I thought of consequences?

If I believed in wishing, I'd wish to turn the night back into the innocent morning. And like in the old tales, I'd be willing to pay any price for it.

But wishing isn't any good, nor is regret. I've got to find another way to undo the harm I've done.

At her door I give Sudha a hug, holding her to me tightly. Ramur Ma's watching, ears pricked up, so I can't even say how sorry I am. But Sudha knows. And by the way she presses her hot cheek to mine I know she's forgiven me already.

"Don't worry, this isn't over yet," I whisper. "We'll fight it every way we can think of." Already I'm devising strategies, things I'm going to say to Mother, who I sense is on our side. "And no matter what happens, it'll happen to us both together. I promise."

I wait for Sudha to agree, but instead she draws back a little and looks at me with a slight, ironic smile. As though she knows already what it'll take me years to figure out: promises may be fulfilled, yes, but not always in the way we imagine.

— SEVEN —

Sudha

LYING IN BED in the midst of my suffocating rage, I think, strangely, of Hercules. Perhaps it is because at school we have been studying the legends of Greece and Rome. Though the nuns have cautioned us about the pagan heroes and heroines, I am fascinated by them. They seem closer to me than most of the people in my life. I have felt the blue air rushing beneath Icarus's wings, the ominous trickle of wax down his arms. I have wept with Persephone when the black vaults closed above her head, and then wept again when Ceres took her in her arms the way my mother never does with me.

Tonight I know how Hercules must have felt, trapped in the poisoned cloak sent to him by the one who—he had believed—had only his welfare in mind. My body is pierced by needles of fire, rage against my mother, and my powerlessness in her hands. What gives her the right to control my life, to wall me up in the name of her mother-duty? Wrong, wrong, this society that says just because I was born to her, she can be my jailer.

Earlier tonight, when she pronounced that I must stay home while Anju goes to college, I had an eerie sensation. I felt I was in a dark twisting tunnel which pressed in on me. It took me a moment to recognize it: the birth channel, narrow, suffocating. Only, I was receding up it, going back into the womb, where my mother would keep me, forever and completely engulfed.

Anju, save me.

My bedsheets sting my skin. My pillow is a roasting stone.

Perhaps if I get some water and then go to Anju and lie beside her, listening to her sleeping breath, this night will somehow end.

On my way, tiptoe-silent to the clay pitcher that sits in the passage, I see that the door to my mother's room is open. Slats of light fall across the floor from the moon on the other side of the barred window. Then I see a silhouette.

Anju. I must get to Anju.

But against my will my feet walk me to my mother's door. I stand there, shadow among shadows, and watch her. She holds on hard to the window bars, her body taut, her forehead pressed against the rusting iron. She is weeping, but not in her usual way—woeful theatrical sobs, loud entreaties called out to all the deities. She cries soundlessly, my mother, with only the trembling line of her back to tell me what is going on. Then she raises her face and looks at the moon.

And suddenly an old nursery rhyme comes to me. *Chander Pane cheye cheye raat keteche kato.* I'd forgotten that she used to sing it when I was small, while she rocked my cradle, while she smiled down at me.

I have spent so many nights gazing at the moon.
That must be why you came to me, my moon-faced child.
Let us go into the forest, the two of us, you and I,
so I can sit silent and enjoy your beauty.

To my mother, her life must have seemed like a trick of the moonlight. One moment her arms were filled with silvery promises. The next she was widowed and penniless. Alone in a world of glowering clouds, except for a daughter. Each hour the clouds crept closer, pressed another wrinkle onto her face. Words were all she had to save herself and her child. She picked the cleverest ones and wove them into a careful garland around her throat. Through them, for a while, she could be what she had so achingly wanted, on that faraway morning by the river.

But lately she had felt their fragrance wearing off, their petals drooping. A single strong gust of wind could blow them into nothingness, leaving her cruelly exposed. And now even her daughter, the one person, surely, that a mother should be able to depend on—the one person she had done it all for—was spreading her wings, called away by other songs.

"Sudha," whispers my mother against the bars. "Sudha, Sudha, Sudha." She rubs a hand across her forehead as though it hurts. What word had the Bidhata Purush written on it for her to be seduced so easily by the dream of love? What other word had he written to make her so determined to save me from the same fate? Does she believe—as perhaps all mothers do—that through her daughter she can redeem her life?

Outside, the pipal trees rustle, though there is no wind. They whisper my name in the same longing tones, as though they are familiar with her sorrow, her fear of being abandoned again.

A bird may escape a cage built of hate, of the desire for power. But a cage built of need? Of love's darkness?

I do not go to the cool sarai of water that waits in the hallway. I do not go to Anju, her sweet arms, the solace of our shared rage and rebellion. I walk back to my room, to the burning bedsheet that twists around me like an umbilical cord. All night I lie awake, thinking of many things.

When the first crows announce morning, with their harsh, startled-sounding cries, I know I will not fight my mother's will.

Not, at least, in this.

EIGHT

Anju

I'M FURIOUS with Sudha.

"You can't just let your mother have her way, not in *this*," I shout as I pace up and down her bedroom. "Without a college education, what kind of life are you going to have? You might as well tie a bucket around your neck and jump in a well right now. You might as well put blinkers over your eyes and join the bullocks that go round and round the mustard mill. That's all you're going to be, a beast of burden for some man."

"Anju, please, sit down," says Sudha. "You're making me dizzy." When I sit grudgingly on her bed, she smiles a small, strained smile. She hasn't slept all night—I can tell by the bags under her eyes. Sudha could never handle lack of sleep. Next thing I know, she'll be falling sick.

"But we agreed last night," I fume, punching at the ugly brown bedspread, chosen—of course—by Aunt N. "We were going to fight it together. I've even made a list of the arguments we'd use to get Mother on our side. How can you change your mind so fast? How can you be such a coward?"

Sudha looks at me, her beautiful eyes distressed. And right away I know it's not fear that's making her do this.

"Did Aunt say something to you last night?" I ask suspiciously.

Sudha shakes her head. "I don't want to break my mother's heart, that's all."

"Your mother doesn't *have* a heart, let alone one you can break."

"Anju!" Sudha says reproachfully. "Every person has a heart, but we're not always lucky enough to get a glimpse of it. And every heart, even the hardest, has a fragile spot. If you hit it there, it shatters. I'm all my mother has. I just don't want her to feel that I too have turned against her."

"Fine. So you're going to ruin your life for her? After all the plans we'd made about reading Shakespeare and Tagore together, and learning about the rise and fall of civilizations, and studying the great inventions of modern science—"

"I'll still be learning important, useful things, Anju."

"Right, like how to make pantua and lemon pickle."

"I'll learn a lot more than that. And anyway, you love lemon pickle!"

"Don't joke about it. You'll be wasting all your talents—"

Sudha leans toward me so I can smell the clean neem fragrance of her soap. "Anju dear, don't be so angry. I'm not giving that much up. Really. I thought about it all last night and realized college doesn't matter to me like it does to you. For me, there are other things that are more important."

When I look unconvinced, she says, "Look, I'll prove it. Tell me, what do you want to do when you grow up?"

She uses the old phrase out of our childhood, although surely at almost-seventeen we're quite grown up already. But I know what she means. Our life after we marry. Only neither of us is ready to name that exhilarating and terrifying condition—wifehood—yet.

"I want to run the bookstore," I say. I close my eyes as I speak and smell the place, the mysterious dusty fragrance of cardboard and old paper, the chemical scent of new-printed ink that's been in my blood almost since birth. "It'll be hard to persuade Mother, but I'm sure I can. After all I'm her only child, with no competing brothers. That's why I'm planning to study literature in college—so I can keep up with the latest writers and stock the best books."

"What I want most," says Sudha, "is to have a happy family. Don't you remember the pictures?"

And suddenly I do. As children each week we'd draw pictures of our future life. Mine were different every time—a jungle explorer swinging from vines, a pilot in goggles flying a snub-nosed plane, a scientist pouring smoking liquids from one test tube to another. But Sudha's were always the same. They showed a stick-figure woman in a traditional red-bordered sari with a big bunch of keys tied to her anchal. She wore a red marriage bindi in the center of her forehead and stood next to a mustachioed man carrying a briefcase. Around them were gathered several stick-figure children, their sex indicated by boxy shorts or triangular skirts. I'd secretly thought it all terribly boring.

"Yes, yes," I say now, a little impatiently. "I want a happy family too. But surely there's something else you want to do—for yourself."

Sudha hesitates. A dreamy shyness comes into her eyes. I sigh, because I know she's going to say she wants to marry Ashok. It strikes me that perhaps he's the reason she gave in so easily—to pacify Aunt N while she gathered her forces for what's bound to be the biggest battle of them all.

Then my cousin surprises me all over again.

"I want to design clothes," she says. "Salwaar kameezes. Pleated wedding ghagras with mirrors stitched in. Kurtas for men, embroidered white on white silk. Baby frocks in satin and eyelet lace. I want to have my own company, with my own tailors and my own label, so that customers at all the best stores will ask for the Basudha brand. People in Bombay and Delhi and Madras will clamor for my work."

I look at her face, gone all intense and shiny, and don't know what to say. I'd no idea she felt like this. She's never spoken of it—and with good reason. I can just hear Aunt N shrilling, "A

Tailor! You want to be a Common Tailor and rub kali on your ancestors' faces!"

Just the thought of it makes me mad. Why *shouldn't* Sudha do what makes her happy? Why shouldn't she at least dream about it? So I complete her dream for her. "And one day you'll be selling to the movies. Stars like Rakhee and Amitabh will refuse to dress in anything but your designs!"

Sudha's eyes gleam like the mirrors she wants to stitch into her clothes. "Don't forget the diplomats. They'll be wearing my kurtas and Nehru coats and embroidered saris to England and Africa and Japan."

"And America, don't forget America!"

"And America, of course!" Both of us are laughing wildly now, our current problems forgotten as we swing suspended in that delicious space between belief and disbelief.

If there is a mocking, answering laugh from the honeysuckle-weighted cornices, the Bidhata Purush's attendants eavesdropping, or maybe the demons, we don't hear it.

NINE

Sudha

AND SO the year passes. Sometimes the days are glassy and unmoving, as though I am suspended in a coma, waiting for my real life to resume. Sometimes they jerk ahead, halting and sputtering, reminding me that my brief freedom is about to end. Soon my world will be enclosed by these walls, these pipal trees. While Anju—how far she'll go, leaving me behind. How dull I'll seem to her when she returns from each day outside, bright as a sunflower that's been drinking light. When the time comes for me to break out of my prison, will I have the strength? Or will I be like a too-tame house bird who prefers her cage to the vast frightening blue of the sky?

When I think this, I'm filled with heaviness. Did I give in too hastily? The lavish kindness my mother has started showering on me since I bowed to her decree is no comfort. They stifle me, all those evenings she spends teaching me to tie my hair in the newest styles, shaping my eyebrows into perfect arches, taking me to afternoon tea at the homes of her friends so I'll know how to conduct myself in company. She has me listen in on their conversations, because she says that will teach me the ways of the world. But I am sickened by their always-same stories about the infidelities of husbands and the tricks wives must employ to hold on to them. Thank God Ashok is not like that, I think as I affix an engrossed expression on my face.

Although I haven't spoken to Ashok since our meeting at the movie house, I have seen him. The first time was on our way back from school. Singhji was driving while Ramur Ma sat next to him, ramrod straight with renewed importance. In the backseat we talked desultorily—we knew whatever we said would make its way to my mother. It was one of those heat-warped days when everything wavers in the airlessness—pavements, buses, even the face of the traffic policeman who raised his hand, bringing our car to a halt just before we turned into our street. So that when Ashok appeared not far from our car window, dressed in the same white shirt I'd last seen him in, I thought he was only a figment of my wishing. Still, I froze mid-sentence, and Anju, when she turned to see what I was staring at, froze as well. But she's quick, my cousin, and in a moment she was talking faster, telling a made-up story about a scandal at school, a girl caught cheating during an exam, and how the nuns sent for her parents and told them they must take her away for good the very same day. Ramur Ma was listening avidly, her mouth fallen open, so I was able to turn to the window and give Ashok a smile. He smiled back. I noticed that one of his front teeth was slightly crooked, and at that an illogical rush of love filled me. Now he was taking an envelope from his pocket. A letter! I wanted it more than I had wanted anything in my life. But I closed my eyes to signal no. I think he understood how I felt, for as the traffic policeman blew his whistle and our car moved forward, he touched the letter to his heart. I put my own hand on my heart, and felt it hammer under my palm in exhilaration and frustration and fear, and then—shocked at my own forwardness—I raised my fingers to my lips. The car speeded up—had Singhji noticed? In the rearview mirror Ashok's shirt gleamed like a small white flame until it disappeared. There was an aching behind my eyes, tears I must not shed. I slipped my hand into Anju's, and though she must have been annoyed at the risk I had just taken, she held it all the way home.

I saw Ashok a few times after that, each time at a different spot along our route to school. He would be drinking coconut water from a streetside vendor, or getting his chappal repaired at a muchi's stand, or standing in line for a bus, his bookbag slung over his shoulder. But I knew he was really waiting for me. There was never any opportunity for talk. Our eyes would meet for an instant, a kind of electricity would shiver up my spine, then Singhji would honk his horn at a rickshaw-puller or weave past a fruit seller who was crossing the road at the wrong place, and we would be gone.

So little. And yet, for my starved heart, so much.

Anju and I never spoke of these moments. She too must have seen Ashok. Even if she didn't, she would have known by my distracted air, the way she had to repeat a question—sometimes two or three times—before I answered. Perhaps she didn't want to give these flash encounters further solidity by acknowledging them. Perhaps she believed that if she ignored them they would dissipate into the fume-filled Calcutta air until eventually I remembered them only as one remembers a beautiful dream, with wonder and resignation and a mild, painless regret for what could never be.

TEN

Anju

FINALLY IT'S HERE, in a flurry of mango leaves and hot April dust. The day of our graduation. I run up to the terrace as soon as I wake. The sky's a brilliant cloudless blue, emptied by some magic of Calcutta smog. I throw out my arms and whirl around, singing "Freedom, freedom, freedom!" Generally, I wouldn't behave in this childish way, but today I can't help it. It finally seems real that in less than three months—as soon as summer vacation is over—I'll start in the English honors program at Lady Brabourne College. One of our older cousins who studied there has told me we'll begin by studying the ancient epic *Beowulf*. I've already borrowed it from the library and read it. Sometimes I whisper the names to myself—Grendel, Hrothgar, the brave and beautiful queen Wealtheow in the mead hall, and the little hairs on my arm stand up for joy.

When I stop, breathless and sweaty, I hear someone clapping. It's a desolate, out-of-rhythm sound. I spin around and see Sudha, sitting in the shadow of the water tank—she must've come up here even earlier. There's a funny look on her face. But of course. For her today's the exact opposite of what it is to me. Each hour that passes will be another nail pounding shut the door of her prison.

As the hot terrace bricks burn into my soles, I make myself a promise. From now on, I'll be Sudha's eyes and ears. I'll teach her everything I learn. The world Aunt N's depriving her of— I'll bring it to her.

But I don't have a chance to tell her any of this because Pishi calls us down for our baths. There's going to be a special puja done for us to please the nine planets so they'll bless us with success and pleasant surprises.

Ramur Ma isn't in the car with us today as we drive to school because the mothers need her help with the dinner they're giving to celebrate our graduation. Just a few close family friends—but as with everything in our house, it's got to be done right. Such elaborate preparations usually make me impatient, but this time I must confess I'm excited. The gilt-edged invitations were sent weeks ago, and the gilt-edged responses have been carefully counted. The formal hall has been dusted and aired and new candles put into the chandelier. Aunt N's had the heavy silver dishes from great-grandfather's time polished. Pishi's arranged bouquets of kena flowers in huge brass vases by the front entrance. An hour before guests arrive, Ramur Ma will sprinkle sandalwood powder on a lighted brazier and walk through the house so every room is filled with fragrance. My mother has to handle the hardest task of all: buying a gift for each guest, something small (that's all our family budget allows) yet elegant—for that's how the Chatterjees always thank visitors for their good wishes.

Not having Ramur Ma's watchdog presence in the car makes me giddily festive. "Let's make a list of all the great things about leaving school," I say to Sudha.

"Okay. You start."

"We won't have to put up with Sister Baptista anymore, the way she says, 'Ladies, Ladies, this is most inappropriate,' whenever we express an opinion that's different from hers. Your turn now."

But Sudha's staring ahead, her hands gripping the back of Singhji's seat.

There he is, in another of his infernal white shirts, standing by a bookstall, his eyes searching the road.

Why does this have to happen today of all days?

Before I can prevent her, Sudha leans forward and says, "Singhji, please, stop at the curb."

I'm not sure what Singhji will do, whether he'll listen to the pleading in her voice or turn the car and take us straight back to the mothers. This isn't the same as when she used to give away her lunch sweets to street children. He could lose his job for this.

Singhji doesn't say yes or no. I try to figure out what he's thinking, but that bearded, scarred face is like a shuttered house. After a moment I look away. There's a certain dignity about him which makes me feel it's vulgar to stare.

We've almost passed Ashok—Sudha bites her lip, but she too has her dignity and won't ask again—when Singhji pulls over to the curb with a quick turn of the wheel. "Be quick, Missybaba," he says. He doesn't smile, but his eyes meet ours in the mirror for a breath-space. How is it that in all these years I didn't notice how kind they are?

Sudha's already at the open window, her hands extended, and Ashok hurries over to take them. I'm amazed at how swiftly this happens, how neither of them hesitates the least bit. It's as if they've known each other for years. They remind me of the stories Pishi told us about the great lovers of the myths, Shakuntala and Dushmanta, Nala and Damayanti, Radha and Krishna, how they'd appear to each other in dreams and share their deepest secrets. It's impossible, of course. And yet when I look at Ashok's face and Sudha's, they seem changed. Ashok's face is older and thinner, as though something boyish has been burned away from it by his longing. And Sudha—I almost don't recognize my cousin in this radiant woman. She's so calm, it's as if she's been ready for this meeting a long time. It's as if she knew it would happen.

They speak comfortably, familiarly, like they're picking up the threads of a recent conversation.

"I won't see you again for a long time," says Sudha. "I won't be allowed to leave the house much, now that I'm graduating. Mother's going to start looking for matches for me."

"So soon?" Ashok looks startled. "I didn't think—"

"Before I get into more trouble, she says!"

How can she bear to joke about it?

"My father's away on business, but I'll speak to him as soon as he returns," says Ashok, his voice determined. "My parents weren't going to start on my wedding plans until I graduated from college, but once I explain to them, I'm sure they'll understand."

Is he serious? They must be saints, his parents. They'll have to be, and magicians too, if they are to persuade Aunt N that their son—the black-hearted villain who stole her little girl's heart—is a fit match for Sudha.

"Please hurry," says Sudha. "I don't know how long I can hold my mother off. But do you really think they'll agree? They don't know me—"

"They will, once I've told them—"

"I'm not sure you know me either." But now she's smiling.

He raises her hand to his cheek—here, right in the middle of Calcutta, with the whole world looking on. Is he immensely brave, or merely stupid? "There are ways and ways of knowing." He's smiling too.

Singhji clears his throat.

"I must go," says Sudha.

"Wait, I didn't know it was your graduation. What can I give you? Ah—" He twists at his finger and pulls off a ring. It flickers in his palm like an eye of fire.

Diamonds? From his simple clothes and the way he was at ease navigating the streets of Calcutta I'd assumed Ashok came from a middle-class family. He certainly didn't act like the stuck-up rich boys I'd meet from time to time at birthdays or weddings. But later Sudha would tell me, to my surprise, that his father—a self-made man—owned one of the larger shipping companies in Calcutta.

"No, no," says Sudha. "It looks terribly expensive."

"It is," he says, but without arrogance. "I wouldn't want to give you something second-rate." His matter-of-fact voice as he slips the ring onto my cousin's finger makes me wonder exactly how wealthy his family is.

"But how'll you explain it? How will I—?"

"My things are mine to do what I want with them. And as for you—it can be a secret, until."

"Until!" Sudha repeats the word as though it were a spell.

Singhji starts the car. The lovers—yes, unwilling though I am, I must accept that that's what they are—let go of each other's hands with reluctance, fingers touching until the last moment. They don't wave but watch with concentration until the car turns a corner. I sneak a look at my cousin. I'm afraid she might be crying, but she looks serene and confident as she touches her lips to the ring.

My poor Sudha. Does she really believe Aunt N will allow her to marry a boy from a lower caste, from a family that's made its money in trade? Someone whom Sudha herself decided on, challenging Aunt's authority?

Sunlight catches the ring as we come to a stop in front of the school, and the stones blaze up briefly. Sudha takes it off and slips it into her blouse. "Don't look so worried, Anju!" she says. "I'll give it to you to keep when we get home. That way even if Mother goes through my drawers like she does once in a while, she won't find it. It's only for a little time anyway, till I get married."

Perhaps she's right to hope. Perhaps love and longing *can* make a magic around them. Look how this morning's meeting happened. Perhaps Ashok's determination—if his parents are rich enough—will manage to sway Aunt N.

If not—but I can't bear to think of what that might mean for Sudha. Not yet.

The storm starts late in the evening. After the ceremonies at school, the final assembly where Sister Baptista surprises us all by bursting into tears. After the dinner at home, which goes off wonderfully, without any of the hitches Aunt N gloomily predicted. All the guests arrive on time, laden with gifts and good wishes. They claim that the cauliflower korma is incomparable, and the rasogollahs are as soft as clouds. They admire us profusely when we walk in wearing the matching pink Benarasi saris that Mother has bought us for the occasion. Even the teatime aunties have only kind things to say. The mothers are exuberant, each in her own way. Pishi keeps wiping at her eyes, telling anyone who will listen that God is great, who would have thought that after the great tragedies they'd been through, the house of the Chatterjees had so much happiness in store. Aunt N proudly corners guests and shows off our certificates. I have a hard time keeping a straight face when I hear her proclaim, "Sudha's so diligent, and Anju's so smart. We couldn't ask for better girls!"

My mother, though quietest, is the happiest of all, because she's the one who struggled the most to keep the family afloat through the dark times. Is she remembering the many days when she left for the bookstore in the morning and returned late at night, dead-tired, only to have to listen to the slew of problems that had occurred at home during the day. She's had to pay for our success with worry lines and graying hair and chronic heartburn and, more recently, a shortness of breath so severe that halfway up the stairs she has to stop and rest. But tonight she's absolutely elegant in a cream tassar silk, a pearl brooch pinned to her shoulder. When she motions to me to come sit by her and lays her hand lightly on my head, I feel a tumult of love in my heart. I understand why Sudha sacrificed so much to make her mother happy. I'm willing to do the same, I tell myself, but luckily my mother won't ask it of me.

The storm begins in earnest after the guests have left, when Sudha and I are in my room undressing. We switch off the light and open the big window because we both love storms—the dusty electric smell, the dark, spreading wings of clouds, the ecstatic drumbeat of rain. We're too wound up to sleep, so we take a long time to fold our saris and comb out our hair, to wipe the bindis from our foreheads and clean the kajol from our eyes. Sudha slips Ashok's ring onto her index finger and turns her hand so the diamonds glint suddenly in lightning, then disappear, then glint again before the next thunderclap.

"But how can you love someone so much when you've only spoken to him twice?" I ask. "How can you be ready to marry him?"

"It happens," says Sudha dreamily. Dressed only in her petticoat, her open hair spilling like black water over her bare breasts, she goes to stand at the window. A pipal branch breaks off with a loud crash. Wind blows in a gust of rain, and when Sudha turns, I see the drops glittering in her hair like pearls. "I know why peacocks dance in rain, don't you?" says my heartbreakingly beautiful cousin. Ashok, I think, if only you could see her like this! Then I'm jealously glad that he can't.

"How, Sudha?" I persist. I've got to understand this dangerous current that's sweeping her away from the safe shore where I'm left desolately alone.

"I can't explain." Sudha's forehead creases in perplexity, and I see that love is almost as much a mystery to her as it is to me. Then her face lights up. "But I can tell you a story about it, and then maybe you'll understand."

"What kind of story?"

"The story about the princess in the palace of snakes."

It's a fairy tale that Pishi's told us many times But Sudha has a way of retelling things, making them magical and novel. Maybe her voice and words, woven into this rainy night, will help me figure out this love that's so different from what she and I have felt for each other all our lives.

"Once there was a princess," begins Sudha, "who lived in an underwater palace filled with snakes. No one knows who her parents were, or how she came to be in this place."

"Was she unhappy?" I ask. My task in these tellings is to be the questioner of statements, and the interpreter of answers.

"Happy enough," says Sudha. "The snakes were beautiful— green and yellow and gold—and gentle. They fed her and played with her and sang her to sleep. They wove themselves into her hair like garlands."

"Didn't she ever get tired of her palace? Didn't she want to see the outside world?"

"No. Remember, she didn't know there was more to life than that dim green underwater light, those cool palace walls built of coral and sea stone."

"But then—"

"The prince came. He carried a jewel which made the lake waters part so he could reach the underwater palace. It was by chance, really. It wasn't as if he was looking for a princess. She was sleeping when he arrived. When he woke her, she couldn't believe her eyes. When he spoke, she knew she'd never be satisfied with the wordless songs of her serpent companions again."

"And she fell in love, just like that?" I'm a little scornful.

"Just like that."

"Why?"

"Because he was the one to wake her and tell her about the magical universe of men—diamond light on sleek mango leaves, the kokils crying to their mates from the coconut trees. He rescued her from sameness, from too much safety. There had been no mirrors in the palace. When she looked into his eyes, their dark center, she saw herself for the first time, tiny, and doubled, and beautiful. I think that's why she loved him most. Without him she'd never have known who she was." Sudha smiles a tender, inward-gazing smile, and for a moment it's as if she's forgotten the storm, the room, even me. Everyone except Ashok.

Thunder crashes outside again. It sounds like an entire tree has fallen. The impact shakes our room, and for the first time I feel a flash of fear. I want Sudha to continue the story—how the wicked king captures the princess and insists that she marry him. How after many trials the princess is reunited with her true love. But there's a series of urgent thuds, like giant fists, just outside.

Then I realize that they *are* fists. Someone's knocking on our door.

"Girls, what on earth were you doing? I've been knocking forever." Pishi's voice is testy. "Get dressed and come with me right away." Her eyes are puffy from tears, her lips tight with worry. In the flickering, gritty light her white sari billows around her like the garment of a ghost. As we walk behind her down the dim corridor, she adds, so softly that we have to strain to hear, "Gouri's very ill."

ELEVEN

Sudha

OF ALL THE rooms in this mansion that is crumbling under the onslaught of age and ancient memories, I know Gouri Ma's room the least. It has always been her haven, the one place where she could go to when she was tired of our squabbles, the other mothers' heated arguments, the never-ending stream of bills. In a life lived largely for the sake of others, it was the one place that was her own. Late at night sometimes strains of sitar music would come to us from behind the closed door, or a faint scent of rose incense, so pure and sweet that I'd want to curl up inside it. But though Gouri Ma never said it, we all knew her room was out of bounds unless she invited us in. Even my mother respected that. So today as we crowd into it, I feel like an invader.

Everyone is here: my mother, Pishi, Ramur Ma, a couple of the older servant women who have been with the family from before our birth. Even Singhji, whom I have never seen inside the house, carries in a couple of medical bags behind a thin, intense-eyed man we don't know. Old Dr. Ganguly, our regular physician, must have been unable to make it through the storm. The new doctor is already preparing an injection. There is a hospital smell in the air, disinfectant and fear, as he says, "Make space, please, the patient needs air," but no one listens.

Gouri Ma lies on her side with her legs pulled up. Her breath comes noisily from someplace far inside her chest. Once in a while she grips the bedclothes with her fists as though to squeeze the pain out of herself. She keeps her eyes tightly closed. Worse than the pain is the helplessness she must feel as she lies here with all of us watching, my proud aunt who has always kept to herself her weaknesses, her desperations, the many nights of private pain that must have preceded this public one.

"Someone needs to move all these people out of here," says the doctor irritably as he puts a stethoscope to Gouri Ma's chest. I turn to Pishi for direction, but she clutches the bedpost, frozen, as though it were the mast of a foundering ship. Singhji is the one who guides us out, sending the servants downstairs and telling my weeping mother that Memsaab needs to pull herself together, for the sake of the girls if nothing else. In his scorched, ruined face, his deep-set eyes are stern with unexpected authority. Under their gaze, my mother's wails gradually subside into sobs. He brings us chairs so we can wait in the corridor, shuts the passage window through which rain is sweeping in, wipes the floor with an old cloth he has procured from somewhere, and seats himself on the ground at a respectful distance in case the doctor needs him.

The night limps on. The grandfather clock downstairs chimes, and its hollow echoes fill my skull. There are flapping sounds at the window. A bird, seeking shelter. Or is it something else? I know the old stories: When someone is very ill, spirits who were close to her in life come down to earth to take her back with them. For Gouri Ma this would be her husband, my uncle Bijoy, that gentle, trusting man who came to a premature, watery end. Would his spirit look like his body had at death, bloated and trailing river weeds? Would it glare at me, accusal-eyed? I glance guiltily at Anju to see if she knows what I'm thinking. But her face is as wooden as the chair she is sitting on, her eyes like black holes gouged into her face. I am afraid to touch her, to pull her back into this fear-filled corridor from wherever it is that she has gone.

The flapping noises have grown deafening. I can't stand them any longer, though no one else seems to hear them. Shivering, I stumble to the window, fling it open. *Please*, I whisper, though I among all of us here have the least right to ask. *Please don't take her yet. We need her so much.* There's an answering sound like a cry. A wet wind slaps at my face—or is it the ghost, displeased that the daughter of the man whose madcap scheme led them both to their deaths dares to speak to him? Is there a swamp smell, a phosphorescent streak in the outline of hands swirling away into the darkness?

Anju doesn't notice—she's still gone—but my mother says in annoyed tones, "Sudha, what's wrong with you? Look what you've done. Now the passageway's wet again. Close that window at once."

Is it then, or hours later, that the door to Gouri Ma's room creaks open? I hear the doctor's low voice giving Pishi instructions. Diet, he says. Temperature. Tests starting tomorrow. Give her these tablets if there's more pain. Call me if there are any sudden changes.

Pishi turns to Anju. "Your mother wants you."

"Make sure you don't excite her," admonishes the doctor as he hands his bags to Singhji. "Her condition isn't good at all. I'd rather she didn't have any visitors at this time, but she insisted."

Anju's eyes reach for mine, entreating. I can feel her fear in the salt taste in my own mouth. But when I rise to follow her, Pishi stops me. "Alone, Gouri said."

That's how it is sometimes when we plunge into the depths of our lives. No one can accompany us, not even those who would give up their hearts for our happiness.

My cousin opens the door to her mother's room. The odor of phenol and urine seeps into the corridor, the heartbreaking smells of the shamed, powerless body, and Anju walks in.

I lie awake in Anju's high white bed, waiting for her. After the doctor left, Mother ordered me to my room, but I crept from it as soon as she fell asleep. I couldn't bear the thought of Anju having to face the rest of the night alone.

I imagine the sickroom, the way the bedside lamp must have thrown a little light onto the mahogany fourposters so they glinted red-black, the pulse's erratic beating in Gouri Ma's throat as she lay propped against pillows. She would not have struggled to sit up. She would not have wept. An intelligent woman, she would have saved her energy for the important things. Her voice would have been soft as tearing silk.

What words did my aunt use to admit failure and fear, to unravel the dreams she had woven around Anju since her birth? I don't know. When Anju finally staggers in, and I ask if she's all right, she gives in to laughter, a hysterical laugh that goes on and on, spiraling upward until, afraid that someone will come to check on what's wrong, I put my hand over her mouth.

Anju is silent now. Only a small shudder shakes her from time to time. I make her lie down. She turns on her side to make space for me, and I lie down too, as we've done so many times. I cover us with the bedspread and stroke her hair until her limbs let go a little of their tenseness. Just before she falls asleep she gives a great sigh. "Remember how I used to laugh at Pishi's sayings? Well, I've just learned not to."

"What do you mean?" I ask, my throat tight with dread.

"Remember how she used to say, be careful of the words you speak for they might come true? Remember how I promised you, the night your mother decided to shut you up at home, that I'd make sure the same things would happen to us both? Well, they have."

"What do you mean?" I repeat, stupidly. My cousin's words make no sense to me.

"Don't ask me any more tonight. I can't talk about it."

I hold my cousin as she sleeps and try vainly to decipher what she said. But I cannot imagine Gouri Ma, even in illness, speaking like my mother. Finally I give up. It is too late, and I am too tired. Or perhaps fear has short-circuited my brain. Anju's head fits into the curve of my shoulder as though she were a child. Her eyes dart beneath their lids. I pray for her to have sweet dreams,

Anju, whose waking life has fallen in shambles around us. The storm passes, the wind transforms itself into a morning breeze, the ghu-ghu birds begin their cooing. Slowly the sounds of the waking household surround us, strangely soothing. A sweeping broom, water being pumped from the tube-well, the clatter of milk cans. After a while, even though I hadn't thought it possible, I too drift into sleep.

And thus for a few hours I am spared the news that what Gouri Ma suffered last night was a mild heart attack. When the doctor warned her that the next one might be far more severe, she decided she must get Anju married as soon as possible.

TWELVE

Anju

THE BRIDAL preparations are in full swing, and since my mother is too ill, she's turned things over to Aunt N.

Aunt's created an entire regimen for us. Each morning we start by eating almonds which have been soaked overnight in milk. (This, Aunt has declared, will cool our systems, calm our minds, and improve both our dispositions and our complexions.) Then we have to do a half-hour of yoga and calisthenics (to give us endurance, which we're sure to need as wives, and prevent the sagging of various body parts, which might be offensive to our future husbands). Then we must apply turmeric paste to our faces (more complexion improvement) and keep the pungent, itchy mask on for half an hour while Ramur Ma rubs warm coconut oil into our hair. (Long, well-oiled, obedient hair symbolizes virtue in women.)

At bathtime we scrub ourselves all over with pumice stones. ("Nothing enhances a husband's affections like silk-soft skin," says Aunt. She's taken to startling us with these nuggets of Kama Sutra–like wisdom. Earlier Sudha and I would have shared a good laugh over them. But nowadays I'm too heartsore.) After lunch we lie in bed with eau de cologne–soaked cloths over our eyes. Sometimes I can't believe this is happening to me. Surely it's a dream, this slight damp pressure on my lids, this sweetish smell that settles in my clothes. This stunned lassitude that keeps me from rebelling.

Soon it's time to get up for our afternoon lessons. A kerosene stove's been set up on the upstairs balcony and a middle-aged Brahmin woman whom Aunt has hired demonstrates elaborate desserts such as gopal-bhog and pati-shapta, which I know I'll never be able to duplicate. We help with the preparations but stay away from the stove: One of Aunt's friends has told her a story about a bride who got burned a week before her wedding, which was, of course, immediately canceled. The Brahmin lady also gives us lessons in the intricate laws of orthodox Hindu cuisine: milk and meat products mustn't be mixed. Nonvegetarian items must be cooked in separate vessels. The left hand must never be used when serving food. Once I asked her what the point of all these rules was, but she looked at me uncomprehendingly.

Finally, when the seamstress comes to teach Sudha sewing, I get an hour off. I'd like to get away to the terrace, but Aunt has declared that on no account are we to expose ourselves to sun. Nor are we to cry—baggy red-rimmed eyes would undo an entire month of her efforts. So I try to focus on a book and not think of my mother.

The doctor says my mother needs to undergo bypass surgery, but she refuses. She says she knows too many people who died from the infection afterward. She can't take such a risk, not until Sudha and I are married. She's doing everything else the doctor wants her to—going for short, careful walks, working fewer hours, cutting out fats. But all it's done is make her lose a lot of weight, so that her cheekbones press up sharp as mountain ridges through her skin.

Mother's often angry nowadays, mostly because her tiredness forces her to stay in bed when there's so much to be done. She's moved downstairs into an annex off the main hall because climbing stairs has become too difficult. I wonder if she wakes up sometimes in the middle of the night, disoriented to find herself, after thirty years, in a new bed. Does her hand reach for the familiar bedpost carved with grape leaves and find itself closing on dark air?

She's also decided to sell the bookstore. We just don't have enough money otherwise, she's explained to me, for two weddings. Two dowries. Dowries are a slippery issue, I've come to learn. A good family never demands a particular amount of money, or a certain list of items. That would be too gauche. And so the bride's party has to anticipate their wishes and go beyond them, because if they don't, it might affect their daughter's future.

I can't imagine the bookstore not belonging to us. Maybe Mother can't either. Maybe that's another reason why she's so angry. She's nursed that store fiercely all these years, spent more time with it than with me. It must be awfully hard for her to think of some stranger sitting at her little desk in the back, ordering trashy romances and potboilers to fill its shelves.

At first I tried to get her to reconsider. "I can help you run it while I go to college," I pleaded. "I'll take care of all the details—I know a lot of them already, and Manager-babu can teach me the rest."

Mother shook her head with finality, as though the papers had been signed already. When my face fell, she took my hands in hers and said, "I'm sorry, Anju, I've let you down, haven't I? All your plans for college—and now the bookstore. I was going to leave it to you—in your name, not your husband's—to run as you wished. I guess there's a lot we hope for that never happens." She paused for breath, then said, "But I'll promise you this much, Anju Ma. I'll arrange your marriage with a man who lets you go to college—and lets you work too, if you want it."

"But *why* must I get married in such a hurry?" I cried angrily. "Why can't you just get the surgery done instead? Why are you so scared? The doctor said it isn't that dangerous anymore—"

I could tell by the way Mother pressed her lips together until they turned white that I'd made her angry. But all she said was, "I can't take such a big chance. What if I die? Who else is there to take care of you and Sudha? To make sure you get a good match?" Then she lay back, eyes closed, and Pishi, who'd come in with a glass of lime sharbat, motioned worriedly for me to leave.

In the evenings when the terrible June heat ebbs a little, we gather around my mother, making a special effort to be cheerful. Pishi turns on the radio so Mother can listen to the songs of Tagore, which she loves. Ramur Ma brings in the tea tray, and Aunt Nalini pours. We use our good cups on these evenings. At first Mother protested. But when Pishi said, "What are we saving them for? What can be a better occasion than this, while the family's still together, before the girls go off to their husbands' homes?" she didn't argue. Perhaps she was thinking that pretty soon she might be gone too.

The cups are quite beautiful, painted on the inside with dragons, so that each sip you take uncovers a little more of their green, glittery scales.

"A traveling Chinese prince gave them to your grandfather," says Pishi. "He said the dragons had special powers. If you could please them, they would grant you a wish."

"How would you please them?" Sudha asks. All these years, and she's still the girl who believed in falling stars and demons.

"He wouldn't tell us that. He said we each had to discover it for ourselves. Otherwise the wish wouldn't work."

"Nice trick!" I mutter. But when my cup's empty, I stare at the dragon inside. That's how foolish I've grown in my desperation. The dragon's wings seem to flutter, just a little. Its ruby eye gleams. Perhaps it's a cousin of the magic serpents of Sudha's tale? Make my mother well, I command it. But my tone isn't right. Offended, the dragon flicks its tail at me and turns back into porcelain.

Toward the end of the evening, the mothers discuss prospective bridegrooms. We aren't allowed to be present at these discussions. The mothers don't want to fill our heads with romantic ideas which might come to nothing. Once the men have been screened and initial talks conducted, we'll be given details of the lucky ones.

So when the song hour ends, Aunt N says in a falsely jovial voice, "Now run along, children." Pishi unlocks the Godrej safe that stands in the corner and takes out several thick yellow envelopes addressed in the matchmaker's spindly writing, and the mothers draw close to examine the offers one more time.

"I think we should see them too," I said once. "Maybe the ones you choose aren't the ones *we'd* like."

Pishi looked undecided, but Aunt said, "Precisely. You'd like all the unsuitable ones, and then we'd have weeks of arguments."

"Trust us, Anju," said Mother. "We want your happiness even more than you do."

What could I say after that?

From what I've overheard Aunt N say to the teatime aunties, so far the offers have been disappointing. Maybe the mothers have set their standards too high. Or maybe nowadays smart men don't want marriages arranged by some old fogey of a matchmaker. Personally, I don't care if the process takes years. Perhaps I could cajole the mothers into letting me attend college meanwhile? But then I hear Mother coughing anxiously, a thin, tearing sound. I see the strain lines around her mouth, like cracks in porcelain, and I'm ashamed of my selfishness.

Sudha's anxious too. She won't talk about it, but I know she's wondering if Ashok's proposal is sitting in the almirah in one of those yellow envelopes. Surely the mothers wouldn't discard it without telling us? Or did his parents decide not to make an offer at all?

As the months pass and I watch her eyes grow haunted and sooty, my sympathy for Ashok begins to fade. I wonder angrily whether Ashok even told his parents about Sudha. Maybe he was only in love with the idea of being in love. It was enough for him to play-act the wan hero who waits by the roadside for his beloved's chariot to pass by. Perhaps marriage was never a part of it.

Tonight Sudha sits on my windowsill and stares out at the September night where white clouds glide like carefree swans. We've started a few halfhearted conversations, then broken them off distractedly.

Soon it'll be the month of Durga Puja, which is considered unsuitable for weddings, and all talks will stop for a while. So far Mother has shown us only two offer letters. One was an old zamidar family like ours; the other had received a title fifty years back from the British. Both families were quite aware of their importance and their sons' impeccable marital credentials. Pompous asses, in fact. Mother must have felt that too, for when we begged her to say no she didn't disagree. Even Aunt N went along with the decision, though in her typical way she reminded us that Calcutta was filled with spinsters who wept every night into their pillows, regretting their earlier finickiness.

When I see how thin Mother has grown, how she stoops over the cane she's recently started using, I feel a balled-up rage swelling in my throat until I think I'll choke on it. She tried hard to keep her illness a secret, but that's impossible in this city of a million watching eyes. Maybe that's why we aren't getting offers for the bookstore. They're waiting like vultures for us to grow desperate. And why we aren't getting good marriage offers either. Wives must be good breeding stock, and people don't want to have anything to do with hereditary diseases.

I'm jerked back to the present by the sound of Sudha weeping softly. I go to her and rub her back, wishing I could make her feel better. Helpless fury drives me to clichés. *That blithering idiot*, I think. *That lily-livered coward. What on earth is he doing?* It makes me even angrier when I remember I was the reason they met in the first place.

"Listen," I tell Sudha. "I'll go to Mother and tell her about you and Ashok, how much you care about him, how you wouldn't be happy marrying anyone else. If she's concerned about him being from a different caste, I'll remind her of Priya Aunty's son who went to Oxford and brought back a British wife, and now look how everyone adores her."

Sudha stops crying. Her eyes widen. She's listening very carefully.

"I'll ask if Ashok's family made an offer, and if they haven't, I'll ask Mother to approach them. And if they aren't interested in our proposal, then we can put the whole thing behind us and go on with our lives, knowing we did our—"

"No!" Sudha says with startling energy. "I don't want you saying anything to Gouri Ma."

"But why? You love him, right? All this waiting's making you crazy, right? Why shouldn't I ask her then? Why should we women always wait for things to happen to us?"

"No, Anju. If Ashok really loves me, if he really wants to marry me, he's got to make the first move."

Really, Sudha can be so stubborn. "This isn't the time for false pride," I tell her. "Besides, how do you know he hasn't?"

"Well, if they've turned down his offer, he's got to come up with another plan. And he will. If he really loves me, he will."

I stare at Sudha's face, the spots of feverish color high on her cheeks, the faraway, unfocused look in her eyes. What does it remind me of?

And then I know. During those fairy tales we acted out as children, when Sudha was always the captured princess I had to rescue, she'd have the same tranced look on her face. In the course of rescuing her I'd run into trouble—that was part of the game—my royal horse tripping as I climbed hills formed out of human skulls, or a sea serpent grabbing me in its coils—but she never attempted to help me. Instead she'd sit on the bed with clasped hands and a concerned expression on her face while I writhed around on the floor, grappling with the monsters she'd imagined. Once, exasperated because it wasn't much fun playing this way, I asked her why.

She looked at me in surprise. "But it's *your* job to overcome obstacles and prove yourself," she said. "That's what princes are supposed to do. If I helped you it wouldn't be the same."

I'm not sure when Sudha started getting caught in the enchanted web of the stories she loved so much and told so well. When, in some place deep inside her impervious to logic, she turned Ashok into the prince who has to save her from the clutches of the wicked king. Once he managed to place her on his milk-white steed, she'd follow him faithfully to the ends of the earth. But until then the rules of the story didn't permit her—and, by extension, me—to help him.

"Please, Sudha," I try one more time. "This is your life, not some stupid fairy tale in a book. Things never happen the way those stories say they do. And even if they did, I'm sure the princesses didn't just sit and—"

"Promise me you won't interfere, that you won't say anything about Ashok to Gouri Ma," Sudha says. Did she hear even a word of what I just said? In the milky moonlight her face has taken on a phosphorescent, fanatical glow. "Promise!" Her eyes bore into me until I mutter a grudging okay.

"Thank you, Anju!" she cries, throwing exuberant arms around me. "I knew you'd understand. Now we'd better get to bed. If Mother sees dark circles under our eyes tomorrow, we won't hear the end of it for weeks."

But I remain standing at the window long after Sudha's gone. The night air, foggy now, wraps itself around me like a damp, mildewed shroud. I can't see. I can't breathe. I'm afraid Sudha's making a terrible mistake, and I, whose job it is to stop her, don't know how.

THIRTEEN

Sudha

I AM DESPERATE.

A proposal has come in for me, one which all the mothers agree is a wonderful one. It is from a family in Bardhaman, a town which is not too small and not too far away. The Sanyal family—that's their name—is distinguished and wealthy, but not too much so. The groom, Ramesh, is also fatherless. At Mr. Sanyal's death, greedy relatives had tried to swindle Ramesh's mother out of the family business. "But she was too smart for them," Pishi says. "She foiled their wicked plans and ran it most successfully—just like your Aunt Gouri—and made sure her three sons lacked for nothing."

She was charming too, on the phone. And frank. "I'll tell you right away, in spite of his name, my son's no god of beauty," she had said to Gouri Ma with a laugh. "That's why I'm looking for a beautiful bride. My motives are quite selfish, I'll admit: I want good-looking grandsons!"

The son who is no god of beauty has a high-ranking job with Indian Railways that requires a great deal of traveling on his part. I am not to worry, says my prospective mother in law. I will not have to go to all those godforsaken places where new rail lines are being laid down. I am to stay home with her and be the daughter she never had. She is looking forward to turning the household over to my care and spending her time with her prayer beads. And oh yes, dowry is of no concern—what with the son's salary, and the profits from the recent sale of the business, they have more than enough.

"Imagine that, no dowry demands!" says my mother, impressed. "Of course *we'll* still give Sudha a magnificent trousseau. We don't want people to say later that the Chatterjees were tight-fisted at their daughter's wedding."

Pishi examines the photo of the bridegroom, the long lean body, the dark skin, the plain face, the slightly receding chin. "He's not too ugly for our Sudha, is he?" she asks.

"Nonsense," says my mother. "I've seen far worse."

"His eyes are kind and intelligent," Gouri Ma says. "He'll know how to appreciate Sudha. That's the most important thing. Why, they'll all love her sweetness and sense of duty."

If only she knew how bitter I feel, how undutiful. My chest is on fire, as though I have swallowed a nestful of red ants. I think I am going mad.

Ashok, where are you? Have you forgotten me?

Because I don't know what else to do, I go looking for Singhji. He helped me once. Perhaps he would do it again.

After lunch when the household sleeps, I throw aside the eau de cologne–soaked cloths and rise from my bed. I tiptoe past the soft snoring sounds, and the drone of ceiling fans. In the downstairs hallway, I freeze for an instant when I hear a cough. Then I am outside, running along the gravel driveway to the small gate-house, where our gatekeeper—when we had one—used to stay. On the afternoons when Singhji is not needed, more and more nowadays since Gouri Ma rarely goes to the bookstore, he rests there. Gouri Ma had offered to let him have the room perma-nently, but Singhji declined in his polite, taciturn way. Perhaps he liked the distance, the ability to shrug us and our troubles from his mind when he went home at night.

I knock on the door. My heart beats heavily, out of rhythm. It is most improper for the daughter of the house to knock on the chauffeur's door, even if he is old enough to be her father.

Singhji's shocked face mirrors my thoughts when he opens the door. "Sudha Missybaba, you shouldn't be here, especially now that your marriage is being fixed," he says as he tries to tuck in the ends of his turban with fingers that shake a little. I notice the furrows cutting into his mottled, fire-slicked forehead, the way he holds on to the door, for a moment, as though dizzy. "Someone might say something bad."

What had I thought he could do for me, this poor aging man whose brief rest I have disturbed?

The afternoon smells of honey from the trumpet flowers that have spilled over the wall of the gatehouse. It is unfair that there should be so much beauty in this world when my heart is breaking. I can no longer control the tears I have been holding back so long.

A look of distress passes over Singhji's usually expressionless face, and he puts out his hand as though he would like to touch my arm. "Don't cry, beti," he says finally. "Crying does no good. I learned that when I lost my family." He looks past me into the air, and I wonder if he is remembering the child he once had. Perhaps that is why he called me *beti*.

"No, crying does no good," says Singhji again. "We must make a plan."

FOURTEEN

Anju

TODAY THE SANYALS are coming to see Sudha.

I was afraid because I didn't know how she'd take it. She's been acting strange ever since their proposal came in. Sometimes she'll lie with her face buried in her pillow, so still that she could be dead. Sometimes she'll stare blindly at the pipal trees for a whole hour. She still won't let me talk to Mother about Ashok. On the rare nights when I can get her to sleep in my room, I'll wake to find her pacing back and forth, twisting the edge of her sari into a rope. When I tell her she'll drive herself crazy if she keeps doing this, she'll push me away impatiently. "I wish I were that lucky!" she'll say in a bitter, not-herself voice.

Sudha's prospective mother-in-law didn't give us much notice. She called the night before and said they were coming to Calcutta on some business and would like to stop by in the afternoon for a few minutes. We were not to worry about a meal or any such formalities. They just wanted to see the girl.

But of course Aunt N wouldn't have any of that. "It's a test!" she insisted. "I've heard of things like that! And later they'll complain that we didn't show them respect. It'll give them an excuse to mistreat my poor Sudha—or maybe break off the wedding." I wanted to say in that case maybe we shouldn't be thinking of getting Sudha married there, but since Mother's illness I've been trying not to cause trouble.

Aunt wouldn't rest until she made Mother call them back, and after a lot of back and forth it was decided they should stay for tea. The rest of the evening the household was in turmoil. Aunt set the servants to cleaning everything, just in case Mrs. Sanyal decided to take a little walk around the house. Once she and Pishi finally reached agreement on the tea snacks they should serve, she dispatched Singhji to the evening bazaar to get the freshest ingredients.

Then there was the matter of what Sudha would wear. Aunt wanted something extra fancy, with lots of zari work, while my mother felt that simplicity was best. They had Ramur Ma bring down whole armloads of saris, which Aunt draped around Sudha one after the other. I was afraid Sudha would explode after the eighth or ninth time—I would have. But she sat there silently, with a sleepy-looking smile on her face. "See," whispered Aunt to Pishi, "she's already dreaming of her husband-to-be." But I knew my cousin better, and that smile worried me. What worried me even more was that when I questioned her about it when we were alone, Sudha wouldn't answer. She only gave me a hug and said, "Not yet, Anju dear. Talking about it might bring bad luck. I'll tell you later."

The Sanyals arrive a whole hour late.

"That's nothing," Aunt N will say later. "I've known of cases where the boy's family decided to arrive a whole *day* late—all the food spoiled, the girl's family going crazy, and the bride-to-be weeping and wailing, wondering if someone had slandered her, and will the match be broken off. It's just to show who's in control."

If something like that happened to me, I'd be so mad I'd break the match off myself. Why should the boy's side always be the one in control?

Mrs. Sanyal's good at control. I can see it in the way she handles her entourage, which consists of Ramesh, his younger brothers, and three or four female relatives whose exact relationship to the family isn't quite clear. It's very subtle—a glance here, a little cough there. And suddenly the female cousins would stop in the middle of a less-than-refined joke, and the boys would put back the singaras they'd heaped onto their plates. Even Ramesh would stop staring at Sudha and begin a polite, if somewhat boring, conversation with my mother.

I'm not sure how I feel about Ramesh. He must be very capable—else how could he hold such a high governmental post?—but I'm not taken with his thin sharp nose, his hair slick with Brylcreem and combed down too precisely, his mouth, which is set in worried lines—except when he looks at Sudha. For he's quite smitten. We can all see that.

I'm not surprised. Even when she was a scab-kneed girl in an old frock, there was a radiance about Sudha so that men couldn't stop themselves from looking—and looking again. Women too stared, whispering behind their hands, and more than once a well-meaning aunty warned the mothers "to keep an eye on that one, so much beauty's bound to land her in trouble." And today in her dark blue dhakai sari, with a thin gold chain that gleams at her throat, she's irresistible. Little tendrils of hair curl around her face like a halo as she pours the tea and takes it over to each guest. Her anklets tinkle like wind-bells. She answers Mrs. Sanyal's questions without a trace of the irritation I'm feeling for her: what was her favorite subject in school (embroidery), what is the proportion of sugar and water in rasogollah syrup (one to two), what she thought should be a woman's most important duty (taking care of those she loved).

Mrs. Sanyal's so impressed that she says she has no more questions, we can be excused. As we leave we hear her telling Aunt N it's clear how much effort she's put into raising her daughter. (I almost laugh aloud at that.) She sees no reason to delay the happy event. Why not have the pandit look for an auspicious day next month?

Sudha must have heard her too, but not a tremor crosses her face. Not even when we reach my room and I tell her, "I just hate the way women are paraded in front of prospective grooms—like animals at the fair. How could you put up with all those stupid questions so calmly?"

"Because I had to make sure Mother would be pleased with me. And because I know I don't have to marry Ramesh," says Sudha. She pulls me up and whirls me around the room, then bursts out laughing at the look on my face. "Don't worry, dear dear Anju. I haven't gone crazy. I just got a letter from Ashok—"

"But how?"

"Singhji told him about the proposal. Yes, our Singhji! He found out where Ashok lived and went and met him. He's been such a support—I can't thank God enough for him. Anyway, Ashok wrote that he really loves me, that he's been anxiously waiting to hear from us. Yes, he persuaded his parents, and they sent us a proposal quite some time back. But my mother"—here Sudha's lips twist in bitterness—"must not have thought it good enough for our illustrious family. Anyway, we're going to meet tomorrow, and he'll figure out what to do."

I sit down hard on the bed, at once terrified for Sudha and amazed that she'd taken such a bold step. I'm also confused, and that makes me angry.

"I thought you said we had to wait for Ashok to act, that we couldn't help him!"

"But we *didn't* help. I just got the news of my troubles to him, like the princess Rukmini did with Lord Krishna, remember that story? Ashok's doing all the rest."

I fight back a pang of jealousy. All our lives Sudha had looked to me to plan things for her. Now that usurper in a white shirt had taken my place. But mostly I feel sad. Even if they met (where?) at such great risk, what solution could they come up with? By now Aunt's probably orchestrated the entire wedding, from flowers to food to which musician would play the shehnai and who would take the groom-gift to the Sanyals the day before the ceremony.

"We'll meet at the Kalighat temple early tomorrow morning. I'm going downstairs right now to tell Mother that I'd promised the goddess I'd pay her a visit, alone, before my wedding. She'll be in such a good mood, I know she'll say yes."

Luminous with her faith in her prince, Sudha kisses me on both cheeks and runs down the stairs, leaving me to cross my fingers for luck and hope to God they don't think up something too crazy and dangerous.

FIFTEEN

Sudha

WHENEVER I'VE BEEN to the Kalighat temple before this, it has been a cacophony of human and animal clamor— priests yelling and shoving at confused temple-goers who mill around like sheep, vendors calling out their wares, lost children wailing, crippled beggars crying for alms, goats bleating as they are dragged to sacrifice. So it seems eerily quiet this dawn, only the sweepers washing the steps of the temple, and the first flower sellers setting up garlands of bright orange marigolds and jasmines white as new-cooked rice. I buy a hibiscus garland, red like the sindur that married women wear, and make my way in.

The stone vault which houses the deity is dim with incense and holy mystery. Later in the day it will be crowded to suffocation, but for now things are quiet, so the priest allows me to stop before the gleaming black image. Since morning I have been rehearsing prayers, all the things I want, but now as I look at the huge eyes of the goddess, rimmed in gold and red, I cannot remember any of them. The goddess appears a little displeased— she knows I have used her as an excuse for a rendezvous of a very different nature. But after all she herself has known love. It is said in the Puranas that she left home against the wishes of her father to follow Lord Shiva, her beloved. So I think she forgives me. When I lay my head on the silver pedestal at the foot of the image, it is cool and smells of sandalwood paste, and I feel comforted.

I see Ashok as soon as I come out. As agreed, he is standing by the Shiva shrine at the far end of the temple. It is the first time we have met alone, and I grow unexpectedly shy when he takes me by the hand and leads me to an alcove. But time is short—Singhji, who is waiting outside, has told me that we should return home within the hour—so my shyness will have to wait until our wedding night.

"Are you well?" Ashok asks me, looking closely at my face. "Did they come for the bride-viewing already?"

I nod wordlessly. He himself appears somber, as though the decision to marry has propelled him into adulthood. There is a new line between his brows. I want to smooth it away. I want to kiss him. I want to laugh and cry, all at once. Finally I say, "They've set the wedding date a month from now."

Ashok thinks carefully, counting on his fingers. Then he says, "Your mother's turned down my offer once already. There's no way she'll agree to our marriage, now that you've received a more 'suitable' proposal. We must elope."

My heart heaves with panic. *Elope.* I am dizzy at the finality of the word, like a door slammed behind me for good. They will disown me. Never again to enter that old marble mansion that has always been home, never again to see the mothers, never to hold my dear Anju close, for comfort and for joy. Can I bear it, even for Ashok's sake?

"We'll do it in two weeks, as soon as you turn eighteen," says Ashok. "That way your mother can't force you to return, or annul the marriage."

"How did you know when my birthday was?" I ask, amazed.

For a moment he looks mysterious. "I have my ways!" But then he gives in to a smile—already he cannot keep secrets from me—and says, "I asked Singhji."

I hadn't realized Singhji kept such close count of my birthdays. But Ashok is giving me details: where we'll go, who'll perform the wedding, how long we must remain in hiding afterward. Singhji has promised to help. I need bring nothing with me. Ashok is confident that his parents would take me in—even before the wedding, if he asks. But to protect them from my mother's accusations, he will not tell them of our plans until the marriage has taken place.

"Don't look so worried, Sudha. Don't you trust me?"

I touch that dear crease between his brows. His skin smells of a soap whose name I do not know. "I trust," I say and sway toward him. That is how we kiss our first kiss, behind the great black Shiva Lingam. His lips are a shock of heat. His fingertips linger on my throat. For the rest of my life, passion will mean the smell of crushed hibiscus and champak incense, this prickling in my palms, this damp slippery stone under my feet.

Then, out of the corner of my eye, just out of focus, I see a young woman, quite lovely, dressed in a village cotton sari—an old-fashioned design one does not see nowadays. Next to her is a tall, fair stranger, his fingers still red from the wedding sindur he has just put on her forehead. He turns her audaciously to him for a kiss—he must be a rule-breaker too. Her body takes on a shivering, like a flowering tree in a spring wind, and over her face, which is oddly familiar, flit joy and regret and excited fear. I swing around urgently—I must find out who they are—but they have vanished.

No matter. In my bones I know them—the shades of my parents, impressions left in this temple air from their marriage day twenty-one years ago. Did they appear to remind me of their story? Or to warn me about mine?

Daughter and mother, mother and daughter. Though we would like to think otherwise, how our lives echo each other's.

When I look back from the temple gate, Ashok is still standing near Shiva's shrine. Soundlessly, he mouths something. I watch the shape of his lips saying *my wife*, and my heart dissolves into honey. Two weeks. How can I live for two whole weeks without him?

I lie on the newly washed terrace floor, the matting cool against my skin, and stare at the night sky. The darkness is diluted by the lights that seep upward from this never-sleeping city. I would ask Anju the names of the constellations that glow faintly through the haze, but she has fallen asleep, her head on my pillow, her breath warm and moist on my cheek, and smelling of cloves. So I repeat to myself the only one I know, Kalpurush, the black warrior with his curved, glittering sword.

I am sleepy too, but I force myself to stay awake. I am looking for falling stars. I need two of them, just at midnight, because I must make two wishes. One for myself and one for Anju—because today a promising proposal has arrived for her from a reputable Calcutta family, the Majumdars, whose only son works in America.

Not that Anju believes in falling stars. They are nothing more, she says, than burning meteors which have no power to help anyone, not even themselves.

I know. But I know also that there may be many sides to something all at once, many realities. A ball of flaming gas hurtling to its doom can, if you believe strongly enough, give you your heart's desire. The death of a star, the birth of a new joy in your life. Isn't that how the universe balances things?

I have not said this to Anju. How hard it is to explain wondrousness—even to her whom I have loved since birth. I hope she understands, though sometimes I wonder if true understanding is ever possible between people.

Earlier tonight when we stole up to the terrace after dinner, and I told her what Ashok and I had decided, I was certain she would be delighted for me. Instead she was distraught.

"Sudha, that's too big a risk. What if things don't turn out the way he says they will? All you have is his word that he'll marry you once you run away with him. What if"—she hesitated, then plunged ahead—"what if he has his way with you and then changes his mind?"

"I *know* he's telling the truth. I *know* I can trust him." I felt the anger shoot through my veins like a poison. "You don't know what love is, that's why you can say something so mean—"

Anju let my accusation pass. "Sudha, listen to me," she said patiently. "Even if he's telling the truth, or what he believes to be the truth, there's no guarantee his parents will take you into their home. If your mother had accepted their proposal, it would have been different. But now you'll be a runaway girl who's lost her reputation. From a family that's already antagonized them. What if they don't recognize your marriage?"

She was putting into words the fears that had jostled unshaped inside me all day. Perhaps that was why I put my hands over my ears and cried, "Enough. I won't allow you to slander Ashok. I've made up my mind about what I'm going to do, and that's that!"

Anju stopped then. She bit her lip hard to keep in the words that wanted to pour out, the angry words, the cautionary words, the loving words. For of course she knew what love was, my sister who would have given all her happiness for mine. "I'll have to help you then, I guess," she said.

Later we talked about Anju's possible marriage to the young man who would be arriving soon from America. All we knew about him was his name—Sunil—and his occupation—a computer scientist. Anju confessed that she was scared. My heart ached to hear that, my brave cousin who had never been afraid of anything in her life.

"To think that I'll have to go and live with a stranger. That I'm supposed to belong to some man I haven't even met as soon as he puts a garland around my neck. Oh, why can't I just remain single? Why must I be yoked to a man like a cart to a buffalo?"

I sighed in sympathy. I would have been afraid too, if Ashok had not saved me. I tried to point out the good sides of marriage to her. A home which in time she would come to rule. A man to wake her with moonlight kisses, to glance at her across a roomful of people with a heat in his eyes that would shake her heart for joy. The babies, with their sweet milk-and-cinnamon smell, to sing to sleep at her breast.

"Milk-and-cinnamon, hah! Dirty nappies, dripping with pee and worse, that's what babies smell like," said my unmaternal cousin. But perhaps she felt a little better, for she threw an arm around me and went to sleep.

I couldn't sleep, though. The morning's thoughts kept ricocheting in my head, all I would lose when I gained Ashok's love. Anju's arm, soft with sleep, circled my neck. Regret welled up in my mouth, bitter as the quinine Pishi used to dose us with. I, the renegade daughter. Would I even be allowed to see Anju again?

Now Anju frowns in her sleep, battling the demons of her dream world just as she has always fought, in her waking life, anyone who will not let her be herself. I smile a little, but inside I am crying. O my Anju, you who have never learned to bend with the wind, what will happen if you marry the wrong kind of man?

Carried from afar by the night breeze, I hear chimes. It is the clock at St. Paul's Cathedral, beginning to strike twelve. And suddenly we are plunged into total darkness, an ocean of ink. For a moment I am startled into terror. But it is only one of the power outages that plague us throughout the year in Calcutta.

The darkness is a cresting wave. It sweeps me up out of my body until I float among the stars, those tiny bright pores on the sky's skin. If only I could pass through them, I would end up on the other side, the right side, shadowless, perfectly illuminated, beyond the worries of this mundane world.

I hear the clock again. Its relentless chimes force me back into the cramped confines of my body. Midnight is almost gone. I search the sky desperately. Then, on the last strike I see it, a flash to the left, a small scar of light, already healing, my falling star.

But only one.

One star for one wish.

Opposing desires battle in my heart for Anju and me, pulling me this way and that. But finally I ask for a wonderful marriage for my cousin, a husband whom she will love with all her being. I know I will have to pay for my wish, for that is the way of this world on the wrong side of the sky, where there is never enough happiness for all of us.

Ashok, Ashok, cries a receding echo in my heart.

Still, I am glad that I gave my wish to Anju.

On the breath-end of that wish, just as the star burns out, comes a startling thought. If only Anju and I, like the wives of the heroes in the old tales, could marry the same man, our Arjun, our Krishna, who would love and treasure us both, and keep us both together.

It is a ridiculous wish, maybe even immoral. But before I can take it back, I am interrupted by Pishi's heavy steps as she pants her way up the stairs, scolding us all the while for being here by ourselves, under the clammy night dew that is sure to make us sick, when all good young women in Calcutta are fast asleep in their beds.

SIXTEEN

Anju

OUR STARS must be really well aligned this month, Aunt N keeps saying. First Sudha's marriage is all set, then I get a proposal, and now someone wants to buy the bookstore.

Her optimism's somewhat misplaced. Sudha's marriage is all set, yes, but not in the way she imagines. I shudder to think of what'll happen after the elopement, all the scoldings I'll have to face—because of course they'll blame me too. But for Sudha's sake I'm willing to put up with it.

As for my marriage proposal, it hasn't progressed far. My maybe-in-laws are waiting for His Highness to arrive from America. There's been some kind of a crisis at his computer company, and he has to take care of things like defective chips and malfunctioning motherboards. As soon as he gets here, his family assures us, we'll have a bride-viewing and they'll let us know his opinion.

I'm in no hurry. He can take the slowest boat back, for all I care. And as I've said to Sudha, they can call it a bride-viewing all they like, but they'd better realize that it's a groom-viewing as well. And if I don't like what I view, you can bet your life my opinion's going to be known too.

The bookstore is, indeed, being sold. One of the other booksellers in Calcutta has made us an offer. It's a poor offer, and he's only going to pay us half the money up front—but Mother accepted it. I begged her to hold out, but I could see in the smoky hollows under her eyes how afraid she was that she wouldn't be around by the time another offer came.

The buyer wants an inventory done before he takes over, and I ask Mother if I can help Manager Babu with it. It'll give me a chance to see the place I'd woven so many dreams around one last time before it becomes someone else's.

But when I get there, I'm not so sure it was a good idea. All the old employees come up to me to say good-bye. They call me Anju Didimoni, little sister, little jewel, and reminisce about how I was just a girl in pigtails when I started coming to the store with Mother. They wipe their eyes on their dhotis and wish me luck with my marriage. Awkwardly, they ask about my mother, whom they call Rani Ma. They tell me how she's been a mother to them all these years. How she gave Jiten the money for his father's eye operation. How when Palash fell from the bus and broke his leg and had to stay home for two months, she didn't cut a paisa of his salary. And when Manager Babu suggested that she let go old man Manish, who's just about blind, she said she couldn't fire someone who's given the store fifty years of his life. Listening to the stories, I begin to understand all those late nights when she sat with the account books, trying to squeeze a little more money from them, and I'm ashamed that I thought I could do better than she had.

The new owner wants to change the name of the bookstore, so today the big red and yellow board that has said Chatterjee and Sons Fine Books for over seventy-five years is coming down. I watch the workmen struggling with ropes and ladders. Someone loses his hold, and the board falls with a crash, cracking in two. I try to stay calm, as Mother would. It was being sent to the go-down anyway, to be chopped up into firewood, I remind myself. But when the new board goes up, I can't bear to watch. I climb onto a chair and furiously begin to pull down books from the science and technology shelves, the section of the store I care least about.

That's when the man comes into the bookstore.

He's elegantly dressed in a traditional kurta with gold buttons, refreshing at a time when so many young men are wearing skin-tight pants and glittery disco shirts. His gold-rimmed spectacles are charmingly old-fashioned and intellectual-looking, and when he asks me if we stock any books by Virginia Woolf, he wins me over completely.

Woolf's been a favorite of mine since the time I stumbled upon one of her books at the store. It was a beautiful old leather-bound volume, printed in England, with an intriguing title: *A Room of One's Own.* When I put my nose to the thick pages, they smelled totally unlike our Indian books with their sweet rice-glue binding. I thought of it as the smell of distance, of new thinking. That smell stayed with me a long time. It stood for something I wanted but didn't know a name for.

When I took the book to my mother, she held it for a while without saying anything. Then she told me that my father had ordered it a few months before he died. I could have it if I wished.

I spent many afternoons reading and rereading the book, which was a long essay rather than the stories I usually preferred. I understood only a little of what the author was saying. But I felt her sadness and her fire. I could see her standing in front of a hall filled with women—for the preface said the essay was originally a speech—demanding that they cast off their blinders and stand up for their rights. She would not have raised her voice, but the passion in it would have pierced each woman's breast like a shaft—as it did mine. It surprised me that my father would have wanted to read such a book. I imagined his hands holding it as he lay in bed late at night, long after Mother fell asleep. I saw the warm light from the lamp falling onto his fingers as he turned the pages. Maybe he'd frowned, turning the ideas over and over in his mind as I was doing. Maybe he'd drawn his breath in sharply, in sympathy and indignation. For the first time in my life, I found I could think of him without bitterness.

When I got older, I persuaded Mother to order all of Woolf's novels, and whenever she allowed me to accompany her to the store, I'd go into a corner and devour them. I was afraid someone would want to buy one before I finished it. But they were never popular with our Indian literati, who much preferred Dickens and Hardy and E. M. Forster.

Now I bring down the full set and start extolling Woolf's virtues. I talk of her style, which is like a river with unexpected turns. Her perceptiveness. Her symbols. Her women with their doomed artistic souls who are unlike any others I've met—in life or in books. I hope I can find a good home for at least one or two of them before the new owner condemns them to some termite-filled storehouse. And this intelligent young man with laughing eyes would appreciate them, I can feel it.

When I pause for breath he tells me that my eloquence has convinced him to buy the entire set!

I wrap them up for him inexpertly but proudly. I try to act cool and professional, like a real salesperson, but when he asks me if I'm one of the staff, I burst out laughing. Manager Babu gives him a severe look designed to put people in their place and informs him that he's been talking to Miss Anjali, the owner's daughter.

The man doesn't appear to be put in his place. "Ah, Miss Anjali, no wonder you're so well read," he says. "Are you in college, studying literature maybe?"

I can tell from Manager Babu's expression that he thinks such a question is terribly forward. He'd like to send the young man on his way, but just then someone yells that the new board's dangling precariously from a hinge, and he has to rush outside.

I tell the young man no, I'm not in college, though that's what I wanted more than anything in the world. I try to keep the sadness out of my voice, but I think he hears it.

"More than marriage, even? I thought that's what most young women your age dream about."

"I don't have to dream about it," I say acidly. "It's going to happen to me any day now, probably as soon as Mr. America gets here."

"Mr. America?" He lifts an eyebrow.

I explain to him about Sunil and his malfunctioning motherboards. I know I shouldn't, but there's a certain sympathy in his gaze that makes me want to confide in him like I've never confided in a man before.

"Oh dear," he says. "He sounds awfully boring."

I'm struck by the ridiculous desire to grab the sleeve of his kurta and say, "Don't go." Or even, shamelessly, "Marry me." For surely a man like this one would allow me to continue my studies. I could go to one of the all-women's colleges. That would be proper enough, even if I were married. Maybe we could even read Woolf together.

Yes, Anju. And maybe the moon will turn into a monkey and fish will fly in the sky.

I slide the package across the counter to him. But instead of taking it, he puts his hand over mine. I'm shocked. Did he read my mind? What if someone sees us? But he smiles such an open, friendly smile that I don't snatch my hand away.

"I know your name, Miss Anjali," he says. "Don't you want to know mine?"

I stare at him. A suspicion makes my heart leap. But surely not. I couldn't be that lucky.

"It's Sunil. Yes, Mr. America himself! No, don't be embarrassed." He gestures at his clothes. "Forgive me for the deception—I had to see you for myself—you as you really are, not at some unnatural bride-viewing ceremony, swathed in silks and jewels, sitting silently with your head lowered. Though now that I've seen you, I don't believe you'd ever sit silently with your head lowered, would you?"

I laugh with him, but uncomfortably. I'm not sure if he means it as a compliment.

"May I tell you," says Sunil, with a funny little formal bow, "how taken I am by your vivacity. You deserve every one of your dreams. If you do me the honor of marrying me, I'll try to make them come true."

The blood pounds through my skull in wild elation. I can't

think of anything to say. I, whom the mothers always scolded for being the talkative one!

"Shall we shake on it?" asks my American husband-to-be. But it's a statement more than a question. His voice is smooth like new molasses. And confident, as though no woman has ever turned him down.

I can understand why they wouldn't.

I clasp his hand as firmly as I can—otherwise I'd surely float away, my heart is so light. Now that he's discarded his glasses, I see his eyes have little flecks of gold in them. Already I adore his crooked eyebrows. I look forward to the evenings when we'll read *To the Lighthouse* to each other.

As soon as I get home I'm going to apologize to Sudha because she was completely, absolutely right. Love happens, and so do miracles.

SEVENTEEN

Sudha

ANJU'S IN-LAWS have come over to set up the details of the wedding. It is not really a bride-viewing, because everyone knows that the bride and groom have met already—the whole servant mahal has been buzzing with the gossip, and not just in our house.

Sunil's mother, a sweet, ineffectual woman who gestures a lot as she speaks, is extremely apologetic. "Our Sunil, he had to take things into his own hands! Didn't even inform us ahead—or else I'd have begged him not to do it. But he just asked around and found out where the bookstore was. That's what happens when you live in America for so many years, I guess! I should be thankful that he even agreed to marry a Calcutta girl." From her tone I can tell that, in spite of his escapades, or maybe because of them, she is immensely proud of her son.

"He knew quite well that if he brought back one of those American memsaheb wives, he wouldn't have been allowed into the house," says Sunil's father, who is obviously the ruling force here. He crosses his scissor-thin legs, clad in dark, foreign-looking pants that Sunil must have brought for him, and eyes with disfavor the shell-shaped sandeshes Pishi has spent all morning preparing. He waves away the hot kachuris stuffed with spicy peas and shakes his head at the steaming milk-tea. He does agree to drink a glass of michri water, but only after he has been assured that the rock sugar has been bought from a reputable store, and the water is boiled. I am glad Anju will only have to live with him for a year—until her visa arrives—and not for the rest of her life.

Sunil, though, seems pleasant and thoughtful. He helps Anju take the teacups around to everyone. In America men must do things like that. Then he begins a low-voiced conversation with Gouri Ma. *Promise*, I overhear, and *as much education as she likes*. I see Gouri Ma's thin face light up. My heart warms further toward my future brother-in-law, and when he looks up I offer him my brightest smile.

Sunil's father, Mr. Majumdar, doesn't like it when the conversation is not centered around him. He clears his throat loudly to ask Gouri Ma how her disease is progressing. I can tell from Gouri Ma's face that she considers such a question inappropriate, but she says, politely enough, that she has a lot more energy nowadays.

"Perhaps it's just the relief of knowing that both our girls are going to be well settled," she smiles. She beckons to me. "Sunil, I want you to meet Sudha. She's my other daughter, the sweetest child, and so talented with the needle, you wouldn't believe."

I blush. Praise from Gouri Ma has always meant so much to me. I join my palms to do a namaskar to Sunil, but he puts out his hand and says, "Oh no, you can't be so formal. We're going to be related, after all." I feel awkward, but I guess this is the way they act in America, so I put my hand in his.

Mr. Majumdar clears his throat again—he would rather his son behaved in a more dignified, bridegroom-like fashion—and says, "Well, there's just a few details to wrap up now. Since our son likes your daughter so much, we've decided to form the alliance here. Though to be frank with you, a couple of the other families—for example, the Bhaduris of Bowbajar—had offered a significant dowry."

"Father!" says Sunil. "We agreed there was to be no dowry discussion!"

"Please don't interrupt me," says his father. "I said I wouldn't ask for a dowry, and so I won't. No doubt Mrs. Chatterjee, who comes from a fine background, already knows what's fitting in this respect. Anyway, a good reputation has always meant more to me than all the money in the world. That's why I broke off talks with the Bhaduris. We found out there was some old scandal in the family, an unmarried aunt who committed suicide—you can guess why! I wasn't going to be associated with any of *that*. Better a penniless, ugly girl, I said to my wife, than one whose family is stained with immorality. And there are far too many such families. You'd be amazed, Mrs. Chatterjee, at what we've been discovering—secret relationships, pregnancies, runaway girls brought back by force—"

I stare at his lips, the way they twist as he speaks. Terror opens inside me like a chasm into which, at any moment, my soul could disappear. I turn to Anju, but Sunil is whispering something to her. There's a small, blissful smile on her lips as she begins to whisper back. I can tell she has not heard a single word Sunil's father has said.

Oh, Anju, if only you hadn't fallen so much in love. What will happen to you now if I run away with Ashok?

"Actually," continues Sunil's father, "our talks with the Bhaduris had progressed quite a bit. But as I told my wife, even the best match, I'll break it. Even at the last moment. It's a matter of family ijjat, after all. Even after the wedding, I'm prepared to send the girl back to her parents if I find something ugly, like—"

"Please, Majumdar Babu," Gouri Ma interrupts. "Not in front of the children! Anju and Sudha, why don't you show Sunil the garden? Anju? Are you listening, Anju?"

We walk out. I want to hold on to the walls, but they are undulating like waves. When we reach the garden, the sun is a parched emptiness in the sky because Sunil's father will never let him marry a girl whose cousin eloped with a man she met in a movie house.

"I'll be back in a minute, Sunil. I want to show you my father's copy of Woolf," says Anju. She rests her hand on his arm. Already it is an intimate gesture. "Sudha, I'll meet the two of you in the jasmine arbor."

Her footsteps fly over the gravel. Her voice is happy as birdsong. I'd been afraid she would ask me why my face is so flushed, but she's far too much in love.

Sunil has noticed, though. "Are you okay?" he asks as we walk toward the bower. "Maybe it's the heat." He has a kind voice. "Here, lean on me." He guides me to the bench inside the arched bower of jasmines, a place I've always loved. But today the scent of the flowers is too sweet, dizzying. The ground is full of black pocked mouths, opening to swallow me. No matter what I do, I will be the cause of pain. If I run away, I will break Anju's heart. If not, I will break Ashok's. I shut my eyes, stumble. "Careful," says Sunil, and grabs my arm.

What ill karma have I performed that I should be plagued with having to make such a choice?

Then it comes to me. It's not my karma I'm expiating, it's my father's. My charming, thoughtless father who brought heartbreak to the Chatterjee household once already.

It is only right that this time it will be his daughter's heart which breaks.

We're sitting on the bench now. I take deep breaths and try opening my eyes. My head has cleared a little. I am deeply embarrassed. Then I notice that Sunil's hand is still on my arm. His face is too close to mine, and he is staring at me with an intent, dazed look.

"You're so beautiful," he says in an altered, sleepy tone. "I've never seen anyone like you, either in India or America. If only I'd met you before I met your cousin—"

And suddenly, in a whole new way, I am very afraid. "Please let go of me," I say. The words come out scratchy and hoarse, almost inaudible.

In slow motion, as though he is underwater, he drops his hand and moves to the other end of the bench. There is a slight sheen of sweat on his forehead. His chest heaves like a runner's. "That was unforgivable," he says, pressing his fingertips into his eyes. "I don't know what came over me."

I see that he means it, that he is as startled by his act as I am. Somehow this makes me feel worse, as though I were to blame.

My lungs hurt when I try to breathe. My throat is too dry for speech. What could I say, anyway? And then I hear Anju's footsteps, light and rapid. "Sorry it took me so long," she calls breathlessly. "I'd misplaced the book. Hey, Sudha, don't tell me you've been sitting here all this time without speaking a word!" To Sunil she says, "She can be shy at first, but once she gets to know you, you won't be able to shut her up!"

I hear Sunil say, formally, "I look forward to that." Is it only I who hear the catch in his voice? I'm afraid to meet his eyes, to see if they still have that drowning look in them. I feel absurdly guilty as I tell Anju I have a bad headache, I want to go and lie down.

"Will you be all right?" she asks. "D'you want me to go with you?" But already she's sitting down next to Sunil, her shoulder touching his, and opening her book. I do not blame her. I know how it is when your blood keeps exact pace with a man's blood-beat, when you cannot think of anything except the fact that he is there next to you. All you want is to be alone with him, forever. Your only memories are of the satin heat of his lips, the flight of his hands over you like blackbirds, the wild, thorny smell of his body, which is like no one else's. Did you have a life before him? You don't know. All you know is that if you did not see him again, you would die.

I am happy for Anju, truly I am.

"I'll be fine," I say. "Don't worry about me."

I walk back to my room, my chest filled with splintered glass.

With each step, *AshokAshokAshok,* I am learning the landscape of loss.

That night I write the letter, explaining to Ashok why I cannot elope with him, not even after Anju is married. The next morning I give it to Singhji along with Ashok's ring, which I have taken from Anju's drawer without her knowledge.

"Are you sure?" asks Singhji. He looks unhappy.

I nod and feel the burn of tears start again down my cheeks. I am thankful that in front of Singhji, at least, I need not hide them.

"But, beti, why? You needn't be afraid—Ashok Babu has planned every detail perfectly. He's the kind of young man who can be trusted—a true pearl, as we say in the Punjab—"

I trust him with my whole heart, I want to cry. But it's best that Singhji believes I am doing this out of fear for myself. There must be no hint, no whisper, that could get back to Anju and make her suspect the real cause.

"Please go now," I tell him. "And don't bring back a reply. I've made up my mind."

When I enter her bedroom that evening, Anju is sitting by the window, gazing out into the darkness. All day I've been teetering on the cliff-edge of that thin laughter whose other name is tears, and seeing her there almost sends me over.

I have to call her name twice. She turns to me with a vague smile. I do not need to ask who she's thinking of. She reaches for my hands, her movements slow, dreamlike. I make myself smile as I grip her fingers.

"How brightly the stars shine tonight, Sudha," she says. "I feel like I've been asleep all my life, underwater, like the princess in the palace of snakes. I might have stayed that way forever—about as alive as a mollusk!—if fate hadn't sent Sunil into my life. And to think he loves me! *Me!* Isn't that the greatest magic of all?"

"Yes," I say. What other answer is possible? Then I add, "I've decided not to elope with Ashok. I'm going to marry Ramesh instead."

"What are you saying?" Anju's whole body goes rigid with consternation. Her eyebrows draw together like the fuzzy caterpillars we used to find in the garden when we were little. "You *love* Ashok! How can you even think of living without him?"

Sweet Anju of the caterpillar brows, you who have just learned what passion is, your words scald me like lava. Now comes the hardest part—for you must not know the truth. You who are going to have a difficult life already, I fear, with your father-in-law whose bloodhound nose can sniff out every indiscretion, and your husband who thinks I am the most beautiful woman he's ever seen. You who would never let me give up Ashok if you knew it was for your sake.

"I've been thinking about what you said," I tell her. "You're right. The risk is too great. What if things don't turn out the way Ashok says they will? My life will be ruined. It's better I marry the man the mothers have chosen for me."

"To marry someone else when you love Ashok—to think of him touching you"—a shudder goes through Anju's entire frame—"if I were in your place, I could never, never, do it!"

Her words are like bullets exploding in my chest. It takes all my willpower to form a smile. "Maybe I'm learning to be more practical, like you told me to be!" What I am learning is deception, how to joke while I dig a hole deep enough to bury my heart. "Didn't you always complain because I was too much of a dreamer?"

Anju looks into my face questioningly, and my insides tremble. Will she see my lie, as she has so often in the past? But slowly the lines on her forehead fade. Blurred by new love, today her mind cannot fix itself on anything except Sunil—the surprising warmth that wells up from under his skin when she touches his arm, the way the hollows under his cheekbones hold an entire chiaroscuro of light and dark. She runs a hand distractedly through her hair and says, "I don't know, Sudha. When I told you not to elope, I wasn't in love myself. Now that I am, I see things differently. It'll be safer for you this way, but will you be happy?"

I nod. *I'll be happy in seeing you happy, dear Anju.*

"Are you sure you're doing the right thing?" Anju asks one last time.

"I am," I say. *I am righting my father's wrongs.*

Earlier today Singhji brought me back a note from Ashok.

I was angry, but Singhji said, with unusual vehemence, "I couldn't just hand him your letter and turn tail like a dog, not when I knew the boy needed someone to talk to."

I knew I shouldn't ask, but I couldn't stop myself. "What did he say?"

"He said, 'She can't mean it. She can't play like this with my life, with her own life.' Then he threw the letter at me and yelled, 'Tell her this is carrying generosity for her cousin too far.' He paced up and down for a while, then he added, 'How does she expect me to live without her? Does she think love's a tap to be turned on and off at will?' "

I could see his face, the way he must have ground his fists into his eyes as he spoke. No, Ashok. Love is not a tap. It flows and flows like blood from a wound, and you can die of it.

"Finally he said, with a rough laugh, 'I never thought Sudha's cousin would become my rival for her love. I never thought that if that happened, she'd win.' Then he wrote you that note. Beti, if you could have seen how he was hurting, you'd change your mind. And you still can. It's not too late. Things will work out for Anju Missybaba, I'm sure."

"No, Singhji, you didn't hear what Sunil's father said. He'll break off the marriage if there's any scandal now. He's already done it once, with another girl. Even after the marriage, he'd send Anju back—he's capable of it. And Sunil—who knows if he's strong enough to stand up against his father? No, Anju loves Sunil too much for me to take that risk. What I'm doing—maybe it'll make up for—"

"Make up for *what*?"

"For things that were done to her before she was born," I said, then sighed, suddenly tired. It was too much to explain, even to a sympathetic listener like Singhji. So although I could see from his distraught face that he wanted to talk further, I told him I was unwell and needed to lie down.

Now I take out Ashok's letter, though I do not need to. I know it by heart already.

Sudha—
Did you believe I was going to be magnanimous, like the lovers in the old myths? Did you expect me to forgive you and wish you happiness with your new husband? Well, you're wrong. This is what I'm going to wish for you: that you too will be let down by the one you love most. You too will be rejected for another. Your heart too will feel as though someone ground his boot heel into it.

Ashok, do you think my heart does not already know what that feels like?

Slowly I tear the note into tiny pieces. I hold my cupped palms outside my window until the wind takes them away into the darkness, like flakes of sloughed-off skin from the Bidhata Purush's feet.

I focus on the sky with all my strength. Sometimes the pain is so deep, the only way to survive it is to keep one's attention on something immense beyond human sorrow.

If there were a falling star now, I know what I would wish for. I would wish Ashok a new love, one that held no hurt in it. If there is such a thing.

EIGHTEEN

Anju

CRAZY LOVE has turned my life upside-down.

Now that I'll be a married woman in a week, the mothers have grown indulgent. I'm allowed to write to Sunil—every day if I want. I've bought myself scented paper, a purple pen. How I would have scoffed at such things earlier! For the moment at least, I've traded in Virginia Woolf for Elizabeth Barrett Browning. *How do I love thee?* I copy out painstakingly, in my best handwriting, more love-struck than Sudha ever was. Or have I taken on, in some strange way, a part of her nature? I thumb through Tagore's poems to find lines to express the swallow-swoop of my heart: *Aaji . . . mane haiteche sukh ati sahaj saral. Today I sense how simple happiness is.* Every day I run to the gate when the postman comes. Sunil isn't much of a writer. But when the mail does bring me a letter in his square handwriting, it's like iridescent bubbles are bursting inside my chest. Perhaps because I've told him how much I want to travel, he usually writes about the places he wants me to see: Lake Tahoe, King's Canyon, Baja. I whisper the names to myself at night before I sleep. They fall from my tongue like mysterious, alien jewels.

Even in my delirious state, I'm worried about Sudha. She's gay enough as she goes through the day's whirl with the mothers, choosing gifts for her in-laws, looking at jewelry patterns, getting her palms painted with mehendi. But every once in a while her laughter sounds brittle and too loud. There's something desperate in the way she pirouettes in front of a mirror as she tries on a gold-worked shawl. And then I wish guiltily that I hadn't listened to her. That I'd gone to my mother and explained about Ashok.

Once I tried to talk to her about it.

"Okay," I said. "I understand why you didn't want to risk everything by running away. But Ramesh isn't the right husband for you. You don't even like him—I can feel it."

Sudha said nothing.

"Why don't you wait a bit?" I begged her. "I'll tell Mother to look for someone else for you. You don't *have* to get married at the same time as me—"

Sudha cut me off fiercely. "I don't care who I marry—they're all the same to me. All I care about is not having to live in this house with all its memories once you're gone." As she swiveled away, she whispered something I didn't quite understand: "How could I stand to remain here without you, Anju, when you're my only reason for remaining here?"

Two days before the wedding, Mother calls us to her room. I know it's something important because Pishi and Aunt N are there too, looking tense. No one speaks when we enter, and Pishi draws the curtains and locks the door behind us. The heavy wooden bar gives an ominous creak as it slides into place. My mother struggles to sit up in the bed. There's a small bottle of nitroglycerine tablets on the side table—she must've overexerted herself and had chest pains again. I imagine the burning, like red-hot fingers gripping her lungs. My usually sensible mother—oh, why's she so stubborn about not undergoing the surgery she obviously needs? I want to rub her back with some of the root-and-herb oil which seems to help with the pain, but I know she hates having anyone fuss over her.

"Girls," she says. "There's something I must show you." She takes a worn-looking jewelry box from the side table. It must be another one of those ugly heirlooms from my grandmother's time—maybe a bulky armband or a fat, moon-shaped comb—which Mother's been sending to the jeweler to be remade into something finer to suit our taste. Then she adds, "Perhaps you can help us decide what's to be done with it."

I'm amused that she's even asking us because usually the mothers make all such decisions on their own. Do they think we're wiser now, just because we're getting married? Don't they see that in my current love-struck state, I'm barely capable of rational thought? I look at Sudha to check if she's got the joke, but she's staring at the box, eyes flared and—yes, afraid.

When Mother opens the box, my eyes widen too. Because inside is the largest ruby I've ever seen. Even in this dim light the jewel shines redly, with an angry energy.

Sudha makes a small sound like a moan. She presses her knuckles against her mouth to cut it off.

"This is what your fathers left behind when they went off," Mother says.

I feel dizzy, off-balance, like I'm being thrust back in time. Anguish stings the back of my throat like old sand. Anguish and rage. The rage which had made me punch the walls of my room because I had nothing to say when my schoolmates taunted me for not having a father. I hear myself saying, in a lost child's voice, "How could he leave us like that?" How many times I'd asked Mother that, only to have her send me away without an answer. Today, finally, I know I can make her tell me if I want.

Then I realize something. I no longer want it. Even truth can come too late. My father's motives mean nothing to me any more. I have Sunil now. My own man, more precious than any ruby, who'll never abandon me.

Pishi and Aunt are watching Mother, who seems at a loss. It's as if they're waiting to hear what she'll say. I wonder whether they each have a different story about what happened, and which of these—if any—is the true one. Is there ever a story that can capture the whole truth? I've a feeling that if I retell this one to my children, it'll have transformed itself by then into something quite new.

Except I'm not going to. I've no interest in passing on the tale of two overgrown boys who went off adventuring without a single thought about what would happen to the women they left behind. Who thought excitement would taste sweeter than all the pleasures of home. If storytelling is how we keep alive those who are gone, then I enthusiastically condemn my father and uncle to oblivion.

But Sudha speaks into the shadowed silence of the room. "They went because, like all men, they wanted to win something amazing, something everyone would admire them for." Her eyes are opaque as stormy water, and her face has gone blank, like a room where someone switched off the light. "It's all true, then," she says, in a strangely despairing voice.

Mother looks as if she wants to ask Sudha what she means, but finally she just sighs and rubs at her chest. "It happened a long time ago. If it weren't for the fact that we can't decide what to do with the ruby, I wouldn't even show it to you at this auspicious time."

"That stone's brought us nothing but bad luck ever since the day it appeared in this house," Pishi bursts out. "I say we get rid of it. I've been saying that all these years, but neither of you would listen. We should sell it and use the money for wedding expenses—God knows we need—"

"Now, Didi," Aunt N interrupts excitedly. "You know we'd never get a fair price for it. Those jewelers, as soon as they see us women, they'll know they can cheat us blind. I say we keep the ruby. It's just a stone. How can it bring bad luck?"

I hadn't expected Aunt, with her amulets and soothsayers and weekly *pujas* to keep the planet Shani from casting his evil eye on us, to turn so pragmatic all of a sudden. She must want this ruby badly.

Mother, impartial as usual, says, "My idea is to have the ruby cut in two and made into pendants for each of you girls."

"But that would ruin its beauty—and its value," protests Aunt.

"What's your solution then?" Mother sounds irritable. They've reached this impasse before, I can tell.

To my surprise Aunt lowers her eyes. Her cheeks redden like a bashful girl's. For a moment I can see how beautiful she must have been before the shock of her husband's death turned her into a grasping, scolding, fearful woman. She takes a deep breath and lets her words tumble out. "I think Sudha should have the ruby, seeing how Anju has so much more. Besides, it was her father who brought it to us in the first place—"

"That's not fair, Nalini," Pishi says sharply, "and you know it. Why, if any one of the girls is to have it, it should be Anju. Because if your husband hadn't put all those wayward ideas into Bijoy's head, he would still be here today."

I'm taken aback by the naked animosity in Pishi's voice. It's true that throughout our childhood the mothers disagreed on how things should be done, and sometimes even argued hotly. But the next day they'd be the best of allies—if not friends, united against us. Sudha and I used to joke about how they were like the holy trinity, Brahma, Vishnu, and Shiva, keeping our little domestic world on track. Had it been a facade all this time, carefully constructed to keep us from guessing how fragile the foundation of our household really was? Now that we were almost married and no longer needed to be sheltered, cracks were widening underfoot, the ground beginning to shift.

Sudha's been staring at the stone as if there are invisible letters on its fiery surface that only she can read. Now she says, decisively, "Pishi's right. I want Anju to have the ruby."

"You brainless girl," cries Aunt N. "You don't know what you're saying!" She turns to my mother in agitation. "Don't listen to her, Gouri Di."

Mother starts to say something, but I interrupt. From somewhere a thought has come to me, so lightning-sharp, so clearly not *mine*, that I know it's the correct answer.

"The ruby must be put back in the vault." I even sound different, my voice full as a temple gong. "It's not really ours. None of us has a right to it. Not until—"

"Not until *what?*" asks Pishi. But I shake my head.

"She's right," says Mother, sounding startled. The other mothers nod as well. They all look relieved. Mother hands me the box and asks me to take it back to the bank tomorrow.

I feel very grown-up as I walk down the corridor alone. It's a little scary. In my hands the box is lighter than I thought it would be. Sudha's gone off to her room, saying she needs a nap. I'll have to wait to tell her the part I held back from the words that had been sent—there's no other way to say it—to me. *Not until we've suffered even further, not until the house of the Chatterjees is reduced to a heap of dusty rubble.*

As though it were only a matter of time.

NINETEEN

Sudha

IT IS THE day before our weddings, and the house is filled with frenzied activity. Hordes of men are at work stringing up lights and setting up an enormous tent on the lawn. In the court-yard behind the kitchen, hired cooks bustle around huge clay ununs, constructed for the occasion, where curries and dals are bubbling. The air is pungent with the aroma of mustard fish and tomato chutney, for many of our out-of-town relatives have ar-rived already and must be fed. This morning Pishi gave us, with much pride, two lawn handkerchiefs on which she'd embroidered good-luck lotuses twined into our initials with red silk thread. Now she has disappeared into her room to make our wedding garlands. The other mothers are equally busy with last-minute details.

Only we, the brides, have nothing to do. We asked Pishi if we could help, but she shooed us from her room—it is bad luck, apparently, for brides to touch their garlands before the proper moment. We wandered through the chaos downstairs for a while, but it was disorienting, the way people—even the servants we had known all our lives—watched us with awe and a certain respectful formality, as though we'd been transformed by our bridal status into anointed beings.

So we are back in our rooms now, where we are to rest ourselves—as though that were possible in the midst of all this hallah. Anju lies on my bed, reading a book. Trying to read, I should say, for in the last half-hour she has not turned a single page. I sit by her, twisting the tendrils of her hair around my finger, as I have loved to do since I was little. So many sadnesses are swirling through my mind. Images of the life I have known all these years, the sense that I am leaving it irrevocably behind. When I return next it will be not as a daughter of the Chatterjees but a daughter-in-law who belongs to her new family.

My traitor memory brings me another image: a young man waiting in blazing heat by the roadside, his lips on mine in the dim alcove of a temple smelling of incense and foolish hope, that brief dazzling time when I believed that I was to be his. Unbearable now, so I turn to my cousin and say, "Remember when we were little, the time we played hide and seek, how you locked yourself into the almirah where Pishi keeps her clothes?"

"Yes," laughs Anju. "And how terrified I was that I'd suffocate to death in there—but of course you came and rescued me!"

"And remember the time when we ate panipuris from a street vendor outside our school and got sick?"

"Indeed I do! And that delicious jeera water the man gave us afterward to drink. It was well worth our upset stomachs!" Anju sits up, animated. "Remember those make-believe games we used to play? How you always insisted on being the princess!"

"Only because you liked being prince better!" I retort.

"And remember that old house near the Ganges where that man—I think he was some kind of great-uncle—lived? We went there once, for a wedding."

I close my eyes and see the building, yellow plaster fallen away in chunks, a roof crusted with mossy growths. "We climbed up to the terrace on one of those old spiral staircases attached to the outside of the house—I was sure I'd fall down, but you wouldn't allow me to stop."

"Silly!" says Anju, laughing. "You know I'd never have let you fall!" Then her eyes take on a faraway look. "Wasn't there a room on the terrace, a locked room? Wasn't there a boy?"

At first I can't remember, but then I see him, a boy not much older than us, beckoning from behind a barred window, his eyes strangely slanted, his fingers fat and pale as earthworms. He'd made grunting noises we couldn't understand, and when we ran away, frightened, he'd beaten on the bars and wept.

"Remember how all the women scolded us when we came down and told them what we found? How later Pishi explained to us that the poor boy had been born with some kind of brain defect?"

I nod. The memory makes me shiver. What would Anju's father-in-law say if he knew of the hidden boy? Would it qualify in his books as a scandal?

"You know, Sudha," says Anju, playing with the glass wedding bangles on my arm. "There'll be no one to whom I can ever talk this way again, who'll know what I mean without explanation." Her eyes are full of tears. And suddenly the fact that we are leaving each other cuts into me like a whiplash—the way truths do, sooner or later, when you have kept your gaze turned deliberately away from them. But I must not cry. Once I begin I will not be able to stop, I have so much to weep for. So I say, with false gaiety, "You'll have Sunil! He'll soon mean more to you than any cousin!"

"Don't joke," says Anju, and from her stiff voice I can tell she's deeply offended. "My love for you is totally different." She drops my hand. "I'm going to see if Mother is back. I want to make sure she doesn't tire herself out."

I should go after Anju and soothe her, and say I didn't mean it, but I am filled with a heaviness that keeps me from moving. Can it be true that nothing can take the place of a true love, not even another love? One part of me longs to believe it. But if it were—how then would I live the rest of my life with this torn-out hole in my chest? And yet I would not want to change what I've chosen. Oh, if only the weddings were over, and all choices behind me forever.

There's a knocking on my door. It is Singhji with a pile of letters and packets. I'm a little taken aback. Except for the night of Gouri Ma's heart attack, he has never come into the house. Besides, it is Ramur Ma's job to bring up the mail. But perhaps on this topsy-turvy day she cannot be found. When I ask him in, he shakes his head but looks around with a shy curiosity. I wonder what he makes of the heavy furniture and the dark-hued oil paintings which go back to before I was born. When I was younger, how I had hated them. But Mother said it was disrespectful to the spirit of our Chatterjee ancestors to change anything. Perhaps she had been embarrassed to admit she didn't have the money. I'd consoled myself with the thought that when I got married I would have the room I wanted, light and airy, with an oleander-pink bedcover and flowers in a slender silver vase, but now that it is about to finally happen, the prospect is joyless.

I shuffle through the pile of letters without enthusiasm. For weeks now people who cannot come to the wedding have been mailing us little blessing-gifts. I am about to tell Singhji to take the whole lot down to Gouri Ma when I notice a small, fat packet without a sender's name.

Later Pishi and I will examine the envelope—a common, brown-paper one bearing a central Calcutta postmark and my name printed in blocky letters—over and over, but at this moment I pay it little attention as I tear it open. And all of a sudden my lap is full of money, hundred-rupee notes—scores and scores of them, it seems, spilled from the packet. I gasp in shock. Even Singhji, who is always so calm, has clapped a hand over his mouth. *Who?* I feel in the envelope for a letter, but there's nothing. And then as I sift through the notes I see it, a small slip of paper on which is written, in flowing Bengali characters, *To Sudha: May your life be as full of joy as mine has been of sorrow. Your Father.*

My brain feels short-circuited, my heart twists as though the last drop of blood is being wrung from it. If it weren't for the money, I would have thought it a cruel joke, but here it is, a lapful, more money than I had ever imagined.

My father, alive?

"Why, beti," whispers Singhji in awe, "there's enough here for Ashok Babu and you to live on for years."

Temptation runs through me like an electric shock. But finally I shake my head. All the money in the world will not help me if Anju's marriage is broken off.

I hand the other packages to Singhji and motion him to leave. I know he sees my fingers trembling. I know I can trust him not to speak of what he's seen in this room. For that I feel a brief thankfulness—then the jagged rock that is my heart lacerates me. *Alive, all this time, and never came to us. Never came to help us when we needed it so much, never came to see me, his daughter, to hold me in his arms—*

Singhji's eyes are full of a wondering sadness as he takes the packages from my hands. Even after he leaves I feel his emotions swirling around me, compassionate as a rain-bearing wind. He would like to do something to help me. But he cannot. Nor can my father. It is too late now. Eighteen years too late.

In Pishi's room I close the door and brace myself against it. The smell of the flowers, damp, cool, temple-like, assails me. Rajani gandha, bel, jui. White as grinning teeth. White as lightning in night storms. White as the widow's dress my mother has been wearing in bitterness for so many needless years. The door is shivery-cold against my back. I shut my eyes tight and wish, as I did when I was a child, that time would double back on itself and give me back my life as it was half an hour ago. The serenity of ignorance. The innocence. But the weight in the bundled-up anchal of my sari will allow me no escape.

"What's the matter?" Pishi rises in concern, holding a gorgeous creation of jasmines and white roses with silver thread woven into it. It is my wedding garland—she'd drawn out the design weeks ago. "Are you ill?"

I can well imagine how I appear, my face bloodless against the dark mahogany of the door, my chest heaving.

"Shall I call the doctor?" asks Pishi. She puts out her hand to feel my forehead. I want to crumple against her as in childhood, to let her lead me to bed, to sleep away what has just occurred as though it were a fever dream. But I am a woman now. So I hand her the letter in silence.

When Pishi looks up from the letter, the paleness in her face matches mine. She does not say what I desperately want her to: that it must be from some heartless prankster. And when I let go of my sari-end so the banknotes I had gathered into it fall in a rush to the floor, she draws in her breath—but it's not so much the sound of shock as of a fear fulfilled. We stare at the pile of money, suddenly bright in a ray of sunshine that has struggled in from between the shutters she closed to keep the flowers fresh. It strikes me that my father—*but he's dead*—must be rich. The thought fills me with fury as I remember our years of scrimping and scraping, my mother's endless complaints, Gouri Ma silently pushing herself until the worry spread its tentacles through her arteries.

The forgotten garland crushed in her hand, Pishi bends down to touch the bills. They make a dry shuffling sound, like someone walking on dead leaves. When she straightens, it is slowly, painfully, as though in a matter of minutes she has grown immensely old. In her fist the garland is a rope of bruised blooms, white and red.

Red?

I pry open her fingers and see the needle embedded in her palm. "Pishi!" I cry. She looks down, but it is as though she doesn't see it, doesn't feel the pain. I take a deep breath and pull it out, pressing down on the wound to stop the blood. The garland that was to have been mine lies crumpled on the floor, blood-defiled. I wonder if this means bad luck, then want to laugh. How much worse can my luck get?

I am trying to remember where Pishi keeps the iodine with

which she used to clean our skinned knees. I rummage in her chest of drawers, and after a while I find the bottle. There's no cotton wool, so I dip the edge of my sari in the brown liquid and hold it to her palm.

"We never did go to identify the bodies." Pishi speaks indistinctly, as though she were immured in glass. "Your mothers were in no state to travel, and I had to take care of them—and Anju and you as well. Besides, the police said there was no point. The bodies had been in the water for a while, and the fish had got to the faces. The police had the moneybags that were in one of the men's pocket—they said that was identification enough. So they sent the bodies back in sealed caskets and we cremated them. But now I'm thinking—someone could easily have—"

"What are you saying?" I whisper. The iodine has stained my sari a burnt-paper brown, a color that will never come clean. I taste the nauseous yellow of bile in my mouth. So many times in my life I thought I was afraid. Now I realize that until this moment I did not know what fear was.

Pishi looks away. "There were three men, remember? One of them could have slipped his moneybag into another man's pocket after he'd—"

I put my hands over my ears, but the phrase already pounds its rhythm inside my skull.

Killed him. Killed him. Killed him.

"My father!"—the word sticks in my throat, the most distasteful word in the world. "No!"

But the pictures have already started flashing through the thunder roaring in my brain, through the mingled odors of iodine and wedding flowers and blood.

I am seeing a boat rocking in a river that winds along the swamps of Sundarban. Monkeys yammer hideously in the vine-choked trees overhead, and in the distance one can hear the howling of hyenas. Mosquitoes buzz and buzz, and tempers are short. It is too hot, there's not enough wind to guide the sail, and the three men are tired of rowing and of cooking their own meals, now that they have sent the bearers away for safety's sake. The elation they felt on finding the cave—for indeed they have found it, and gathered their rubies, and tied them securely into their waistbands—has been replaced by a strange depression. Because they have adventured and won—and are no different from when they left their easy Calcutta existences. And it is in this frame of mind that my uncle Bijoy picks a quarrel with my father one evening when their partner is at the other end of the boat, cooking the night meal. He tells my father what he knows, and accuses him of being an impostor, a liar, a cheat who took advantage of the goodness of the Chatterjees.

And my father? Does he deny it? Does he plead for forgiveness? I do not think so. A black rage breaks over his face that Bijoy should have spoiled things just when luck had at last smiled on him. Rage mixed with shame, which is the worse kind. Before he realizes what he is doing, he has picked up an oar and hit my uncle over the head. The *thwack* of wood hitting flesh ricochets through the forest. The body slumps, sacklike, into a corner of the boat. And when the partner comes running, crying *What was that?* there's nothing to do but swing the oar again.

Does my father weep, then, kneeling beside the man who had loved him like the brother he never was? No. I will not give him tears. Dry-eyed, teeth clenched, he lifts first one body, then the other—how like sleeping children they are, slack-limbed and trusting in his arms—to drop them over the side. But first he raises their shirts to untie the pouches. Is it hard for him to touch their still-warm skin? To slide his moneybag into the pouch where he knew Bijoy kept his, feeling, under his fingers, a still-beating heart? Does he shudder when he hears the first splash, and then, like an echo, the second? Does he jump, startled, when, from the shore, he hears a pack of jackals yelping their displeasure?

And that night, when the white moon rises in the ink sky and a pair of night birds circle the mast, crying like the souls of the dead, is he frightened then, my father? Does he wish the act undone, the act that has cut him off from his wife and coming baby, forever? The act that will force him to change his name and, with only the baleful red glow of the rubies for company, move to some faraway city. But no, the postmark on the envelope said Calcutta. A shudder goes through me as I realize he has been inhabiting the outskirts of our lives for years, watching us. Maybe he sat in a taxi across the street when school was done and Anju and I came strolling out. Maybe he brushed against me when we went shopping in the crowded corridors of New Market. Maybe he stopped outside our gates late at night and watched the lights go out one by one, and imagined my mother and me in our beds. What thoughts might go through the head of a man like that? Through and through and through, until one day, eighteen years later, he sold a gemstone and stacked the banknotes in a pile and picked up a pen and wrote, *To Sudha.*

Ah, Mr. Majumdar, what would you make of this, the scandal to top all scandals?

"Sudha," says Pishi urgently. "Pull yourself together. No one must know that your father has reached out for you from the darkness of the death world."

A corkscrew of laughter is boring its way through me. What did she think I was going to do, shout it from the rooftops?

"You must decide what to do with the money." Pishi's voice is anxious.

It's hard to focus on details. Finally I say, "Take it to Kalighat for me. Give it to the beggars. And have a puja done for my uncle's soul."

"I am so glad you said that." Pishi lets out the breath she's been holding. "It's blood money, yoked to misfortune."

"I have to go," I say. I must be alone, must try to make some sense of who I have become today.

"Sudha," says Pishi, putting out her hand as I stumble to the door, "Whatever your father did, it's not your fault."

But I shudder away. Words have no power to comfort me. To touch me is to be contaminated. Because once upon a time a man raised an oar and brought it down on another's head. His rage is a river that runs through my body, and its waters are my blood. That is the blessing-gift my father has sent me.

TWENTY

Anju

IT'S HORRIBLY HOT in the wedding tent. I'm suffocating under the thick weight of incense and the wail of conch shells and the jabbering of wedding guests. The heavy gold and red Benarasi I'm wearing isn't helping either. I'm standing right in front of Sunil, but I can't see his face because the women are holding up a silk sheet between us. They'll lower it only after the priest finishes the mantra he's reciting to bring us good luck. It's a thousand-year-old mantra from the Vedas and defines luck as cattle and horses and vassals—and the one hundred sons I'm supposed to present to Sunil. A wicked laughter's beginning to bubble up behind my throat as I listen. I've got to control it until Sunil and I are alone. Unfortunately, that won't be until the fire ceremony and the puffed rice ceremony and the bridal flower-bed cere-mony and a hundred other such ceremonies are over. Still, when it finally happens we'll laugh together, and it'll be a better begin-ning to our married life than a hundred mantras.

The mantra's very long, and the priest chants it in a singsong voice that makes me want to yawn. But it isn't proper for brides to yawn, so to distract myself I watch my husband's feet, the only part of him visible under the edge of the silk sheet. I admire the curve of his arches, the cleanly clipped toenails. Thank God his toes don't sprout stiff black hairs like so many men's do. (I'm an authority on male feet—in the last few days I've touched at least a hundred belonging to elderly relatives to whom I'm supposed to show respect.) At the end of the wedding I'm supposed to touch

Sunil's too, to acknowledge him as the head of our household. Maybe if no one's watching too closely—or even if they are—I'll tickle them instead.

Somewhere off to the side, Sudha and her husband are going through the same ceremony. I know I should be focusing on the silk sheet—my eyes are supposed to meet Sunil's as soon as it's lifted, for that's the moment of auspicious seeing—but instead I crane my neck to look for Sudha. No luck. All I see is the flash and glitter of bangles and earrings, the bright stippled tints of a hundred silk saris. It feels as if all of Calcutta has crowded itself into the space between us.

If I could just see Sudha's face, I'd feel better. Something happened to her yesterday afternoon after I lost my temper and stomped off. If only I hadn't. Because when I came back she was lying on the bed, covered all the way up to her head in a thick bedspread though it was a hot day. I could tell she wasn't asleep, so I pulled the cover off. She didn't move. Her face was dripping with sweat and she kept her eyes closed until I shook her and called her name, and then she looked at me like she didn't know who I was. It reminded me of the time when one of the maids had spilled a pot of boiling dal on herself. Huge blisters had sprung up on her arm, and Pishi had made her put it in a bucket of ice water until the doctor arrived. "Does it feel a little better?" she'd asked after a while. The girl hadn't answered. She'd just stared at her with the same animal look of baffled terror.

Once I would have known, even without Sudha telling me, what the problem was. But recently it's like a fog has drifted between our hearts. At first I'd blamed Sudha for it. I told myself she was purposely distancing herself so it wouldn't hurt her so much when we had to say good-bye. But now I wonder, as I stare at my husband's feet, if maybe it wasn't just as much my fault because I'd been too drunk with my newfound desire to pay attention to her silent distress.

"Anju! Anju!" The women have let the sheet fall and are calling my name.

"Here's her husband, right in front of her, and she's dreaming about someone else!" one jokes.

I blush and raise my eyes to Sunil's. He's smiling, eyebrow raised. He'll probably tease me about it later, too. *Who was it you were thinking of so intently that you almost let the moment of auspicious sight pass?* But when I explain my worries about Sudha, surely he'll sympathize. I expect no less of a man who loves Virginia Woolf.

Now we exchange the garlands that Pishi has made for us. Jasmine and rose and night-blooming gardenia. I'll never smell them again without feeling Sunil's fingertips brushing my throat like a flame. The ends of our garments are tied together, and we walk seven times around the sacred fire. My hand feels so right in Sunil's strong, warm grasp, like a nesting bird that's found its home. "My heart is yours, as yours is mine," I repeat after the priest, pronouncing each word as clearly as I can. "For seven lifetimes will I follow you to the ends of the earth." Sunil's hand tightens on mine, and I know he's heard the conviction throbbing through my voice.

The ceremony's going to continue for a long time—the putting of sindur on the woman's forehead, the recital of more mantras, the official giving away of the bride, the recital of even more mantras. But as far as I'm concerned it's done, because I feel joined to Sunil, for ever and ever.

We're supposed to move to a different part of the tent for the next ritual, but I ask Sunil to wait a moment. I want to watch Sudha complete her seven circles around the fire. How beautiful she looks. *More beautiful than she's ever looked in her life,* I hear the guests whisper as they admire the chandan marks on her forehead, the translucent flush on her cheeks, the way she lowers her thick lashes modestly as she follows Ramesh. But then they've never seen her bare-breasted on a stormy night, her soul flashing in her eyes.

At they walk, Sudha stumbles over the edge of her sari. Ramesh turns quickly to keep her from falling. But she has righted herself already and moves back just a fraction so his arm won't touch her. Her face is a shell, with whatever had been alive inside scraped away. It frightens me. It's as though I'm seeing the old tale enacted again—the princess of the snakes who has lost her beloved and been captured by the stranger-king. Now she has no other choice but to follow him to his barren kingdom.

A great sigh shakes me, all the way to the core of my heart. Oh, Sudha, why did you do this to yourself? And me, too busy with my own unforgivable pleasure, why didn't I stop you?

Sunil mistakes the reason for my sigh.

"Yes, she's lovely, truly lovely," he says.

There's nothing unusual about his words. All my life I've heard men—and women, for that matter—admire Sudha, often much more extravagantly. But there's something in Sunil's voice that makes me give him a sharp glance. "The loveliest of women—" he murmurs, very softly, then breaks off. He keeps gazing at Sudha—almost as if he isn't capable of moving his eyes away. His face is naked and open, like a house with no curtains. And because I'm so deeply in love myself, I recognize exactly what I'm seeing in there.

A long time ago, in school, I'd watched a movie of a California redwood tree that had been struck by lightning. It hadn't burned up, as one would have expected, or been charred black. From the outside, it looked almost like the other trees. But one day a man leaned against it—and the tree crashed to the ground. When they looked inside, they saw that its entire core was hollow, and filled with ash.

I feel like I'm that tree.

I go through the motions of the rest of the ceremony. Sunil marks my forehead with sindur. I slip a ring onto his finger. We chant more prayers for conjugal bliss. When Sudha passes by us, following her husband with listless steps, Sunil's voice falters as he says, "And I will protect you and treasure you and love you as my Lakshmi, my goddess of prosperity."

How is it no one else notices this?

But of course I'm overwrought. Light-headed from the wedding-day fast, I'm reading too much into a glance, a pause. And even if I'm not, how can it matter? Sudha will remain here while Sunil and I go to America. After this night, he'll probably never have the occasion to see her again. Even otherwise she'd never betray me, not in a million lives. Still, in spite of all my logicking, my mouth is parched, my fingers shake and spill things, and when we stand up, I too stumble and Sunil has to grab my elbow.

In the banquet hall, everyone mills around us, offering congratulations. The mothers weep a little as they bless the bridegrooms and kiss Sudha and me. Then we're seated at the bridal table at the far end of the hall, the four of us facing the guests, Ramesh, then Sudha, then Sunil, then myself. Ah, what a comedy of errors, what a crooked quadrangle of love! Ramesh—the only one who's in high spirits—asks Sunil a million questions about America. Sudha stares down at the traditional banana-leaf platter in front of her as though she's never seen one before. A slight film of sweat adds a dewy glitter to her face. I watch my husband trying to answer Ramesh without looking at Ramesh's wife. I watch him trying to be considerate to me, telling me, a bit distractedly, to have a little food, maybe a bite of the fish fry. Asking if I feel well. I sense that he's distressed by the emotions that have swept over him like a flash fire. That he would like to behave honorably. And I—I'm so scoured by rage and helpless love and jealousy that I can't trust my voice to make a civil response. Yes, for the first time in my life I'm consumed by jealousy of Sudha, sister of my heart.

After the meal, we stand up to leave our table, Ramesh, then Sudha, then Sunil, then me in the rear. Sudha pulls her handkerchief from her waistband to wipe her face, and when she puts it back, it falls to the ground behind the table. It's the special handkerchief Pishi embroidered with good luck lotuses—I have an identical one tucked into my blouse. I'm about to alert her when Sunil bends to pick it up. I'm the only one who sees him slip it casually into his kurta pocket.

It doesn't mean anything, I tell myself. He's just waiting for the right moment to return it. But the rest of the evening a cold trembling takes over my legs, and the blood pounding in my ears seems to howl with derisive laughter. *Fool, fool, fool.*

How a single moment can destroy your entire life, crush all the happiness out of your heart if you let it. But I won't let it! I can't! It would bankrupt me—I've poured so much of myself into Sunil.

When Sudha and I are alone for a few minutes in the room where the women will come to dress us in our Bashar clothes for the long night of singing and jokes that follows the wedding, I ask her, "How does it feel?"

"What?" says Sudha as she pulls the heavy wedding garland from her neck wearily, letting it drop to the floor. "To be married?"

"No. To have my husband be crazily in love with you," I say bitterly. But already I'm sorry for what I've said. Why am I blaming my innocent cousin for what's not her fault?

"What are you talking about, Anju?" Sudha says, her voice anguished. I take a step toward her. I'm about to throw my arms around her neck and apologize. But she shrinks back and holds up her hands, as though she doesn't want me to touch her. The look that flashes in her eyes is an emotion you can never mistake for anything else, especially if you've felt it yourself.

It's knowing guilt I see on my cousin's enchantress face.

Words crowd my mouth like gravel. I must spit them out. "Sudha, how could you do this to me?"

"Anju, no, wait," Sudha cries. But I walk out of the room, lurching under the weight of the lesson I've learned less than one hour into wifehood: how quickly the sweetest love turns rancid when it isn't returned. When the one you love loves someone else.

BOOK TWO

The Queen of Swords

TWENTY-ONE

Sudha

DOWNSTAIRS IN the Bardhaman house it is noisy with festivity, but upstairs where I wait alone it is quiet enough for me to hear the thick, faltering beat of my heart. I am sitting in the room that is to be mine from tonight, on the high, garland-twined bed which used to belong to my husband's parents, and his grandparents before them. Still dressed in the heavy purple silk I'd worn for the bridal feast, I am sweating a little, but mostly I'm cold with fear. The warnings of the teatime aunties echo in my ears. Someone has laid out my night-sari—a lacy, diaphanous affair—helpfully on the bed, but I cannot stand the thought of undressing, cannot stand the thought of what must follow, a stranger's hands groping over me in lust and ownership.

I had gone through the wedding ceremony in a fog of numbness. I wrapped myself in it gratefully as though it were a magic shawl that could shield me from my life. I stood and sat and stood again, repeating mantras, smiling when I was expected to. If I could keep myself from feeling what I was undergoing, I told myself, then it wouldn't become real. At some point I would wake to find I had dreamed it all. But the shawl of numbness tore when Anju looked at me with loathing and accused me of snaring her husband. There is nothing now to keep me from the full, chill weight of my despair.

My bridal night. How often in the last year I had daydreamed it. The tenderness with which my husband would lift my veil, his

157

lips on my shy eyelids like an invitation. The words of endearment with which he would unlock the secrets of my body. Now I dread those very things.

Ashok, what poisons are burning through your brain tonight? When I think of your letter, *you too will be betrayed by those you love*, black laughter wants to burst from my heart. Your curse has come true already, for isn't the hatred in the eyes of my dearest cousin for whom I gave you up the worst of betrayals?

I hear footsteps on the stairs, the raucous laughter of the young men escorting Ramesh to the bedroom. He says good-bye to them and shuts the door. The sound of the bolt is like a bullet. As he walks toward me, I cannot stop myself from trembling. I clasp my hands tightly—I will not give him the advantage of knowing how frightened I am. He sits on the bed—but lightly, and not too close. We are silent—I am incapable of making light conversation, and he does not seem interested in it. When he leans over to take my hand, I flinch. Ramesh starts to say something, then stops. He works his fingers between my stiff ones and looks down at them, the dark and fair latticed together. "Do you find me so ugly?" he asks finally.

Astonishment makes me glance up into his eyes. It is not the question I expected my self-assured husband—for so he has appeared to me through the ceremonies—to ask. I can hear the disappointment in his voice, and the hurt. Somehow they lessen my fear.

Perhaps Ramesh was always conscious of his plainness, but these last few days must have been hard for him, with relatives exclaiming constantly over my looks. Many husbands would have grown irritated at so much attention being heaped upon their wives while they were ignored, but he'd been patient enough. Even when an old gentleman called me "the goddess Lakshmi come to earth," the smile on Ramesh's face hadn't faltered.

But now the sadness in his words strikes a chord in me. Growing up my mother's daughter, I know what it is to feel inadequate. I do not want to be the cause of someone else feeling that way.

If Ramesh had been a woman, I would have put my arms around him and assured him that the problem was not in him but in the unbearable situation in which I found myself trapped—and who but myself could I blame for that? But I cannot take the chance of him misunderstanding such a gesture. So I focus my gaze on my silver toe rings, their small faraway glitter, and force myself to speak. "This is so new—I can't—I'm sorry—" The words come out whispery and unconvincing.

But Ramesh gives a relieved laugh. "I understand completely. I don't believe in forcing such things. I'd be happy to give you—us—time to get to know each other."

We lie side by side after he switches off the lamp, careful not to touch. I'm tense all over, not sure I can trust him. I have heard too many stories from the aunties. But Ramesh talks in a slow, soft voice, pausing courteously from time to time for a response. He tells me about his work as an engineer, how much he loves it. How exciting it is for him to be faced with a problem to solve. The way he visualizes projects long before they come to pass, the lean, shining lines of a new track laid over terrain everyone else considers too difficult. The clean arc of a railroad bridge over a gorge that plummets into mists.

"There's nothing like the sound a train makes as it passes over such a bridge—that giant, hollow, echoing sound. Maybe sometime I'll take you with me so you can listen," Ramesh says.

I nod. In the dim light that seeps up from the courtyard below, his eyes are still and shining, focused on my face.

"By the way," he adds, very casually, "let's not tell anyone about what we've decided tonight, okay?"

I want to laugh. It's not as though I have an entourage of confidantes around me. But I know what he is really saying: If my mother-in-law knew of our platonic arrangement, we'd both be in a lot of trouble. Already I have overheard her telling several of the admiring relatives at the wedding about her hopes for the imminent birth of the handsomest children the Sanyal family ever saw.

"All right," I say. I will never love Ramesh—only toward one man can I feel that wrenching whirlwind emotion, soaring to heaven, flung down to hell, both at once. But our little conspiracy makes me feel we can be friends.

TWENTY-TWO

Anju

I LOVE being married, as long as I don't think too much about it. It's like floating on a giant bed of cotton candy, incredibly light and pink and sweet, but with sudden hollows into which you can tumble any minute. And then the stickiness grabs hold and won't let you up.

Being married is like what I imagine drinking wine to be, tipping up your head and letting the cool liquid pool into your mouth, a little bit of it trickling down your chin. And as long as you keep drinking, you're safe from being hung over.

But why am I projecting shadows onto a landscape of sunshine? Sunil's a most attentive husband. Almost every day he takes me someplace where we can be alone—so we'll get to know each other, he says, before he has to return to America, leaving me behind to wait for my visa. We stroll around Victoria Memorial. We sit at the edge of Rabindra Sarobar, throwing petals into the water. When he describes America to me, it seems almost as amazing as the fairy kingdoms of Pishi's tales. "You can be anything in America, Angel"—that's his special name for me—he says excitedly. "You can be what you want." Sitting there with my head on his shoulder, under the fragrant Hasnahana bushes with the sunlight making golden ripples on the lake, I believe him.

Marriage has changed me in unexpected ways. When I'm with Sunil, I'm like a dog with new puppies. I resent all intruders—and everyone is an intruder. When we visited my mother a couple of weeks after our wedding, as brides and grooms traditionally do,

I'm ashamed to say I had to work hard to hide my impatience. The house I'd always considered imposing seemed suddenly decrepit—it was as if I could hear the marble and mortar crumbling to pieces around me. And the mothers seemed smaller, shrunken, as if they were collapsing inward, into the void Sudha and I had left behind. When Pishi took Sunil away on the pretext of showing him the house so that Mother could ask me if he was treating me well, I was annoyed and answered in sulky monosyllables. How quickly my loyalties had shifted. Even if I'd had a problem with Sunil, I wouldn't have told her. That was why I said yes so fast when she asked me if I liked my in-laws.

I do like Sunil's mother. She's truly good-hearted and very fond of Sunil. I know she'd have liked to spend more time with him during his short visit, but she never complains when Sunil goes off with me for the whole day, returning only a little before his father comes home from the office. She'll happily make us a cup of tea and tell me stories about Sunil's childhood, laughing as she remembers the time he almost set the kitchen on fire with his science experiment, or how afraid he used to be of spiders. At such times she looks beautiful.

But when Sunil's father is around, Sunil's mother turns into a different woman. She bends her head and speaks in a watery whisper, or hunches her shoulders apologetically as she rushes to fetch what he's shouting for. He shouts a lot, Sunil's father. I think he enjoys it. Just as he enjoys quoting derogatory passages about women from the Hindu scriptures. I'm still too new in the family to be a target of his outbursts, but I've seen him eyeing me once or twice as he says things like, "Women and gold are the root of all evil."

I'm sitting at my dressing table, wearing a starched-stiff Bengal sari with lots of gold-work, trying to arrange the end in a veil over my head. The veil keeps slipping off, so I have to pin it on with bobby pins. Once I went down to dinner in a flowery kurta that Sunil had bought me, but his mother rushed up and begged me to go and change before his father saw me. She looked so scared that I didn't have the heart to argue. *Tyrant*, I think, as I clasp a fat jeweled chain around my neck. But as Sunil says, what the heck. I only have to put up with him for a year at most, until my visa gets here, and for Sunil's sake I will. I smile at my reflection, imagining how Sunil will remove my clothes later tonight, his lingering hands transforming me not into the old, familiar Anju but a wild and magical woman.

That's what marriage is, transformation into wondrous and terrifying selves we could never have dreamed.

In the dining room, Sunil's father is already seated at the head of the mahogany table. I help Sunil's mother carry in the dishes. We serve Sunil's father first, then Sunil, who sits at the other end. Then we eat—except that she's always jumping up to see if she can give the men a second helping of something or other.

Sunil's mother is a fervent cook. Like so many women, cooking is how she expresses love. Her task would be a little easier if Sunil's father weren't so finicky. Still, she manages to create dinners that are works of art. Tonight she's made a musoor dal with green mangoes, which Sunil's father says is excellent for cooling the temper—not that it's helped him any. There's aged basmati rice (easy to digest), mashed potatoes with steamed bitter gourd (to cleanse the blood), and a curry of ladyfingers with sautéed ginger (to stimulate the digestive organs). I've also brought in a raita of yogurt and cucumbers (a rejuvenator) and a big plate of tangra fish, cooked crisp so they can be eaten whole (more calcium that way, says Sunil's father). While I'm arranging all this on Sunil's father's plate, my mother-in-law hurries in with a small covered bowl, which she places next to Sunil. Then, looking absurdly guilty, she busies herself with serving Sunil.

None of this, of course, has escaped my father-in-law's vulture eye.

"What's that?" he asks.

"Nothing," my mother-in-law stammers. "Just a little dish I made for Sunil, nothing you care for, that's why I was putting it on this side—"

"Bring it here, Anjali," says Sunil's father. I consider disobeying him—but then he'll just make my mother-in-law do it. I glance at Sunil for direction. He's staring straight ahead, his jaw stiff, so I do as I'm told. Sunil's father lifts the lid. We peer down together at the dark brown paste inside—it's a tamarind chutney, rich and smooth, glistening with little flecks of chilies. It must have taken Sunil's mother a long time to prepare.

In one swift motion Sunil's father flings the bowl across the table at Sunil's mother. There's a fleshy thud, then a metal clatter as the bowl falls to the floor.

I stare in dizzy disbelief at the sauce spilled across the table, the dark stains spreading over Sunil's mother's sari. Nothing in my life has prepared me for this. What upsets me the most is the meekness with which she lowers her eyes and doesn't even wipe her spattered arms.

"Haven't I told you never to make that unhealthy stuff?" thunders Sunil's father. "Haven't I told you I can't stand the smell? Who pays for the food you eat in this house? Answer me."

Sunil's mother's lower lip quivers. How humiliating it must be for her to be treated this way in front of her new daughter-in-law. I want to take her away, to wipe her wet cheeks and soiled arms and shake some anger into her so she'll never allow that man to do this to her again. But when I start toward her, the harsh ricochet of Sunil's father's voice stops me.

"Sit down, Anjali. Where d'you think you're going?"

I'm about to tell him where, when Sunil pushes back his chair and stands up. The slam of his fist into the table is louder than his father's voice. "Enough! I'm sick of you bullying my mother. Sick of you always insisting that we do what you want. As it happens, I was the one who asked her to make the tamarind chutney—"

Sunil's father's jaw falls open. He's not used to rebellions.

Then he too stands up. The two men face each other across the table, their faces identical in twisted rage.

"So this is what you've learned in America, how to defy your father? Who was it that sent you there, I'd like to know? Who bought your ticket? Who paid all your expenses so that you could—"

My handsome, laughing husband whom I love so much stares at his father with pure hatred in his eyes. His face is murderous—if he'd been a stranger I met on a street somewhere, I'd have fled from him.

"Don't worry, I'll be happy to pay back every paisa and more," he says. "I don't want to live indebted to you, being reminded of it every day of my life. Like my poor mother. And let me tell you something, if I see you mistreating her one more time—"

"Quite the hero, aren't you?" spits out Sunil's father. "Want to impress your new wife, hunh? I wonder how impressed she'd be if she knew about your American exploits, all that drinking and whoring—yes, yes, don't think the stories didn't get back to me—"

But here my mother-in-law, who's been frozen with shock until now, pulls me into the kitchen and shuts the door, so that all I can hear are muffled roars that remind me of bulls fighting.

Late that night I lie in bed alone, my stomach hurting with hunger and distress. I can't stand the idea of having to face Sunil's father ever again. How can I stay in this house with him and Sunil's mother, that poor, broken woman, as everyone expects me to, for a whole year after Sunil leaves? How can I reconcile the tender, caring Sunil I know with the enraged stranger downstairs, ready to smash in his father's face?

But most of all Sunil's father's crude accusations tear me open with their malevolent claws. *Drinking and whoring.* I wish Sunil's mother hadn't pulled me away before I could hear Sunil's response. I wish that doubt didn't shift its ugly coils inside me like a snake coming awake. I wish I had someone who'd know just what to make of this crazy evening with her cool, calm vision. I wish I had Sudha.

And with that realization I'm crying, my stinging salt tears soaking my bridal pillow. I haven't allowed myself to think of Sudha for a whole month, since the moment I turned on her so unforgivably after our wedding. Haven't called her, haven't even asked the mothers how she's doing. Every time the topic came up during my brief visit home, I changed it deftly. Deep in the core of my jealous heart, I knew she wasn't to blame for that spellbound look on Sunil's face—ah, but I can't bear to think of it. That's why I've kept myself drugged with the romance of his words, the passion of his touch.

This is how love makes cowards of us.

The door swings open. Sunil flicks on the light. I blink in its sudden glare and wipe my eyes quickly, not wanting him to see I've been crying. But of course he notices.

"Angel," he says, putting down the packet he's carrying to take me in his arms. "I'm sorry about tonight." He holds me tightly. His hands stroke my hair. I burrow my face into his chest and smell the American cologne mingled with sweat, the best smell of all. We hold each other, comforting and being comforted. I press my lips into his palm, murmuring words that one might say to an injured child. The house of marriage has many locked rooms. Tonight we've opened one and entered in.

He's kissing my eyelids now, his breath hot on my face. I open my mouth to him, shrug off my clothes and pull at his. My bones are remolding themselves to fit against his, our skins have melted together, seamless, to form a map of desire. We move in urgent harmony, cry out in unison, lie damp and triumphant in each other's arms. How vulnerable he is after lovemaking as he nuzzles, infant-like, at my shoulder. How could I have ever been fool enough to doubt him?

166

Later, we sit cross-legged on the bed, eating. Sunil has brought me luchis and alu dum—all the way from the railway station because the neighborhood stores were closed by the time he and his father finished with each other. I take big starving bites of the crisp, fried bread and the spicy potatoes. I tell him it's the best-tasting meal I've ever had. He catches my hand and licks my fingers one by one, and I shiver.

"You taste better," he laughs, pulling me down to him.

I'm not unwilling, but first there's something I must ask. "Please don't take it wrong," I start hesitantly, "but when you leave, can I go back to my mother's house?"

For a long moment Sunil stares into space, his lips thin. Have I angered him? When he looks at me, though, there's only sadness in his eyes. "Maybe that would be best," he says. "I'd hoped—but—will you come and see my mother once in a while? She's taken a liking to you, and as you've seen, there aren't too many pleasures in her life."

"Of course," I say, relieved. I'm touched too by his concern for his mother. We decide I'll visit her in the afternoons when his father is at work.

"Now that we've taken care of business," Sunil says with a mischievous grin, "it's time for pleasure!"

What quicksilver moods he has! But I'm equal to them.

"Pleasure!" I grin back as he nudges me onto the pillow and begins to kiss me, little kisses along my collarbone, then lower, until I gasp in shocked delight. Ecstasy has taken over my body. I'm cotton candy in his mouth, melting. I'm sweet wine, intoxicating us both. I'm the luckiest woman in the world.

Sudha

IN MY HUSBAND'S house, I am always the first to wake.

No one forces me to do this. Ramesh, who is not the sort of person to force anyone to anything, would rather have me stay warm under our platonic quilt until the alarm clock rings. And as long as I join my mother-in-law for morning tea so that we can go over the day's plans, she's satisfied.

But this early hour when I sit at our bedroom window, shivering a little in the cool air as I watch the sun rise over the pond, the mists shimmering off the bamboo grove—it is precious beyond words. It is the one time I have to ponder my life. To feel the shape of this new woman I am becoming. Who is this Basudha who applies to the parting in her hair, after bath each day, an unwavering line of sindur to ensure her husband's prosperity? She puzzles me as she looks out from the mirror with her grave, grown-up gaze. A ring of keys weighs down the end of her sari, but she bears the weight well.

There's a story behind the keys. A few days after the wedding my mother-in-law called me to her room. I went a little fearfully, for though she had been kind enough to me so far, already I realized she was a strong-willed woman and used to having her own way. I had seen her reduce servant maids to tears with a single glance. But all she did was take the ring of keys off her sari and place them in my hand. "Natun Bau," she said—that is what they all call me in this house, New Wife—"this is your home now. You must learn to take charge of it." The cool brass of the keys in my hand was an astonishment, as was the look in her eyes—a mingling of reluctance and resolve. Giving up responsibility was something new for her, and difficult. But she was determined to do it. She must have steered her family through the rocky times that followed her husband's death with the same determination.

Brought up on the cynical tales of Mother's friends, I had equated a mother-in-law with tyranny, with someone who would fight me tooth and claw for control of her house and her son. But my mother-in-law was more complex than that. Already I could feel, emanating from her, solid as a wall of fire, her loyalty to the Sanyal family. That was why she gave me those keys, symbol of shared power—not so much because she liked me—she hardly knew me, after all—but because I belonged to the family now. But God protect me if I let the Sanyals down. She would never forgive that.

In spite of myself, I felt the stirrings of a reluctant awe. When I married Ramesh, I'd told myself that I would not get close to any of the Sanyals. I would do my duty, and no more. But this was a woman worth admiring.

"I'll try to do a good job for you, Mother," I said, and touched her feet in the traditional gesture.

"May you be the mother of a hundred sons," she responded formally, using the traditional words. But her hand rested for a gentle moment on my head.

For the first time since my marriage, I loosened my grip a little on the pain I had been holding on to desperately, a raft in my sea of stormy loss. Love's grand passion was snatched from me, yes, but perhaps there could still be quiet affections in my life. Perhaps I could learn to think of this woman as a mother, and this place as a home.

So now I am the keeper of the household, its many cupboards and pantries, trunks and storerooms. All except the double-locked steel Godrej safe that holds the money and the wedding jewelry. Those keys are still kept by my mother-in-law. I do not mind. I have responsibilities enough. It is so different to live in a household of men, not just Ramesh but his two teenaged brothers with their wild, coltish energy who have drawn me in with their artless demands. They burst into my room at all hours with small crises: a button to be sewed on, a lost schoolbook to be located. They keep me busy with requests for new snacks when they return each afternoon from school. They regale me with gory details about the cat cadaver in the biology lab, or the latest fight on the football field. I have happily accepted the job of making sure they leave for school on time. And though I am only a few years older than they are, something sweet and maternal opens in me as I straighten their lapels and make sure they have not forgotten their lunches.

But morning, before I am plunged into responsibility, allows me time to remember the Sudha I used to be. It seems impossible that I was the girl who ran panting to the terrace to wish on a falling star, who begged Pishi for stories of princesses and demons and saw herself in those stories. Who loved a man, once, so deeply that when she pulled him out of her heart, like a golden thorn—but no, I have promised myself I will not think of that anymore.

When I think of my past, I think most of Anju. There are so many images woven into the fragile filaments of my brain. Anju playing hopscotch with me up on our terrace, intent on victory, but always giving me a damp, generous hug if I won instead. Anju, her eyes dark with mischief, persuading me to eat onion piajis from the vendors. And later, her eyes dark with compunction as she held my head while I threw up in the bathroom. Anju flushed with anger, defending me from Mother's scoldings. Anju with her dreams of college ended, weeping in my bed. Anju with her face like a starry night as she told me of Sunil. But always at the end I see Anju at our wedding feast. Behind her thin, gold-glittery veil, her eyes are chiseled from black marble as she looks from Sunil to me and back again.

That veil seems to have frozen into gold ice between me and

Anju. After Sunil returned to America and she went back to the mothers—she never did tell me why—I called several times to ask how she was. I would sense in her pauses and her broken-off replies that she missed Sunil, that she longed to talk about him. Yet if I asked how he was faring, all alone in America, she answered curtly, as though she did not trust me with the details of her husband's life. We would end up speaking inanities— weather, food, films—the way we had vowed never to. After I hung up I wanted to cry. I wanted to hate Sunil with his easy American charm. Sunil who had whirled his way into our lives, as thoughtless as a tornado. But how could I when my cousin's happiness was so intertwined with his? I wanted to demand of God if this was my reward for giving up my happiness for Anju's sake. But that was a foolish question. I did what I needed to. Being rewarded had nothing to do with it.

But today as I lean into the window bars, I've put those old sorrows away. I am so excited I cannot sit still. A song rises into my mouth and I hum it softly, so as not to wake Ramesh. Yesterday, after a long silence, Anju called to tell me that her visa had arrived, that she would leave for America in three weeks. I could feel her exhilaration throbbing through the phone cord. A frost-knife twisted in my gut. My dear cousin, how far she would be going from everything familiar. From me. I prayed that she would be satisfied with what she found on the other side of the world.

"Please come to Bardhaman so we can be together one last time before you go," I begged.

Anju hesitated. I could hear her thinking up an excuse, as she had done every time I invited her. But finally, uncertainly, she agreed. She is coming today. My heart shakes with the joy of it. But I am also a little afraid. What will she see when she looks at my new household with her clever, critical eye? At the new me?

TWENTY-FOUR

Anju

ALL THROUGH the train journey to Bardhaman I'm sweaty and uncomfortable and angry with myself. Why couldn't I just have told Sudha I was too busy? It's going to be terribly awkward, both of us trying to find safe topics to discuss, tiptoeing around Sunil's name as if it's a lake of drowning sand waiting to suck us in, like in Pishi's stories.

The first-class compartment is stuffed to bursting with all kinds of people—passengers and beggars and vendors selling everything from sugar-dipped candy to magic cures. Most of them are traveling without the benefit of a ticket. This upsets my sense of justice and makes me feel put upon. I glare at the old woman squatting by my feet beside a basket of smelly, squawking chickens. She scratches her armpit and gives me a betel-juice-stained grin.

The mothers hadn't wanted me to travel by train. They'd arranged for Singhji to drive me down, but I'd refused. I was old enough to travel by myself, I said. It was only a few hours by train. Singhji would drop me off at the station and Sudha would pick me up at the other end. What could be safer? And hadn't they themselves said, all these years, that once I was a married woman, they'd no longer have to worry about my reputation?

"I'm concerned because you've never traveled anywhere alone," Mother said. "And the trains get terribly crowded," said Pishi. They looked so distressed that I was about to give in when Aunt N piped up, "There you go, being difficult as always, always insisting on your own way. What's your father-in-law going to say if he hears we bought you a ticket and put you on public transportation, like a common servant girl?"

Mention of my father-in-law put me into a foul mood, and I argued and argued (wasn't I going to America in less than a month? And how would I learn to travel alone unless I traveled alone?) until Mother said, Fine, if that's what I wanted I could have it. So now I sit here smelling like chicken droppings, with no one to blame but myself.

Finally the train lurches to a stop at Bardhaman. My clothes are stuck to my back, my eyes red from engine smoke. I step down, fully prepared to be disagreeble. But when I see Sudha, her face bright with a simple, generous joy, the walls I'd set up so carefully collapse around me like a house of cards. Inside my heart it feels wet, like new rain. I drop my bags and throw my arms around her. In spite of all my insecurities, in spite of the oceans that'll be between us soon and the men that are between us already, I can never stop loving Sudha. It's my habit, and it's my fate.

I dislike the house as soon as I see it. There's something ominous about the hulking brick structure that makes me shiver as I stand before a door massive enough to keep out whole armies of invaders—or is it designed to keep people in? I hear the grate of a bolt, the door swings open, and I'm face-to-face with Mrs. Sanyal.

Years later I'll think back on this, our first real meeting, and try to reconstruct what I saw. It would be hard to keep the details from being colored by what came afterward, but this much I'll be sure of: Though Mrs. Sanyal is most pleasant, when she looks at me I feel a focused intensity in her gaze, like a ray of sun through a magnifying glass, as if she's trying to figure out whether I'm a good influence on her daughter-in-law, or a bad one.

"Come in, dear Anju," she says. Behind her there's an enormous wall panel carved with fierce-looking figures, clawed and weaponed. She sees me staring at them and smiles. "They're yakshas. They guard our house. Come in, come in. I'm glad you're finally here!" I'm about to thank her when she adds, "Ever since she knew you were coming, Natun Bau's been so excited she hasn't been able to concentrate on a thing!"

The rebuke beneath the pleasant words is quite clear. I cast a quick glance at Sudha to see how she'll handle it and am baffled to see her smiling. When she replies, I hear only respectful affection in her voice. "I know, Mother. I've been no help to you at all. But now that Anju's actually here, I'm sure to do better."

As Sudha leads me upstairs to an oppressively large guest room crowded with oppressively large furniture, I wonder, didn't she hear what I heard? Or have I grown overly sensitive because of Sunil's father-in-law?

Below us, Mrs. Sanyal calls sweetly, "Natun Bau dear, once you settle your cousin, don't forget it's almost time to start rolling out the rutis for dinner."

Throughout the visit, little things bite at me like ants. The way Sudha serves the family at dinnertime, even Ramesh's younger brothers, cleaning up their spills and removing their dirty dishes. The way her smile doesn't falter when one of the boys pushes away his plate, telling her—the cheeky brat—that the fish curry didn't turn out right. The way, whenever Mrs. Sanyal calls her, she drops what she's doing—even abandoning me in the middle of a conversation with an apologetic "Why don't you rest for a while, Anju"—to go to her.

But what bothers me most is that Sudha's so determinedly cheerful. It's not that I want her to be unhappy. But this bustling young woman who does everything so well—from supervising the maid as she milks the cows, to putting out quilts in the sun, to frying fresh singaras for Ramesh's brothers when they get home from school—isn't the dreamer I've admired and been exasperated by, loved and wanted to protect. Can she really have cut Ashok so cleanly out of her heart, like a cancerous growth? Or is she hiding something from me?

One afternoon, sitting under the neem tree in the courtyard while Sudha mends Ramesh's socks, I ask her if she doesn't get tired of all the work she's made to do. "Why is it *you* that has to count out the dirty clothes for the dhobi and then count the clean clothes he brings back? Why is it *you* who has to make up the market list each day and hand out the spices for grinding and cut the vegetables for lunch and dinner? Why is it always *you* who runs up to the terrace to check on the—"

"But, Anju," says Sudha, looking at me with amusement, "no one makes me do anything. I like helping my mother-in-law. After all, she's getting old and frail, and has worked so hard all her life—"

To me, Mrs. Sanyal looked tough as alligator hide and fit enough to outlast us both by decades. But Sudha always did have a tendency to see only what she wanted.

"The servants do all the heavy work, but you know how it is—" Sudha nods her head wisely, just as Mrs. Sanyal might. "They'll steal the clothes off your back if you don't watch them every minute."

Oh my princess of the snake palace, is this what you've dwindled into?

I try once more. "Doesn't it bother you that Ramesh is always going off to faraway places, leaving you alone with his family?"

Sudha shrugs. "He can't help his job, and they're my family too. Besides, when he's here, he's so kind, I have nothing to complain about."

I want to shake the platitudes from her mouth. Is kindness enough to satisfy you, as if you're a stray dog? I want to say.

Forget Ashok, but what about your other passions? Your own clothing design business? Taffetas and silks and satins and eyelet lace?

Is this what marriage is, this settling for the mediocre? The thought terrifies me.

A dappled sunlight falls over Sudha as she picks up a ripped pant belonging to one of the boys and continues her mending. Her stitches are neat and precise. Is it a trick of the dusty afternoon light that her face seems suddenly far away, like an anemone at the bottom of the sea which might disappear in a swirl of sand if the current changes even a little?

It strikes me that that's how fragile her happiness is.

What right do I have to judge my cousin for the ways she's chosen in order to survive? What right do I have to be disappointed because she no longer sees herself as the heroine of a romantic tale? Who am I to say that small joys are less valuable than a passion which shatters your life?

And so, for the rest of my visit, I focus on what we have. We talk about the mothers and the old house, all the great times we've had there. I compliment Sudha on the new dishes she's learned to make, and ask for second helpings. When Ramesh goes out of town I sleep with her in her big bed, and when she falls asleep, I press my face into the cloud of hair spread over her pillow and breathe in the smell, so that I'll carry it with me to America. When it's time to leave we hold each other for a long time. Marriage has complicated our lives, divided our loyalties, set us on our different wifely orbits. Revealed things we must keep from each other. Never again could we live together the way we did in our girlhood, that time of simple and absolute raptures. It would be too dangerous.

But no matter how far we travel from each other, our hearts will always be inseparable.

When Singhji picks me up at Howrah station, I lean back against the familiar cushioned seat and close my eyes. The childhood journeys I took in this car were so much simpler, though then I hadn't recognized them as such. Tears are seeping from under my eyelids. It's not simply the sorrow of parting—surely that wouldn't leave me with this sense of prickly dread. Little images explode against my eyelids, getting all mixed up. When just the three of us were out for a walk, Ramesh put his arm around Sudha. But when Mrs. Sanyal's around, he hardly even looks at her. The bowl of chutney Sunil's father threw at his mother, how it arced through the air, staining it a dejected brown. The day a neighbor lady brought over her little grandchild, Mrs. Sanyal smiled her hard smile and said, *Soon I'll have one to show you too.* Sunil's eyes had glittered like light on the edge of a knife when he fought with his father. *Drinking and whoring, don't think the stories didn't get back to me.* Later in bed he hadn't bothered to deny the accusations.

"Is something wrong with Sudha Didi?" Singhji's voice makes me jump. In all these years, I don't remember him ever initiating a conversation. Against the darkness of his beard, his scarred face looks paler than usual. Of course he'd be concerned! He always did have a special bond with Sudha, a conspiratorial friendship, right from the time he'd stop the car so she could give away her lunch sweets. And he'd taken some big risks to help her with Ashok. I wish I'd been more thoughtful and agreed to have him drive me to Bardhaman. Now he probably won't have the chance to see her for a long time because Mrs. Sanyal didn't believe in Natun Bau going to too many places.

"She's just fine," I assure him. "Everyone in her new home likes her."

"They are lucky to have her." He nods his head with emphasis, then adds, kindly, "And your new family is lucky too."

Impulsively I ask, "Singhji, do you think we're going to be happy in our husbands' houses?" Immediately, I'm irritated with myself. What can I expect this old man to say except the meaningless traditional responses: *Of course,* or *I'll pray for it.*

But I'm wrong. "You must make your own happiness, Anju Didi," Singhji says with a passion that takes me aback. "You must be wise enough to recognize it when it comes. And if it doesn't come in spite of all your efforts, you must do something about that as well."

I want to ask what one can do to capture a truant happiness, but we're at the gate already, and at the end of the worn driveway, under the cracked marble of the entry arch, I see the mothers waiting, their tense, eager faces like lights flickering in a gale.

TWENTY-FIVE

Sudha

SOMETIMES WHEN I realize that over three years have passed since I placed the wedding garland around Ramesh's neck, I cannot quite believe it. My days have such a sameness to them, a hypnotic placidity, like a pool into which nothing ever falls, leaf or stone or human life. I float on this pool. I know I am needed; I know I am liked. And so I am not unhappy.

Even sex with Ramesh—for after a few months, one night he put his hand on my breast and I let him, it was his right after all, and he'd been patient enough—is only a minor inconvenience. For I have discovered that if I try hard enough, I can shut down my mind while things are being done to my body.

I'm glad to know from Anju's letters that her life is very different from mine. The quiet rhythms of my existence would have driven her to desperation—I saw that even in the brief space of her visit. Her restlessness, though she tried hard to hide it, made me restless as well. It affected the others too. The boys were more demanding than usual, and Ramesh quieter. And my mother-in-law, who is usually busy with her own work, would come by a dozen times on the merest of pretexts, almost as though she were keeping an eye on Anju and me. And so when it was time for Anju to leave I was sad, but not unhappy. Much as I loved her, she reminded me of all the things I had chosen to give up.

So perhaps it is best that now all we have of each other are our letters. Letters are so much more comfortable, so much less complicated than people. In them the world can be reduced to an inch-wide window, can be idealized like a touched-up photograph. This is truer of my letters than Anju's, which vibrate with all her feelings and opinions. But since they are reduced to the rectangular white silence of paper, I can enjoy them without worrying about whom she might offend with her frankness.

Even then there are problems. In Ramesh's family, the day's mail is passed out at dinner. My heart starts beating fast as soon as I glimpse, among the bills and boys' magazines and advertisements for Ayurvedic remedies, the blue aerogram from America. When it is handed to me, I glance through it very quickly, only taking in half, because in a minute my mother-in-law will ask how Anju is getting along. From her cool, clipped tones I know she feels I should show her the letter. But no matter how much I want her approval, I cannot do that. It's something I promised Anju during her visit.

At night, after everyone has gone to bed, I go into the bathroom. I switch on the dim bulb and lean against the water tank to read the letter one last time, slowly, intensely, trying to commit every word to memory. Through the rustle of the sheet, I can hear Anju's eager voice trying to show me her world. I picture the bedroom she has decorated with the silk bedspread we bought together at the Maidan fair, the vase of bulrushes she and Sunil picked during a hike, the Chinese dinner they had last weekend. I try out the delicious, exotic syllables, *chow fun, mu shu, braised tofu*, delighted that she is experiencing so many brave new things. In my reply I address her as *Anju, mistress of chopsticks*. On the day she writes that she has started taking classes at her local college, and describes for me the strange American chairs with little desktops attached to them, I weep for joy.

Next day when I am alone in the kitchen, I take the letter from my blouse, where I have kept it all night, and drop it into the unun. As it warps into ash, I wonder how Anju gets rid of my letters. Not that she has much cause to. My letters are as wholesome and bland as the milk-and-mashed rice that is fed to babies.

Because I, Sudha, who was for so long the keeper of secrets, no longer have secrets worth sharing. This life I have built over the cinders of my passion and my pain, this life where I have redefined happiness as usefulness—how blameless it has been, how unremarkable. Until today.

Today the household is in a flurry, because Ramesh's Aunt Tarini, his late father's sister, has come to visit us from Bahrampur. She has brought with her a retinue consisting of her oldest son and his bride of six months, her ayah, her chauffeur, her doctor, and various impoverished female relatives who serve as her confidantes and spies. My mother-in-law is determined to impress them all, even if it kills her.

It is a rivalry that goes back decades, Ramesh has told me, to the time when my mother-in-law was a new bride in this house, and Aunt Tarini (just a girl herself) had wrinkled up her nose and said, "Oh my, is this the jewelry your father gave you for your wedding? Why, even our maidservants wear better things!" My mother-in-law did not come from a rich family—her father had been forced to mortgage his house to raise her dowry—and Aunt Tarini's insult had lodged in a deep place inside her, festering. Years later when Aunt Tarini's husband took a mistress and moved into a separate house, she'd been heard to remark that she understood perfectly why the poor man behaved as he did. To which Aunt Tarini retorted that at least *she* hadn't driven her husband to the cremation ground.

When I got married, Aunt Tarini gave me a silk sari just like the one my mother-in-law had bought me to wear during the Bardhaman ceremonies, but with more gold embroidery on it. In retaliation, my mother-in-law presented Aunt Tarini's daughter-in-law with a monstrously heavy seven-strand gold necklace at her wedding last year. Ramesh had protested, in his quiet way. We can't really afford it, he said, and besides, what's the point? But she brushed his words aside like flies, as she always did when he disagreed with her. And he gave in, as he always did at such times. This morning, when Aunt Tarini arrived, she brought six suitcases filled to the brim with gifts for our family, including the servants and the neighbors. I shudder to think what my mother-in-law will do when, later in the year, it is time for our annual visit to Bahrampur.

I am sitting on the kitchen floor, instructing the maid about which spices to grind—we are preparing a daunting feast, enough to give Aunt Tarini a week-long heartburn—when my mother-in-law hurries in. At first I think she has come to check on the lobsters that our fish seller delivered this morning, the hugest I've ever seen, clanging their claws angrily at the bottom of a steel pail. Bahrampur has no seafood worth speaking of, and my mother-in-law has gleefully confided in me that she can't wait to catch the look on Aunt's face when the lobster curry is served.

But when I look more closely I can see that she is furious. Her lips are clamped shut and there are thunderbolts in her eyes. It unnerves me to see her like this, for I've always thought of her as a large, rooted banyan, spreading her comforting shade over the family.

"What's the matter?" I ask, wishing that Aunt Tarini had never left Bahrampur. "What has she done now?"

My mother-in-law glares at the maid, who scurries out. "It's Deepa," she says, her voice volcanic.

Deepa is Aunt Tarini's daughter-in-law, a plump, sweet-faced girl with hardly a word to say for herself. At her wedding my mother-in-law had seemed to take a liking to her. *Isn't she pretty*, she'd said to various relatives. *Why, she's almost as pretty as Sudha*. And, *It's good she has a placid nature—she'll need it with that Tarini*.

What could the placid Deepa have done to put my mother-in-law into such a state?

"She's pregnant," my mother-in-law breathes venomously and looks down at me with accusing eyes.

The concrete kitchen floor seems suddenly icy. My knees are ice too. My thighs. Blocks of ice clatter into being in my chest. For the last two years Ramesh and I have been trying assiduously for a baby, but with no success.

How much I want a baby to fill the empty spaces inside me! Somewhere in those unending nights when I lay beside Ramesh trying not to think of Ashok, the longing for a baby swept over my entire being until it became larger than the love I had left behind. I do not know exactly how it happened. Perhaps it was because I felt motherhood was my final chance at happiness. Perhaps I believed it would give me back what wifehood had taken away. Or perhaps it is just that desire lies at the heart of human existence. When we turn away from one desire, we must find another to cleave to with all our strength—or else we die.

Certainly the desire for a grandchild has been central to my mother-in-law's life as well, though she tries to hold back her anxieties. Still, every month she asks me eagerly if I've had my period. And when I nod guiltily, the silent disappointment in her eyes is worse than anything I can imagine her saying.

Today, however, she isn't silent. "After that woman told me she was going to be a grandmother," she spits out, "she shook her head with pity. *How long has it been since Ramesh has been married?* she asked innocently, as though she didn't know it to the day. *My goodness, is it over three years already? I'd get Sudha checked by a doctor, if I were you.* Then she broke off to pat her daughter-in-law's arm. *Go and lie down, Deepa Ma,* she said, sweet as sugar-water. *After all, we wouldn't want anything to happen to my grandson, would we?* I asked her how she could be so sure it was going to be a boy, and she said they'd stopped by at a fancy medical office in Calcutta where they have machines that can look into a woman's stomach and tell you everything."

My mother-in-law kicks at the steel bucket, starting up a frantic clatter of claws. All her plans for victory over Aunt Tarini have come to nothing. Even the largest lobster in the world is no match for a grandson, after all.

Then she looks at me, eyes narrowed and speculative, and I see she is not going to give up so easily. She's making plans, and while she makes them she eyes me with a new coldness, as though I were something inanimate, a rock perhaps in the path of her goal, something for her to climb over. Or blast away.

TWENTY-SIX

Anju

I BALANCE THE bag of groceries on my hip and brush my short hair from my face as I try to unlock our apartment door. The key sticks in the lock, as usual, and I have to jiggle it—quite a feat, considering that I'm also holding on to Sunil's newly cleaned jacket. I can feel the bag of groceries beginning to slide. I make a frantic grab at it—there are eggs inside—and lose the jacket. The letters I just got out of our mailbox scatter all over the doormat. Bills, pizza coupons, a computer-generated flyer addressed to Single Resident. Under the Memorial Day sale announcements from Sears I glimpse a distinctive cream envelope. My heart begins to beat unevenly even before I see my name written in my mother's neat script because lately there's been no good news from home at all.

"Shit!" I say, bending awkwardly to pick things up. "Shit!" Of all the American terms I've avidly gleaned in the three years I've been here, it's my favorite. It's explosive, exact conciseness expresses how I feel a lot of the time. But I'm careful to use it only when Sunil isn't around because he thinks it isn't lady-like. I point out that I hear far worse from him when he's driving. He claims that's different.

The door finally opens with a protesting *kreek*, but I wait a bit before going in. Even now, I don't like walking into an empty apartment. There's something about the air—unpeopled and stagnant, like it's from the bottom of a well that dried up a long time ago—that makes me uncomfortable. That's when the longing for the house of my childhood shakes me the most. How irritated I used to be at the constant commotion—milkmen, vegetable sellers, Ramur Ma shouting at the neighbor cat who'd sneaked into the kitchen, Pishi calling me to go for my bath. Now I'd be glad to see even the teatime aunties!

Inside, I drop everything on the kitchen table and collapse on the couch. I've been out since morning—first I took Sunil to the train station, then I went to my classes, then I caught up on some assignments at the library, then the grocery, then the dry cleaner's. I'm in a terrible mood—hunger always does that to me. That, and the fact that there's nothing to eat unless I cook it first. Of the many realizations I've had since I came to America, the foremost one is that I hate cooking.

Not that there's time to cook. I have to pick Sunil up from the station in thirty minutes, and it'll take me a good fifteen just to get there. So it'll have to be frozen burritos again. I know what Sunil's going to say. Well, he won't really say anything, but he'll give me that look, as if his life is one big burden and guess who's responsible. That look always provokes me into a fight, and tonight I don't want to, I've got to save my energies for the letter from India. So I drag myself off the couch and throw together onions and tomatoes and a few spices for a rice casserole to go with the burritos. I leave the stove on low, though Sunil's warned me that it's dangerous, wipe my hands on my jeans, and take the steps two at a time. Of course I hit every red light on the way to the station, and the motorist behind me honks and yells "Fucking Eye-ranian" because I'm not quick enough to make a left turn before the signal changes.

It's not what I imagined my American life would be like.

After dinner—which has turned out surprisingly good, the casserole a success in spite of my cavalier handling of it—we settle down, Sunil at the computer, me on the couch with my books and the letter, which I'm still not ready to deal with. Sunil has put a jazz tape into our old player. The room fills with notes drawn out like threads of airy gold, at once melancholy and exhilarating. As they seep into me I have to admit that I was being overdramatic earlier. I have a tendency to do that, as Sunil's pointed out.

Sunil's shoulders lean eagerly forward as he works on a program. Sometimes I get angry that he pays more attention to a machine than to me, but at other times I watch him, fascinated. There's something reverent in the absolute attention he gives to the numbers flickering across the neon screen. Watching his fingers move effortlessly across the keyboard, I feel I have a deeper insight into him than if we were merely talking.

I need all the insight I can get, because Sunil's the original man with a hundred faces. Even after all this time I can't tell which ones are really his, and which are masks pulled on for effect. He writes devotedly to his mother every week. He never mentions his father, though every month he sends him a sizable money order, more than we can afford. Once I asked him about it and he said, shortly, that he was buying back his freedom. When I was sick last winter he sat up all night, massaging my feet with Vicks, holding a basin for me to throw up in. But another time when I'd run out of writing paper and looked in his desk drawer for some, he yelled at me for not respecting his privacy.

Unlike some of the other Indian husbands I know, Sunil's always encouraged me to feel comfortable in America. He taught me to drive and introduced me to his colleagues at work. He bought me jeans and hiking boots, and when I said I'd like to see how I look in short hair, he said, "Go for it!" He's taken me to malls and plays and dance clubs and the ocean. And finally, though money is short, he's been enthusiastic about my going to college to get a degree in literature.

But when one evening I suggested we read some Virginia Woolf together, he shook his head emphatically.

"All that arty-farty stuff is not for me."

"But you bought the whole set from our store," I said, perplexed and disappointed. "I thought you really liked her work."

"Nah. In the introductory letter your mother had written to us she'd mentioned that she was one of your favorite writers, so I thought that would be a good way to start a conversation."

My cheeks burned. I felt cheated. Used.

"And then when I saw how you got all fired up about her, I thought it'd be nice to get the whole set for you. It cost little enough in dollars," said Sunil. He picked up one of his computer journals and leafed casually through it, unaware of—or unconcerned by—my distress. It was obvious he didn't think of his actions as deceptive.

I thought back to the young man that I'd fallen in love with that day. How the light had shimmered around his cream silk kurta. Now the table lamp threw distorted shadows of our silhouettes on the cramped apartment walls. Was this always how dreams of romance ended? Did the same thought cross Sunil's mind when he saw, waiting for him across the Caltrain parking lot, a tired, irritable woman with tangly hair and spice-stained jeans?

There are days when Sunil takes the car to work and doesn't come home until midnight. By then I'm crazy with worry and anger. I know he's not in the office—or at least he's not picking up the phone—and when he finally returns and I explode with accusations, he just shrugs and says I have to let him live his life too.

"What does that mean?" I scream at him, holding him by the lapels. "What the hell does that mean?" All the time I'm trying not to examine him for signs—slurred words, the smell of alcohol, or worse, a stranger's perfume. I'm hating myself for what he's reduced me to, sniffing at him when he returns like a suspicious bitch. And he'll pull my hands from him calmly, and go into the bathroom to brush his teeth.

Sometimes I think of leaving Sunil and returning to Calcutta, but I know I never will. It's not from fear of the gossip I'd have to face, nor because of how sad and anxious Mother would be. It's not even because a life left behind, cauterized like a wound, cannot be opened up at will for one to step back into.

It's because in some dark, tangled, needful way I can't quite fathom, I love Sunil more now than ever before.

What is hardest for me to understand is how Sunil feels toward Sudha. For the longest time we never brought her name up. He'd ask about the mothers from time to time—he's courteous that way—but he wouldn't say a word about Sudha, not even when he picked up the mail and there was a letter from her in the stack.

For a while I was happy to have it that way. Our wedding day was still too close to me. In spite of all the times we made love, all the sweet words Sunil whispered afterward into my hair, all I had to do was close my eyes and I could see the look on his face as he stared after Sudha, as he picked up the handkerchief that had fallen from her waistband. I'd never seen that wide-pupiled, out-of-control look on him again, not even at the height of our love-making.

But silence has its own insidious power. Because we wouldn't speak of her, Sudha sat between us on the sofa as we watched TV. Her hand brushed ours at table as we reached for a jug of juice, a carafe of wine. Setting off on a weekend drive, we'd catch her eyes in the rearview mirror, and when at night we lay in bed, we'd have to reach across her phantom body to touch each other. I was afraid of this Sudha we'd created. She wasn't the cousin

I loved, with her fears and fanciful imaginings, the girl who'd wanted so much and settled for so little. This Sudha, frozen in her bridal finery, remote and mythic as the princess in the snake palace—how could I hope to be her equal in any way? How could I claim my husband back from her?

And so I began talking, just a little at a time, telling Sunil about our childhood. The escapades, the punishments. Sunil never said anything, but his entire body would grow still as I spoke, like he was listening with every pore. Still I continued, telling him about Sudha's reluctant love for her mother, her dreams of creating designer-label clothes, her belief in falling stars. I took special care to paint for him images of Sudha as a wife, how well she played that part, how cherished she was in her new home, and how happy. Perhaps I exaggerated a bit, but it's only human, isn't it, to want to protect what belongs to you?

As I spoke, I realized how much I'd been missing Sudha, how much I longed to tell her about my troubles. In my letters, I'd only presented the best and brightest parts of my American existence. Was it out of a desire to save her from worry, or out of a need to let her know what a wonderful marriage Sunil and I had?

Sudha's letters were no more honest than mine. Sometimes I'd get one, full of a wonderful description of Durga Puja in her in-laws' home, or telling me how exciting it was when Ramesh took them all to the inauguration of a bridge he'd designed. But these were only surface things, and reading them I'd want to shake her because she wouldn't let me past them into her real life.

Mother's letters were a little better, although she minimized everything that might worry me, not realizing that it only made me more anxious. She'd write that she hadn't been well, and immediately I'd imagine her doubled over with chest pains. She'd write that money was a bit short, and I'd picture the mothers living on rice and water. I've asked her a hundred times to sell that white elephant of a house which constantly needs repairs—the land it's sitting on is worth a great deal—but she always writes back that that's unthinkable. It's the only home Pishi knew, and Aunt

Nalini as well. She herself had lived there all her adult life, and wanted to die there.

Recently, though, mother's letters have been mostly about Sudha, and they're the ones I'm most worried by. That's why I sit here holding the cream envelope, scared to open it.

The first hint that things might not be well with Sudha came from one of the teatime aunties whose sister lives in Bahrampur and knows Ramesh's Aunt Tarini. Apparently Aunt Tarini had been going around telling people something must be wrong with Sudha, look how it was four years already and she didn't have even one baby to show in all that time. Aunt N took the affront personally and was ready to write her a nasty letter saying there was nothing wrong with *her* daughter, how about *their* son, but Mother wouldn't let her. Foolish gossip, she said, is best ignored. Surely if there were a medical problem, or her in-laws were treating her badly, Sudha would have told them.

When I read that, I sighed. My mother's world was so bounded by the simple, angular lines of honesty that she'd forgotten how it was to be torn by conflicting loyalties.

But a few months later Mrs. Sanyal called Mother to say they were getting a little concerned, nothing to get anxious about, still, they thought they'd take Sudha to see one of the ladies' doctors in Bardhaman. Mother asked to speak to Sudha, but Sudha answered in monosyllables, saying only, over and over, Don't worry, I'm okay. But what else could she have said with Mrs. Sanyal listening?

What bothered me most was that all this time I'd been getting letters from Sudha as usual. They were cheerful as ever, and not one had mentioned a word about any of this. I could understand her not wanting to bad-mouth her mother-in-law, but why couldn't she have written to me of how she felt about not becoming pregnant? Together we would have grieved and raged and thought up a way of coping, as we used to do as girls. The fact that Sudha no longer turned to me when in trouble, that instead she preferred to—there was no other word for it—lie, worked itself deeper and deeper into me, the way Pishi used to say a broken needle tip would if it became embedded in our flesh, not resting until it found our heart.

The doctor in Bardhaman, writes my mother today, pronounced that Sudha was completely normal, and for a few weeks matters seemed to have settled down. But now Sudha's mother-in-law wants a second opinion. So she's going to bring Sudha to Calcutta to be checked out by a leading gynecologist.

I'm furious as I read this. I picture Sudha lying on an examining table, the awkward helplessness of her splayed legs, the doctor's callous hands searching and prodding inside her. How violated she must feel. It makes me shudder with revulsion. For once, I agree with Aunt N—Sudha's husband should be the one going to the doctor. My books fall to the floor with a thud as I stand up to pace restlessly around the room.

"What's the matter?" says Sunil.

I tell him, my voice rising as the angry words tumble out. "It's so unfair. Why is it that everyone always thinks it's the woman's problem? Why is it that the woman's always guilty until proved innocent? And even after she's proved innocent, as in Sudha's case, she has to continue to suffer. Why?"

"There aren't any answers to a lot of *whys* in the world, Anju. It's just how things are done. Sudha's mother-in-law isn't as bad as some of the others. You must have heard the stories when you were growing up in Calcutta—all the things that happen to childless women—"

I glare at him. It isn't just what he says—and the underlying insinuation of *childless women* that gets me. It's his tone, infuriatingly calm, as if we're discussing the ancient Christian martyrs instead of my cousin's life.

Maybe it's because I'm all worked up, but I seem to hear something else in his voice. *See how lucky you are to live in this free and easy American culture, to have a magnanimous husband like me.*

"You don't care a bit about what happens to Sudha, do you?" I shout.

"You don't know what I care about," says Sunil, very quietly, his voice like a knife sliding from its sheath. But I'm too upset to stop.

"You probably don't even see anything wrong in treating a woman that way," I say. "You probably agree with all those Indian men who see a woman as nothing more than a baby machine."

"Kindly don't shout, Anjali," says Sunil coldly. I can tell he's really upset by the fact that he uses my full name. "Once in a while you should actually listen to what people are saying before attacking them. If you took a good look at your life, all the things you're allowed to do, maybe then you'd be a little more—"

He breaks off abruptly, but of course I know the word he's left out. *Grateful, grateful, grateful.*

Sunil grabs up his keys from the kitchen counter, shrugs on his jacket, opens the apartment door, and is gone almost before I realize it. Gone without kissing me as he always does when leaving, gone without saying he'll be back.

I stand in the middle of the empty room, my lungs bursting with the words I haven't yet had a chance to say, and feel the startled sting of tears. We've had some big fights before, but he's never left me like this. I feel a prick of premonition, as though my life's turning, like a boat in a gale. What if he doesn't return? says a small scared voice inside my head.

"Of course he will," I say, speaking aloud to calm myself. "See, the computer's still on." But when the voice asks, Now that he's found out how easy it is to leave an argument in anger, what if he does it again? And again? I have no answer.

I pace some more, kick the furniture. End up in the kitchen where I gulp down mouthfuls of Rocky Road ice cream straight out of the carton. It's not my fault that he can't handle his temper, I mutter. He should have understood how upset I was about Sudha. I weep some more out of self-pity. It's an unfair world where not only are we women expected to have husbands but we're supposed to feel grateful for them as well.

Then I'm ashamed for indulging myself like this. Pull yourself together, Anju, I tell myself. This isn't about you. Use the few brains you have to think of how you can help Sudha. Because you've got to help her, whether she asks for it or not. It doesn't matter that she didn't tell you what's going on. She's still the sister of your heart, the one you called out into the world, the one you're responsible for.

I pick up a notepad and start jotting down ideas. I'll make sure my mother insists on Sudha spending a few days with her in Calcutta after the checkup. I'll call Sudha then and make her tell me the whole truth. How bad things are with her mother-in-law. What part her husband's been playing in all this. What she herself wants. And when I've found it all out, I'll know what to do.

— TWENTY-SEVEN —

Sudha

WHEN I WAS a child, I could depend on people being a certain way. All those I was closest to—Anju, Pishi, Gouri Ma, even my mother—I knew what angered them and what made them happy. Though their actions surprised me sometimes, their motives never did. In spite of their surface complexities, at their hearts there was a certain simplicity. I had believed that was how all people were.

Now, looking at my mother-in-law, I am no longer sure.

My mother-in-law is like a sunlit field of flowers. You are drawn into it, admiring, then suddenly you are caught in the stinging tangles of a hidden bichuti vine. The roots of the poisons in her run deep, beyond my powers of digging. What vindictiveness is stored in her from the days when she was a young bride, looked down on because of her parents' poverty? How hard is the crust which formed over her heart in the early days of her widowhood, when her husband's relatives turned against her? What terrible vows did she make during those sleepless nights and desperate days which taught her that she could depend on no one? How naïve I had been to think what such a woman extended toward me was as uncomplicated as love.

On the way to the specialist in Calcutta, my mother-in-law doesn't say much. Mostly she stares stoically ahead, past the front seat where Ramesh is sitting beside the driver, into the hot dusty glare of noon. From the slight movement of her lips I think she's repeating the names of God. But I am wary of guesses where she is concerned. Earlier while we waited at a level crossing for a train to pass, she told me, not unkindly, to be prepared for whatever the doctor might say. One of her friends' daughter-in-law had to go into surgery right after an examination like this—they'd found something seriously wrong with her tubes—but then she ended up with two sets of twins.

Does she mean this as a warning, or a message of hope?

One thing I do know—she is upset that Ramesh is with us, and that he and I will stay on in Calcutta without her. She would have liked to finish my checkup, get the mandatory visit to the mothers over as quickly as possible, and take me back to Bardhaman—her territory—the same day. But when Gouri Ma had called last week, Ramesh was the one to pick up the phone. And when she told him how much the mothers missed me, and how much they would like a chance to have the two of us stay with them for a few days, he innocently promised we would do so.

Oh, what a scene there was when my mother-in-law learned what he'd agreed to.

"Am I dead?" she said to him—not shouting, no, that wasn't her style, but her voice cold and crackling like snakeskin. "Am I dead that you think you can arrange whatever you want, do whatever people insist on without even asking my permission?"

Ramesh replied that it wasn't just "people." It was his wife's aunt, whom he was supposed to respect like his own mother, wasn't he?

My mother-in-law looked at him, her face expressionless. And Ramesh, who orders hundreds of men around every day, seemed to shrink. Who knew the history between mother and son, how long ago she had started staring him down like this? But whatever was in her glance, it worked on my husband like a nail does on a car tire. Although he did manage to say that he saw nothing wrong in us spending a little time with the mothers, his voice wavered unconvincingly, and in a few minutes he added that if she really didn't want us to, he would call Gouri Ma and make excuses. Watching the Adam's apple in his throat bob up and down as he swallowed, I felt pity and despair squeeze my chest like a pair of burning hands.

My husband was a kind man—I had known that for a while now—but in front of his mother he was like a leaf in a gale. If there ever came a time when she turned against me—and since Aunt Tarini's visit such a thing no longer seemed impossible—what support could I count on from him?

Sitting in the car now, I shift my legs carefully. I am holding a large box of sandesh in my lap. They are specialties of Bardhaman, thin-shelled and sweet, and filled with rose water. A gift from my mother-in-law to the mothers, with whom Ramesh and I are to spend the night and part of tomorrow. For once Ramesh had backed down, my mother-in-law turned around and said we should go. Otherwise folks would say that the Sanyals did not keep their word. Control, that was what she wanted, to make people dangle from her hands like puppets, and there was nothing Ramesh or I could do to stop her.

The realization had glazed my mouth with fear.

Ramesh drops us off at the specialist's. He is to run a few errands for his mother, then pick us up. My heart sinks as I watch my only ally leave. He might be weak, but he had held me at night after the humiliation of the previous examination, and wiped away my tears. Not that he could ever gauge the depths of the aching emptiness inside me. Not that he could long for a baby as I do, every cell in my body yearning toward motherhood even while I resent the way my worth is measured by it. Now I shiver as I wonder what this doctor will find. Will I have to have an operation, as my mother-in-law hinted? Or am I barren, as the servants whisper, and thus beyond all reprieve?

The specialist is a grizzled old man with bushy white eyebrows and a booming voice which makes the nurses scurry about. But to me he speaks kindly as he checks my blood test results from

Bardhaman, and his hands, examining me, are gentle. After he is done he tells my mother-in-law that absolutely nothing is wrong with my system.

"But you knew that already," he adds impatiently. "The other doctor must have told you the same thing. Instead of dragging this poor girl uselessly all over the place, have you considered the fact that the fault might lie in your own genes?" He scribbles a name on a pad and holds it out. "Here's the name of a colleague of mine your son should see, if you're really interested in a grand-child."

My mother-in-law's face doesn't give away her fury—only someone who has been watching her carefully, as I have these past months, would notice the way her chest rises and falls under the precise pleats of her sari. She reaches out with a polite smile to accept the paper.

The doctor puts the sheet in her hand, then takes it back and turns to me instead. "Maybe it's better if you give it to your husband," he says. "Men have a foolish pride about these things sometimes, and you might be able to persuade him better than his mother can."

I almost laugh out loud at that. Oh, Doctor Babu, you might know many things about women's bodies, but you need lessons in reading their circumstances better.

But maybe he has read something. For he looks straight into my eyes as he closes my fingers over the sheet and gives my hand a squeeze. "And don't let anyone tell you it's your fault that you're not getting pregnant," he says. "Because it isn't."

From behind I can feel my mother-in-law's disapproval settle over me like a sheet of lead. I don't dare nod agreement, but I hope he sees the gratitude in my eyes.

On the way out, I say I need to use the bathroom, and there I memorize the name and phone number on the sheet. I am glad of that, because as soon as we are out in the front office, my mother-in-law snatches the sheet from my hand and says she'll keep it safe in her bag. I'm not to say anything about the doctor's foolish newfangled ideas to Ramesh, she knows her son, he wouldn't like it. If someone *has* to tell him, it should be her. But not until she's tried some other things.

I nod meek agreement. I am learning my mother-in-law's lessons well, how to hide the plans whirring busily inside my head behind a face as empty and sweet as a mask made of sugar.

That night Ramesh and I sit down to dinner with the mothers, giddy as children escaped from school. According to my plan, which no one knows, I have dressed myself in a gauzy scarlet chiffon sari and a low-cut blouse that I'd put away until now as too revealing. In celebration of the doctor's verdict, the mothers have prepared a feast of my childhood favorites—fried brinjals, puffed-up golden luchis, sautéed red spinach, curries of shrimp and chicken and mustard fish, rice pudding with raisins and pistachios. When I see them all set out on the table, carefully arranged in the cut-glass dishes that the family has always saved for special occasions, I want to cry for love. It must have taken them the whole day, for now, except for Ramur Ma, all the house servants have been sent away. I take double helpings of everything, and as I eat, I talk and gesture animatedly with my hands to ward away the tears. Because tears are not part of my plan tonight. Nor is sadness. And so I pull my attention away from the mothers who hover around us like lost moths. The way their wrinkles—so many more than before—are like the new cracks that have appeared in the walls, as though an evil fairy had shaken an aging-dust over the whole house. I tell a joke, a really funny one, and throw back my head to laugh. My gold-drop earrings swing against the sides of my throat, long and cool and sparkling like me. I let my sari end slide just a little off my shoulder. Behind the pleasure in the mothers' eyes I see surprise—this is not the Sudha they know. And Ramesh, I feel his eyes on me too. He watches the edge of the sari, the way my flesh gleams warm against it. There is a confused desire in his eyes. Is he thinking how different I am when I sit at his mother's table? Is he wondering who I really am?

Ramesh, I wonder the same thing about this duplicitous, laughing self who will not let me feel all that is boiling inside, anger and sorrow and anxiety. Scintillating Sudha, witty Sudha, driven by the power of my desperate desire. For the baby I *must* have, the baby who is waiting inside me like the dream of a furled leaf, I will do whatever I have to tonight to charm you into agreeing to see the doctor whose name and number I've stamped onto my brain.

That night, for the first time, I initiate our lovemaking. For the first time too, I leave the light on, as Ramesh has often asked. Immediately I wish I had not, for he looks at me with such startled pleasure, such naked hope in his eyes, that it wrenches at me. It tears open a memory I had sealed away, another man who once looked at me like that. But I am getting better at turning from things I cannot stand to think about.

We make long and arduous love, and then, as Ramesh lies holding me tight to his chest, his breath still coming in gasps, I ask him about going to see a doctor. He agrees at once.

"I was going to suggest it myself, once we were alone," he says, moving his arm away. "But you didn't give me a chance." The light has left his eyes and in the lines of his lips I read a small reproach. *You didn't have to pretend, didn't have to use your body like that.*

For a moment I feel ashamed, sullied. I put a contrite hand on his shoulder. But tonight I cannot hold on to guilt. Relief makes me float into a weightless sleep. In my dream I am a purple kite with a long spangled tail. The wind pulls me up, up, up. The clouds kiss me and I kiss them back. *Baby,* I whisper into the blue breathless sky, *Baby, I've made everything ready for you. Come soon.*

TWENTY-EIGHT

Anju

THE PHONE CALL home is a major disappointment.

I should've known. It's always like this. I plan and plan, I even make a list of all the things I'm going to say. For sure this time, I think, we'll communicate. I'll get them to see what I'm saying, why it's so important. But when I'm finally on the phone and hear the voice at the other end, Mother's or Pishi's, so small and tinny, it's like we're on different planets. We talk too fast, both sides aware of the growing phone bill. In our hurry we interrupt each other, pouring out concern and advice. *Do what the doctor says*, I admonish Mother. *Go on a vacation, all of you. Don't just sit in that gloomy old house*, I tell Pishi. *In fact, why don't you sell it and go live in a nice new flat. Drive carefully*, they say back to me. *Tell our son-in-law not to stay out late. We've heard how dangerous the streets of America are.* Aunt N comes on the phone briefly to tell me not to study too much. *You'll get dark circles under your eyes, permanent ones.* After we've spoken our *I-love-you*s and *hundred-blessings-to-you-both*s and hung up, I wonder in frustration if we were even speaking the same language.

"It's not their fault," says Sunil. "You expect too much from people. You want them to understand instantly where you're coming from. You want them to agree with everything you say. But *you've* changed since you came here. You see the world differently now. You can't convey that over a telephone line, not without it costing a fortune."

That's the other problem with calls to India. Money. We've

been short on money ever since Sunil started sending those astronomical amounts back to his father. Now when I call home—and I make it a point to do so when Sunil's there, because I don't like being underhanded about such things—I can hear him counting the minutes inside his head. He won't say anything about it openly—he's too proud for that. And I'm too stubborn. Why should *I* give up speaking to my mother just because *he* needs to prove something to his father? But silence has never been a solution with us, and usually a day or so after I've called India we find a pretext to fight.

All these things are in my mind as I go into the bedroom and shut the door. I'm more nervous than usual because I'll be speaking to Sudha, which I've only done once a year since I left India, on her birthday, and that didn't count because we never could really say anything meaningful with her mother-in-law hovering like a hawk. This is my one chance and I mustn't blow it, because who knows when that harpy will let Sudha come to Calcutta again.

It takes forever to get the connection, even though it's Saturday morning, and then to get Sudha on the line. In the background I hear my mother asking everyone to come to the living room, she has a new Tagore tape she wants to play for them. Bless her, she knows how important it is for me to have some privacy. I hear the door close, and finally Sudha and I are on our own.

"Sudha, tell me what's happening," I say.

She's a little startled by the urgency in my voice, I can tell it in her silence. But then she's always known I'm no good at preambles.

"Everything's okay," she says. "The doctor said I'm fine, I can have children—"

"I know that," I interrupt impatiently. "Ma told me that already. But how's your mother-in-law treating you? And your husband."

"Ramesh has been wonderful. Last night he promised me he'd

go and see the doctor and do whatever is necessary, and already this morning he's set up an appointment with him. But we aren't going to tell my mother-in-law any of this."

I guess that answers both my questions.

"Has she been pressuring you a lot? Does that bother you? Do you even want a child right now? I know I don't—and fortunately, Sunil doesn't care either way."

"Oh, Anju!" Sudha breathes into the phone. I haven't heard that tone in her voice since the time—how long ago it seems—when she used to tell me about Ashok. "I want a baby more than anything else in the world. Your life is different. You've got college, and Sunil. Who do I have to love, to call my own?"

I hear my bedroom door open. Sunil comes into the room. I scowl at him to indicate that I want him to leave. He ignores me and starts rummaging in the dresser drawer.

"I do wish my mother-in-law didn't feel so strongly about it, though. I can see how important it is to her, but it makes me so tense that—"

I wait, but that's all Sudha will say. How can I break through that cactus fence of foolish loyalty she's built around her?

"Perhaps you and Ramesh can go somewhere together, just by yourselves, like a little holiday?"

"Anju!" Sudha starts laughing, but it's not a happy sound. "You've really forgotten how things are in a joint family, haven't you? I can just see my mother-in-law smiling sweetly and waving good-bye as Ramesh and I drive off into the sunset, like in your American movies!"

Stupid me. She's right. But I won't give up so easily.

"Why don't I speak to Ramesh for a minute? Maybe I can persuade him—"

Sudha's very quiet. Have I upset her by suggesting I can succeed with her husband where she can't? But when she speaks, it's about something so different that it shocks me.

"Anju, remember the bus stop at the corner of Rani Rashmoni

Road, the one we passed every day on our way back from school? Well, this morning Singhji took Ramesh and me for a drive that way, and I thought I saw—he was wearing a white shirt—just like—"

There's a loud clatter as Sunil drops something, and Sudha breaks off abruptly.

I place my hand over the mouthpiece and glare at Sunil. "Can I *please* have a little privacy?" I whisper angrily. He glares back at me, looks pointedly at his watch, and leaves, slamming the door. Oh, he's going to be one sorry guy as soon as I get off the phone.

"Sudha," I say, carefully. I'm stepping on unsure ground here, speaking things perhaps better left unsaid. "Are you sure it was him? Did it upset you? Do you want to talk about it?" But the moment is lost.

"I can handle Ramesh," Sudha says. Her voice is cool and slightly tinged with displeasure. She picks up our earlier conversation so smoothly, it's as though I imagined what she said a moment back. Then her voice deepens with concern of a different kind. "It's Gouri Ma you need to have a serious talk with. This morning I ran into her on the upstairs landing. She'd just climbed up, and her face was white and she was panting. It scared me. You know how her doctor suggested an operation even before our wedding—well, I think she shouldn't put it off any longer. Don't listen to her excuses, although I'm sure, knowing Gouri Ma, that she'll have some good ones."

"Sudha," I say, "Wait, first tell me—"

But she's slipped away already, without the answers I want so badly, Sudha, who's learned a new elusiveness. So I spend the rest of the call arguing with my mother, who's even more stubborn than I am.

Sunil and I never do have that fight.

When I speak to her, my mother says she doesn't want the

doctors cutting her up. She would rather die in peace, in her own home, when the time comes.

"And when it does, no doctor can save me anyway. I'm beginning to believe what they say in our holy books, that the moment of our death is written by the Bidhata Purush on our foreheads as soon as we are born. Why spend the little money we have, money that your Pishi and Aunt Nalini can live on, trying to stretch out my life? I've lived long enough and done all I needed to. Now that you're happily settled, I'm ready to move on."

The finality in her voice frightens me. It's too serene, too fatalistic. Not like the mother I know. It's as though, while I was caught up in my American life, she'd been loosening the ties that held her to this world. Any moment now she'll cast off the last one and go spinning off into space.

When I hang up, I bury my face in the pillow and weep. I think of my sick mother, my beleaguered cousin, my husband who's probably hunched in front of his computer, lost in cyberspace. Or maybe he's taken the car and gone off somewhere in his anger. How quick and eager I was to come so far from my family, not knowing how much I was giving up, and how little I would gain. I'm like one of those ghosts in Pishi's tales who can see disaster coming to her dear ones but is unable to intervene. She shouts out warnings, and they hear only the wind moaning in the bamboos. She puts out her ghostly arms to hold them back from misfortune, but they walk right through her, because even in their memories she's no more substantial than fog.

At lunchtime Sunil comes looking for me. When he sees my swollen face and red eyes, he bites back whatever he was intending to say. He brings me a cool, wet towel and a couple of aspirin—he knows crying always gives me the worst headache. He holds me like one would hold a child who's had a nightmare and rubs my back and tells me he's there for me if I want to talk. When I shake my head, he nods equably. A few minutes later I hear him on the phone, ordering takeout Chinese from the Golden Dragon, my favorite restaurant. When the food arrives, he sets it out on trays and brings it to the bed, fragrant steam rising from the little red and white containers of fried rice and chow mein and Kung Pao chicken. He fills a plate and hands it to me and starts telling me about a funny incident at work. Like a child I allow myself to be consoled by food and warmth, the voice of a loved one and his touch. We sit back against propped-up pillows, and as I eat I snuggle into Sunil's shoulder. The monsters haven't gone. I know that. They're waiting, under the bed, in the closet. But I don't have to deal with them until it's dark, until loneliness oozes up again around me like river mud.

TWENTY-NINE

Sudha

MY BRIEF RESPITE passes in the sighing of a single breath, and already it is time for us to return to Bardhaman. I go for a last walk in the garden and see with sorrow how overgrown it is, the weeds spilling onto the graveled driveway, the mansa cactus pushing up its thorny leaves through the few remaining roses. The new owner of the bookstore never did pay the mothers fully, in spite of a court battle, and for a long time there hasn't been enough money to hire a mali. Pishi tells me in her letters that Singhji does what he can with the garden, but it is obviously too much for him to handle.

I pull dead flowers and yellowing leaves from a jasmine bush and think of Singhji. He too has aged more than he should have in just four years. When he climbs out from the driver's seat, it takes him a moment to straighten up. After money became a problem, Gouri Ma decided she would sell the car. She broke the news to Singhji as gently as she could. Much as they hated it, she said, they'd have to let him go. But Singhji refused to hear of it.

"You can try to sell that old metal pile—I doubt you'll get much for it," he said with a great frown, "but you can't get rid of me so easily! You're the only family I've known for more than twenty years. How can I leave you now, when you're all alone? And where would I go anyway? I'm too old to start over in some rich upstart's household, to put up with their kicks and curses."

"But I don't have the money to pay you, Singhji," Gouri Ma said.

"I don't need a salary. I saved a good bit of what you paid me over the years—being a single man, what expenses did I have? It'll keep me till God sees fit to call me to Him."

Mother had agreed happily, but Gouri Ma would not hear of it. They argued back and forth until Pishi suggested that Singhji give up his rented room and stay full-time in the gateman's cottage. They'd take care of his meals as well. So he moved his few belongings over, and each day, morning and evening, Ramur Ma took over a covered tray of food for him, grumbling all the way. But deep down she was happy about it, as were the mothers. It was a relief, Pishi confided to me, to have a man around the house again—and such a handy one, too, who always knew how to repair a leak or fix a broken hinge on a window.

I decide suddenly that I'll go see Singhji. But maybe it is not such a sudden decision. Maybe it has been growing in me since this morning, when Singhji took us for a ride along the old roads we used to travel as girls, and I thought I caught a glimpse, a figure in a white shirt out of a dream, and looking into the rearview mirror, I met Singhji's sharp, knowing eyes.

"Sudha beti," says Singhji, opening the door so quickly that I wonder if he has been waiting for my knock. He is dressed already in a crisp kurta pajama set and an immaculate white turban—he is to drive us to Bardhaman in a little while—and beyond his shoulder I see that his room is clean and spare, like himself. In his ravaged face his eyes light up in a pleasure so heartfelt that I am ashamed that I did not come to see him earlier. And now that I am here, it is purely to satisfy my own selfish need.

Singhji brings a stool. I am touched by the meticulous way in which he takes a small towel and wipes it before motioning for me to sit. Is this how it's always going to be in my life, love and caring denied to me where I expect them, and given when I am not looking?

I want to express my appreciation, but there is no time for courtesies. "Was it him?" I ask bluntly.

"Yes." The smallest of words, but enough to throw my heart off the course I had charted so carefully for it.

"But how?" I whisper.

"He knew you'd be coming. He's been in touch with me. We meet every month. He asks for news of you."

My palms are sweating. My pendulum heart swings from wild happiness to consternation. "What have you said?"

"Everything."

The staccato reply brings heat to my cheeks. Perhaps it is just that Ashok should know all my humiliations. That he should have the comfort of saying, *See what happened to her because—* Still, I feel betrayed. "You shouldn't have told him anything," I say accusingly. "Why did you?"

"Because he's waiting for you."

"What do you mean?" My hands are shaking. My stomach feels as though I am on a runaway train.

"He hasn't married. He still loves you. He told me to tell you that he didn't mean what he wrote in that first angry letter. He wishes all will turn out well for you. But if you ever need him, he'll be there. Oh, beti—" A sigh shakes Singhji. "If only you'd listened to me and gone away with him."

I close my eyes against the sharp pain of what might have been. I want to ask Singhji how Ashok looks. If he is well. Are his eyes the same? His blunt-cut, responsible fingernails? The smell of his hair, like sunlight and smoke?

But that is the way to only more unhappiness. And danger.

Outside I hear Pishi calling, "Sudha! Sudha! Where *has* that girl disappeared to?"

"Here," says Singhji, handing me an envelope. "He sent you this. If you want to send back a message, I will take it."

There's no time to read, so I fold it up and thrust it into my blouse. So many words are whirling in my foolish, greedy heart. I push them all back. "Tell him to marry," I say. "Tell him to forget me."

"Might as well tell the ocean not to throw itself on the rocks," says Singhji dryly.

Halfway through the journey back to Bardhaman, I cannot bear it anymore. I say I have to use the bathroom. In the ill-lit, foul-smelling toilet of a roadside dhaba, I tear open the envelope. There is only one line written on the sheet inside. *Come with me.* My heart hammers so hard, I have to hold on to the wall. I fold the sheet, hide it in my blouse, and splash water on my face. Still, my cheeks burn, and when I come out Ramesh asks in concern if I am coming down with something. I keep my eyes closed the rest of the trip, telling Ramesh my head hurts. The car lurches over potholes. Ramesh's arm around my shoulders grows to an unbearable weight. Ashok's words are searing themselves against my eyelids. I allow myself a small thrill of hope. I could run away, yes. My mother-in-law would be happy, Ramesh would forget me soon enough, and Anju is so far away that even the farthest ripple of my action cannot touch her, especially since—my mother gleefully informed me of this—Sunil and his father are not on speaking terms. Would my act be evil, or good? I am not sure, and I am not sure I care. *Live for yourself this one time*, my heart sings. And the child I long for so much, who is to say I cannot have that child with Ashok? Then it would be a doubly loved child, doubly precious, because it belonged to both me and him.

The car groans to a halt in front of my in-laws' house. I am surprised when I open my eyes to find that the day has turned dark. Rust-colored clouds hang over the brick building. The ominous heaviness of the afternoon light—as though a storm is rising—emphasizes the hard contours of the house and makes me reluctant to go in.

I must say something to Singhji—though what I have not decided. Maybe I can speak to him while Ramesh is supervising the unloading of our baggage. But before I get a chance, my mother-in-law comes bustling out. From the newly starched sari she's wearing, I can tell she is about to go somewhere. I give an inward sigh of relief. That will allow me to take refuge in bed and think things through.

"Ah, here you are finally!" she says. "How is it you're so late?" She throws an accusing glance at Singhji. "I've been waiting and waiting. I was afraid the auspicious hour would pass, but luckily you got here just in time."

My brain feels stiff and cramped, like my legs. What is she talking about?

"Come on, Natun Bau." It's telling, I think, as she grabs my hand, that she still calls me New Wife, though it has been almost five years now. Perhaps to her I will never shed my newness to become a true part of this household. She pulls me to the other side of the courtyard, where I see the family car and chauffeur are waiting. "There's no time for dawdling. We've got to start right away."

"But, Mother," Ramesh protests as he follows us. "Where are you taking Sudha? She hasn't been feeling well. She needs to rest—"

I blush to hear the caring in his voice. If only he knew what I had been thinking in the car, while he held me so tenderly.

"She'll be fine!" says my mother-in-law in a testy voice. "Stop fussing over her and go drink some cha. I'm taking her to Goddess Shashti's shrine in Belapur."

"What shrine is that? I've never even heard of it!" Ramesh is displeased too, and for a moment I think he will put out his hand and pull me away from his mother. "I don't think Sudha should go anywhere right now—"

"There's a lot you haven't heard of, my boy. While you were wasting time in Calcutta, I've been making inquiries. The goddess is very powerful. All kinds of women have had babies after visiting her. I've already contacted the priest, but in order for it to do us any good, we must get there during the auspicious hour, before the sun sets."

And before I can say anything to Ramesh or to Singhji, she's pushed me into the car and nodded to the driver. The engine clanks to life, the car sputters, raising clouds of dust, and we are on our way.

Soon we've turned onto a mud road which winds through coconut palms and ponds filled with mosquito plants. It is a road I do not know, taking us deep into the rural landscape, bamboo forests and fields of mustard flowers, abandoned wells beside crumbling huts, taking us westward to where the sun glares at us from a tear in a black cloud.

"Pray, Natun Bau," says my mother-in-law. "Pray to the goddess for a son." She is still holding on to my wrist. Her nails bite my flesh, and her lips move feverishly all the way to the shrine of the goddess of childbirth.

I walk by myself down the dark, winding corridor to the inner courtyard of Shashti's shrine. Only the actual supplicants—the childless wives—are allowed in here, for which fact I'm immensely thankful, because it means my mother-in-law must wait reluctantly on the stone bench by the main gate.

I am a little frightened as I walk, unsure of what to expect. A part of me wants this place to be fake—the product of greedy priests preying on superstitious minds—so my mother-in-law can be proved wrong. But the part of me which used to love the old tales longs to believe that this is a site of true power compared to which the most potent modern drug is less than dust.

The old priest at the gate pressed a handful of flowers into my palm along with a piece of string, but gave no further instructions.

"Go, go," he said when I tried to ask. "When you get there, you'll know what to do."

I blink as the courtyard bursts upon me in a sudden blaze of heat and wailing sound, too much to take in all at once. There's a shadeless, airless square paved with bricks that burn my naked feet, and when I squint upward, the clouds seem to have all disappeared. Each wall of the courtyard is painted with a shape—an eye, an enormous, white eye, which stares out with the goddess's unblinking, all-seeing gaze. I find it hard to look away from. Is that a shallow pool in the center of the courtyard, edged with concrete? And in its center, not a deity, as I'd expected, but a small square of earth with a tree I cannot recognize. Everything hurts my eyes—the harsh white paint, the glint of water, the shimmering leaves of the tree. But they are not leaves, for as I watch, a woman—I realize, suddenly, that the courtyard is full of women, weeping young women—a woman wades across the pool to the tree and ties something to one of its branches. I walk closer and see it's a pair of gold earrings. The tree is weighed down with such offerings—neck chains, bracelets, toe rings, armbands, a fortune's worth. I'm amazed they have not been stolen. The goddess must truly be powerful to inspire such reverent fear.

The women are strewn around the courtyard like plucked blossoms. From their dust-wrinkled saris and wilted faces, it seems that many have been here for several days. Some lie face down on the heat-baked bricks, weeping quietly. Some lean into the pool, praying aloud, their tears falling into the water. Some are writing on slips of paper which they tie, along with their jewelry, to the tree. Some sit as in a trance, their gaze turned inward, listening to things I cannot hear. Next to me a woman beats her head in a steady rhythm against the concrete edge of the pool, calling, "Mother, Goddess, speak to me, save my life." Sorrow fills the courtyard, the air is acrid with it as with smoke, it stings my eyes. I want to weep too, not for me but for us all—for rich or poor, educated or illiterate, here we are finally reduced to a sameness in this sisterhood of deprivation.

I feel I should pray, so I kneel and place my head on the bricks. But I am too distracted. When I close my eyes, unrelated images flash across them. Ramesh drinking tea as he leafs through a paper, a stray cat I used to feed as a child, the Shiva temple where Ashok presses his marigold-scented lips on mine, the back of Singhji's turbaned head as he drives Anju and me to school, the way a fugitive sorrow flits across Anju's veiled face as she watches Sunil watching me at our wedding. So much unfulfilled desire in this world, so many people in need of help. What—who—shall I pray for?

The woman who's been beating her head on the concrete sits up and looks around confusedly. She is just a girl, maybe sixteen or seventeen, and pretty in her rural, dark-skinned way, though right now her forehead is bruised and bleeding and there is an unfocused look in her eyes. I am torn between pity and revulsion. I want to comfort her, to bathe her forehead and hold her by the hand. But also I want to run from this horrifying place, so like—the image comes to me from a class I took in my final year of school—one of the circles of Dante's Inferno. Desperately I try to remember that there is a saner world where women study and work and go shopping and visit the cinema with their girlfriends, where it is permissible for them to live normal lives even if they cannot be mothers. I repeat to myself the names of classmates who I've heard have become doctors and teachers and famous dancers, but they are too far away. Reality is this bloodied, weeping girl next to me. A sludgy fear clogs my throat. How long before I too am driven to a similar desperation?

The girl makes a wheezing sound in her throat. Against my better judgment I lean closer to listen, and between my breasts Ashok's letter crackles like a bay leaf that has been thrown into scalding oil.

"I heard the goddess. She spoke. But I didn't understand

215

her. She said"—here the girl's voice grows low and guttural, as though it is someone else's—"*you must choose between your two loves, for only one love is allowed to a woman.*"

The girl's words make me shiver in spite of the heat. The air around me is startled still. The white eye bores into me.

The girl clutches at the edge of my sari with chipped nails, her words coming in gasps. "But I don't have two loves, not even one. Or else why would I be here like this, waiting and fasting for two days now? You explain it, Didi. You look like a school-educated woman. I'll tell you my story. You tell me what the goddess meant. Three years this monsoon, I've been married. Haven't had any babies. My husband's family's been upset with me ever since the wedding. They say my parents didn't give them enough, even though my poor father gave them everything he had. I tried to run away home, but my parents sent me back. They couldn't afford my weight on their shoulders, they said. I understood that. I accepted my in-laws' slaps and curses. But now they're planning something else, I know it. I overheard the whispers at the women's lake. They want to get my husband married again. He'd be happy enough to. He never did care for me, thought I was too dark from the start."

"Will they send you back to your parents?" I ask.

The girl shakes her head. Her nostrils flare like those of an animal ringed by fire. "By the rules of our community, they'd have to return my dowry then. But if I die, if there's an accident, like what happened a few months back to the washerman's wife, while she was cooking—"

Her words lacerate my skin, nails of rust and ice. I've heard of such "accidents."

"But if I'm pregnant, they wouldn't do it. They'd forgive me all my faults if I can give them a son. That's why I'm here. I decided I wasn't going to leave until the goddess gave me an answer. Now she has, and I don't understand it."

But I do, I think, as I watch the girl, who has broken into sobs. If those are indeed the goddess's words—and they must be, for this poor girl is incapable of making them up—then I, Sudha, am the one they're meant for. I am the one who wants it all, the passion of a lover, the adoration of a child. The one who was foolish enough to believe that it is possible for a woman to possess so much happiness.

I slide from my arms a set of thick gold bangles that Gouri Ma had given me and hand them to the weeping girl. When she stares at me, open mouthed, I tell her, with all the conviction I can muster, that the goddess wants her to have them. They are to pay for her and her husband to visit the Bardhaman hospital—they must do it together—so doctors can see if there is a reason why she is not getting pregnant. "Tell your in-laws," I end, "that unless they do this within a month, a great disaster will fall on their family."

She nods mutely. An amazement of fear and hope flickers over her face like a flock of butterflies. Then she is gone.

As for me, I wade across the pool to the tree. I reach into my blouse and take out Ashok's letter. I long to read it one last time, but I don't. I tie it to a branch. I am not weeping, though inside me a new-painted rainbow is fading into blackness. *Ashok-AshokAshok, once again I am losing you.*

Anju would say I am crazy to heed the words of this half-hysterical girl. But she is only repeating a truth I had accepted long ago into the core of my pessimistic heart, a truth that passion made me briefly forget: a death for a life, one love sacrificed for another. That is the nature of this world. And as for my choice, had it not been made already, made and sealed with my virgin-blood, during those never-ending nights I could not have survived otherwise in Ramesh's bed? Because a child is yours in a way even the most solicitous lover can never be. Carved from your bones, borne into the world upon your breath, the flame you cup carefully in your palm against the coming dark.

I let the crushed petals fall from my hands into the pool. As I walk out, the wall beside me wavers in the heat. But the eye on it watches, unmoving and satisfied.

My mother-in-law looks up suspiciously as I reach the gate. "Done already, Bau? Why, the priest tells me some of the women have been here for three or four days."

I say nothing, but the priest peers into my face and replies, "She's done. It's in the goddess's hands now." When I touch his feet before leaving, he intones the old blessing, "May you be the mother of a hundred sons."

Just one child, I think. *That would be enough for me.* And as though he has heard, his old face creases into a smile. "Very well," he says, and sprinkles my head lightly with holy water.

"What did he mean, *very well?*" asks my mother-in-law once we're in the car. But she doesn't expect me to know and goes on to another matter. "I see you've left your gold balas at the shrine. Let's hope the goddess is pleased with that."

"I know she is," I say, and I do. In this world of uncertainties, it's one thing I am sure of. I close my eyes to evade further questions. The way back is jerky, pothole to pothole, but for comfort I have the girl's hope-lit face, hidden behind the raw red of my eyelids.

THIRTY

Anju

FOR A FEW weeks now I've been uneasy. I'm tired all the time. I want to fall into bed in the middle of the afternoon and stay there for at least a year. At the oddest moments I go crazy with hunger, but only for certain things—mango achar flecked with chilies, or pizza for breakfast. Halfway through eating I have to throw up, right into the kitchen sink. Fortunately, my bouts of vomiting occur mostly after Sunil leaves for work, so I don't have to answer his questions. My breasts hurt all the time, and if I bump into something, pain explodes in them like fireworks gone wrong. The very thought of cooking dinner puts me in a bad mood. "Make it yourself," I mutter to Sunil from the couch, where I've started spending a big part of my day. And a big part of my night as well.

"What's the problem?"

"You thrash around too much," I say grumpily. "I can't get a wink of sleep."

"It must be your time of month," he says, in that superior male tone that makes me want to scream. "You've been bitching about everything."

That's part of the problem. It *is* my time of month, and nothing's happened. But it can't be! We've been taking precautions. I've worn that awkward, slimy diaphragm-thing, much as I detest it, whenever we had sex because I know how important it is that we don't have a baby now. Sunil and I can't afford one. More important, I must finish college, which I'm loving more than anything else in America.

But the nausea won't go away, and finally I buy a pregnancy test, and sure enough, the strip changes color. I'm so upset I burst into tears—just like those bimbos on the soap operas, which I watch from time to time to see how brainless American TV can get. And though I know it's wiser to wait until he's home, I can't stop myself from phoning Sunil.

When I tell him, there's a long pause at his end—the kind they call *pregnant*, I think hysterically. Then he says, "Are you sure?"

"No. I made it up. It's my idea of humor in the morning." But as soon as I say it, I'm sorry. Sunil doesn't respond well to sarcasm, especially from me, and right now I need him on my side.

"No need to snap at me," he says irritably. "You were the one supposed to be careful, weren't you? Wasn't that our agreement?"

"I was," I admit. My throat stings with guilt as though I just swallowed a cactus. "I did everything the little booklet said—" I'm a failure, I know it. A moron who can't even follow bold-print instructions.

Another silence. What if he says I should have an—? Terror thuds out-of rhythm in my chest. *A-bor-tion. A-bor-tion.* An impossible, monstrous word. On the other hand, how'll I take care of a baby? What'll happen to all my plans for my future?

Then I think of Sudha, who'd give anything to have this child I'm carrying so grudgingly, and I feel so ashamed that I burst into tears again.

"Hush, Anju," Sunil says, with one of his sudden turn-arounds. Now that he's reduced me to tears, his voice is kind. "It's not a disaster. We would have had a baby anyway, sooner or later. So we'll have to plan and budget more carefully than we thought. We can manage that."

"Really?" I breathe, light-headed with relief. "You really think it'll be okay?"

"Of course it will. Now go wash your face and lie down and rest. I'll come home as soon as I can."

I wash my face and in celebration I make myself two large mango achar sandwiches. Even when I throw up right afterward, it doesn't upset me. When I lie down, I'm too excited to sleep. For the first time since I found out, I allow myself to imagine my baby—he or she must be no larger than a grape—clinging tenaciously, cleverly, to my insides. I place a hand over my lower belly and think I feel a special warmth, a tingly light, the clean, pale green of a California grape, radiating into my hand. A big, foolish, sentimental smile spreads itself over my entire face.

Then I remember that I'm going to have to tell Sudha.

Once Sunil gets used to the idea of the pregnancy, he can't stop talking about our baby. I'm surprised at how boyishly excited he is, how willing to let me see it. I'd thought only women felt this way.

Sunil comes home earlier nowadays. He's brought home a stack of healthy eating books from the library and often cooks for us, carefully balancing proteins and carbohydrates and using only extra-virgin olive oil. Each day he makes me a drink of hot milk and crushed almonds, which he insists will increase the baby's brain power. He tries hard not to fight with me because he's heard that might affect the baby's personality. His computer's gathered an inch of dust because he's too busy compiling lists of baby names, writing them out in Bangla and English. From time to time he'll try one out on me. Do you like the meaning? he'll ask, his forehead squinched up. Do you think it's easy enough for American tongues? He particularly likes to talk about the things he wants to do with the baby. They're predictable enough—visits to the zoo, playing ball in the park if it's a boy, taking her to dance class if it's a girl—but the urgency with which he speaks makes me wonder what gaps in his own childhood he's trying to fill.

Ever since the doctor confirmed the pregnancy and said the baby was doing fine, he's been dying to call India and tell our mothers. I'm the one who keeps putting it off.

"But why?" Sunil asks, his brow knotted. "Don't you want them to know? They'll be so happy."

"Give me another week," I say. "Let it be just our secret for one more week."

The truth, which I can't tell Sunil, is that I'm afraid. Afraid of the silence that's bound to be there at the other end when I tell Sudha, who's got to be the first to know. I can't write about this to her—something this vital has to be spoken, voice to human voice, not conveyed through cowardly black squiggles on a page. I can already hear her suck in air at the irony of it—that I, who hadn't wanted a child at all, should become pregnant so unthinkingly, with such unfair ease, while she— She'll hurry into speech then, speaking too quickly to show me she doesn't mind, that she's happy for me, and really, she *will* be. Because that's the thing about us human beings when we really love someone, we can be happy even while our heart is breaking.

I spend a lot of time planning my speech, picking the right words so she won't be hurt. When I finally get up the nerve to call—on a Saturday night, to make use of the low rate—one of Ramesh's brothers picks up the phone. Sudha's still in bed, he says. He'll go call her. I'm puzzled. It's past nine in the morning in India—Sudha never sleeps that late.

It seems to take Sudha an awfully long time to get to the phone. From the kitchen where he's fixing us hot cocoa, Sunil stops stirring, though he doesn't say anything. I'm just about to hang up and try later, when I hear Sudha, with a breathless little catch to her voice, like she's run all the way, saying, "Anju, are you still there? Sorry, I was sleeping. What is it? I was worried—you hardly ever call from America."

All my carefully rehearsed words take flight like pigeons startled by a gunshot.

"Sudha," I blurt out. "I'm going to have a baby. I had to tell you." I pause and swallow. The silence is awful, like a vacuum sucking me into the small black holes of the mouthpiece. "Sudha," I cry, "I'm sorry."

"Dear, silly Anju," says Sudha. There's a wobble in her voice. It takes me a moment to realize it's not from tears. "Why should you be sorry?" Her laughter spills through the phone lines, as bright as pomegranate juice. "I'm so delighted I could dance—remember, the way we used to clasp hands up on the old terrace, and whirl and whirl until everything became a blur of light? I'm delighted—for us both. I wanted to wait another week to let you know, so I'd be surer, but there's no need because inside me I'm certain already. I'm going to be a mother too! Oh, Anju, how I wish we could be together now!"

The same longing racks my insides, as physical as one of my overwhelming hungers. "I'll write to you every single week, promise," I say, dizzy with this gift that's just made my pregnancy perfect. There's a hundred questions milling around inside my head. What's Sudha's mother-in-law saying now? Did Ramesh finally go to the doctor? Did they manage to get away on a little vacation as I'd suggested? I hope so! That way I can tell my little nephew or niece, *You know what? If it weren't for my wonderful idea, you wouldn't be here!* But our time is up. "I'll keep you posted on everything that's happening," I call out urgently, "and send you photos of how awful I look. You must do the same."

"I will," says Sudha.

I stand at the window after I hang up, sipping the rich, sweet cocoa that Sunil has handed me, looking out at the chocolatey dark. High above, there are halos around the stars, like in a Van Gogh painting. Two babies, coming to us together! It's a wonderful world, more wonderful than I deserve, and I vow to be a good person for the rest of my life—gentler and calmer and less selfish, like my cousin—so I can measure up to it.

THIRTY-ONE

Sudha

WHEN I WAKE from my afternoon nap, the sun has painted the walls of my bedroom a gentle gold. I rub my eyes, trying to remember the dream I had, something soft and warm like the quilt I am curled under, but it plays hide-and-seek at the edge of my mind and will not let itself be caught. I stretch, catlike—no, more like a tigress. I am filled with power and potency and well-being, with the beauty of my sleek, ripe body.

I come downstairs and join my mother-in-law, who's having her evening tea. "Had a good nap?" she asks pleasantly, then calls, "Oh, Dinabandhu, bring Bau Ma some cha." Now that I'm expecting, she has taken to a more affectionate form of address. She even puts down the paper she's reading to chat with me until the steaming cup of ginger tea, reputed to be particularly excellent for pregnant digestive systems, arrives.

Since the pregnancy, my mother-in-law's taken over a lot of my duties. She doesn't want me bending over a hot unun, or lifting sacks of rice and lentils from the storage room, or running up to the terrace to check on the pickles set out in the sun.

"You should let me do some of it, Ma," I say sometimes, feeling guilty. "I feel useless—and bored."

"My dear!" Her eyes take on a dewy softness, as they often do nowadays. "What are you talking about! You're doing the most useful thing of all. And as for bored, why don't you ask Ramesh's brothers to run to Biren's shop and pick up a new video movie for you?"

Yes, now that I am pregnant, all things—within the boundaries of my mother-in-law's notions of seemliness—are permitted to me. I can ask my brothers-in-law to run errands for me. I can sleep in late and lie down in the afternoons, and no one is to disturb me. Should I wish to be alone, I can go to the balcony and sit in the shade of the neem tree as long as I want. Women get moody at this time, my mother-in-law will whisper to the maids. They have to be humored. At mealtimes I am served first, even before Ramesh. After all, as my mother-in-law dryly remarked once, his job is done. I am given the best portions—the coveted fish heads stewed with lentils and sprinkled with lemon, the crisp, golden-brown fried brinjals, the creamy top layer of the rice pudding that I love. When my mother-in-law called Calcutta to tell them my news, she asked Pishi about my favorite dishes. Now she makes sure Dinabandhu cooks at least one of them every day.

At times, embarrassed, I try to protest.

"Eat, eat, Bau Ma," smiles my mother-in-law, counting out, by my plate, the expensive prenatal vitamin tablets she's had shipped from Dey's Medical Stores in Calcutta. "Remember, you're eating for my grandson, too." Even the fact that Ramesh, back from a trip to Murshidabad, has brought me a whole boxful of the silk saris which the region is famous for, does not bother her. Perhaps she thinks they are keeping her grandson warm.

At night after dinner we all sit and watch video movies. My mother-in-law likes me to watch comedies, or holy stories from the Ramayana. They'll have a good effect on her grandson's personality, she says. She was not pleased the other day when Ramesh's brothers brought a video of the Rani of Jhansi, the widow-queen who led a rebellion against the British in the 1850s and died valiantly on the battlefield. Too much bloodshed, she complained. But I was fascinated. The Rani was so wondrously brave. When the priests proclaimed that as a childless widow she should devote her life to prayers, she boldly told them that her subjects were her children and she had to take care of them. She donned male garb and, a sword in each hand, led her soldiers into battle. Even when her forces were overwhelmed by the British guns, she didn't give up. Fallen on the battlefield with a fatal wound, she scintillated with a desperate, abandoned joy. I watched that movie twice.

"I guess it's all right for queens to be that way," said my mother-in-law. "But I much prefer someone womanly and gentle-natured like our Bau Ma!"

Sweetness, sweetness all around, and yet why do I feel dissatisfied? Why does the inside of my mouth pucker up as though I have bitten into a sour plum? My mother says I should be down on my knees, forehead to the floor, giving thanks that my in-laws are so caring. But as I walk the prescribed mile around the terrace in the evenings, I cannot seem to forget that measuring look in my mother-in-law's eyes when I couldn't get pregnant. I am even suspicious of Ramesh. The most innocent of his questions—do I feel nauseous anymore, would I like him to rub my back—raises my hackles. If in bed he slips a hand, careful and cupped, over my belly, I shrug it away impatiently, though I know I'm hurting his feelings. All of this love and caring, I want to shout, is it for Sudha, or for the carrier of the new heir of the Sanyals?

Stupid girl, my mother would say. What's the difference?

But there *is* one. I sense it. Walking around the terrace in the suddenly sad evening hour when the stars seem very far and dim, I wish Anju were here. With her keen logic, she would find the right words to give shape to my misgivings. She would tell me that I am right.

Chief among my inscrutable mother-in-law's inscrutable actions is this: She has kept my pregnancy a secret. Except for the mothers and Anju, no one outside our household knows. Not even Aunt Tarini.

"I was sure she'd send her a telegram, first thing, with an even bigger box of sweets than the one Aunt gave us," I say to Ramesh one day when he comes home early to join me on my evening terrace walk. (He's allowed to do such things now.) But he too cannot figure it out.

"Maybe she's afraid of you getting the evil eye from envious people. Or maybe she's decided not to stoop to Aunt's level anymore," he replies. "Maybe she promised that to Goddess Shashti if she gave her a grandson."

"That's the other thing that bothers me," I say irritably. "The way she's so sure it's going to be a boy. What if it isn't?"

"Let's hope it is, or else she'll surely blow a gasket," says my engineer husband. The image, applied to my dignified mother-in-law, is so ridiculous that it makes us both break into guilty laughter.

Today as I finish my tea, my mother-in-law slides an aerogram across the table at me.

"From Anju," she says, as though I had not recognized that pale blue I've come to love. "I hope your cousin is well. It must be hard for her, all alone in that faraway country, without a mother or mother-in-law to help her through this time," she adds, kindly.

She has grown very kind recently, my mother-in-law.

Maybe I am being unnecessarily hard on her. Maybe this *is* her real nature, and that other, during those doctor visits and that afternoon at the shrine, was the cruelty that sometimes rises in us when we are desperate.

"If you don't mind," I say, standing up, "I'll read it as I take my evening walk."

"Not at all, Bau Ma, you go ahead," she says. As I start up the stairs, she calls from behind, "Don't stumble on anything though, while you're busy reading."

As always, I can hear Anju's voice in her letter. Amused,

extravagant, frank—and right now, very, very happy. She tells me how strange it feels to be pregnant, how she loves and hates it at the same time. How sometimes when she's alone she takes off her clothes and stands in front of the mirror, examining the changes—the dark line of hair pointing downward from the navel, the nipples dark and glistening as the prunes she soaks overnight for her constipation, the luscious, obscene swell of her abdomen. *Am I breathtakingly beautiful, Sudha, or overwhelmingly ugly? I can't decide.* I smile. *Beautiful, Anju,* I whisper into the sheet. She scolds me because I haven't sent her a photo of myself in return for the one she mailed me last month. I sigh. I'll have to explain to her that my mother-in-law thinks taking photos at this time brings bad luck.

When Anju tells me how Sunil has changed, I am glad for her. Perhaps now I will be able to shrug off that faint unease I have been carrying since the wedding, my fear that Anju needs him more than he needs her. The anticipation of fatherhood seems to have wrought a remarkable transformation in him. He thinks nothing of driving clear across town to Mumtaz Cuisine to fetch her fresh-made rasogollahs, her latest craving. In the evenings he massages her swollen feet with pine oil. He's already opened an account at his credit union—not that they have anything to put in it—for the baby. *He's like one of those hundred-year redwoods he took me to visit,* Anju writes, *with their woodsy-smelling barks that you just can't stop yourself from leaning on.*

The part I love best is when Anju writes about her baby. He/she is big as a lemon now—she knows this from her pregnancy book. The last time she went to the doctor, she listened to the baby's heartbeat. It was like a runaway engine, full of furious energy. That's when she realized how much she loved this little creature inside her, more a part of her life already than anyone else could ever be. *I can die for him—or her—Sudha. I can kill.* When I read that, I have to stop walking, because something thick and hot and molten is welling up in me like lava. *I too, Anju,* I think. *I too.*

The next part of her letter is hard to read. It has been written and rewritten, daubed over with some kind of chalky correcting paint until the paper is lumpy. Finally, impatiently, Anju has scratched it all out and written below, *I'm really worried about something Ma wrote in her last letter. Remember that time when we went to visit one of our great-uncles in an old, crumbly house near the river? Remember the retarded boy locked up in the terrace room who scared us so much, and how Pishi explained he'd been born with a birth defect? No one had paid him much attention—they'd thought of him as some kind of freak accident. But one of our cousins just gave birth to a baby with the same problem. Ma wrote that it's probably not hereditary, but she thought I should tell the doctor and go through any tests he suggests. I showed the letter to Sunil, and he's already set up an appointment for next week. But Ma must have told you this already so you can get your baby checked too.*

I hold the letter scrunched tight in my fist. I am breathless, as though someone has punched all the air out of my lungs. I can feel the cold prickle of sweat between my breasts. Gouri Ma hasn't written a word of this to me. Gouri Ma, who loves me like a daughter, who would never want harm of any kind to come upon me. There's only one explanation for her silence: she knew—as Pishi had suspected she did—that my father was an impostor, unrelated to her husband. She knew my baby and I were at no risk, for we did not share the Chatterjee blood.

I squeeze my eyes tightly shut to keep the tears in. All this time, somewhere in that place where unreasonable hope hides, I had nursed the idea that Pishi had been wrong. She was old, and it had all happened a long time back. She could have got the facts a little mixed up, embroidered the parts she'd forgotten. Now I no longer have that comfort. And as for not being at risk, who knows what diseases ran in the veins of my father the wastrel? What murderous genes he has planted in his grandchild?

I tear Anju's letter into tiny bits and go straight to the kitchen.

Veined with her pen strokes, the pieces gleam blue one last time on the coals before they begin to char. Don't regret what you can't change, I tell myself, shivering, my arms hugging my belly. But what I am really thinking is, *If only I could burn away my past like this.*

That night, while I am at dinner, my mother phones. She is all agitated about our cousin's baby—the idiot boy, she calls him. "I went to see him today, and you could tell there wasn't a bit of brain behind the walls of his skull, the way he just lay there. And his mother, the poor girl, I don't think she's stopped crying ever since the doctor's diagnosis." Now her voice goes shrill with virtue. "I thought to myself, Nalini, this is no time for false family pride. Not that Sudha, God bless her, is going to have a problem. After all, *my* side has never had any such happenings, not in fourteen generations. Still, you must tell Sudha's mother-in-law, so that Sudha can get that test done, amio-something, you know, with the injection needle. No, no, girl, don't tell me you'll tell her later. I want to talk to her myself."

Wearily, I call my mother-in-law to the phone and return to the table. I stare at my plate without appetite although Dinabandhu has cooked a jackfruit curry specially for me. Foolish, interfering woman, I think angrily. Now my mother-in-law will be all stirred up, like a nestful of hornets. There'll be more doctor visits, more people poking and prodding at me. All for no reason.

But there's something else bothering me, some unnameable apprehension.

"Yes indeed," I hear my mother-in-law saying from the hallway. I'm perplexed by how gracious her voice sounds. Why isn't she more upset? "I agree. You acted most responsibly. No, I won't waste any time. In fact you'll be happy to know

I'd been thinking along the same lines—one can't take any chances when dealing with the heir of an old, bonédi family like ours. I've already set up tests for Sudha. She'll be going in next week. Yes, of course, I'll call you with the results right away."

$\mathcal{A}$nju

THE DOCTOR'S waiting room is decorated in pale blues and pinks designed to soothe nervous parents-to-be. But they don't do Sunil and me much good as we fidget in our plush chairs. I wonder how Sudha's doing—she should have got her amniocentesis results yesterday. I shifted my date to match hers, so we'd both know around the same time if our babies were okay. I hope Ramesh went with her to the doctor, instead of that crusty old mother-in-law of hers. I hope he held her hand the way Sunil is holding mine. I doubt it. In India men don't do those things—at least not the men I've seen. But I'll know everything when I call her tonight.

The doctor is forty-five minutes late. He's busy with a delivery, the nurse informs us smilingly. I give her a glare. Sure! He's probably pacing his office right now, agonizing about how to break the news to us. I glance at Sunil, hoping he'll flash me one of his quirky smiles. I want him to lift his eyebrows in that amused way that says, *There you go again, Anju, with your overactive imagination. Didn't the doctor tell you that the chances of a problem for women your age are very slight? He really only ordered the test because you insisted.* But Sunil dabs at his upper lip, avoiding my eyes, and when I clasp his palm it's as damp as mine.

What will I—we—do if . . . ? My mind freezes on that thought. I stare at the cover of the magazine on the table in front of me until I can feel the face of Princess Di being tattooed into my brain.

But just like Sunil says, once again I've tortured myself needlessly. The doctor breezes in, smiling plumply, waving a report. All is well with our baby—and it's a boy! We follow him with sheepish, relieved grins to the examination room, where he goes over the results of some other tests with us. He's concerned about my blood pressure, and the fact that my sugar's too high. He wants me to rest a lot and cut out the salt and the sweets. I nod dutifully but I'm only half-hearing him. I'm rehearsing all the things I'll say to Sudha tonight. I can't wait to tell her my news, and to hear hers!

On our way home, Sunil and I stop at the Golden Dragon to celebrate. We splurge on hot and sour soup, spring rolls, eggplant in black bean sauce, sweet and sour shrimp, and pork chow mein. Recklessly, I eat a whole plateful of the extra spicy (and extra salty) Kung Pao chicken. Sunil tries to stop me—but halfheartedly. He can see how much fun I'm having.

"Relax," I tell him. "I know my body better than that doctor does. I won't even get heartburn, you'll see. Happiness is the best digestive tonic in the world!" As proof I show him the fortune in my cookie. It reads, *A wonderful event is about to occur in your life.*

"It is," says Sunil. "Because I'm going to take you home and make love to you."

And he does. The tenderness with which he kisses the curves of my breasts and hips makes me cry. I can't even remember what the word *sorrow* means. Afterward, I lay my head on his damp chest, which gives off a scent like newly cut grass. His breath is gentle and rhythmic like deep-sea waves, and though I don't intend to let it, it pulls me into sleep.

I jerk awake, my heart pounding with the feeling that I've forgotten something crucial. It's after midnight, way past the time I promised Sudha I'd call her. Shit! I should have set the alarm. I aim a glare at the sleeping Sunil—it's all his fault, the seducer!—

and drag my body over to the phone. My sleepy fingers fumble with the numbers, and I have to start over a couple of times.

One of the brothers-in-law picks up the phone at the other end. When I ask to speak to Sudha, he hesitates. She's resting, he finally says in an uncertain voice. I insist, so he tells me to hold. He's gone for a long time. I chew the inside of my cheek and watch the phosphorescent dial on the clock.

Sudha's voice, when I hear it, is a dead monotone I hardly recognize.

"Are you sick?" I ask, scared. "Shall I call back some other time?"

"No," she says, then adds, with obvious effort, "How's your baby?" Her words slur like she's been drugged.

"He's fine," I say. A huge, awkward silence looms between us, filled by the question I don't dare to ask.

"My baby—she's okay too," Sudha says, then makes a small, choking sound. "Can't talk anymore now," she says.

The line goes dead.

I sit in a daze, holding on to the phone. The muted dial tone buzzes in my ear for a while. There's a bunch of metallic bleeps, then a female American voice instructs me politely to replace the receiver. I obey. My arms are made of wood, my joints stiff and unoiled. What could be wrong? If Sudha's okay and her baby's okay—could it be Ramesh or her mother-in-law? No—if it were that, Ramesh's brother would have been more upset. Are they giving Sudha a hard time because it's a girl? No, that would sadden her, but it wouldn't make her break down like this.

It's something else, something devastating, something—a chill travels down my spine as I think this—she couldn't talk about in front of her in-laws. So it's no use calling her back. I'm going to have to wait for her to call me. But where—and when—in that watchful household will she ever find the privacy for that?

I hold myself tight and rock back and forth, trying to dislodge the icy dread in my chest. Something horrifying is looming over Sudha, spreading its dark, scaly wings.

"Nonsense," says Sunil when I finally wake him and sob out my incoherent fears. "If there was a problem, your mother would have known. She'd have called and told me, even if she didn't want to upset you. Come to bed. You'll make yourself sick carrying on like this."

I sob some more, but Sunil's voice is confident and commanding, and thankfully I give in to it. I snuggle down in bed and push my aching spine against him. His hand finds my hip and strokes the stretch marks that line it like silver seams. His breath ruffles the small hairs on the back of my neck, makes me sleepy. But he himself is wide awake. I know it in the hard precision of his shoulders, the too-still way he holds himself, like a wild animal might in the presence of danger. Just before I drift off the thought comes to me that perhaps he's worried too. Perhaps—and I'm not sure if I should be happy about it, or disturbed—under his nonchalance, he cares more about what happens to Sudha than he'll admit.

The next day I stay home, although I know I'll miss my psych midterm with Professor Warner, who doesn't allow makeups. I'm afraid to leave the phone even to go to the bathroom, though by now it's past midnight in India. But I imagine Sudha tiptoeing down the dark staircase of the sleeping house and lifting the receiver with trembling fingers. I have to be here for her.

Around midday I can't hold out any longer. I call my mother. But just as I guessed, she knows nothing. She thinks I'm overreacting. Still, she promises to phone Sudha right away, and to call me back if anything's wrong. But I have a feeling she won't get through to my cousin past that dragon of a mother-in-law.

By evening I'm exhausted from waiting. My shoulders ache like I've been pushing a huge rock uphill. All I've managed to force myself to eat are some Saltines dipped in milk.

Sunil's face grows heavy when he returns from work and sees me lying on the sofa by the phone, still in my nightgown, wads of Kleenex strewn around me. "Anjali," he snaps. "This is ridiculous. This kind of obsessive behavior won't help either you or your cousin. All it'll do is hurt my son."

His son. Worried as I am, the statement intrigues me. This little life inside of me, which I've been thinking of as totally *mine*, already belongs to so many others. Grandson, cousin, son of his father. It's the same with Sudha's baby.

While I mull over the complexity of these claims, Sunil pushes me into the bathroom. "Take a long, hot shower," he orders. "I'll call you if the phone rings." He hands me a new bar of the Mysore sandalwood soap that we save for special occasions. By the time I come out, he's made me some tomato soup and a grilled cheese sandwich.

I'm suddenly ravenous. I take a big bite of the sandwich. "It's the best grilled cheese I've ever tasted," I tell him. A sweet, long-ago memory resonates in the air between us, and over the steaming soup we smile at each other.

I'm having a nightmare, one of those where you know you're dreaming, but that doesn't make it any less scary. In my nightmare my baby's trapped somewhere underwater, far from me. He lifts a tiny black receiver to call me for help. I hear the muffled ringing of the phone and try to run to it, but my limbs are like stone. A submarine wind starts to blow. The water, quiet till now, rushes swirling around my little boy, rips the phone from his fingers. There are faces in the torrent, human faces—Ramesh, Sudha's mother-in-law, Aunt N, Sunil. But as I watch, their features flatten out, their skin grows black and scaly, and their tongues forked. They're serpents now, throwing their coils around my baby, pulling at him. His face crumples as he begins to disappear into the writing, looped mass of their bodies. *Anju,* he cries. *Anju-Anju-Anju.* Then he's gone.

"Anju, wake up," Sunil says. He's leaning over me, shaking my arm gently. I jerk my arm away with a stifled scream—I can't help it—the dream's still too vivid in my mind. "Come on," he says impatiently. "It's a person-to-person call for you from India. Maybe it's Sudha." He thrusts the phone into my numb hand and settles himself at the foot of the bed. *Please go,* I mouth at him, but he's busy clipping his nails.

There's a lot of disturbance on the line. I can hardly hear Sudha's voice as she says hello.

"Speak up," I say. "We've got a bad connection." But then I realize that's not it. She's in some kind of public place—there are bells ringing, people shouting questions, the clang of machines, the distant roar of a bus. My heart begins to pound crazily. Her mother-in-law would never let Sudha go somewhere like that—and certainly not alone.

"I'm at the main post office," says Sudha, her sentences short and jerky. "Couldn't talk from home. Took a cycle-rickshaw here while she was taking her afternoon nap."

"Sudha, what's wrong? I've been worried sick. Has something happened to Ramesh, or your mother-in-law?"

"No," Sudha says. "They're fine," she adds with venom.

Then she says, "They want to kill my baby."

"What?" I'm sure I've heard it wrong.

"My mother-in-law wants me to have an abortion."

The bed tilts and rocks, threatens to throw me off. The room turns brown at the edges, like burning paper. I grope dizzily for Sunil's hand. It feels stiff and cold.

"Sudha, how can that be?" I finally manage to say. "After all the pressure she's been putting on you to get pregnant—?" But a part of me knows already.

"When the test showed that it was a girl," Sudha's voice is a hollow echo, "my mother-in-law said the eldest child of the

Sanyal family has to be male—that's how it's been in the last five generations. She said it's not fitting, it'll bring the family shame and ill luck. But I think it's really because of Aunt Tarini's grandson—"

Aunt Tarini's grandson? I'll have to ask Sudha to explain that some other time.

"Isn't she afraid that you might not have a baby at all?"

"No. She says that once Goddess Shashti has smiled on a woman, there's no fear of that."

"But Ramesh?" I say, my voice high and cracked with outrage. "What about him? He's a good man, a modern man. Surely he doesn't think the same way as—"

Sudha laughs. It's a terrible sound, full of bitterness and relinquished hope. "He *is* a good man. But he's no match for his mother. When he told her it wasn't necessary, he'd be happy with a girl, she just looked at him with those hooded, dispassionate hawk-eyes until he looked away. Then she said I wouldn't even have conceived the baby if she hadn't taken me to Shashti's shrine. I waited for him to tell her about the doctor he'd been seeing, about the special vitamins and injections, but I guess he didn't dare. She accused him of forgetting all the hardships she'd been through after his father died—the times she'd gone hungry so the children could eat, the nights she'd lain awake worrying, the insults she'd endured. She asked him if a pretty face outweighed all of that. Oh, she was cruel. She chose words that went right into him, like steel hooks with poisoned tips, until finally he just gave up."

"What d'you mean, gave up?"

"He covered his ears with his hands and walked out. I ran after him—I was beyond shame by now. You can't let her do this to me, I said. He looked at me and his eyes were funny, as if he didn't quite know where he was. Remember the time when our cousin Poltu put his finger into an electrical outlet and almost died? Remember the look in his eyes right after? That was how Ramesh looked. He said to me, Please, Sudha, let me be for a little while. I put my hands on his arm and shook him. I can't let you be, I shouted. I need you to help me, to protect our daughter. But he plucked my fingers off his arm as though I was speaking a strange language he'd never heard before and walked out of the house. He came back some time late last night, I don't know when, and shut himself up in the library. I haven't talked to him since. I can't depend on him, Anju. I know my mother-in-law's made the appointment for the abortion already. She's not telling me when. If I don't go of my own will, she'll find some other way of getting me there—maybe drug me, who knows. She's capable of anything, once she makes up her mind."

I'm too stunned to speak. I know about the abortion of girl babies. Every once in a while there'll be a story about it in *India West*. And last month "60 Minutes" had featured the abortion clinics that have sprung up all over India, now that amnio tests are so easily available. I'd been outraged as I watched the rows of cots lined up against a dirty wall, the women lying on them with their faces turned away. But it was a remote outrage, and the scene, dim and greenish as though taken in underwater light, was something that could never happen to me, or to anyone I loved. So I had believed.

"Your time is up, madam," interrupts the operator's voice with its heavy Indian accent.

"Anju," Sudha calls desperately, "what am I going to do?"

My brain is like stone, my tongue also.

"I've put in three more minutes' worth of change. That's all I have," Sudha says. "Hurry, Anju. Anju! Are you there?"

I'm trying desperately to think. "Do you have anything else with you? Any other money?" I ask finally. I'm afraid to hear her reply. From her letters I know already that her mother-in-law keeps the keys to the safe.

But Sudha surprises me.

"I have five hundred rupees. I took them from Ramesh's desk drawer. And all my jewelry that wasn't in the safe. Just in case."

"Just in case what?" I want her to say it. I need her to say it.

"Just in case I decided not to go back." Sudha's voice is stronger now. I think she needed to hear herself say it too.

"Well then, that solves our immediate problem. Take the next train to Howrah station, then take a cab home. The mothers will take care of you."

"It's not so simple, Anju." Sudha's voice has a catch in it. "Just before I called you, I called Calcutta. Mother picked up the phone. When I told her, she said I mustn't leave, absolutely not. My place is with my in-laws, for better or worse. She's afraid they'll never take me back, and then what would happen to me? Everyone will think they threw me out because I did something bad. They'll think my baby is a bastard—" Her voice breaks on the last word.

I'm breathless with disbelief. "You should have told her they're forcing you to have an abortion," I finally manage to say. Surely even Aunt N would then see Sudha has no choice but to leave.

"I did. She thinks it's the lesser of the two evils." Sudha starts crying in great gasps. "My own mother."

"Time's up," comes the operator's bored voice. For a moment I wonder if she'd been listening in, and what she made of our predicament. But maybe she heard calls like this all the time, lives breaking, certainties destroyed, disillusionment staining the air like smoke from a house you thought would never burn.

"One step at a time," I tell Sudha, putting all the confidence I don't feel into my voice. "Things will work out somehow, you'll see. I'll call you in Calcutta."

Then the line goes dead.

"You shouldn't have told her to go back to your house," Sunil says even before I've replaced the receiver. "She might have been able to work things out with her husband had she stayed.

Now her mother-in-law will have the perfect excuse to convince Ramesh to get a divorce—"

I'm so angry my whole body's shaking. I start to tell Sunil exactly how stupid his thinking is, just like a man's. How could a man understand what Sudha's suffering? How could a man, who'd never held life inside him, know what it would mean to be forced to give up that life?

Then I feel it, a small but definite movement, deep in my belly, cool and silver as a fish jumping. My baby! He reminds me of what's most important.

I clamp my lips shut. Once I start to fight with Sunil, I won't be able to stop, and right now I need to focus positive energy on Sudha. Sudha, who's taking a rickshaw to the train station. Sudha, who's leaving the security of wifehood with nothing but a bag clutched in her hand.

I pick up a pillow and go to the living room. I lie down on the sofa and close my eyes. I keep my palm pressed tight against my belly, drawing warmth from my baby, drawing strength. Against the dark lining of my eyelids Sudha stands on a dust-choked platform as the Calcutta train pulls up with its shrill whistle and hot diesel smell. She places her small foot—so elegant, so fragile—on the compartment steps, and begins her hard journey.

$\mathcal{S}udha$

AS I STAND under the cavernous, soot-stained ceiling of Howrah station, which magnifies every sound into an eerie echo, it comes to me that in all my life I've never traveled anywhere alone. I am shocked by the enormous noisiness of this place: the huge wall clock whose minute hand moves in reluctant jerks, the yells of the vendors pushing carts stacked with yellow mausambi fruit over which clouds of flies buzz excitedly, the red-uniformed coolies who think nothing of shoving you aside as they run up the platform carrying fat hold-alls on their heads. The entire place smells of sweat and urine—and hopelessness. The odor is intensified when I pass the homeless families huddled on their jute bedding, holding out begging bowls. Pity and nausea rise in me as I fumble for a coin, and I cannot repress a shudder. If it weren't for the frail protection of the mothers, would I too be on a pavement by now?

And the men—the station is full of men. They brush against me purposely, they spit out wads of betel leaf near my feet and bare their teeth in a grin when I jump away, their bold, leering eyes travel over my body—a woman alone is fair game, after all— as they wonder why I have no baggage. Why no one has come to meet me. There's a sinking feeling inside me. Is this too something I will have to get used to? For a moment I am tempted to climb back on the train and return to the seeming-safety of the big brick house in Bardhaman.

Somehow I find my way through the press of the crowd to the

taxi stand. There's no line—there never is in Calcutta—and the only way to get a taxi is to push past the others and jump into one. I watch helplessly for about fifteen minutes, then plunge into the fray in desperation, shouldering my way between strangers, no longer caring whose foot I step on. My hair comes loose, someone's kurta button scratches my cheek, someone else whose face I cannot see in the crowd takes advantage of the melee to grope at my breast. I swat his hand away furiously and kick at the ankles of a fat man blocking my path. He turns to say something nasty, but his mouth falls open at the ferocious scowl on my face. I jab at his paunch with a determined elbow, and finally I'm in a taxi, mopping the sweat from my neck, trembling. Maybe this is how the Rani of Jhansi felt the first time she went to war. I give the driver the address, using my sternest voice so he will not be tempted to take me around the long way, and sink back into the seat.

Being alone in a taxi is a little frightening. I remember stories I've overheard, Mother's friends whispering about girls who had been kidnapped and sent to the Middle East. But I cannot afford fear. Who knows how many places I'll have to go alone, now that I am no longer the daughter-in-law of the Sanyals? Then I remember I'm not alone. My daughter is with me, my sweet daughter, a flame flickering in the center of my body. When I remember that for her my in-laws' house, guarded by its hosts of weaponed yakshas, is the most dangerous place of all, I am no longer doubtful about what I have done.

Ramur Ma opens the door when I ring the bell. She gives a shriek of surprise and clutches at her bosom, so I know my mother hasn't told anyone about my phone call. "Sudha Didi, goodness, is it really you! Where's Ramesh Dada Babu? Don't tell me he let you travel all by yourself in your condition! O Nalini Ma, Gouri Ma, O Pishi Ma, come quickly, see who's here!"

I sit awkwardly on the edge of the sofa in the living room, holding my purse tightly with both my hands, feeling like a stranger in the house where I was born. And like a stranger, I am not sure of my welcome.

"O my God," says my mother, who's the first to arrive. Her hand flies to her mouth. "So you went ahead and did it, you stubborn, impetuous girl. O my God, what'll we do now?"

It's what I expected, but it still stings. I blink away the tears as though I were a girl of twelve. Can't she tell, can't she ever tell, that I need someone to hold and comfort me?

"What do you mean?" asks Pishi, who has followed close behind. "And what kind of way is that to greet your daughter who's visiting you after so many months? Come, Sudha Ma, let me see how pretty you've grown now that you're about to become a mother. Oh, how happy I am to see you! But Ramur Ma's right, our son-in-law shouldn't have let you come all by yourself. You look terribly tired." She rubs my back and gratefully I let my head sink onto her shoulder.

Gouri Ma hurries in now, her welcoming smile a little perplexed. I can see her searching the room for my baggage. She's wondering why Ramesh's driver hasn't brought it in yet from the outside.

This is the most painful part, having to go over all the sordid details again, watching the horror growing in Gouri Ma's eyes, watching Pishi clenching a corner of her sari in her fists.

"I told her not to," hisses my mother. "I told her to grit her teeth and put up with it, and try for another pregnancy. A woman can have many children, after all, but a husband is forever. But no, Madam had to do it her own way. *Now* what'll we tell our relatives? Uff, she's smeared kali forever on the Chatterjee family, to say nothing of my ancestors."

I want to say something barbed about her ancestors, but it's too much effort. My back aches dully, and all I want is to lie down in the familiar room of my childhood and pull the bedcover up over my head.

"Enough now, Nalini," says Gouri Ma. Her breath comes unevenly and I feel wretched for having added to her troubles. "Sudha's old enough to make her own decision, and I can see why she's made it. It's up to us to support her—"

"There you go again, Didi," my mother says, "encouraging her to be headstrong. No wonder she's been having trouble with her mother-in-law—"

It's like my childhood replaying itself. I would laugh if it were not so painful.

"Bas, bas, Nalini," says Pishi. "The poor girl's about to faint, she's that tired, can't you see? Let's feed her and get her into bed, then you can cry and call on the gods all you want." She takes me by the hand and guides me down a corridor. "Here, Sudha, wash up in this bathroom. There have been some changes in the house. We've had to close off the upstairs—there were a lot of leaks after the monsoons. I'll tell you more about all that tomorrow."

Dinner passes in a daze, a frugal meal of rice and dal and sautéed spinach, sadly revealing of the mothers' financial circumstance. I brush away Pishi's apologies—the unun has been put out for the night, she says, or else they'd send Singhji to the market for some fish to fry up hot for me.

"It's delicious, just like this," I tell her, and it is. I didn't know how starved I had been for food served with love, food I could eat without choking on the strings attached to it. Food for Sudha, not for a receptacle for the heir of the Sanyal family.

After dinner I lie down in the makeshift bed the mothers have fixed in the pantry. Tomorrow they'll have a bed carried down, Gouri Ma says. She bends over to ruffle my hair. "We're all glad you're here, Sudha," she smiles. "Even your mother. It's just her habit to complain—you know that."

"I'm sorry to cause you so much trouble," I say.

"Nonsense. Aren't you our daughter, tied to us not only by blood but by all the years of your life?" Gouri Ma's eyes hold mine. I know what she is really saying. *No matter who your father was, you are you, and you belong here. As will your daughter. Because ultimately blood is not as important as love.*

I breathe out in a deep, satisfied sigh and snuggle into my pillow. Long after she has turned off the light, I feel Gouri Ma's soft touch on my hair, like a blessing. Next door I can hear the mothers talking, their voices rising and falling in argument, trying to figure out what they should do. The sounds relax me. Even a sudden burst of anger from Gouri Ma, or my mother's extravagant wails, are familiar as childhood lullabies, with their plaintive refrain of concern. I know the beat underlying them so well, I could tap it out on my bones.

"It's the beat of the caring heart," I whisper to my daughter. And together, soothed, we sleep.

The next morning, because my mother insists, Gouri Ma calls my mother-in-law. She tells her I am here, that I am well, that I want to keep the baby. Could she possibly work out a compromise, so both families can save face and be happy?

My mother-in-law is gracious, with the graciousness of someone who knows she cannot be persuaded. If I return at once and go through with the scheduled abortion, she will consider my foolish act of rebellion forgotten. If not, she is afraid she will have to set the divorce proceedings in motion.

But what does Ramesh say to all this? Gouri Ma says. She asks if she can speak to him.

My mother-in-law informs her that he is not available. He agrees with her, of course. She sounds surprised that anyone would even need to ask.

After she hangs up, Gouri Ma takes my hands in hers. "I didn't have much hope concerning your mother-in-law," she says, "but Nalini made such a fuss that I made the call. We should contact Ramesh, though. I'll send Singhji to his office—"

I think for a while of his soft silken eyes, his hesitant hand cupping my belly. The way his mouth wavered into weakness when his mother raised her voice. The way he held his hands over his ears and begged, *Sudha, please, let me be.*

"He knows where I am," I say finally. "If he wants us, he can get in touch with us easily enough. And if he doesn't want her"—I touch my stomach—"then I'm not for him either."

We do not hear from Ramesh. The next week a peon delivers divorce papers to our door. Under "Reason" is typed "Desertion."

I take off my wedding bracelets later that day, wipe off the sindur powder in spite of my mother's lamentations.

"O Goddess Durga! What will people say?" she cries. "A pregnant woman without sindur on her forehead! What shameful names will they call your child?"

I offer her a nonchalant shrug, but I'm pierced by a shaft of guilt. Is my audacity laying my daughter open to condemnation?

Surprisingly, it is my usually diffident Pishi who comes to my rescue. "Why should she care anymore what people say? What good has it done her? What good has it done any of us, a whole lifetime of being afraid of what society might think? I spit on this society which says it's fine to kill a baby girl in her mother's womb, but wrong for the mother to run away to save her child." She's standing now, her chest heaving, her face flushed. I've never seen her this impassioned, nor, by their expressions, have my mother or Gouri Ma.

"When I came back to my parents' home as a widow, how many of society's tyrannical rules I followed! How old was I then, Gouri? No more than eighteen. I packed away my good saris, my wedding jewelry, ate only one meal a day, no fish or meat, fasted and prayed—for what? Every night I soaked my pillow with guilty tears because I was told it was my bad luck which caused my husband's death.

"Men whose wives died could marry as soon as a year had passed. They didn't stop their work or their schooling. No one talked about their bad luck. We even have a saying, don't we, 'Abhagar goru moré, Bhagya baner bau, the unlucky man's cow dies, the lucky man's wife dies!' But when after three years of being a widow I begged my father to get me a private tutor so I'd at least have my studies to occupy me, he slapped me across the face. I considered suicide, oh yes, many times in those early years, but I was too young and too afraid of what the priests said— those who take their own lives end up in the deepest pit of hell. So I lived on in my brother's household. What else could I do? But though he was kind—and you too, Gouri—I knew it was charity. I had no right in this house—or anywhere else. My life was over because I was a woman without a husband. I refuse to have our Sudha live like that."

A stunned silence follows her outburst. Gouri Ma wipes her eyes, and even my mother bites her lip and looks down.

"You're right, Didi," Gouri Ma says finally. "What do you think we should do?"

"Sell the house," says Pishi without hesitation. "Like that Marwari businessman has been asking us to do for a long time."

Both Gouri Ma and my mother breathe in sharply. I too am shocked. This from Pishi, the upholder of family tradition!

"What is it but a heap of stone anyway?" Pishi continues. "The true Chatterjee spirit, if there is such a thing, must live on in us. Us, the women—and the little one who's coming, whom we must be ready to welcome. For heaven's sake, Nalini, don't look so tragic. You won't be out on the street. The money we get from the sale of the land alone will be enough to buy a nice little flat somewhere convenient, Gariahat maybe, and pay for Sudha's delivery. We must make sure she goes to a really good doctor. And, Gouri—I don't want any more excuses from you—I want you going for a checkup next week, and if the doctor still says you require surgery for your heart, I want you to get it done right away. Sudha and our granddaughter will need all three of us through the hard times to come—you most of all, because you know the most about surviving in the outside world."

"Yes, Didi," Gouri Ma says with a new meekness. A smile begins to form on her lips.

"And you, girl," says Pishi to me, "go take a nice bath and shampoo the last of that red from your forehead. The Sanyals are the ones who have lost out, not you. You've got a whole life in front of you, and it's going to be such a dazzling success that it'll leave them gaping."

I too can't help smiling. When Pishi pronounces it with such gusto, my future seems a possibility. I bend to touch her feet, then Gouri Ma's and my mother's.

"Ah, but what kind of blessing shall we give you?" Pishi says with a wry smile. "To say that you should be the mother of a hundred sons seems hardly appropriate, isn't it, when a husband is no longer in the picture?"

And suddenly I know. "Bless me that I might be like the Rani of Jhansi, the Queen of Swords," I say. "Bless me that I have the courage to go into battle when necessary, no matter how bleak the situation. Bless me that I may be able to fight for myself and my child, no matter where I am."

"We bless you," say the mothers.

In the shower I scrub until the last vestige of red is washed down the drain. I am washing away unhappiness, I tell myself. I am washing away the stamp of duty. I am washing away the death sentence that was passed on my daughter. I am washing away everything the Bidhata Purush wrote, for I've had enough of living a life decreed by someone else. How easy it seems! What power we women can have if we believe in ourselves!

My optimism's temporary, I know that. The next months will bring many troubles, many doubts. Still, my heart is filled with lightness. I open my mouth and let the sweet clean water flow into it. In my womb, my daughter pirouettes with joy to hear me sing.

THIRTY-FOUR

Anju

ALL WEEK I toss and turn on the lumpy sofa to which I've banished myself. Sunil came over the first night and asked me to go back to bed with him, but when I told him to leave me alone, he didn't ask again. My uneasy sleep is punctured by dreams like wisps of torn clouds, where Sudha's face fades in and out, sometimes entreating, sometimes weeping, sometimes wide-eyed in fear. Each morning I wake with a backache and a sinking in my chest. I've spoken to Sudha twice since she came to Calcutta, and both times she's been in good spirits. Still, I can't stop thinking of what Sunil said. Did I make the wrong decision for Sudha, misled by my American-feminist notions of right and wrong? Have I condemned her to a life of loneliness?

As the week passes, I work myself deeper into depression, certain I've ruined Sudha's life. This morning I hand Sunil his coffee in moody silence and won't return his good-byes. When he tries to kiss me, I turn my face away. "Oh, Angel!" he says, throwing up his hands. But when he comes home in the evening, he hands me a bouquet of irises in that deep blue color which I love, and when he hugs me, he holds me to him for an extra moment.

All this only reminds me of the little tendernesses now lost forever to Sudha. Still, I bring my pillows back to the bedroom.

We make love that night after a long time. It's wonderful, but afterward I'm caught in a strange restlessness. I toss and turn, then finally sit up. "I can't stop thinking of Sudha—I hope she's okay."

Sunil acts like he's sleeping, but a telltale furrow springs up between his brows. He probably doesn't want to hear any more about Sudha—I've been going on and on about her all week—but I can't seem to stop.

"I wish I could do more than just call her once in a while."

"You've already done too much." Sunil sits up too, abandoning all pretense of sleep. "You've made the kind of decision for her that you should never make for someone else. What if things don't work out, and ten years down the line she blames you for all her troubles?"

"Sudha's not like that!" My voice is shrill, eager for a fight. That's what I need—to attack someone, anyone. Maybe that would still those doubting voices inside my head. "You don't know how it is between the two of us—I don't think you've ever loved anyone the way we love each other. Sudha's like my other half—how could I just sit back and let her mother-in-law and that jellyfish of a husband force her into an abortion she didn't want?"

"Don't get so worked up," Sunil says, mildly enough. "It's not good for you."

"Worked up! *Worked up!* You'd be worked up too if people were trying to kill—no, murder—your baby niece."

Sunil doesn't comment on that. Instead he says, "But how's she going to live now? You've told me that the mothers have money troubles of their own. Surely she wouldn't want to be a burden to—"

"Of course she won't! She'll get a job."

"Doing what? She has no training, no experience."

"She could—" I press my fingers to my temples and will a solution to come. "She could supply the local boutiques with needlework. You don't know how talented she is—"

Sunil gives me an ironic look. "You really believe it's that easy, don't you?"

"Not easy, perhaps, but not impossible either," I say. I *have* to believe in possibility. How else can we bear the enormous weight of life?

"What about the social stigma? Just like Aunt Nalini said, there'll be a lot of talk."

I sigh. "There's always talk. You have to ignore it."

"That's easy for you to say, Anju. You're safe here in America. Sudha's the one who'll have to face it every day. What kind of life will it be for her, alone with her daughter for the rest of her days—for who'd want to marry her after this? A social pariah—" There's an odd harshness in Sunil's voice, a raw, grating note under the cruel words, as though it hurts him to say them. I press my knuckles into my eyes—I must figure out that note, what it means—but all I can see is my cousin walking down a street holding her daughter's hand, while the neighbor women whisper from verandas and the neighbor children run behind, calling out wicked names.

"Maybe her mother wasn't so wrong after all," Sunil says. "Maybe the abortion would have been the lesser of the two evils."

I stare at my husband. At the dark, heavy shapes of the words he has just released into the air between us. How little I know of this man. How little we ever know of the men we rush into loving.

"Why don't you come out and say it was okay for Mrs. Sanyal to demand an abortion," I finally whisper. "Why don't you say Ramesh did the right thing, siding with his mother. Maybe *you'd* have wanted me to have an abortion too, if we'd been in India and my baby hadn't turned out to be a boy."

"Anjali—" says Sunil angrily, but I don't wait to hear any more. I stalk from the room, slamming the door behind me. I know what I just said is unfair—or is it? Questions riddle me until it feels as if I have pins and needles all over my body. How can Sunil be so unfeeling toward Sudha's plight? Does it mean he'd be the same way toward me, if ever I got into trouble? Does he love me at all? What if something happened to our baby—

would he love me still? Pregnant-woman fancies perhaps, the kind that come to us all when we're alone, but I can't stop them.

And Sudha, who's going to be alone all her nights—what fancies are taking sudden flight in her mind, like a flock of frightened birds? Does she put out her hand in her sleep, searching for Ramesh's familiar shape? Does she miss the way a body molds itself against another in bed, fused by need and familiarity? Is she already regretting the path I've made her take? Will she, as Sunil warned, look back on this day and curse me?

I can't think straight anymore. I've lost all sense of perspective.

I curl myself onto the couch, shivering a little because I've left my blankets in the bedroom. *Please*, I close my aching eyes and pray. *Please, just let me sleep.*

Then the memory comes to me, so intense that I can feel again the cold slimy jelly which the nurse rubbed onto my skin. She's sliding the monitor back and forth over the mound that is my stomach as she prepares for the ultrasound that will show me my baby. At first he's a vague blob on the screen. Then as the image is enlarged I see the delicate curl of his perfect fishbone spine, the small bump of his penis. He waves his arms and legs in a graceful underwater dance, though as yet I don't feel any of it. The green radium blip on the screen, not unlike the stars Sudha and I used to watch on those long-ago summer nights, is the beat of his heart.

That ultrasound had changed everything, made my baby real in a whole new way.

I know it must have been the same for Sudha.

I go to the coat closet and get out a bunch of jackets. I put a couple under my head and cover myself with the rest. I still can't say, for sure, that I gave Sudha the right advice. Nor can I tell what its repercussions will be. But my breath steadies, and my heartbeat. And when I feel the idea leap up inside me, I know my baby has thought it into being. And like my baby, it's perfect.

I'll bring Sudha and her daughter to America. Why not! She

can sew clothes for all the Indian ladies here and maybe—finally—open that boutique she dreamed of. She can live in her own studio apartment down the road—that way she'll have her independence. Every afternoon I'll take my son over to play with her daughter, so the two of them can grow up together, as dear to each other as we were. We'll give them matching names: Prem, god of love, and Dayita, beloved.

Prem and Dayita, I whisper aloud. Prem and Dayita, children who'll be loved like no child has ever been loved before.

Tomorrow I'll think of all the prickly details, how to get them here, the kinds of visas, how much it'll all cost. I can get a job and save for their tickets. That way I won't have to ask Sunil for a single penny. Tomorrow I'll go to my college library—I know they're looking for an assistant. I won't even tell Sunil about it. It'll be my secret, mine and my baby's.

Tomorrow, I say to myself, smiling in the dark.

There's something I'm forgetting, some crucial element of the equation without which the answer will turn out wrong. Something that tinges my triumph with misgiving. But I'm too exhausted to figure it out.

The last thing I imagine before I sink into a viscous sleep is the astonishment on Sunil's face when he sees the airline tickets.

— THIRTY-FIVE —

Sudha

I BEND awkwardly over the steel trunk to stuff in two more towels, then press down on the lid with all of my pregnant weight. When it creaks to a reluctant close, I straighten up with a relieved sigh. I wipe my sweaty face and rub at my lower back, which has been one constant ache all week. There's an ache inside me too, a desolation as I watch the movers dismantle the last of the furniture we're taking with us—two fourposter beds, the smaller of the dining tables, a cupboard—and load them on to the lorry. Today is the day we move to our flat. It's also the day the construction company starts tearing down the house—I can't call it our house anymore—so they can begin building the twenty-four-story apartment complex that will take its place.

The end of an era, of a lifestyle. The end of sitting on the mossy roof while Pishi oils my hair and tells stories of her father's time. The end of picking jasmines from the garden bushes to make garlands for our puja altar. The end of opening the door to a long-unused room and smelling, in the dust, the yearnings of those who lived here ages ago.

If I feel desolation, how much more must the mothers be feeling. And I, Sudha, breaker of homes, am the one who has brought it into their lives.

But when I come out on the corridor, I'm faced not by tragedy but drama. Mother rushes down the stairs, calling out to the movers to be sure to use the proper padding before they load her mahogany almirah. "Singhji, Singhji," I hear her shout. "Are you

255

ready? I've got to get over to the flat before the movers get there, or else they'll surely put everything in the wrong place." A truck from the Sisters of Charity rolls up and Pishi and Ramur Ma carry out armloads of household goods we've decided we no longer need. There's a phone call for Gouri Ma. The auctioneers who took our antique furniture held a successful sale and will be sending her a check soon. They might even be able to get us some money for the car. A gentleman at the auction was interested in vintage models. Yes, yes, says Gouri Ma and jots down figures. Years seem to have fallen away from her face. Some of it is due to the successful surgery she had two months back, but a lot of it happened after she made up her mind to sell the house.

"I think we'll be very happy in our new place, don't you?" she tells me as she hangs up. "Be sure to rest well in the afternoon. We'll put you to work decorating it this evening." She waves her notes at me as she hurries off. "There's going to be enough money to buy a very nice cradle for our baby, and you'll have to decide where to put it."

Isn't it funny, I tell my daughter—for she and I have taken to having long conversations nowadays—how we spend so much time holding on to the old ways, not knowing how refreshing change can be? How, like a wind from the Ganga, it can sweep clean all the dust we've accumulated in the crannies of our mind?

She nods wisely inside me—already she is wiser than I, this child whose life was almost torn in two in the tug of war between change and the old ways. Isn't it funny, she adds, that sometimes the thing we've feared most, year after year, turns out to be the best thing that could have happened to us?

I think about last week, when the final divorce papers were delivered to me from the court. I looked at the wax seal, colored an ironic sindur-red, scared of how I would react. This was the final disgrace for a woman, the final failure. That was what I had been brought up believing. I waited for despair to break over me like a flood wave—but it didn't. There was a sense of great tiredness, yes, and some sorrow. I had worked so hard at loving my in-laws, at being a good wife. I felt as though I'd spent years of my life pushing a rock uphill—and the moment I stopped, it rolled right down to the bottom. But there was also a huge relief, and a small hope. I signed my name at the bottom of the form with a flourish, and was surprised to find my mouth curving in a smile. We were starting anew, my daughter and I, and because there were no roles charted out for us by society, we could become anything we wanted.

It's from moments like this that history is made, I tell my daughter, as much as it is from wars and treaties and the deaths of kings. But most times we don't realize it.

She begins to reply, but at that moment Ramur Ma shouts from downstairs, "O Sudha Didi, Gouri Ma wants you to come to the living room. Someone's here to see you."

How inconvenient, I say to my daughter, wiping my hands on my dust-streaked sari. Just when I was about to go for a bath. Who do you think it could it be?

I have no idea, she says, sounding as irritated as I at the interruption.

With all its furniture gone, the living room is a cavernous emptiness, echoing under my steps. It takes a moment for my eyes to get accustomed to its shuttered dark. And then I see, on one of the two wicker moras that Ramur Ma must have set up hastily, a man is sitting. And even before I recognize his face, gaunter than before, and bearded, I know him by his white shirt.

The ground buckles up around my feet. I have to hold on to the wall.

"Sudha," says Ashok, and his voice is the same as years ago, the brown-sugar voice that I kept strenuously from my dreams all through my marriage, all through the breaking up of it.

I wonder at the fact that the mothers have allowed him into the house. Is it because I no longer have a reputation left to lose?

Or could it be something else? But I cannot think straight. My heart beats erratically, as though I were still that naive girl in the cinema hall, balanced on the threshold of adulthood, my eyes dazzled by its neon magic. My foolish heart, as though the world has not taught me a hundred bitter lessons since then. It makes me infuriated with myself.

Perhaps that's why my voice comes out harsher than I intended. "Why did you come here, Ashok? Is it to look down on me in my time of trouble, and say, *If only you'd listened to me*? Well, let me tell you, though this isn't how I expected my life to turn out, I've no regrets for what has happened. None. And I'm not ready to give up either. I'm going to fight for my daughter and myself, and I'm going to win."

Ashok is taken aback by my attack—I can see it in the hurt surprise in his eyes. "I'm not here to gloat. How could you think that?"

"I don't want your pity either," I say belligerently. That would be even worse, somehow—to see pity in the eyes that had once looked at me as though I were truly a princess out of a fairy tale.

"I'm not here to offer you my pity." Now he's smiling a little. The gentleness with which he speaks only makes me want to cry. And that would be worst of all, to burst into tears in front of Ashok. I turn to leave. I will keep my dignity, even if I have nothing else.

"Stop, please." Now he's off the mora, standing in front of me, his hands held up. But he doesn't touch me, nor I him. This much, at least, the years have taught us. "Aren't you even going to give me a chance to tell you why I came?"

I push past him.

"Sudha!" he calls from behind me, part laughing, part exasperated. "You're as stubborn as ever!"

I almost stop. I want to tell him he is mistaken. Or maybe he never knew me. Just as I never really knew him. I am not stubborn. I am quiet, forbearing, gullible and dutiful. That is why he is not the father of the baby I am carrying.

"I wanted to say this properly, not blurt it out to your back, but you give me no choice. Sudha, I want to marry you."

An incredulous joy spurts up in me, but I will not give myself to it. It must be a mistake—of Ashok's tongue, or my ears. And even if he did say what he said, he might regret it in a moment—or a week, or a year. And then how could I bear it?

"Why would you want to marry me?" I speak roughly, gesturing toward my ungainly belly, my bare forehead. "Why would anyone?"

"Am I just *anyone*?" Ashok says, but I notice that his eyes shift away from my stomach. "I've been asking myself the same thing ever since Singhji told me you'd come back home. Because I knew, that very minute, what I was going to do. And the answer is, I can't imagine being happy with anyone else. After your wedding, my parents tried many times to get me to marry. They arranged gatherings where I'd run into attractive young women. They even persuaded me to attend a few bride-viewings. I was so angry with you, I almost agreed to get married, just to spite you, to show you I didn't care. Thank God I came to my senses before I ruined another life along with my own.

"Instead, I threw myself into the family business. In my spare time I took up sports, went mountain climbing. Parachuting. The riskiest things I could think of. I hoped they'd keep my mind off you. Nothing worked. You were an obsession, a drug in my blood.

"I tortured myself further by meeting with Singhji and making him tell me everything he knew about your married life. I hated your husband, that monkey with a pearl necklace around his neck. I couldn't stop picturing him with you—even though it made me feel like someone was squeezing my throat in both his hands—at small, intimate moments. Accepting a cup of tea from you, putting out his hand to tuck a stray strand of hair behind your ear as though it was his right. When I heard your in-laws were pressuring you because you weren't pregnant, I wanted you to have a baby and be happy. But not really. What I really wanted was your marriage to fail. I wanted you to have no one but me to love." He shuts his eyes and presses his fingertips into his temples, and when he opens them, uncertainty blends with shame in his eyes. The beginnings of age lines bracket his mouth, and a muscle jumps nervously in his cheek. I see that he is no prince after all, though he has tried manfully to be one because I wanted it so. He is human, like me, racked by the same demons, the same treacherous need.

I walk into his arms then, and it is as though I have completed a movement I began long ago in the Kalighat temple, one of those complicated dance sequences which take you all the way across the stage before you can return to where you started. I touch his chest. In spite of its tumultuous rise and fall it seems a solid place, a place where one may build a shelter to last a lifetime.

We sit on the steps of Outram Ghat and watch the long tremble of the ferryboat's lights moving across the darkening waters of the Ganga. It is evening. The street lamps cast warm yellow pools of glowing around us, the jhi-jhi bugs chirp sleepily. We talk a little, Ashok and I, but we are not uncomfortable with silence. It is enough to be with him. To touch his hand—its square knuckles, its slight rasp of hair—is to be filled with the presence of miracle. So much of what we might speak of is external anyway. Secondary. The events of our lives have marked us, yes, but they have not changed our essential selves, no more than an avalanche changes the rock-heart of the mountain slope over which it crashes.

When a distant clock chimes eight, we rise, Ashok helping me carefully to my feet. The mothers do not like me to stay out late, although now that our wedding is merely a matter of time, they have no objection to us seeing each other.

Ashok maneuvers himself around my belly so he can embrace me. Inside me, I feel my daughter squirm. Suspicious of men—as she has ample cause to be—she has not been entirely happy with this recent development. *You'll like him,* I tell her. *He'll be a good father to you.* She maintains a mutinous silence. At opportune moments—such as this one—she kicks out hard.

"Oof!" says Ashok. "Not again! I'm beginning to think she doesn't want me anywhere near you!"

I laugh. He joins in, but it is an edgy sound. On the way home, he does not touch me again.

Last week Ashok brought his parents to meet me. His father, in whom I see how Ashok will look in twenty years, did not speak much, but his smile was kind. His mother took my hands in hers and squeezed them tightly. In a voice soft as rain she told me how delighted she was to see Ashok marrying at last.

"He's loved you for so long, my dear. Sometimes nowadays I wake up at night and he's standing by the hall window. I ask him what the matter is and he tells me he's too excited, there's a hot, sparkly feeling in his chest, the night is so magical with its moon-lit clouds, how can anyone just lie in bed."

"Mother!" Ashok protested, laughing. "You're giving all my secrets away. Now Sudha's going to be impossible to live with."

I love watching Ashok's hands as he drives. The deft, minimal turns of his wrist. The way he rests two fingers lightly on the steering wheel as the car glides ahead, smooth as a swan. Some-times he drives with only one hand and brings my hand to his lips with the other. He kisses each separate finger, then the hollow of my palm.

Oh, Anju, how I wish you were here so I could tell you face to face how it feels. Whoever knew that when I scrubbed away what the Bidhata Purush had written on my forehead, I would uncover this? A rosy happiness has dyed my body through and through. Happiness beyond deserving. It frightens me.

"But will you be happy with me?" I ask Ashok. "I'm no longer that star-eyed girl you fell in love with. I don't think I can trust anyone so completely ever again. I don't know if I can love anyone except my daughter so completely." A frown marks Ashok's face as I say this, but I force myself to continue. "And my past—it'll always be there, reminding you that my body was another man's first. Will you be able to live with the fact that when I came to you I was no longer a virgin?"

"Did you love him?"

I consider the question. I have felt affection for Ramesh, and often pity. At times we have been comrades pitted against a stronger, more ruthless force. But love? No.

"Then I can live with it," says Ashok. I want to believe the sureness in his voice. I *will* believe it.

Our kisses are long and starved and urgent, they are full and sharp as wild fennel. They are golden as butter in sunshine. We kiss with a strange urgency, as though we do not have a lifetime of kissing ahead. Is it because, being older, we know how grudgingly the world hands out its gifts, how eager it is to snatch them back?

Tonight when we have reached the apartment and I am about to get down from his car, Ashok catches my hand and holds it against his mouth. I feel little puffs of heat on my fingertips, his delicious breath. Then he says, "Do you truly believe in honesty between lovers?"

"Of course."

"Then I must tell you something that has been tormenting me the last few days, and you must promise to consider my request."

I nod nervously. The car is suddenly full of shadow, like the bottom of the sea on a stormy day. What can it be? Perhaps he wants a big wedding? Perhaps it's something to do with his family? Whatever he wants, I cannot imagine denying it to him.

He looks out across the sea-shadows, hiding his emotions—as men do—behind his darkened, distant gaze.

"I'm no saint, you must remember, just an ordinary man with my own limitations."

Is he about to confess to a secret vice? A mistress? An illegitimate child that he wants me to take in as my own? No matter. If he can accept my past, I can accept his.

"While I don't care about your previous marriage"—Ashok looks away as he speaks—"I don't think I can welcome your daughter as fully as she deserves."

I am too shocked even to pull my hand away from his. "What do you mean?" Disks of dizzy light flash across my vision.

"Please, Sudha." Ashok speaks pleadingly, rapidly. "Don't be angry. It's better that I speak the truth now, rather than have it come out later through a hundred veiled resentments. I discussed this already with your Aunt Gouri, who's a very intelligent woman. She understood me completely and agreed that it's the best thing for us. You and I need to be alone, at least in the beginning, so we can build a strong relationship. The mothers will be happy to keep your daughter and make sure she never lacks for love. I promise I'll give her every opportunity that money can bring. You can visit her whenever you want. Perhaps, after we've had little ones of our own, she could even come and stay with us, like a dear niece. No, Sudha, don't push me away like that. Think about it, please. Talk about it with your mother and aunts. You promised me you'd consider it—"

"I'll consider it," I say tonelessly. Somewhere inside me a

tornado swoops down, lifting a matchstick house into an exploding sky. Shards fall like rain, piercing my skin, thorning the ground. *In dreams begin follies,* says a voice like a forgotten poem. I walk carefully through the thorns, one foot in front of the other, not looking back. Behind me the car door sighs shut.

THIRTY-SIX

Anju

I LOVE WORKING. No. To be honest, the work part is so-so. What I really love is earning my own money. What a feeling of power it gives me to take my own check to the bank and put it into my own account! The first time I got my check, I made the teller cash the entire amount into one-dollar bills. I held the pile of money in my hands for a whole minute, breathing in that green scent, the scent of freedom, and then I gave it all back to her to deposit into my account.

"Why'd you do that?" she asked, obviously annoyed.

"To make it real," I said. She stared at me. I could tell what she was thinking. *Crazy foreigner.*

I don't think the American students who work with me at the college library would understand it either. They're constantly bitching about how tired they are, how work doesn't leave them enough time to have fun. They joke about wanting a rich uncle who'd pay their bills so they wouldn't have to lug carts of library books up to the stacks. They'd probably laugh their heads off if I told them how, growing up in India, I'd have given anything to be allowed to work at our bookstore. How it didn't always feel so good to be given everything I needed. How sometimes I'd wanted to be able to give too.

Since getting married I've felt this more and more. Not that I can accuse Sunil of stinginess. When money's short, he'll do without things rather than ask me to cut back. I can feel the strain it puts on him, though, so once or twice I offered to take up a job. But he got all huffy and said he's quite capable of feeding his own wife, thank you. If that isn't a typical Indian male!

That's why I've had to be so careful about keeping this job a secret, only working weekday hours—though weekends pay better—and opening an account at a different bank. I've even asked my supervisor not to call me at home, though it embarrassed me no end to do that. But my supervisor, an older black woman who looks like she might've been through troubles of her own, had nodded understandingly and not asked any awkward questions. I'm beginning to think I won't even tell Sunil about Sudha's tickets—I'll just send them to her and swear her to secrecy. I shudder when I think of tax time, when I'll have to hand him my W-2. But, like the heroine of one of my favorite books says, Tomorrow is another day. I've got plenty of other things to worry about right now.

Today I'm particularly worried because when I go for my monthly checkup, the doctor isn't pleased at all. My blood pressure's still too high, he says, and my sugar doesn't look good at all. Have I been eating what I should, and at the proper intervals?

I hang my guilty head. I do pretty well early in the day. Even when I have to go straight from class to work, I pack myself apples or an egg sandwich, things I can eat on the run. But by the time I get home, I'm tired and cranky. That's when I'll eat half a jar of sweet chutney, or a big bowl of ice cream. It's the least I deserve, I'll tell myself, refusing to listen to the scolding voice in my head. Then when Sunil comes home and makes us a virtuous, balanced meal of rice and low-salt dal and such, I'll only pick at it, complaining that it's too boring and bland.

Maybe I'm under too much stress, the doctor continues sternly. Maybe I should consider dropping out of school for a quarter.

"I can't do that," I tell him, horrified.

"Why not?"

I stare at him mutely. How can I explain to him how hugely important college is for me, a second lease on life after the first had been snatched away from me in India? How can I explain how hard Sunil and I had worked on our budget in order to pay for these classes? Or that—perhaps worst of all—if I dropped out of school, I'd no longer be eligible for the library job, and all my dreams of having Sudha start a new life here with me would be shattered?

"Well?"

"I won't get a refund if I drop out now," I blurt out. Which wasn't even what I meant to say.

"You'll have to decide, of course, whether a few dollars are more important to you than your baby," says the doctor coldly.

Although I've always liked him until now, suddenly I hate my doctor. Stupid, supercilious man. What does he know about my circumstances? About my cousin's? Why I need the money so badly that I have to keep working even when some days I feel dizzy after bending over and picking up an armful of books? Does he think I'm doing it just for fun? Then I remember that he doesn't know about my job. He'd probably go right through the roof if he did.

"I might have to put you on bed rest if I don't see any improvement by your next visit," he warns as I leave.

I mutter curses under my breath all the way to my car, but he's managed to scare me. The next few weeks I'm a model eater—I smile through my steamed broccoli and drink gallons of prune juice and remember my iron pills and give the ice-cream aisle a wide berth when I go grocery shopping. During my work breaks I lie on the women's restroom couch and practice my Lamaze breathing, and at home I study in bed, feet propped on pillows to help my circulation. By my next visit I feel a lot better, and the doctor actually smiles when he looks over my test results.

"I guess we'll let you stay on your feet a while longer," he says.

We'll let you! Who does he think he is, Queen Victoria?

But all the way home, with a brief stop at the bank to deposit my latest check, I sing Bengali nursery rhymes loudly, cheerfully and—I must confess—unmusically to Prem. No matter. When Sudha gets here, she'll teach him all the right tunes.

At the apartment, I munch on carrot sticks as I hide my bank book in the back of my underwear drawer. And suddenly I'm overcome—as I often am nowadays—by sadness. How easy it is to trick Sunil, who for all his shortcomings isn't the kind of man who looks through someone else's drawers. Although I'm not doing anything *wrong*, although I'd do it all over again for Sudha, I feel guilty. Along with the guilt come two thoughts. First: How little husbands and wives know of each other. I'm willing to bet every penny in my bankbook that Sunil can't even imagine me being capable of such duplicity. And second: If I can hide so much so easily from Sunil, who is both more resourceful and more complex than I am, how much might he be hiding from me?

THIRTY-SEVEN

Sudha

EVERY AFTERNOON in our new flat, while the mothers rest in the bedrooms and Ramur Ma snores on a mat on the kitchen floor, I sit at the small desk by the window, sketching clothes for the two babies. Singhji, who is now officially retired but stops by each day to see if there are errands to run, dozes in an armchair. As I draw, the jangling of tram bells and the cries of vendors from the dusty street below seem to recede. Sunlight drizzles through the leaves of the tamarind tree outside onto little confections of caps, all lace and silk and ribbon. Woolen booties with birds worked into them, so our children will soar over every trouble. Pants made of softest malmal. White muslin dresses with shadow-work for the hot summer that's coming up for Dayita. Checkered wool shirts for Prem, his name embroidered over a little pocket, for the rainy California winter. From time to time Singhji wakes to cluck his tongue admiringly over the pictures I've drawn. It's bad luck, of course, to actually stitch anything before the babies are born. But the mothers have conceded that designing them is harmless. I think they sense the happiness my work brings me, the way it keeps me from dwelling too much, through the long, still afternoon, on the uncertainty that is my future.

I adore the names Anju has given our children, Prem and Dayita, the way she calls them children of love. My daughter especially needs such a name, for apart from this little household, there is no one on this entire continent who cares for her. I cannot forget that—I *must not* forget that—through these coming weeks, which are sure to be filled with pulled-out, painful arguments about what I should say to Ashok.

My mother is absolutely against my turning Ashok down. "Go ahead and agree to whatever he asks now," she says. "You can always change a husband's mind, especially if you're giving him what he wants in bed." When I look shocked, she says irritably, "Come on, Sudha, you're not a child anymore. Be a little practical. If you'd thought of these things earlier, you might not be in this state today."

If you had agreed to Ashok's proposal earlier, I think bitterly, I wouldn't be in this state today either.

"Hush now, Nalini," Pishi says. "You know our Sudha never was the self-serving kind, thinking one thing while speaking another. But you're right in advising her to marry Ashok. He truly is a fine man. Not many girls get a second chance like this. We'll gladly take care of Dayita—and we'd do a good job too, among the three of us. Isn't that so, Gouri?"

Pishi, I know you will. But can even three grandmothers take a mother's place?

"Yes, yes," says Gouri Ma. She is staring out at the tamarind pods, which hang like swollen black fingers from the branches, and I think I sense a certain hesitation in her. But when she speaks, she only says, "All Ashok wants is a few years alone with you. That's not too much to ask, is it?"

Don't tempt me, Gouri Ma. Already I'm too weak. Already I want too badly to clasp the hand of love Ashok is holding out to me.

"Indeed it isn't," my mother says. "I've known men who've insisted that women send children from an earlier marriage to the orphanage—"

"We were talking again yesterday, Ashok and I," says Gouri

270

Ma. "He agrees that when Dayita is of school age, she can spend all her holidays with you—"

"Summer, puja time, Christmas," says my mother, counting them off on her fingers. "What more could you want?"

I want the man who is to be my husband to love my daughter unconditionally. Perhaps it is too much to ask. But having settled for too little once, I'm not willing to do it again.

"It's not like we're trying to get rid of you, my dear," Pishi adds. "You know how much we love you. But we've learned, all three of us, how hard it is to live out your days without a man. Unfortunately, the world hasn't changed that much since we lost our husbands."

"At least people were sympathetic to us because we were widows," says my mother. "What do you think they're going to say to you?"

"Dayita's my daughter," I say. "She needs me. How will I face her later when she asks me why I abandoned her for the sake of my own pleasure?"

"Listen to her!" my mother protests. "Is it abandoning the child to leave her with three loving grandmothers?"

"In my heart I would be abandoning her," I say, looking straight into Gouri Ma's eyes. They are cloudy with sadness, as though she knows how stony the road I've chosen will be. But she understands.

"Don't prod the poor girl any more, Nalini," she says. "Let's see how things turn out. Let's hope Ashok will change his mind."

But I do not hope for that. On the day Ashok sent my matchstick dreams crashing, I promised myself I would no longer place my hopes on a happiness that was held in someone else's hand. I weep my tears in secret, and they scald me like molten iron. But when I write to Ashok that I cannot give Dayita up, no matter how much I love him, it is with an unfaltering hand.

Last night I dreamed of Prem. He was blue as Krishna, and floating like a snowflake in milky light. He stretched out his little hands to us, Dayita and me, and said, *Come*. I woke in tears, not knowing why I was crying. All afternoon a residue of melancholy sits on my heart like silt. I try to clear it by designing a quilt, but my patterns turn out wrong, and my wastepaper basket is full of crumpled sheets.

Perhaps I am distracted by the letter I received from Anju yesterday.

In the letter Anju wrote she wants us to come to America. America had its own problems, she said, but at least it would give me the advantage of anonymity. No one in America would care that I was a daughter of the Chatterjees, or that I was divorced. I could design a new life, earn my own living, give Dayita everything she needed. Best of all, no one would look down on her, for America was full of mothers like me who'd decided that living alone was better than living with the wrong man.

I read the paragraph over and over. What Anju said opened up an avenue I hadn't considered. This way I would not be a burden on the mothers, who had already used up too much of their limited resources on me. And now that Ashok had come and gone again from my life, meteorlike, leaving a smoky, searing trail behind, there was nothing to keep me in this country.

And yet I hesitated. This little flat, already familiar. The mothers' glad cherishing. And over there: the ways of an alien land, an alien people. The fear of being a burden once more.

Because though Anju did not mention him, Sunil was there, in the gap between every word. When Anju wrote that a man could never appreciate what I was going through, I understood what it meant. When she wrote she was working, secretly, to save money for my ticket, I understood that too. Sunil did not want me in America.

I did not blame him. It was natural enough that a man should want to keep what was his for those who were his—his wife and his son. And if there was something else behind his reluctance, the shame of a heat-fused afternoon in a garden narcotic with honeysuckle and lost control, I understood perfectly that he didn't want a reminder of it.

Neither did I.

I locked the letter away in my trunk. I did not mention it to the mothers.

I'm better off in Calcutta, I tell myself now as I begin to trace a pattern of blue on blue. So many women are surviving here on their own—I can too. Surely my skill with the needle must be worth something. This quilt, it will be a test. I'll stitch it, then have Singhji take it to the Anarkali Boutique on the corner of Rashbehari junction. Maybe they will like it and place an order for more.

From who-knows-where, a sudden wind blows grit into my eyes. When I raise my hand to rub at them, it snatches away the paper I am drawing on. I lunge for it but the wind is too quick. The sheet tumbles over the sill and disappears under the feet of the multitude of passersby below. Involuntarily, I shiver. Is this the Bidhata Purush's chill, vindictive breath warning me not to stitch into my life patterns he has not placed there?

Stubbornly I pull out another sheet and begin to draw again. I *will* prove myself. I *will* be in charge of my fate. I *will* pattern a new life for myself. I swat away the superstitious unease that buzzes in my ear like gnats.

The new design is even more beautiful than before. Concentric circles of lotus buds, the spiral of death and rebirth, and in the center, a single opened flower to symbolize freedom from this earth-bound life that we humans have crowded with our complex sorrows.

Almost every evening we have visitors. Relatives, friends, old neighbors and new ones. More people than ever visited us in the old house. They come out of curiosity to see how the Chatterjee women are dealing with their reduced fortunes. They come to express their sympathy, but they stay to watch in amazement and not a little envy.

Along with the old house, the mothers seem to have shrugged off a great burden of tradition. Perhaps, ironically, I helped it happen. For now that I have come back neither wife nor widow, now that I have let go of all that society considers valuable, what is left for them to fear? Away from those ancient halls echoing with patriarchal voices which insisted that foremost of all they must be widows of the Chatterjee family, for the first time they can learn to live their lives with a girlish lightness.

The mothers have joined book societies and knitting classes. They go for walks around Victoria Memorial. They volunteer at Mother Teresa's Shishu Bhavan and (chaperoned by an insistent Singhji) attend all-night classical music concerts from which they return, cheeks flushed with the early morning cold, humming a song in the bhairav raga. They take day trips to Dakshineswar and bathe in the Ganges. After they have prayed at the temple, they eat singaras on the river steps while the afternoon sun dries their hair. Already they are talking of a trip to Darjeeling in the summer. It wouldn't cost much—Gouri Ma's cousin brother has a bungalow he's offered to her many times, the mountains would be lovely and the weather cool for Dayita, we'd get to drink the best tea, fresh-packed from the local cha-bagan, and go see the sunrise from Tiger Hill.

"It's not *right*," says Sarita Aunty, who is visiting today, between large, disapproving bites of the sandesh Singhji has fetched from Ganguram Sweets down the street.

The mothers have cut down on cooking too. Except for a few dishes Pishi makes for me from time to time, they leave the kitchen mostly to Ramur Ma. On rainy evenings they order crispy lentil-stuffed dalpuris from Ganguram. And once I caught them at the panipuri vendor's, snacking from shal leaves right there by the mini-bus stop.

"But you never used to allow Anju and me to do that!" I protested. "It isn't fair!"

The mothers smiled benign smiles.

"You can eat whatever you want now," my mother said, her tone expansive. "Now that you're all grown up."

"Yes, why not?" said Pishi.

"Once you've had the baby, that is," Gouri Ma added.

"It's not *right*," says Sarita Aunty once more, swallowing the last of her sandesh and licking her fingers daintily clean.

"What's not right?" my mother asks Sarita Aunty now, a trifle belligerently.

"You know, taking Sudha and the baby around to Darjeeling and all, like that—"

"Like what?" says Pishi, also belligerent.

"Well," stammers Sarita Aunty, backtracking, "the child will be so small, just a few months, will it be safe to expose her to all kinds of outside germs?"

"Don't worry," says Gouri Ma, smiling sweetly. "We'll keep our granddaughter well protected, and her mother too, away from germ carriers."

But of course we all know what Sarita Aunty really means. *It isn't right that you should have so much fun when Sudha's disgraced you all by leaving her husband. What are things coming to! Instead of making sure she regrets what she's done, you're acting like you're pleased about it. And that baby—you can plan to treat her like a little princess all you want, but we know what she is. A girl without a father. A girl whom no one wanted, except her willful mother.*

All evening after Sarita Aunty leaves, the mothers are extra kind to me, extra cheerful. They tell me stories of when I was little, how naughty I was. They hope my daughter will be naughtier, so that I'll finally realize what troubles I put them through. They bring out the gramophone and play the records I used to love, folk tunes and nursery rhymes, *Ata gache tota pakhi,* and *Dol, dol, dol.*

I laugh obediently at the jokes. I sing with the record:

The parrot flies to the custard-apple tree
The bees are in the pomegranates
I call and call you, little bride
Why do you not speak?

Later, though, after everyone has gone to bed, I sit at the darkened window and watch the fireflies flickering on and off in the shrubs below. Along the night wall a soundless lizard leaps to swallow a bug. Somewhere far away, an owl, bird of sorrow, cries out in the voice of a child. In my belly Dayita moves sleepily, heart-achingly, confident of protection.

How long can the mothers guard my child from the ugly words, the insults flung at her by people far crueler than Sarita Aunty? How long can I? I can provide for her physical necessities—the owners of the Anarkali Boutique have asked me to become one of their regular suppliers—but what will I say the day Dayita asks me where her father is? And when I tell her—for if I do not, others will be only too happy to—and she asks me why he and his mother wanted her to die, how will I explain it? How will I keep her from believing that she is worth less than nothing? How will I ever wipe that stain from her heart?

I rise in the dark and unlock my trunk by feel. I grope inside until I find the cool, smooth American paper. Anju's promise of reprieve. Anonymity. I hold it to my cheek until it is warm, until it is like holding onto Anju's hand, and I begin to reconsider.

THIRTY-EIGHT

Anju

ALL WEEK I've been dragging myself through the hours, more tired than I've ever been in my life, wondering how I'm going to get through the rest of my pregnancy. But finally Friday's here, and am I glad! Friday's my best day, just a couple of classes, no work. I plan to put in a solid afternoon of studying—not at the main library where my co-workers are always interrupting me to chat, but on the deserted top floor of one of the graduate branches. I'm winded by the time I make it up the stairs, but there's a comfortable old couch where I put up my feet—and then, before I know it, I've dozed off. When I wake with a start, heart thudding, it's almost evening. Shit! I'd counted on getting the groceries before I picked Sunil up from the station. Now I'm not even caught up on my homework, and worst of all, the niggling pain I've had all week in my lower back has gotten worse, probably from lying scrunched up on this couch, which isn't halfway as comfortable as it looked. When I straighten up, the pain spreads to my stomach as well. I try to massage it away. Just below my ribs I feel a familiar bump—my son's head—and even though I'm hurting, I smile. You're in the wrong position, kid, I whisper, patting him. But I'm not concerned—he still has three months to turn around.

I get to the station in record time, maneuvering the car around corners like a regular James Bond—and there's no Sunil. I wait for the next two trains, growing more anxious by the minute. My back's killing me. In exactly five minutes I'm going to have to use the bathroom, or else. Finally I give up and drive home, and the first thing I see when I open the door is my dear husband, sitting comfortable as you please in the recliner, watching TV with a mug of beer in his hand. It's enough to give a saint apoplexy.

"What the hell happened to you? Do you know how worried I've been?" I shout over my shoulder as I rush to the bathroom. The pain in my stomach, which must have been caused by an overextended bladder, is a little better now, and I return to the living room ready to do battle. But I'm taken aback by the expression on Sunil's face. It's not apologetic, as I'd have expected, but furious.

God! Something awful must have happened for him to come home early like this. Did he get laid off? I'm ashamed of the selfish thoughts that begin to explode one after another inside me like a string of firecrackers at Kali Puja: Will the insurance still cover my delivery? What'll I feed our baby? And, I'll never be able to bring Sudha over now.

"What's wrong?" I whisper finally, sitting down. I reach out to touch Sunil's shoulder, but he shoves my hand away.

"Nothing's wrong with *me*," he says in a hard voice.

"Why are you home early then?"

"I had to visit a client close by, so I just took a cab home. I tried to call you—I left several messages"—he jerks his chin at the answering machine—"but you were nowhere around."

"I fell asleep at the library."

"Sure you did!" Sunil's voice is heavy with sarcasm.

I look at him in surprise. "What do you mean?"

"Then what's this?" he says, and jabs at the answering machine button. "I found this when I tried to erase my messages."

"Anju," says a female American voice. "I hope I got the right number for you—you didn't have it on file." It takes me a moment to realize that it's the woman who sometimes fills in for my supervisor. My heart gives a sick lurch. "Sorry to disturb you at home, but we're desperate. Three of the stackers have come down with the flu, and with exam week just around the corner, the library's a mess. I know you don't like to work weekends, but could you possibly come in for a few hours tomorrow? Call me as soon as you get this message—"

If thunder could whisper, it would sound like Sunil's voice. "How long has this been going on? And why? What did you need so badly that you had to get the money for it secretly, like this?" There's a desperate hurt beneath the anger in his eyes.

"It's for Sudha," I blurt out. "I'm saving for her ticket. I had to do it this way because you didn't want to help." Someone seems to be pulling apart the bones of my lower back with both hands. If only this were all over, and I could go lie down.

I expect an outburst from Sunil, but he's oddly silent. In the darkening evening, an expression flits over his face, gone before I can catch it.

"You *had* to meddle, didn't you?" he says finally. A cracked tiredness runs through his voice. "You couldn't leave well enough alone."

"What do you mean, meddle?" I say. I'm tired, too—too tired for fighting, too tired for diplomacy. "Sudha's my sister, the person I love most in the world. You yourself told me how hard life would be for her in India, now that she's now married anymore. How can I just leave her there to suffer?"

"Go to bed, Anju," says Sunil with a sigh. "You look awful. Now I know why you've been so tired and irritable these last months—you're working yourself to death. I'll bring you some hot soup, and then I'll call that woman and tell her you're quitting."

I jump to my feet with the last of my strength. "You'll do no such thing," I cry. "I'm not quitting. I'm perfectly fine. I *will* keep working. I *will* bring Sudha to America, whether you want it or not."

"Please, Anju," says Sunil. "Go lie down. You're all worked up."

"Don't treat me like a child." I'm shouting now, gasping for breath. Someone's smashing the bones of my pelvis with a steel hammer. "I won't let you control me like your father controls your mother. I won't let you—"

And then the pain's so bad I have to double over, but not before I've seen the stricken look in Sunil's eyes. There's a sticky wetness between my legs, a dark stain begins to spread down my pants. There's a smell like rusting metal in the air. Did I lose control over my bladder?

Sunil mutters something as he grabs the phone.

"No," I cry, lunging to knock it from him.

"Stop it, Anju," he says, trying to ward me off with his free hand. "Calm down. I'm not calling your work. I'm calling an ambulance."

The firecrackers explode inside me once more, taking me with them.

When I come to, the pain is intense, a hot light that blinds me even through the dull haze of medication. But worse is the hollow feeling I have, that sense that it's too late.

When I get up the courage, I touch my belly. Low down, there are bandages, seals of a disaster I've somehow stupidly slept through. And though I'm still swollen, I can tell my baby is gone.

I'm not sure what happens next. The tears which stream their course down the sides of my face until they pool into my ears like warm blood. Or the crisp, starched nurse who smiles an unbearably cheerful smile and comments on the fact that I'm awake. Or the screams that spurt out independent of my will because inside my throat there's a bottomless fountain, as in the tales Pishi used to tell when I was too young to understand that life can be crueler than any story. Or the hands holding me down, the needle piercing my flesh, the burning squirt of more numbing medication. But finally there's Sunil, stroking my hair, saying I must be brave.

"Tell me," I say. My voice is a hoarse, grating thing. It shows nothing of the helpless rage building to explosion inside me. When Sunil hesitates, I grasp his hand with all the strength I can call up, letting my nails sink in. I want him to hurt, to feel at least a pale echo of what I'm feeling. "Tell me everything."

They'd rushed me, bleeding heavily, to the hospital. They'd brought me to an operating room as soon as they could, and performed a C-section. But by then his heartbeat had stopped.

"I want to see him," I whisper, but Sunil shakes his head. The body's been sent away already. Even otherwise, the doctor had advised against it. The best thing for me would be to put the whole incident behind me as soon as I could—and this way, the baby would be less of a reality.

Oh, the stupidity of men. I'd held him inside me for six months. I'd talked to him every day since I knew he was there. He'd pulsed against my flesh with the minute brightness of a star, giving me guidance and courage. Through the thin lining of my skin, I'd touched the curve of his head. Nothing they did could lessen the wrenching reality of what he'd meant to me.

I try to argue with Sunil, but my tongue's heavy from the tranquilizer, and I see from his eyes that he's made his decision.

It's hard to form words with lips numb as leather. But I must know one more thing before I go under. "What did he look like?" I ask. The sounds are so slurred I'm afraid Sunil won't understand, but he does.

"He was beautiful, with tiny hands like starfish."

Sunil's eyes grow unfocused, remembering. The softness with which my usually unpoetic husband speaks startles me. "Something had been wrong with the cord, it had cut off the oxygen, so he was blue like a—baby Krishna."

I'm amazed, again, at his words. But of course they're exactly right. I can see the translucent blueness of my baby's skin glowing through the darkness of my tight-shut eyes.

"He was so beautiful," Sunil repeats. The bitterness in his voice pries my eyelids open. A brilliant rage is flickering over his face, like electricity in a storm cloud.

I know then I was mistaken earlier. Hearts break in different ways, a father's no less than a mother's.

"My baby, I killed him."

I'm not sure whether I've spoken the words or only thought them from within the hot bands of steel that are squeezing my throat. But from the sudden, profound stillness of Sunil's body I know he's heard me.

"Don't be silly, Anju," he says, after a pause.

That pause—the enormous, accusing weight of that pause. It makes me turn my face into the antiseptic smell of the hospital pillow and shut my eyelids tight, tight, tight.

I'm not going to open them ever again.

THIRTY-NINE

Sudha

THEY TRIED to keep the news from me because they were afraid of what I might do, but I suspected. I smelled it in the air of the flat, cold suddenly in spite of the blistering April sun outside. Cold and heavy with the smell of white chrysanthemums, though it wasn't the season for them. White chrysanthemums, the kind we drape over bodies at funerals. Sometimes I would wake at night and think I heard sobs from Gouri Ma's room. I would walk over, and she would be sleeping, the bedspread covering her face—but too soundly, not responding when I called her. And there hadn't been a letter from Anju in over a month.

"She must be busy, or maybe just not in the mood—you know how pregnant women get sometimes," says Pishi when I tell her how worried I am. "Your job right now is to eat well and rest well and exercise properly, and most of all, to not worry."

"But don't you think we should at least call?"

"Actually, Sunil called the other morning, when you were out for your morning walk—"

"How is it you didn't tell me?" I ask, annoyed.

Pishi sighs. "I'm getting old—I guess I forget things sometimes." She does look old suddenly, and weary. The skin under her eyes hangs loose and purple. Has her arthritis been acting up again, keeping her awake at night? "Anyway, they're both doing quite well, so you can stop being so anxious."

I peer at her eyes—are they more red-rimmed than usual?— but she avoids my gaze and goes off for her bath.

When another week passes without a letter from Anju, I call. I call at our usual time, morning in India, evening in America. Anju is always back home by now, fixing dinner and grumbling about it. But this time no one picks up the phone, and though I leave her a message, she doesn't call me back.

"That's strange," I tell the mothers after a couple of days have passed. "Surely Anju would call back—after all, I hardly ever phone her. She must have known it was important."

"Maybe they've gone on vacation," offers my mother.

But I'm not satisfied. I'm going to call again, I decide. When the mothers are not in the house.

The mothers have been unusually reluctant to leave me alone recently, so I have to wait until it is time for our weekly trip to the temple. We all get ready to go, and then I tell them I am too tired.

"Come on—it's not far," my mother insists. "It's bad luck to say you'll go to the temple and then change your mind."

"We can take a taxi," Gouri Ma says.

I yawn loudly. "I really think I need to take a nap."

"Maybe I should stay with you," Pishi says.

"No, no. Please go, all of you, and pray for Dayita and me. I'll just be lying down anyway."

By the time I convince them to leave, it is almost noon. Midnight in California. I am sorry I have to disturb Anju, but this way she will certainly be home.

Sunil is the one who picks up the phone, his voice sleepily bewildered and young. A voice I would not have recognized—it has been so long—if I had not known. I feel a moment's awkwardness—the last time we spoke was on that ill-fated afternoon in the garden—but I push it away. I am calling because of Anju, I tell myself firmly. Besides, we are both adults now and have been through enough of life's hardships to know which things deserve our care, which are best left alone. When I tell him who I am, he pauses—is he too thinking of the jasmine arbor?—then says somewhat abruptly that Anju is sleeping. He doesn't want to disturb her—she doesn't sleep very well nowadays. "I'll tell her you called," he says, sounding as if he is about to hang up.

"Wait," I call, "wait," and then like a thunderclap an idea comes to me. It is worth a try—at least this way I will know if I have been worrying needlessly all this while, as the mothers claim. "Is Anju doing better now?"

I cross my fingers as I speak. Please God, let Sunil say, What on earth are you talking about?

Instead he says, in a startled voice, "So they've told you! I thought they weren't going to until your delivery. No, she's not better. In fact, she's worse than she was right after she lost the baby."

The words strike me like a fist in the center of my chest, knocking the air out of me. When I can breathe again, it is a wheezy, jerking sound, and I cover the mouthpiece so Sunil will not hear it. Oh, Anju, Anju! How did this happen? And I nowhere near you to help at this terrible time.

"I've only told Anju's mother a little bit of this—I know she has a bad heart—but I'm going crazy keeping it all to myself," says Sunil. "She won't get out of bed. Actually, the sofa. That's where she sleeps nowadays. She won't take her antidepressants. I'll set the tablets out by her plate when I leave for work, and when I come back they'll still be sitting there. She's lost a lot of weight—when I take her hand, it feels like a very old woman's, with the skin sliding over the bones. She'll only eat if I actually spoon the food into her mouth."

The words pour through the phone and widen into a pool around me. Now they are rising past my ankles, my shins. "And she won't talk. She hasn't spoken a single word since I brought her home. She blames herself, I think. I tell her she mustn't—

but my words have no effect on her. Once I tried to tell her how much I was suffering too"—here Sunil pauses, clears his throat—"I thought that would break the barrier between us—but she just covered her head with the pillow. That's the same thing she does whenever I ask if she'd like to go visit her mother in India. The doctor wants to put her in a nursing home for a while, but when he told her about it during our last visit, her whole body started shaking, and her eyes went wild and skittery, like a trapped animal's. I can't bear the thought of sending her away. But I don't know what else to do. I don't have any more leave left and she isn't getting any better."

I find I am hugging my stomach tightly, as though Dayita too would slip away otherwise, like my beautiful, elusive Prem.

Not now, Sudha. Think only of Anju now.

"Maybe you can help," Sunil says. "Can you?"

I think desperately. The inside of my head is filled with a roaring sound like a distant fire, with whirries of dust raised by the Bidhata Purush's furious passing. And then I know.

"Is she awake now?" I ask. "Then put the phone to her ear."

He does it, and I start speaking. The inside of my mouth is caked with dust. Dust embroiders the lining of my lungs. It presses down upon me like an unkept promise, it sucks up my voice. But I make myself go on.

"Once there was a princess who spent her girlhood in a crumbling marble palace set around with guards. They told her what was proper and what was not, and held up their poison spears before her face if she attempted to stray outside the boundaries they had drawn for her. When she was old enough, she married, obediently, the king they had selected for her. The firecrackers at the wedding were so loud that no one could hear if her heart was breaking. And when she got to her husband's house, she had no trouble adjusting, for it was exactly the same as the house she'd grown up in, except that the guards were fiercer, and their spear tips more poisonous.

"All went well with the marriage until the queen was due to give birth. Then a soothsayer discovered that the baby was a girl. Aghast at the idea that their future ruler might be a woman, the guards aimed their poison spears at the queen's belly so they could destroy the baby before she could be born. The king, petrified with fear, could do nothing to protect her."

I stumble over the painful words. This is not the story I had meant to tell Anju. But it has taken its own necessary shape, and I must follow where it leads.

"The queen was terrified too, but she placed her hands on her belly to gather courage from her unborn daughter. And she felt something being passed into her hands through the wall of the womb. Looking down, she saw it was a sword, a flaming sword made of light, and then another, one for each hand. Whirling the swords around her head like the Goddess Durga, like the Rani of Jhansi, the queen left the palace, and none dared prevent her.

"Along the way the queen met many people, but though they loved her and her newborn daughter, they were frightened by the thought of the guards who might be pursuing them. Still others were made uneasy by the unearthly brightness that emanated from them both by this time, for suffering and courage calls forth that brightness in us. Thus none dared to give them shelter.

"The queen kept searching for a new home. Some days her heart was low and she wondered if her daughter and she were doomed to travel the earth ceaselessly, but she never gave up. Until the day she reached the ocean's edge and there was no place further for her to go."

I come to a halt. The words I've been following through the labyrinth of memory like Theseus followed his ball of string have run out. What shall I do now?

Then, very softly, I hear Anju's voice. "But suddenly the queen heard someone say, 'Don't worry, dear one. Reach for my hand.' And looking up she saw a rainbow that extended all the way from the other side of the earth to her. You see, in all this turmoil, the queen had forgotten that she had a twin sister who lived in the land across the ocean. The sister was sending her all her love in the form of this rainbow—"

Anju's voice falters, but I take up the story. "The queen held her daughter with one hand and with the other she grasped the rainbow. And her sister pulled her across the ocean, over the gaping jaws of sea monsters, to safety."

Anju is crying now. "Oh, Sudha," she says between sobs, "I need you. I need you so much. I'm starved for you. I was trying so hard to get the money together for your ticket, but I messed everything up."

Oh God! Was that why Anju had the miscarriage? She was working for me, unfortunate me. What have I ever brought her except ill luck?

"Please come," Anju says. "Promise me you'll come at once."

I am shaken by how feeble she sounds, how pitiable. It is how I would have sounded, once upon a time, before I learned that mothers cannot afford fear.

I try to keep my voice even. "I'll come as soon as I can, once Dayita is born. Now listen to me—meanwhile you must do everything the doctor says so you can get better. How else will you help me take care of Dayita? After all, she's your daughter as much as mine."

Anju laughs a shaky, rusty laugh. "Sudha, I can't wait to see you! What fun the two of us will have."

"The three of us," I say.

"I can't believe you'll be here, Sudha, just like old times!" Anju says in a high clear child's voice, as though she hadn't heard a word of what I said about Dayita.

After the mothers return and hear everything, we hold each other and cry. Then we scold each other. "How could you keep something so crucial from me?" I say. "You told us you couldn't come to the temple because you were tired!" they retort. We shake our heads over the fact that Anju refuses to come to India, which would have been so much easier. "Stubborn as ever," says my mother, but Pishi says, "Anju never could stand to be pitied," and Gouri Ma says, "She's thinking about Sudha's life, about getting her a new start." I tell them how Anju would not respond when I mentioned Dayita's name. They say I must be patient with her loss. When I tell them why she was working so hard before the miscarriage, they are silent. Then Gouri Ma takes my hands in hers and says it was a great pity, but I must not feel responsible.

Oh, Gouri Ma—as though guilt were as easy to shake off as water on a lotus leaf.

The mothers marvel at Sunil's generosity—he came on the phone after Anju and I had finished talking to say that he would arrange tickets and visas for Dayita and myself. But something puzzles me. Just before hanging up, he had given a sigh like someone who had been hanging on to a cliff ledge for a long time, someone who finally loosened his hands and felt with a strange relief the air rushing up around his body as he fell. "I tried," he said.

I didn't tell the mothers about that. He had said it very softly, to himself, and I might have heard wrong.

"But what did you say to Anju to get her to listen?" the mothers ask finally. "To talk to you?"

"Oh, just something," I say, unexpectedly reluctant to discuss it. "Something private between her and me."

"Can't you tell us even a little bit?" pleads my mother.

"I told her a story."

"Ah, a story," nods Pishi. More than any of us, she knows the power stories hold at their center, like a mango holds its seed. It is a power that dissipates with questioning, so she merely asks, with an odd, wistful look, "Was it a story I'd told you, Sudha?"

I am sorry to disappoint her. "It's a new story. One I made up, kind of, on the spot."

"Does it have a name?" asks Gouri Ma.

I start to shake my head. Then it comes to me.

"The Queen of Swords," I say.

I write to Anju every day, describing for her the minute, unglamorous details of my pregnancy. At first I was hesitant. I thought it would be too painful for her. But sometimes the only way to healing is through the corridor of pain. Denying the fact that I am going to have a child would do neither of us any good. So I tell her how terrible my indigestion is. How I am breathless all the time. How Dayita keeps me awake all night, kicking. Before I go into the hospital I jot down how the first of the labor pains feel, a cramping like my insides want to fall out all at once. And after I return, I try to find words for the moment they put my daughter on my chest, slippery and wrinkled as a prune, and unbelievably beautiful.

But somehow I cannot bear to send that last letter.

These last few months, Anju has been busy getting ready for me. She is eating the right things and, although she's still weak, is starting to go for walks with Sunil. The doctor has said she can be taken off her medication in a little while. She talked to her professors and thinks she can make up a couple of her classes next semester. She and Sunil have agreed that when she is well enough, she can go back to work if she wants. Best of all, she has started reading again.

Sunil calls the mothers delightedly to say he is amazed at the change in her. Please tell Sudha she's a miracle, he says. I must find a way to thank her properly once she gets here.

As always the mothers love his courteous words, but something about that last sentence troubles me. My mother prods me to send him an equally courteous reply, but I do not. What would I write anyway? *I'm* not amazed. Anju always had the ability to follow through once she had set her mind on a goal.

And the goal—or miracle—is not me. Whether Anju acknowledges it or not, it is Dayita.

"And what a nice miracle you are," I tell Dayita, smiling down at her head, black and fuzzy as the core of a kadam flower, as I nurse her. I try not to think of what I would do if Anju continues to ignore her once I get to America. If she takes a great aversion to my daughter. "It can't happen," I whisper into Dayita's neck as I hug her close, as I breathe in the reassuring smell of milk and baby powder. My words are as fervent as a prayer. "Everybody loves you."

This is certainly true in our little household, where the mothers are always fighting over who gets to hold her and play with her, and who gets to sing her to sleep.

"*I'm* her real grandmother," says my mother. "She even looks like me. Give her to me."

"No you're not," says Pishi, hands on her hips. "It's love that makes a relationship, as much as blood. Plus she's a lot prettier than you ever were. And anyway, you never could burp a baby. Gouri, *Gouri!* Did you sneak up on us and take Daya Moni away again!"

It amuses me to see how proprietory everyone is toward her. Even Singhji takes her from my arms quite unceremoniously and sends me off for an afternoon nap so he can sit in his armchair and rock her back and forth and talk baby-talk while she grabs handfuls of his beard and gurgles with laughter and Ramur Ma hovers around them jealously "to make sure the old man, who's probably never held a baby in his life, doesn't drop our Daya Moni."

So nursing times—one of the few times I am allowed to have my daughter all to myself—are precious to me. That is when I get to examine her all over, marveling anew at the intricate perfection of her fingers and toes, the translucent curved petals of her ears. The riot of recent curls which shimmer against my breast, the small dimple on her chin. I tell her I want her to grow up courageous and strong, more than I ever was. I sing to her and tell her stories. She sucks moistly, noisily, as though oblivious. But I know she is taking in every word.

This afternoon I decide to tell her the story of Prem.

"There once was a boy," I say, "the sweetest of all boys, and the luckiest. When he was the size of a mustard seed in his mother's belly—why even then he was the wisest of children and advised his mother on what to do. By the time he grew as large as a lemon, he knew how to sing and dance and turn somersaults. And when he grew to the size of a pomelo, he could recite the twenty-four scriptural texts from beginning to end. The gods looked down amazed and said, he is too good for the imperfect world of men. So they took him from his mother's womb and made him into a star, so that he would never face the sorrow-thorns that prick us daily. I'll show him to you this very evening, looking down at you with his star-eyes, and he will love you, for you are his little cousin, and you will always have a friend in the skies, to guide you when you need."

The door to my room opens. I adjust my sari and look up, annoyed at the interruption.

"Sudha, have you finished nursing, are you decent?" asks my mother in a coy voice that makes me cringe. "Well then, here's a visitor for you.

I turn to find Ashok, holding a teddy bear twice the size of my daughter and looking a little embarrassed. I am embarrassed too, especially when my mother clicks shut the door purposefully, leaving us together. I hurry to open it, but Ashok puts a hand on my arm, and my heart pitches and tilts. When I pull away, he says, "I owe you an apology, Sudha, and your daughter also." He looks down at Dayita and she—foolish, indiscriminate girl— gives him a huge grin.

"You don't owe me anything," I say, annoyed. Does he not realize how hard it is for me to see him again? Every time I think I have turned the page, he re-enters my life, awkward as a post-script.

"May I hold her?" says Ashok. I hand her to him grudgingly,

but then I have to smile, I cannot help it, even though the memory of how close we'd come to belonging to each other is still like a splinter inside my chest. He looks so nervous—as though Dayita might bite or, at the very least, throw up all over the sparkling white shirt he is wearing. Spitefully I wish she would—it would serve him right for not wanting her—but of course she is being a golden child, cooing up at him and reaching for his face with her fat, dimpled arms.

"I'm not very good at this," he says. "I don't have any practice—no nieces or nephews, you see. But I could learn. What do you think?"

When I scowl at him—I am in no mood for riddles—he says, "I've been thinking a lot, the last few months. What I said to you was wrong, trying to make you choose between your child and me. And especially now that I see the two of you together, I know no one should ever separate you. So"—he swallows, and I realize it is not only Dayita that is making him nervous—"Sudha, will you marry me? Will you teach me to love your daughter?" And he chucks Dayita awkwardly under her chin.

For a moment my greedy, forgetful heart leaps. Ashok and I, that old, tempting dream which began at the movies—but no, its true beginning was in the fairy tales. Now the last obstacle has crumbled, the last mountain of skull-bones crossed, the last monster beheaded. The last, best magic worked: the prince and princess turned into ordinary humans, but still finding each other worthy of love. I watch him holding my daughter and know he will be a conscientious father—and an affectionate one. For if there's any tenderness in him at all—and I know there is—surely my daughter will pull it forth.

Then I remember Anju. Anju waiting so desperately, Anju exercising and eating spinach each day and learning to smile again. Anju, who has already started to clean her apartment in anticipation of my tourist visa, which is due to arrive any week now. Anju, whose father would not be dead except for my father. Whose son would not be dead, perhaps, except for—

"Ashok," I say. I close my eyes tight, dizzy with déja vu. Too late, too late. All my life, the timing of things has been off. "I'm sorry—"

"Don't be," he says. "I heard about Anju from your Gouri Aunty. I understand that you must go and help her. That's not a problem. You're going on a temporary visa—you'll come back after a few months. I'll wait for you. I've waited so many years, what's a little more time?"

My heartbeat evens. Thankfulness fills my mouth, sweet as honey. Ah, for once in my life I will not have to choose between my loves! So when the words come, I am as startled by them as Ashok.

"I'm not sure if I'm coming back at all."

And suddenly I know this: I am going for Anju, yes, and for Dayita, but most of all I am going for me. I am going with the knowledge that this will not be a fairy-tale journey, my winged steed leaping over all obstacles with unfailing ease, but I am going anyway. Do I want to return? And if I do return, will I be happy tying my life to a man's whims again, even if he is a good man? I do not know. The yearning that shoots up from the soles of my feet when I think of Ashok, is it love? I am not sure. It is so different in its nature from the craving pull, gut and sinew and womb, that I feel for my sister and my daughter.

In her last letter Anju had written about her plans for us to start a clothes boutique. We would start small, she would handle the business end, I would be the creative one. At the time I had laughed, but now I think, why not? A future built by women out of their own wits, their own hands. A future where I lean on myself alone.

"Visas can change," I tell Ashok, "like human desires." I hold his hand in mine, and in memory of the passionate dream we once shared, so youthful and innocent and absolute that I expect never to feel it again, I kiss his cheek.

It is a gesture of farewell.

FORTY

Anju

SUDHA'S COMING, Sudha's coming! She'll be here in a week! I'm buffeted between joy and panic—there's so much to be done to get the apartment ready before she arrives. I hadn't expected the visa to come through so fast. I suspect it's because Sunil went to my doctor and made him write a letter about how Sudha's getting here is crucial to my recovery. And of course it is. Not just her getting here, but her staying here. The visa's only valid for a year, but I've heard those things can be arranged. Maybe Sudha can go to college here. Maybe we'll get that business started. Maybe she'll meet someone who'll make up for what she's giving up to come here. But when I think that, I'm racked by doubt. Is there a man in all of America who could love her as absolutely as Ashok does?

The day I received my mother's letter telling me about Ashok's second offer of marriage, I couldn't sleep. I tossed around in bed, even though my mother had written, quite clearly, that Sudha had turned him down. "Sudha didn't want me to tell you about this," she'd ended, "but I feel you should know how deeply she loves you."

I even woke Sunil up once, when my worries got too much for me. "But what if Sudha changes her mind?" I asked him.

"Come *on*, Anju!" he said, irritated. "She's promised you, hasn't she? She seems like a reliable person. She knows how much you're looking forward to having her here. She knows it's going to be good for her too."

"But what Ashok's offering is so wonderful, now that he's agreed to accept"—I swallowed to force myself to say the name—"Dayita too—this is the man she's loved all her life, you understand—I don't see how she can bear to give him up. And even if she can, I'm not sure she *should* give him up, no matter how much I need her. Maybe I should call her tomorrow and—"

"Do what you want, but for heaven's sake, let me sleep now," Sunil said in an angry kind of voice. "In case you've forgotten, I have to go to work in the morning." He turned and pulled the covers over his ears. But some of my anxiety must have infected him. From his breathing I could tell he remained awake for a long time. Maybe even longer than I did, because when I surfaced briefly from a broken dream hours later, I heard him rummaging around in the bathroom closet where I keep my sleeping pills.

I sit back on my heels, sweating. I'm out of breath and frustrated. My heart pumps too hard, and a sharp ache along my scar reminds me that I can no longer spur my body along as though it's a trained animal whose only function is to take me where I want to go.

This room, previously our study-cum-junk-collection-area, is taking forever to set up. Though it's been several months since my surgery, I'm not supposed to lift anything heavy yet, and Sunil's been too busy with a project at work to do more than empty a couple of drawers' worth of his stuff into boxes. He promised me he'd put them in the storage space under the stairs last weekend, but they're still sitting in the middle of the room, waiting for me to trip over them every time I turn around.

I can't complain too much though, because he did get the crib. He found the ad in the flea-market paper and went and picked it up. Set it up, too, all by himself. He could have used an extra pair of hands, but he didn't push me to help him. Not that I could have done it. I couldn't even enter the room. Just seeing him carry it in, part by part, made my hands start shaking. I felt like I was spiraling back into those first dizzy days after I'd returned from the hospital when I'd have to hold on to the edge of the bed because otherwise I'd surely have floated away, I was that empty inside.

Afterward, Sunil came over to where I was sitting by the window, staring out, and touched the back of my neck lightly. "I know you're hurting, Anju. I'm hurting too. But you must pull yourself together. Dayita will be here in a few days—by your invitation, I might add."

"I didn't invite *her*," I mumbled through stiff lips. I couldn't help it, even though it made me feel meaner than hell.

Sunil gave me a look, mingled annoyance and pity. For once I could read what was going through his mind. *Sorry, sweetheart, you don't have a choice anymore. Maybe having to deal with it would be good for you.*

I *do* have a choice, I said to myself. Dayita doesn't exist for me. No other baby does. Sudha will understand—she'll know I can't be forced, not in this. Because it's the least I owe my Prem.

Today I'm determined to empty out the remaining drawers of the desk. We don't have an extra dresser, but Sudha can put her clothes in there, and the top will do very nicely for her knick-knacks. Her mattress, which we'll pick up this weekend, can go in the corner by the window.

I am careful to give the crib a wide berth. A murky energy throbs around it, like in the taboo places spoken of in old tales. It would suck me in if I got too close.

I pull out drawers filled with Sunil's books and papers. Dried-out pens spill out, and college notes written in faded ink. A stapler, envelopes, manila folders, outdated textbooks which he'll never use again but won't let me throw away. As I move back and forth filling cartons, I keep my face carefully averted. I'm safe as long as my eyes aren't caught by the white slats of the crib, by the jauntily swinging red-and-black Mickey Mouse mobile Sunil's described to me.

Before long, I've run out of space. Maybe if I repack the boxes Sunil filled last week, I can stuff a few more items into them. I lift a stack of old bank statements out of one—what a pack rat Sunil is!—and something clatters to the floor. It's an oval wooden container small enough to be cupped in my palm, intricately carved with leaves and fruit in a Kashmiri design. I've never seen it before. Wait!—I have, years ago at our wedding, when some relative presented it to us. To keep something valuable in, he'd said. Like most of our wedding gifts, it was pretty but not very practical, and I was sure we'd left it behind. How on earth did it get here, at the bottom of a box filled with yellowed Merrill Lynch annual reports?

I flick the lid open unthinkingly, expecting it to be empty, but it isn't. A wisp of cloth flutters from it—a handkerchief, my wedding handkerchief, that delicate white lawn bordered with embroidered good-luck lotuses. I bury my face in it, trying to recall that far-off day. It seems I smell the marriage-fire, the priest's reedy, chanting voice, the turmeric rubbed into my skin for luck. The smell of a long-dissipated dream. Did I put the handkerchief in that box? Recently my mind's been like a sieve. But no, I remember quite clearly putting it into the top drawer of the dresser in my bedroom in Sunil's father's house. Sunil must have taken it from there before he came away to America. Who would have thought he was such a romantic!

I tuck the handkerchief into my bra. At dinner I'll take it out with a flourish, tease Sunil about it. It's been a long time since we've had something to laugh about.

Then a terrible doubt takes hold of me. I spread out the handkerchief and examine the initial in the corner, looped in silk thread red as danger, red as betrayal and bitter blood. Just as I'd expected in the deep, hopeless cavern of my heart, it's a B for Basudha.

How could I have forgotten, even for a breath-beat? Is it that the mind, in order to survive, blacks out moments that would otherwise drive it mad?

The scene shivers to life before my eyes once again, as it did so many times during the bittersweet month after my wedding, those nights I lay awake after lovemaking, wondering of whom Sunil had been thinking as he groaned his pleasure between my breasts.

The wedding dinner is over. We rise. Ramesh and Sudha walk ahead, his arm under her reluctant elbow. She pulls out a handkerchief to wipe her face. She replaces it—but no, it falls behind the table. No one notices Sunil bending to pick it up. To slip it into his pocket where he fists his hand around it. No one except me.

Now I hold the handkerchief to my trembling lips. It smells faintly, sweetly of my cousin's body. I wait for the old jealousy to bare its fangs, but all I feel is despair. How many times had Sunil tried to stop me from bringing Sudha over to America? How many hints had he given? *Why can't you leave well enough alone?* I'd thought he was being selfish, stingy. But he'd only been trying to save me.

There's a roaring in my ears like opened floodgates. *You don't have a choice anymore,* says my husband's voice as I'm swept away. Oh, Sudha, now that you're already halfway to America in your mind, what shall we do now?

FORTY-ONE

Sudha

ONCE WHEN Anju and I were children, Gouri Ma took us to the Maidan fair. We loved everything about it, from the smell of boiling molasses at the sweets stand to the brightly colored parrots the bird vendor carried around in cages hung from poles. Best of all we liked the nagordola, the huge Ferris wheel. It would start off creakily, excruciatingly slow, so that we'd stamp our feet and cry, *Faster, faster*. But soon enough our car was hurtling around, the earth disappearing somewhere below, the sky opening around us in a rush, then earth, then sky, then earth again, until we screamed for the wheel to stop its relentless spinning. Yet when it did, we ran as quickly as we could, dizzy and stumble-footed, to stand in line for another ride.

These last few weeks I feel as if I am on that nagordola. After I said no to Ashok, how painfully time dragged its crippled body along. The desire to be gone built like steam inside my heart until I was ready to explode. *Faster, faster*, I chafed until the giant Ferris wheel of the days finally picked up speed and became a mad blur of shopping-packing-tickets-passports-inoculations. Not until this morning at the airport, when I feel the mothers' love pulling at me like a river pulls at your body just before you climb out, do I realize the dismaying finality of this moment. My time is up, and unlike that day at the fair, I cannot pay my coin and climb on again. What I am leaving behind—I cannot articulate what it is, but I know I will not find it, ever, in America. The mothers kiss me, their lips damp and cool on my forehead, that childhood smell of Binaca toothpaste, and I wish I had not been in such a hurry to go.

At the entrance to the security area, Singhji hands me my carry-on bag. It's heavy with Dayita's things, nappies and bottles of juice and extra outfits—how many items such a little person needs!—but wedged into a corner I catch a glimpse of a packet wrapped in brown paper and tied with string.

"What's this?" I ask.

"Oh, nothing," say the mothers, "but be careful, don't lose it." They wipe at their eyes with their sari edges as they whisper blessings. *Goddess Durga keep you. May you be always happy. And brave as the Rani of Jhansi*. When I reach for the packet to see what is inside, they swat my hand away with mock-frowns. "Wait until you get on the plane," they say.

I have been overwhelmed by gifts and good wishes all week. So many from people who I thought did not care, so many from people whose love I had done little to deserve. But then, love is never about deserving, is it? Nor is hate. I learned *that* from my mother-in-law. The teatime aunties brought jars of lemon achar for me and gripe water for Dayita. Neighbors from down the street gave me filmi magazines to read on the plane and churan mix in case I felt airsick. Sunil's mother, as sweet and timid as ever, stopped by with a hand-knitted blanket for Dayita and a message. "Tell Sunil not to send any more money," she whispered. "They need it more than we do. His father's sorry about what happened, but he's too proud to ever admit it. Maybe if Sunil called—? Will you try to persuade him?" Her stricken doe-eyes held mine until I nodded uneasy agreement.

Ramur Ma and Singhji presented me with a silver dish-and-bowl set for Dayita, with her name carved into the edge.

"But it's too expensive!" I said, appalled at the thought of how much of their savings such a gift must have eaten into.

"Oh hush," said Ramur Ma. "Just be sure to send us photos of Daya Moni when she gets old enough to eat from them."

Ashok tried to give me back his diamond ring. When I would not accept it, he gave me a plastic card embossed with my name.

"It's a credit card," he explained.

I knew about credit cards—Anju had written to me about them—but I hadn't known one could get them in India.

"They've just started issuing them," he said. "You can use it in America, and the bill will be sent to me here. I don't want you ever to run out of money, or feel dependent on anyone." He paused, and I wondered if he meant Sunil, and whether by the keenness sometimes given to lovers he sensed my ambivalence toward him. But he couldn't—how could he? I had been very careful to say nothing.

"I want you to be able to give Dayita everything she needs—and most important, to be able to buy a ticket whenever you decide you're ready to come back home." He pressed the card into my hand. "To me," he added.

I started to protest, but he said, "Please—just think of it as a kindness you're doing me, because otherwise I'd be worrying about you every day."

I took it then, but though I appreciated his concern, inside me I vowed I would never use it. Once I had depended on a man who clapped his hands over his ears and said, *Please, Sudha, let me be.* It was my own feet I wanted to stand on now.

Late last night, when the mothers had finished helping me pack my suitcases, Gouri Ma handed me a letter. From the fancy embossed envelope I could see it was a wedding card. "This came a few days ago," she said, her voice cautious. The glitter in her eyes—I could not tell if it was pain or anger. "Didi and Nalini wanted me to destroy it right away, but I felt I did not have the right to."

Even before I saw the Bardhaman postmark, I knew what it was. I knew it with the same kind of instinct that makes you snatch your hand away from a scorpion though no one has warned you yet of what it might do. A wedding announcement for Ramesh. Sent by my mother-in-law. One last swipe from her poisonous claw.

Ah, how much spite that woman had pent up within her.

"My poor Sudha, are you very upset?" Pishi asked. She put out a hand to knead my stiff, high shoulders.

I was. It was not because Ramesh was getting remarried. After all, I myself had briefly considered the same thing. I suspected the marriage was more his mother's idea, anyway. She would have gone around and around him like the grinding stones we use to crush wheat, *What about your duty to the Sanyal family, what about me, I'm too old to run this household all by myself,* until one day he covered his ears and said, *okay, okay, do what you want.* But to send me this card—I could hear her voice between the beautifully looped gold characters on it, taunting me. *See how easily you can be replaced, see what a catch my son is, see what an enormous mistake you made, leaving him.* My skin smarted from it as from a sudden slap.

I took a deep breath, let it out. I could not afford to add the weight of old resentments to all that I was carrying already with me to my new life. My mother was saying something about the gall of that woman, you'd think she'd at least have had the decency to return Sudha's wedding jewelry, now that she's getting a whole new dowry along with a new daughter-in-law, it'll serve her right if Ramesh's second wife turns out to be a shrew. I lifted my arm wearily to stop her.

"Let it be," I said. "It doesn't matter." I did not really feel that way, not yet. But saying the words brought me a moment of ease, as though after having spent hours climbing up a dark, stale stairwell, I had felt on my face a riffle of night air. It gave me hope that with time I would grow into their truth.

The inside of the airplane is quite beautiful, like something out of a movie, all plush maroon walls and shiny fixtures and air hostesses with lacquered smiles. It is the moment I have dreamed of for weeks, but I am too curious to give it much attention. As soon as I settle Dayita with a pacifier, I tear open the brown packet.

Inside is a velvet jewelry box, and a note in Gouri Ma's handwriting. *For our granddaughter.* I sigh, half-amused, half-vexed at the waste of money. It's probably a pair of silver bell-anklets like the ones people are always giving babies. Pretty, but most impractical. As soon as I put them on Dayita, she'll start chewing them.

But when I open the box, I gasp. For inside on a cushion of pale cream silk sits a necklace with a beautiful ruby pendant, shining with a red light that seems to well up from deep within it. It takes me a moment to realize that it is *the* ruby, the one that enticed Anju's father and mine away from their families—one to his death, the other to murder. The last time I looked at it, the ruby had filled me with foreboding, but now, tamed by the lacy gold frame that binds it, it is merely beautiful. Is it because it has exacted sufficient suffering from us? The ancestral house of the Chatterjees is indeed reduced to rubble, and of its two daughters, one is childless and the other without a husband. Only Dayita, the sapling growing from the ruins, is untouched and strong with her infant power.

I slip the necklace over her head without hesitation.

"It's your inheritance, baby," I tell her. "Perhaps you can cleanse it of the film that has gathered around it, the sorrow and cruelty and greed."

The crimson sparkle of the stone catches her eye, and she gives a gurgly laugh and tugs at it. But in a moment she is distracted by something far more fascinating—her socks. I smile as I watch her trying to pull them off. There is something marvelous about the way a jewel which had driven men to acts of folly and desperation lies forgotten on my daughter's innocent chest.

But look, here is another packet in the carry bag. It is actually an envelope, a fat one. When I see my name printed in blocky letters on it, a slow, swollen throbbing fills my head. It is the same writing that was on the envelope of money sent to me on the eve of my marriage. My father's writing.

How did he manage to get this letter in here? Along with his murderous arts, had he learned wizardry as well? Or had he bribed someone in our household?

I want to throw the letter away unopened, but my curiosity is too great. So I give Dayita her bottle and rip open the envelope.

Dear daughter, the letter begins. A shiver goes up my spine as I read the words. My body clenches with an old anger. *He has no right to call me that.* But I go on.

Dear daughter,

By the time you read this, you will be gone, and I will never see you again, for surely I will not live until you return from America—if you do indeed return. Knowing this gives me the courage to write my story, and to beg your forgiveness.

Some of my tale you have heard from your Pishi, though I doubt that the man she painted for you was really me. Who can know a man who lives, as I did, in camouflage? Not even he himself knows who he is.

Let me begin with the part no one else knows: the day we found the ruby cave. The day I thought of, briefly, as the happiest in my life, until events proved it to be the most disastrous.

By this time there were only three of us left in our party, your uncle Bijoy, I, and the man whose great-grandfather had originally discovered the rubies. Haldar (that was the name he gave us), a tall, wiry man with piercing eyes, had let the bearers go the day before. We were very close to the cave, and he didn't want them to come any further. He didn't trust them, he said. Had I been listening more carefully, I might have wondered if perhaps he didn't trust us too. But I was crazy for the rubies and paid attention to little else.

At dawn that day we rowed the dinghy-boat from our launch to the edge of a mangrove swamp and entered the forest, sinking into the marshy ground with each step, hacking at the vines that blocked our way. From time to time Haldar consulted his compass and a little notebook he carried. I managed a look at it once, but it must have been written in some sort of code, for I couldn't understand anything. In an hour we were covered with mud, exhausted, and not a little jumpy—for a number of the vines had turned out to be laudoga snakes, those whiplash-thin green creatures whose bite is said to be so instantly poisonous that no one even feels it. There was no question of stopping for rest—we had to get back to our boat by nightfall when, Haldar said, the tigers came out.

After a while the ground firmed, and Haldar took out the blindfolds and tied them over our eyes. We protested, saying this would slow us down further, that we were so lost in this forest already that we couldn't even have found our way back to our boat. But he insisted. That had been the deal, and if we didn't honor it, he was ready to turn back right then. So, blindfolded, we stumbled behind him, holding the end of a rope he'd tied to his waist, cursing as we bumped into each other or tripped over roots. After a while we could tell, by the change in the air, which was cooler now but musty and damp, that we had entered a cave. The path narrowed to a tunnel through which we had to crawl on our hands and knees— all our fancy safari clothing was in tatters by now—and then suddenly Haldar stood up and gave a gasp. I straightened up too and tore off my blindfold and saw that we were in a huge limestone cavern—so huge that the top of it receded into blackness. Haldar shone his flashlight onto the cavern wall nearest us, and we could see the rubies, embedded chunks that gleamed a dark rust color, like dried blood, against the chalky white. "Ten minutes," whispered Haldar. "One ruby only." We got down to our task silently—somehow it didn't seem right to speak in such an awe-inspiring place. As soon as Bijoy and I had chiseled out our rubies, Haldar replaced our blindfolds. We returned the same way we'd come, falling, bruising ourselves over and over, but this time I didn't feel any of it. I was too busy dreaming of how the ruby would change my life. How with it I would finally make your mother smile.

That night we ate well—Haldar had set a trap for fish before we'd left, and he made a fine mustard curry out of his catch—and we talked gaily of what we'd do with our newfound fortunes. But when your uncle and I lay down in the cabin—Haldar preferred to sleep outside, in the open air—Bijoy said, "Gopal, we have to talk."

I was so exhausted I could barely keep my eyes open. "Can't it wait till tomorrow?" I asked him. "I haven't felt this sleepy in my life."

"I'm tired too," he said, "but no. Who knows what tomorrow will bring, whether any of us will be alive to see it." There was something in his voice, at once anguished and stern, that made me shiver. I rubbed at my eyes and lit the kerosene lantern that we'd switched off. In its flickering light I could see the sadness on his face. With that my sleep fled, because I knew what he had discovered.

"You lied to us," said Bijoy. "You're not my cousin, are you?"

My mouth felt like a tinderbox, dry and flammable, which even a single word would set alight.

"I trusted you," Bijoy said. The words went through me like a knife. All this time I hadn't realized that I loved him more than I had ever loved any man. When he called me *brother*, a sweetness rose up in me. I couldn't bear the thought of him never doing that again.

And so I told him what I'd sworn never to tell anyone—the truth about myself, though I was afraid that it might cause him to turn from me in disgust. The shameful truth of being a bastard in the house of my father, Bijoy's uncle in Khulna. How he'd seduced my mother, a maidservant in his household, then sent her back to her family when she told him a baby was on the way. But her family wanted no part of the disgrace an unmarried mother would bring them. Poor as they were, they had their standing in their community. So my mother returned to Khulna, half-starved, bruised black from the beatings her brothers had given her.

Many women in her position would have despaired and thrown themselves into a well, but my mother was determined to live, and to make a life for me. She bribed the gateman of the big house with a pair of gold earrings the master had given her, the last thing of value she had left, and appeared in front of the master and his wife—who was also pregnant—as they sat at dinner. She threatened to kill herself if her position in the household wasn't restored, and adequate provision made for her baby. Nor was she going to die silently and in secret. She'd set fire to herself in the marketplace and scream out the name of her betrayer with her last breath. And if the master hushed up the scandal with his money, she'd come back as a ghost and haunt his wife. Haunt her until she had a miscarriage, not just this time but every time she was pregnant. She swore this on the head of her unborn child.

How much of this talk would have swayed the master is uncertain, for he was known to be a hard man, but his frightened young wife begged him to give the maid what she wanted. She worked herself into such a hysterical state that finally the master grudgingly said that the maid could come back—but she'd have to work in the cow-barn, and sleep in the quarters above the barn, and never show her face—nor her son's—to him.

That's how my mother hacked out a precarious foothold in a house that wanted nothing of either of us. Life wasn't easy for her as she lived out her days above the cow-barn. The other maids taunted her, and the men servants seemed to think, now that the master had discarded her, she was fair game for them. To protect herself she developed a stinging tongue and a reputation as a witch-woman—but I knew there was never any truth to that. She was ferocious in her protection of me, making sure that I was clothed and fed and sent to school, that no one forced me to do menial work. The children who teased me for being a bastard didn't dare to do so in her hearing. "You're as good as the master's daughter that everyone makes such a fuss over," she always said to me. Still, she couldn't protect me from the furious shame that filled me, nor the ravenous desire for revenge, especially after she died from a fever because no doctor would come to treat her.

I ran away from the cow-barn soon after, before the master had a chance to throw me out. Anger ate into me, anger that the world had cheated me of what had been my right. I spent my days planning vengeance—maybe I would burn the big house down, or abduct my half-sister and sell her to the flesh-merchants. But fortunately for me (for otherwise I'd have lived out my life in the city's jail) the partition occurred. The master lost everything in the riots and fled with his family. And though I've heard the daughter came back, after things quieted down, all that was left of her father's fortune by then was the ruined shell of the house I'd both hated and coveted.

The partition cut me loose from any ties I had in Khulna, and I decided to seek my fortune. I would become an adventurer. Why not? The revenge I hadn't been able to wreak on my father I would exact on others. Somehow or other, the world would pay for what it owed me. That was the way I thought when I fooled your mother into marrying me and cheated my way into Bijoy's house—and his heart. Except I hadn't realized that he would find his way into my heart too.

When I finished my story Bijoy was silent for a long time. Then he put his arm around me. "You are indeed my cousin, whatever the world might say," he told me. Though he said nothing more, I knew he felt for my childhood and forgave me my deceit. And that we would never need to bring this up again.

Something changed in me when Bijoy put his arm around my shoulder. The great burden of pretending to be someone that I was not fell from me, and with it a certain bitterness. If Bijoy could accept me in spite of my shortcomings, if he could see something worth loving in me, perhaps I could too. This would be the treasure—more precious than a hundred rubies—with which I'd start my new life.

As I thought this, the fever of discontent that had plagued me for so many years lifted from my heart, and I fell into a deep, drugged sleep.

I use the word *drugged* intentionally, daughter, for I am sure now that that is what Haldar did to us. I am not sure why he waited until this time to harm us—probably it was so that he could add our rubies to the three to which the ancient warning had restricted him. He must have put something in the mustard-fish, some paralyzing herb, perhaps, for though I wondered at the sounds I heard in my sleep—the engine starting, the waves increasing as the launch made its way to the middle of the river, the thud, the splash that followed it—I was unable to open my eyes. Even when I felt his hands on me, searching my waistband for the pouch holding the ruby, I couldn't move. Only after he heaved me over the side of the launch into the water did panic break through my frozen muscles. The current was strong, and the bobbing outline of the launch was already beginning to recede. I searched the ink-black water frantically for Bijoy but saw nothing. I hoped the water had revived him, too—I didn't know then that he couldn't swim.

Finally I realized that if I was to get back to the launch, I'd have to stop searching and start swimming back. Already my tired muscles were cramping. It took me a long time to make it back to the boat. Luckily, Haldar was so certain of the effectiveness of his drug that he hadn't bothered to take the launch upriver—if he had, it surely would have been the end of me. But perhaps *luckily* is the wrong word. Maybe it would have been better if I too had drowned that night like my brother.

I climbed up over the side of the launch as quietly as I could. Haldar was hunched near a lantern—gloating over the rubies, no doubt. I was on him before he had a chance to look up. I gripped him around the throat, but he was strong and slammed me into the deck. Then he threw the lantern at my face. I could hear the sizzling sound my flesh made as the glass broke. Pain exploded across my forehead, worse than anything I'd known. That's when my hand found the grappling hook. I swung it at Haldar with all the rage of my misshapen, misfortunate life and heard him scream as it knocked him over the side.

I pause my reading here. My lungs have turned to stone—I cannot breathe. The fire, the burned face. No, it cannot be. But I must continue reading.

I had no time to think of what I'd done—but I wouldn't have been sorry even if I had. The shattered lantern had started a fire on the deck. I tried to put it out but it was too powerful. The dinghy was my only chance. As I rowed away, I heard the launch exploding behind me, but I had no time to look. I maneuvered the dinghy toward the spot where I thought Bijoy had been thrown overboard. It was frustratingly slow—I wasn't skilled at rowing and the current was strong. I searched and searched, weaving back and forth across the black water, swinging the lantern, calling his name, battling the pain that raked my face. But there was no sign of a body, living or dead. Finally, after the sun came up and I could see how fast the current swept past the prow of the dinghy, I gave up. I rowed the dinghy ashore and fell, unconscious, on the marshy ground. I had no money or papers—Haldar had taken them, just as he must have taken Bijoy's. As for the rubies, they must have sunk, along with the exploded boat, to the bottom of the river.

I came to consciousness in a nearby village—the adibasis had found me and taken me there. Their ojha did what he could for me with root and herbs. It relieved the pain, but when I looked into a mirror and saw the gouges and scabs, the loathsome crisped-away pinkness, the monstrosity my face had become, I shuddered and flung the mirror from me with all my strength.

I should have contacted the police then, but I was too distraught to think straight. I'd killed one man, and if the police charged me with Bijoy's death too, how could I prove my innocence? In one sense I *was* guilty of it—hadn't I been the one to show him the ruby and tempt him to this ill-fated adventure? I couldn't stand the thought of going back to Bijoy's house, empty-handed, ugly beyond imagination, bearing the worst possible news, to face the condemnation in the eyes of the three widows.

So I disguised myself as a refugee—it wasn't so far from the truth, after all—and made my way down to Calcutta by begging on the trains. I slept on the platform of Sialdah station and agonized over how I would approach the women, what I could possibly say to them. Then I saw the obituary in the papers—for Bijoy and for me.

The announcement gave me a strange sensation—frightening, almost—of having ceased to exist. But it also brought me a certain release. No longer father or husband or cousin, I felt I could once more invent whom I wanted to be.

Coward that I was, I told myself matters had been decided for me. It would be less painful for the women to believe that we had both died. Seeing me would only cause them to remember Bijoy and to regret that I hadn't been taken instead of him. So I found a job in a car mechanic's garage, wore a turban and grew a beard, took on a false name and learned to drive. The money was good, the labor punishing enough that I could sleep at night. Soon I'd saved enough to start a business in a new town, forget my past once and for all. I went—several times—but each time a restlessness I could not understand forced me to return to Calcutta.

Then one day I heard that the Chatterjee women needed a driver, and I found myself standing at the old gate which had closed behind me five years ago, offering to work for whatever they could afford to pay. That is how I became Singhji.

Singhji, I whisper. *Singhji.* It is a sound from a forgotten language whose meaning I cannot decipher. But there is more.

At first I kept my distance from the mothers and spoke as little as I could, afraid I might be discovered. But soon I realized that there was no reason to fear that. People rarely recognize things they are not expecting to see, even when they're right in front of their eyes. And in many ways, I was not Gopal anymore. My frivolousness had been burned away in the fire that night, my vanity and my need to assume importance. What was left was regret, and the realization that through my own wrong choice my family was lost to me forever. The only way I could be with them now was as their servant.

Through the years I watched your mother and you, the two I loved most in that house. I was anguished by your mother's bitter greed, because I knew the part I had played in changing her from the lovely young woman who had stolen my heart by the riverside. Watching you grow into a kind and beautiful girl, I felt exquisite joy—and sorrow too, because I would always be a stranger to you, unable to protect you from your mother's broken dreams. I tried vainly to steer you toward happiness. I admired and anguished over the choice you made so Anju could marry the man she loved. Finally, before your marriage, I gathered all the savings I'd been accumulating since your birth for this occasion and mailed them to you.

But the shock in your eyes as you opened the package taught me that only the good are blessed with the ability to give. How painful it was for me to have to drive your Pishi to Kalighat and watch her give every paisa away to beggars. It was then I realized that, having given up my identity, I'd become like the viewer of a movie who weeps for the characters on the screen but cannot help them. Or was it I who was the character, trapped in the tale I'd fabricated?

On the way back from Kalighat, I gathered up my courage to ask your Pishi as casually as I could what this money was which she'd given away. She told me it was ill-gotten gains, belonging to a murderer who'd destroyed the Chatterjee family through his greed. I guessed then at the story she must have surmised for you out of half-truths, and was shaken at the thought of the hatred you must feel for me. On that day I promised myself that when the time was right I would tell you the whole story and relieve you of the burden of guilt and hate you've carried all these years.

So, Sudha, here is my gift, the only one I have left to give: You are not the daughter of a murderer—not in the sense you've feared all these years.

My one request is that you not tell the mothers who I am. It is too late for that to do us any good, and it will snatch from me the only comfort I possess: that of helping them through the twilight of our lives. And truly, Gopal died long ago, in that night of fire and water, and I am Singhji.

I wish for my granddaughter all the luck that passed me by. I am thankful that I was able to hold her in my arms these few months. I hope when she is old enough, you will tell her the story of her grandfather so she will not repeat his errors. I hope she will be able to love him a little.

I press my knuckles hard against my teeth and welcome the pain. I am caught between sorrow and relief and incredulity. Singhji—my father? I cannot even begin to imagine how he must have felt day after day, salaaming to the mothers and even to us, obediently following orders, the nobleman of an old tale, disguised as the servant. Only in his case, it was a disguise he would never be able to remove. A memory of eyes comes back to me as I think of my father: eyes in their scarred sockets gazing at me in the rearview mirror, noble eyes, sorrowful eyes, eyes enigmatic with a love he knew he could not express, nor I understand. If there is one thing his story has taught me, it is that when all the dross is melted away from the human heart, only gold remains.

Dayita gives a sudden wail, and thankfully I turn to tend to her. I take refuge in the simple acts of motherhood which allow me to push back the letter and its implications into that dark recess where I have stored all the experiences of my life which I have not dared to examine fully. I am afraid they will scorch me beyond recognition, like the girl in a story I once heard, who opens a forbidden door to find blazing behind it the chariot of the Sun God.

But here now is a wondrous thought that has just risen inside me like the sun after a stormy night: If my father did not kill Anju's, then I need no longer carry the guilt which has been with me so long that I have forgotten it once was not a part of me. I need not pay her back with my life for the one her father lost. I examine this idea cautiously, gingerly, as one fingers a newly formed scab to test the healing underneath. And this is what I discover: My feelings toward Anju have not changed. If anything, they are purer, more intense because they are no longer dictated by necessity. I love her because I love her.

By now I have changed Dayita and burped her and rocked her back and forth, but she decides she does not like the airplane anymore. She makes her arms and legs as rigid as she can—it's a new trick she's learned, a most effective one—and screams until her face turns red and passengers crane their necks to see what I am doing to the poor child. I offer her my breast, but she refuses to let me off so easily. Finally, because I do not know what else to do, I begin to whisper a story into her ears. Amazingly, she starts to quiet—she is still crying, but they are soft sobs now. And that is how, poised in the sky between our new life and our old one, the life we cannot yet imagine and the one we've already begun to forget, I tell her a tale to make her heart strong, to graft her life onto. For of all things in this world it seems to me that that is what women most need. I tell her the story—once again—of the Queen of Swords. But as I speak it changes and is no longer the story I told Anju.

I tell her how the Queen of Swords was born an ordinary girl, I tell of her marriage and pregnancy, of how the palace guards tried to destroy the girl baby in her womb. How the unborn daughter gave her mother the courage to leave, gave her the flaming swords made of light so that none dared prevent her from going.

I tell her of the queen's desperation, after her baby was born, when no one dared to give them refuge. How she wandered in many lands with her daughter, until finally she found herself at the ocean's edge, with no place else to go.

"Then," I continue, "she heard a voice saying, 'Mother, don't weep.' She looked and it was her daughter, speaking her first words. The child knelt and touched the swords, and when she did so, they became as one and turned into a silver bird. Its eyes were made of rubies, and its wings shimmered like dual rainbows. The queen and her daughter climbed onto its back, and the bird began to carry them to a new life in a new land. *We'll be happy ever after*, the queen wanted to whisper to her daughter as they flew, but she knew that was not true. Life never is that way. And so instead she held her daughter in silence, heart to heart, and as they traveled each heart drew on the other's strength, so that when they reached their destination they would be ready."

Dayita is asleep when I finish, her limbs loose and trustful.

How wondrous the way her head fits into the crook of my elbow. I have a cramp in my arm but I do not set her down. I hold her like this for a long time, listening to her breathe. The main lights of the plane have been turned off, and in the shadows the ruby on her chest rises and falls with a tiny glimmer, like a bird's eye.

FORTY-TWO

Anju

I'VE ALWAYS thought of myself as an impatient person. It's one of the things Pishi used to scold me about when I was a girl. But now I realize that all this time I never knew what true impatience meant. Even those ecstatic early days with Sunil were nothing compared to what I've been going through this week. I can't sit still. I have no interest in food. But for the first time in my life I've been cooking feverishly until the refrigerator is crammed with all the dishes I remember Sudha liking. Which is crazy because she can cook them ten times better than I can. I've also selected a few American dishes—spaghetti sauce, apple pie, potato salad—my repertoire is admittedly meager. It'll be a good way to start explaining to Sudha about life in this country.

When I mentioned this to Sunil, he was clearly annoyed. "For heaven's sake," he said. "You're not her teacher—or her keeper. She'll learn on her own."

I shouldn't have brought it up—he's been increasingly edgy and irritable whenever I speak of Sudha. And since I discovered the handkerchief I'm awkward too, so whatever I say comes out sounding stilted or overly enthusiastic. Still, once in a while, I *have* to talk about her when the longing to have her here shudders through me like the hot flashes that used to hit me in the first nights since Prem died.

(There, I can speak of it now, without feeling as though I'm sinking into quicksand, my mouth filling with mica and grit.)

The other thing I'm beginning to painfully admit to myself is that I'm a coward in the things that matter the most. I couldn't tell Sudha not to come to America after I'd begged her to do so, but now I'm afraid of what her presence in my home will unravel. Nor have I had the courage to ask my husband whether that handkerchief, folded so carefully into the Kashmiri box, is the forgotten remnant of an old crush, or proof of a continuing obsession.

All these thoughts go around and around in my brain like the bullocks they use in villages to turn the water wheel. I'd go crazy, but fortunately I run out of time. The plane's arriving this morning in an hour and a half—miraculously on time in spite of the heavy rains we've been getting since daybreak. I must be ready to leave in twenty minutes, Sunil yells from the other room. I pull a tray of chocolate chip cookies out of the oven—they've puffed up nicely and are only a trifle overdone. I take a last look at Sudha's room. The monstrous black eyes of the Mickey on the crib mobile bore into me until I shut the door.

"Are you dressed?" calls Sunil.

"I am," I yell back. Looking down at my jeans and too-loose shirt, I wonder briefly whether I should dress up more for Sudha, then shake my head. Nah, such silly things have never mattered between us. What would I wear anyway? I'm too thin for most of my clothes. I still have trouble eating. I know it's my fault, I should try harder, but everything seems to harbor a faint antiseptic odor. Maybe when Sudha gets here.

That's how a lot of my sentences have been ending nowadays. *When Sudha gets here. Everything will be better when Sudha gets here.*

At the airport Sunil pushes his way through the packed crowd outside the customs area—mostly Indians like ourselves, waiting for family members. I follow a little behind him. There's no sign of any passengers.

"What's wrong?" Sunil asks the plump mustachioed man standing next to him. "It can't be that the plane's late—we called before we came."

"I hear immigration's been very picky lately, asking lots of questions," says the mustachioed man. "Why, they even denied entry to someone last week, some kind of a fraudulent visa. I heard it from my friend's mother-in-law—she came on the same flight. She was telling us about the poor young woman, crying and crying as the authorities took her away. Apparently the girl's husband was already here, but she lied about it in order to get a quick tourist visa." He clicks his tongue pityingly. "What some people won't do to try and bypass the legal channels."

My mouth is dry as I listen, and my stomach churns. What if the authorities suspect that I too am planning for Sudha to stay on in America? Would they—? Oh, I'd die if I had to return to the apartment without my cousin.

The crowd presses up against me, smelling of hospitals. Outside the glass walls of the airport, the sky has coagulated into a steely gray. I'm suffocating. I've got to be alone. I catch Sunil's eye and motion toward the rest room, then push my way through the wall of bodies. In the rest room I gulp in deep breaths and splash cold water on my face. When the trembling in my hands is a little better, I make my way back.

The first passengers have begun to trickle through the doors, and the crowd surges ahead, waving and calling. I manage to edge in behind Sunil. He hasn't noticed me yet, and I'm just about to put my hand on his arm when I see Sudha. How lovely she looks in spite of the exhausting flight, her silk sari molded to her slender body, her fine hair escaped from her braid and curling around her face. Even the circles under her fragile eyes add to her charm. She carries a bundle and pushes with her other hand a cart loaded with two enormous suitcases that are entirely too heavy for her to handle. There's a lost look on her face as she swivels her head, trying to locate us. I want to call out, to run to her and gather her to my heart, but my throat is clogged with too much emotion—

love and thankfulness and that old desire to protect. Now she's seen Sunil—a look of relief comes over her face and she stops to wave. Sunil waves back.

"Your wife?" asks the mustachioed man.

I wait for Sunil to explain who she is, but he says nothing. His silence is a block of ice in which I'm trapped. From where I stand I can see the slight smile on his face.

"Lucky chap!" says the man, clapping Sunil on the back. "Oh, there's mine. I'd better go." He hurries toward a spectacled woman who's just as plump as he is, leading three plump girls in identical pink dresses.

Someone jostles me, releasing me from frozenness. I take a few steps back toward the glass wall—I couldn't bear it if Sunil found out that I saw his brief, silent deception. My face is hot with shame, and that makes me angrier, because why should *I* be ashamed. But no, angry isn't a good enough word for the emotion that's bludgeoning my body.

Then Sudha's kissing me, her free arm so tight around my neck that it hurts. I welcome the pain. "Anju Anju Anju," she's crying into my hair. Each syllable falls onto my heart like magic balm. The bundle is pressed up against my chest, not liking it one bit, I can tell that by the way it squirms and mewls.

I press my face against Sudha's face and hold her, not wanting to ever let go. For one illogical moment I wish with all my might that the boundaries of our bodies could dissolve, that our skin and bone and blood could melt and become one.

Squished between us, the bundle lets out a long, protesting wail. When I look, its face is screwed up tight and turning mottled.

"Here, hold her for a minute, will you?" says Sudha.

The blood crashes in my ears, a red tidal wave. I shake my head and begin to back away. I've got to find the words—the words with which to explain to Sudha that it's impossible.

"I really need you to," Sudha says, rubbing her back with a

grimace. "After fourteen hours on the plane with her, I'm done for."

No, I try to tell her. It would be disloyal to the dead. But she's already thrust the bundle into my arms. I'm surprised by how heavy it is for such a small creature. Its solid heft belies its frail appearance. How natural the head feels nestled in the curve of my shoulder. I'd promised myself I'd never hold another baby with the arms that belonged to Prem, but this—this is so *right*. As right as the ruby—yes, I recognized it at once—around her throat. Even the way she butts her face against my breast—she's hungry now—is more sweet than bitter. Inside me, love lets itself down in a rush, uncontrollable, like the milk when your baby cries.

Somewhere to the side, Sudha is greeting Sunil, telling him sorry, she didn't mean to ignore him like that, it's just that she hadn't seen me for so long. He replies formally that of course he understands. But my ears barely register their exchange. I'm occupied by the way my body is unclenching, re-forming itself molecule by molecule, arranging itself around my niece like petals around a flower's core. My forehead tingles as though a new fortune is being written on it. Who would have thought, after all the barricades I'd set up against Dayita in my heart, that in the span of a minute she'd make it hers?

"Babies are beyond explaining, aren't they?" Sudha says in my ear. Her arm is around me again, her voice heavy with unshed tears. I want to tell her not to be sad—because I'm not. And Prem, who's somewhere close, whose presence I feel for the first time since the miscarriage, brushing against my face gauzy as a dragonfly wing—Prem's not sad either. I want to tell her about the nature of radiance, how I glimpsed it fleetingly in the pulse beating in her daughter's throat. But it'll be a long time before I can find the right words.

Instead I slip an arm around Sudha and support Dayita cautiously with the other. Sudha places her arm under mine, so we're both holding Dayita up. If a passerby who had the eyes to notice such things looked at us, she would see that we've formed a tableau, two women, their arms intertwined like lotus stalks, smiling down at the baby between them. Two women who have traveled the vale of sorrow, and the baby who will save them, who has saved them already. Madonnas with child.

Somewhere Sunil drums his fingers on the edge of the baggage cart and says we really should be going, but we don't listen, not right away. There'll be trouble enough later—like an animal I sense it prickling the nape of my neck. I'll deal with it when it comes. But for now the three of us stand unhurried, feeling the way we fit, skin on skin on skin, into each other's lives. A rain-dampened sun struggles from the clouds to frame us in its hesitant, holy light.

ALSO BY
CHITRA BANERJEE DIVAKARUNI

THE MISTRESS OF SPICES

Magical, tantalizing, and sensual, *The Mistress of Spices* is the story of Tilo, a young woman born in another time, in a far-away place, who is trained in the art of spices and ordained as a mistress charged with special powers. Made immortal in an initiation by fire, she travels to modern-day Oakland and begins to administer her curatives. An unexpected romance confronts her with the choice between her supernatural existence and the vicissitudes of contemporary life. Here is a spellbinding and hypnotizing tale of joy and sorrow and one woman's special powers.

Fiction/0-385-48238-8

ARRANGED MARRIAGE

This exquisitely wrought debut collection of stories subtly chronicles the accommodation—and the rebellion—Indian-born girls and women in America undergo as they balance old treasured beliefs and surprising new desires. Each story is complete in itself; together they create a tapestry as colorful, as delicate and as enduring as the finest silk sari.

Fiction/0-385-48350-3

LEAVING YUBA CITY

Divakaruni's third volume of poetry is a deeply affecting collection that explores images about India and the Indian experience in America—from the adventures of going to a convent school in India run by Irish nuns to the history of the earliest Indian immigrants in the United States.

Poetry/0-385-48854-8

ANCHOR BOOKS
Available from your local bookstore, or call toll-free to order:
1-800-793-2665 (credit cards only).